TIME AFTER TIME

This Large Print Book carries the
Seal of Approval of N.A.V.H.

TIME AFTER TIME

LISA GRUNWALD

THORNDIKE PRESS
A part of Gale, a Cengage Company

Farmington Hills, Mich • San Francisco • New York • Waterville, Maine
Meriden, Conn • Mason, Ohio • Chicago

GALE
A Cengage Company

LIBRARY OF CONGRESS CIP DATA ON FILE.
CATALOGUING IN PUBLICATION FOR THIS BOOK
IS AVAILABLE FROM THE LIBRARY OF CONGRESS

ISBN-13: 978-1-4328-6930-4 (hardcover alk. paper)

Published in 2019 by arrangement with Random House, an imprint and division of Penguin Random House LLC

Printed in Mexico
1 2 3 4 5 6 7 23 22 21 20 19

For Stephen, Ziz, and Jonny,
because it happened to all of us

Time after time
I tell myself that I'm
So lucky to be loving you

So lucky to be
The one you run to see
In the evening, when the day is through

I only know what I know
The passing years will show
You've kept my love so young, so new

And time after time
You'll hear me say that I'm
So lucky to be loving you.
— Sammy Cahn and Jule Styne, 1947

If you're lost you can look
And you will find me,
Time after time.
— Cyndi Lauper and Rob Hyman, 1983

PART ONE

PART ONE

1
I KNOW WHERE I WANT TO GO

1937

She wasn't carrying a suitcase, and she wasn't wearing a coat. Those were the things that struck him when he saw her for the first time. It was just a bit after sunrise on a Sunday in early December. Joe was heading across the Main Concourse for Track 13, but there she was — no bag, no coat — standing by the west side of the great gold clock, peering into a window of the information booth. If she was traveling, then she was traveling light. If she was working at the terminal, then she was drunk, or she should have known better. No woman who worked at Grand Central would ever go near the guys in the booth at this hour, not at the end of a long night, when their shifts were finally over, and they were probably handing a bottle around.

Then one of them must have made a pass, because she stepped back quickly, and he

11

could hear them barking and laughing as she turned to walk away. Joe saw how young she was, and how completely out of place she looked. Why was she here at dawn, and what was she doing without an escort? Still, she didn't seem scared by the guys as much as frustrated, even angry. Her eyes were enormous and bright green, and her lips were the same kind of hard-candy red as the stoplight on a signal lamp.

She stepped away from the stir she'd caused but stopped walking after just a few yards. A tramp standing on the marble staircase cupped a cigarette in his hand, flicked off the ash, and gave her the eye.

"Hey, princess," he said. "Can you spare a grand?"

Joe hadn't had his coffee yet, but he moved to her side in just a few steps. Her earrings might have been real pearls, and they dangled from glittering, flame-shaped tops. But "princess"? Joe didn't think so. Her pale-blue dress was smudged and worn, and her shoes seemed old and scuffed.

"You look kind of lost," he said to her.

Behind her, the tramp gave Joe the finger. Another guy whistled from inside the booth.

"I'm not lost," the girl said. "It's just that —"

"What?"

12

"Those men."

"Did you need directions?" Joe asked.

"No," she said. "No, I've been here before."

"Well, what did you need those guys for, then?"

"I was only asking them what happened to the bank on the lower level. One of them said there'd been a little fire, and they all started laughing and saying things like 'Fire down below.' "

She looked at the ground, then back at Joe. "Do you think they could be drunk?"

"Oh, they could definitely be drunk," Joe said.

"How rude."

"Want me to go chew them out?"

She smiled. "You'd do that?" she asked.

She tucked her hair behind her ears and lifted her chin just slightly. Joe realized she wasn't just beautiful. There was something else about her, something vivid and exciting. She made him think of the cats in the tunnels far beneath the concourse: coiled up and waiting, all energy, no telling what they were going to do.

By now, the tramp had moved away, and the guys in the booth were leaving too — disappearing one by one down the booth's hidden corkscrew staircase.

13

"So, you know where you're going?" Joe asked the girl.

"I know where I want to go," she said.

"And where's that?"

"Turtle Bay Gardens."

That was the neighborhood near the East River, just blocks from the YMCA where Joe lived but miles beyond him in all other ways. Turtle Bay was a high-class place with pale, private houses and rich, private people. That meant the pearls were real, Joe thought. But still this young woman seemed happy, even eager, to be talking to him.

Standing this close, he could smell her perfume: a blend of talcum and flowers and something sharper, like wood or whiskey. She was two or three inches shorter than he was. Her hair was a jumble of soft copper wires, and it fell at her neck in a cloud of curls. Her cheeks were smooth and pink, the same shade as the terminal's Tennessee marble floors.

"So why do you need a bank at this hour?" Joe asked. "I thought they'd caught Ma Barker."

She didn't laugh at his joke. She reached into her dress pocket and pulled out a cushion of paper money. The bills weren't green; they looked foreign. "This is all I've got," she said. "I need to get it changed for

14

American dollars."

"There's a branch a few blocks away," Joe said. "But I don't think it opens till nine. Where are you coming from, that you don't have cash?"

"I do have cash. It's just French cash."

"Last I heard, they hadn't laid any tracks under the Atlantic," Joe said. "What train were you on, anyway? And why aren't you wearing a coat?"

This time she laughed — a wonderful, confident laugh, deeper than he would have thought possible for someone who looked so young. But she ignored all his questions.

"Anything else you'd like to know, mister?"

"Didn't mean to be rude," he said.

"You're not!" she exclaimed. "You're being so kind."

He told her his name, and he asked for hers.

"Nora Lansing," she said, extending her hand, as if he'd asked her to dance.

Joe shook it, but hastily let it go. "Your hand's really hot. Do you feel all right?"

"I'm fine," she said.

Carefully, he took her hand back, cupping it now in both of his, as if it were a butterfly. Its warmth seemed to spread from her hand into his, then traveled the length of

15

his spine, like a current along the railroad tracks.

"Nice to meet you, Miss Lansing."

"Nora."

Nora. It was an old-fashioned name, and she did seem a little old-fashioned. Her pale-blue dress had a black collar, black cuffs, and swirly flat black buttons that looked like rolled-up licorice wheels. What Joe knew about women's clothing could fit inside an olive, but he knew the dress looked wrong somehow.

She leaned in closer to him.

"So, Joe, let me ask you this," she said. "Is there any chance you could walk me home?"

"To Turtle Bay Gardens? What about the bank?"

"Well, I wouldn't need to go there, see, if you could walk me home."

Joe looked up at the gold clock and then back at Nora. "I wish I could," he said. "Honestly. But I work here, and I'm late for a meeting, and right after that, I start my shift."

The brightness in her eyes dimmed a bit. Joe realized, with some amazement, that he suddenly felt it was his obligation to bring the brightness back.

"What if I find a cop to walk you?" he asked.

16

"Oh, you're so nice," Nora said. "But I can do that myself. I should have done it in the first place."

By now the Main Concourse was starting to bubble and steam with the morning rush: workers and travelers in seemingly random motion, except for the subtle dance steps that kept them from bumping into each other. No one stopped, unless it was at the clock, the ticket windows, or the blackboard where Bill Keogh stood on a ladder and wrote out the times and track numbers in lemon-yellow chalk.

"Are you sure you're all right?" Joe asked Nora.

"I'm sure."

She circled her left wrist with her right hand. For just a moment, she looked confused, and he hesitated, reluctant to leave her. Then she said, resolutely: "Go ahead, Joe. You don't want to be late."

They walked off in opposite directions, and Joe checked the time as he hurried across the concourse. When he stopped to look back, he was half embarrassed, half thrilled, to see that Nora had done the same thing. Their eyes met the way their hands had: filled with heat and surprise. Finally, Joe turned to leave and, noting the time once more, he started to run.

17

2

As If the Sun Were Rolling By

1937

The meeting Joe was heading for had nothing to do with Grand Central, even though everyone who attended it had a job somewhere in the terminal. This was a prayer meeting run by a porter named Ralston Crosbie Young, also known as the Red Cap Preacher. Like virtually all the Red Caps, Ralston was abidingly polite. He had been carrying passengers' bags and giving directions since the terminal's opening in 1913. But for years now, at least three days a week, he had also been leading prayer meetings in an empty train car on Track 13. Joe had been born and raised a Catholic, and he attended church now only when he went with his family in Queens. Ralston's meetings were more his style. "Listen, man," Ralston frequently said. "God has a plan for your life."

There were several dozen regulars, like

18

Joan, who gave manicures at DeLevie's and always had an eye out for Joe. There were Wallace and Delroy, Red Caps like Ralston who looked incomplete when they took off their hats. There was Doug from the Oyster Bar kitchen, whose shoes scraped the floor with the bits of shells that were caught in his soles; Tommy, the kid who swept the barbershop; and Mr. Walters, who wore a suit and tie, so no one ever quite got around to asking him what he did.

Joe wasn't a regular, but the group always seemed to welcome him. He was thirty-two now, but he'd been seventeen when he'd gotten his first job at the terminal, and even people who hadn't known him for years usually felt they had. In some ways, he still looked like a kid. His mouth, slightly crooked, always seemed to be smiling, no matter what his mood. His ears were mismatched: one straight, the other tipped like an elf's. And though his thick black hair was parted along the tidiest line, some C-shaped locks were always flopping down on his forehead. Despite his youthfulness, though, Joe seemed sturdy in every way. His face was broad and Irish; more friendly than handsome, but steadfast, like his body.

Ralston had already started the meeting when Joe arrived, but he stopped, pointed a

19

slender brown finger at him, and said, "Hoped I'd see you this morning."

Joe pointed back at him, smiling. "Hoped I'd see you too."

Ralston moved some newspapers from the seat beside him.

"Here's your place," he said quietly, and Joe sat.

Joe liked going to Ralston's meetings now and then, but he'd rarely missed the ones that were held on December 5 and January 6. These were special meetings because they took place on special mornings. Clear weather permitting, these were the two mornings in the year when you could stand on certain side streets and, looking west to east, see the rising sun line up exactly with the street grid of Manhattan. The same thing happened on two summer evenings, looking west at sunset. During these sunrises and sunsets, the skyscrapers of Manhattan framed the sun exactly the way Joe had heard the towering rocks at Stonehenge in England did.

Not many people knew about these special days, but those who did waited for them. They were sometimes called the Manhattan Solstices because — due to the particular angle of the New York streets — they occurred several weeks before and after the true winter and summer solstices. In the terminal, they had always been called Manhattanhenge, and a Manhattanhenge sunrise was one of the few things that could bring even old-timers to work at dawn. If you were game to stand out in the cold and dark, you would first see the sky start to lighten, then a small halo on the horizon that slowly grew taller, as if an angel were rising from the edge of the world. Finally, the sun would appear, and the light would come coursing down the street.

If at sunrise, for whatever reason, you happened to find yourself inside instead of outside the terminal, you could see that amazing line of light blast through the middle of the three high arched windows. The sun would flood the floor and make the famous blue ceiling come alive in a wash of pale-purple light. In a place made of marble, limestone, steel, and brass, where almost everyone worked underground, dependent on electric light and attending the constant circuits of trains, Manhattanhenge was a reminder that there was power, order, and beauty in the natural world as well.

Ralston Young wasn't usually particular about what he preached. He could rip a page from a Sears, Roebuck catalogue and

21

find a message from God in it. But today, an hour after December's Manhattanhenge sunrise, Ralston didn't need to look for extra inspiration. Gratitude for the majesty of the Lord's universe, that was what Ralston preached this morning. Gratitude for the way the planets circled the sun, for the way the ancients had built Stonehenge, and for the way William K. Vanderbilt had built Grand Central Terminal.

Joe would have loved to see Stonehenge. It was one of a hundred places he had sworn to himself he'd go someday — if the lousy Depression ever ended and he had the money or got the chance. But Manhattanhenge was pretty damn good itself, particularly when its special light was being praised by Ralston Young in the dimness of an unused train car. Today, Joe closed his eyes and tried to clear his mind, to marvel at the glory of God's handiwork. But he kept imagining Nora disappearing into the crowd — her copper hair, the spark in her green eyes, the licorice buttons on her dress — and all he could think was that he should have asked for her phone number before letting her get away.

Hastily, he stood up.

"You all right, Joseph?" Ralston asked him.

"I'm sorry," Joe said. "Just late for my

22

shift, that's all."

He checked his watch as he sprinted up the ramp to the concourse. In truth, he still had twenty minutes before he was due to start work, and he spent all but the last few of them standing by the gold clock, scanning the crowd for Nora, wishing that he had been the one who'd gotten to walk her home.

Joe Reynolds was a leverman, the youngest in Grand Central's history. His job was to guide the incoming trains through their final miles under Park Avenue and into the terminal. With its two-level layout, Grand Central had forty-eight tracks that could be in use at any one time, and when things got really busy, a new train might roll in every twenty seconds.

Joe was assigned to Signal Tower A, not a tower at all, but the upper room of a narrow, two-story brick sweatbox that was situated under Park Avenue and Fiftieth Street, almost half a mile north of the Main Concourse. Joe's responsibility was to push and pull the levers that, connected by underground cables, moved the tracks from side to side just in time to line up before the trains reached them. In Tower A alone, there were more than three hundred levers, each one numbered, together making up a vast chest-high console that the men called the Piano. The handles were made of brass, and the spots where they'd been gripped so often gleamed like the Red Caps' jacket buttons. There were five signal towers for Grand Central, three men to a Piano, forty or fifty levers to a man, and above each man a panel showing the dozens of tracks converging.

There was not much in a tower room except light and noise and men. There was no idle conversation. There were no cigarettes, no food, no coffee — except at the desks where the tower directors manned the phones and called out the routes and the track changes. The room always smelled of metal and sweat.

It was bright, no matter the season or hour. God had separated the day from the night when he created the world, but when the engineer William J. Wilgus created the tower system, it was always day, and the lights ranged from twinkling to blinding. There were the tiny green emeralds that twinkled on the boards and showed the trains' positions. There were the overheads, so strong that when anyone entered the room, he had to shield his eyes. And finally, there were the bursts of light that came from the trains rumbling past the tower windows. Every few minutes, a flash and a roar, as if the sun were rolling by. The whole thing had its own music, with the rhythms of lights and sounds, and the movements of the levermen, and the directors, setting the tempo from the desks and the phones. The heat from the lights was so intense that the men always worked with their sleeves rolled up, used the showers afterward, and kept a stack of fresh shirts in their lockers. It was exhausting work, but Joe had a knack for it. Like Steady Max Sullivan, who had started training Joe when he was barely twenty, he had mastered a perfect level of alertness, a suitable halfway point between caring too little and caring too much.

There were fail-safes in the system, but the goal was never to need them. Hanging on the wall, in a dusty black frame, was a now honey-colored *New York Times* article from 1913. With a thick black pencil, someone had long ago circled one paragraph as inspiration:

In a signal tower, every moment is an emergency, either actual or possible. "Why, I eat, drink, and breathe emergency in my work," said one of the operators. "It's funny, but you can't surprise me with anything."

3

IT *Is* YOU!

1938

It was a year later, and she saw him before he saw her. He was coming down the ramp that led to the restaurants on the lower level. He was wearing a short black coat and a plaid hat, tying a fuzzy red scarf around his neck. The last time, it had been morning by the information booth, and he'd been kind and gallant about that guy who'd called her "princess." This time, it was just past six in the evening, and Nora was standing outside the Oyster Bar, the terminal's oldest restaurant. She didn't have to speak loudly. She said "Joe," and he stopped cold.

His eyes widened, and he glanced from left to right, as if he were hoping to find a witness. "You again!" he exclaimed. "It *is* you!"

"Nora," she said.

"I didn't forget. Nora Lansing," Joe said. "From Paris."

"Joe Reynolds," she said. "From right here."

He smiled as he undid the scarf he'd just tied. He pulled off his cap and, with one large hand, swept the locks of black hair from his forehead. She had forgotten how kind his face was, in its slightly uneven way.

"Don't tell me you never found someone to walk you home," he said with a grin. "Have you been waiting for me all this time?"

Nora laughed, but waiting for Joe Reynolds was exactly what she'd been doing.

He was looking at her intently now. "Why are you —" he started to say, but apparently thought better of it. He gestured to the restaurant. "How was your dinner?" he asked instead. "Were you brave? Did you try the oyster stew?"

"No."

"The pan roast?" he asked.

"No, I haven't eaten."

"You're here all by yourself again?"

He looked confused and excited, but before he could ask another question, a middle-aged couple, obviously tipsy, emerged from the restaurant arm in arm. It wasn't clear who was steadier.

"Can we, Jack?" the woman asked.

They were just feet from Joe and Nora,

eyeing the famous Whispering Gallery, where people could stand on diagonal spots, backs to each other, yards apart, and — whispering into the corners — have their voices carry above them through the pale zigzags of the arched tile ceiling.

The man sighed so dramatically that he was either teasing or truly annoyed.

"Oh, come on, Jack," the woman said.

"All right, Patsy, all right."

Wobbling a little, they let go of each other and shuffled to their opposite corners.

Patsy kept looking back at Jack.

"Jack," she said, but he didn't turn around.

"Jack!" she barked.

"What?" he shouted back, turning.

"Remember!" she nearly yelled at him. "Whisper! Whisper!"

Joe's and Nora's eyes met in amusement.

"Have you ever done it?" he asked her.

"What? The Whispering Gallery? Of course not," she said. "I'm no tourist. I grew up here. Have you ever done it?"

"Me? The people around here would never let me live it down."

But even as Joe said this, he was ushering Nora into the corner that Patsy had just left.

Standing thirty feet apart, each of them leaned into a corner.

29

"Nora Lansing," Joe whispered into the corner of the alcove. His voice was distant but clear. "Will you have dinner with me?"

"Joe Reynolds," she whispered back. "Only if you're buying."

They turned to each other and smiled the way people do when they learn that they love the same song.

"That's a deal, Patsy," Joe said to her.

"Shake on it, Jack," she answered.

Joe took her hand, then held it tighter, apparently not as startled by its heat this time as he'd been the year before.

"What is it about your hand?" he asked.

"What is it about your questions?"

At Alva's Little Coffee Shop, a skinny, tall woman with close-set eyes greeted Joe with a lipsticky smack on the cheek, grabbed a couple of menus, and used them to swat Joe on his backside. She led them to a red leather booth, leaned against its coat-hook post, and gave Nora a long look up and down.

"So, who've we got here?" she asked Joe, her eyes not leaving Nora's.

Nora tucked her hair behind her ears, hoping she didn't look too disheveled.

"Alva, Nora," Joe said. "Nora, Alva. Alva, haven't you got some coffee to brew? Or someone else to torture?"

"I'll give you a minute," Alva said. She put the menus on the table and used her thumb to smudge off the lipstick her kiss had left on Joe's cheek.

"Well, *she* seems to know you pretty well," Nora said.

Joe shrugged. "Everyone who works here knows everyone."

He took off his coat and put it beside him.

"Now I've got to ask," he said. "Don't you ever wear a coat? It was snowing today. And is that your only dress?"

"I wouldn't have taken you for someone who was interested in women's fashion," she said.

"What, with me wearing fancy clothes like these?" Joe asked. He tugged at the collar of his blue twill shirt, then leaned forward confidentially and touched a smudged part of Nora's sleeve. "Honestly, though. Are you down on your luck?"

Just about everyone Nora had ever known had treated her — either with deference or disdain — like the rich girl she'd grown up being. She looked at Joe with wonder.

"Are you?" he asked again quietly.

She was so moved that she almost couldn't find an answer. Finally, she said: "This is just my traveling dress."

31

"And where are you traveling from this time?" Joe asked her. "Let me guess. China? Peru? New Jersey?"

"Closer to Jersey, I guess," she said.

"As in where?"

"As in it's not important."

"Oh, a woman of mystery," Joe said.

She didn't want to be that. She wanted to tell him everything — everything starting with Paris and going all the way through till this evening. There was something so straight and solid about him that it made her certain he'd understand. But she didn't want to scare him away. Perhaps if he could just walk her home, though, things would be all right.

"What's good here?" she asked him instead.

"Everything except the coffee," Joe said. "What do you like?"

"I like coffee," she said, smiling. "And I like grilled cheese."

"Also, a woman who knows what she wants."

"It's absolutely my favorite," Nora said. "In Paris, they make them with ham and mustard, and they call them croques-monsieurs. If you get them with an egg on top, they call them croques-madames. I don't know why."

"Because women are more complicated than men," Joe said.

Nora laughed, delighted. "Joe!"

He shook his head at her, smiling.

"What?"

"No, nothing," Joe said.

"What?"

"It's just the way you laughed."

"Do you like it or hate it? My mother hates it. She used to say it isn't ladylike."

"It isn't, Nora," Joe said. "It's swell."

She liked how he said her name. It was just her name, but it had been a long time since she'd heard it.

They were still smiling at each other when Alva came back. "What's it going to be, lovebirds?"

Joe ordered a grilled cheese for Nora and a plate of silver-dollar pancakes for himself.

"Coffee too, please," Nora said.

"You'll regret it, believe me," said Joe, and this time Alva swatted him on the head.

"Apart from the grilled cheese," he asked Nora when Alva had gone, "what did you like about Paris?"

A dozen images came to her in succession, as if she were flipping through the pages of one of her sketchpads. The tallest spire of Notre-Dame, which looked like a compass arrow. The attic flat she and her

33

friend Margaret had shared, with its copper-framed skylight and sloping floors. The cafés where the waiters wore black vests and crisp white aprons and where she'd sat outside drinking café au lait and drawing the passersby.

"Everything," Nora said. "I loved every single thing about it. But I think what I loved most was that I got to be on my own. You know, I had a job and a paycheck and a flat, and I guess I just liked feeling like a grown-up."

"A grown-up."

"Yes," Nora said. "Do you know what I mean?"

Joe cleared his throat. "Everyone I know grew up the day the stock market crashed," he said. For a moment, he looked puzzled. "There's something different about you," he said.

"No, there's something different about *you.*"

"About me?" Joe said. "What's that?"

"That you know there's something different about me."

34

4
HERE WE GO

1938

Joe kept trying to fix his gaze on Nora's forehead, her shoulders, the table, his own hands, but his eyes kept drifting stubbornly to hers. He told himself to concentrate harder on what she was saying.

"What were you doing in Paris?" he asked.

"Well, I went after I graduated."

"From college?"

Nora nodded.

"So, did you see the Eiffel Tower? The *Mona Lisa*?"

"Of course."

"And take one of those boat rides on the river?"

"The Seine."

"Right," Joe said. "And Notre-Dame?"

"I did *all* that," Nora said. "I didn't mind being a tourist *there*. But I also worked for an art gallery. And I did a lot of painting."

"You were a painter in Paris?"

"Well, on my best days I was."

"I've never met a painter," Joe said, trying to make it sound as if *that* was the most exciting thing about her.

Now his eyes were on Nora's lips, the same stoplight red he remembered from the year before.

"Have you ever been to Paris?" she asked him.

"I've never been to Turtle Bay Gardens."

She laughed — that deep, unexpected laugh.

Alva brought their food, along with a smirk, and filled two coffee cups. Nora took a paper napkin and placed it elegantly on her lap. Turtle Bay manners, Joe thought. She traced a graceful forefinger around the thick rounded rim of the diner plate, looking at her sandwich expectantly but not yet picking it up.

She asked Joe where he'd grown up.

"Sunnyside," he said.

"Like the eggs?"

"Like the eggs."

"Where's Sunnyside?" she asked.

With his thumb, he slid back the chrome bar on the syrup jar top and spilled a figure eight over his plate of bite-sized pancakes.

"Sunnyside is in Queens," he said.

"Queens?"

36

"Queens is a borough in New York City, Nora."

"I'm well aware of that, Joe," she said.

She sipped her coffee and grimaced.

"I told you it was terrible," Joe said.

"Have you eaten here a lot?" Nora asked.

"Only about a thousand times."

For a while, they sat in silence, at last allowing their eyes to meet. Then Joe used his fork to spear several of the pancakes and took an enormous first bite.

"Eat up," he told Nora. "It'll help the coffee go down."

She held her sandwich up, as if it were a sacrament. She took a bite. "Heaven," she said. Her eyes seemed to fill with light.

It was nearly nine o'clock by the time Alva cleared their plates away, asked if they wanted more coffee, and cursed mildly when they both said no too quickly and then laughed.

Nora asked Joe what he did at the station.

He told her he was a leverman.

"I've never met a leverman."

He smiled.

"But what *is* that?" she asked him.

"I work in a signal tower at the levers that make the train tracks move."

"So, you're like an engineer," she said.

"No," he said, still smiling. "I'm like a leverman."

"Sorry," Nora said. "I guess I don't know much about trains. What does a leverman do?"

"Really want to know?" he asked.

She nodded.

Joe stood up, took a bunch of cutlery from the counter, and, back at their booth, laid two knives side by side.

"Train tracks, right?" Nora asked him.

"And you thought you didn't know much about trains."

Then he used a fork and a spoon and a few other knives to show her the basics of how a lever could make a straight track branch off into a diverging track.

"And you work the fork," she said.

"Right. Except at Grand Central, every leverman is in charge of about fifty forks at a time."

He couldn't help feeling proud when he saw Nora's look of admiration, but it was past nine o'clock now, and Alva was hovering. He looked at the check and put some bills on the table, then hesitated.

"What is it?" Nora asked.

"Your number," he said. "Can I have your number?"

"My phone number?"

"I've got to see you again. Can I call you tomorrow?"

She looked suddenly doubtful. "You can try," she told him.

Joe fished in the pockets of his coat and found a short yellow pencil and the stub of a movie ticket.

"What do you mean, I can try?"

Nora took the pencil and the ticket stub. "Sometimes," she said, "it's hard to get through."

"Too many Romeos on the line?"

"I'd explain it to you if I thought you'd understand."

"Why wouldn't I understand?" Joe asked.

"It doesn't matter," she said. She wrote down her number. "Thank you so much for dinner."

She handed back the ticket, which, with her number on it now, immediately seemed like a ticket for something new. He put it in his coat pocket and, standing close beside her, remembered the gentle wood-and-whiskey bite of her perfume. They started walking toward the Main Concourse and the exit on Forty-second Street.

"What are we going to do about a coat for you?" he asked.

"Don't worry," she said. "I never get cold."

"Here we go," he said gruffly. "Take my

39

coat." He draped it over Nora's shoulders.

"Oh, Joe," she said, her face close to his, as if she were telling a secret.

He smiled at her. "But you can't have my hat or scarf."

"Bossy," she said, but she turned around and slipped her arms into the sleeves. The stiff wool collar brushed her left cheek. She inhaled. "It smells so good," she said. "Like fresh laundry! Has anyone ever told you that you smell like fresh laundry?"

"Oh, sure," Joe said. "All the time."

She laughed again, he realized he was in love, and then they walked up the stairs.

Joe's coat fell all the way past Nora's knees, leaving just a few inches of her blue dress showing. She leaned forward, her face nearly touching his neck this time, and thanked him, her hand on his shoulder. All the day's exhaustion faded. It might just as well have been morning. He opened the door, but now it was her turn to hesitate.

"Come on," Joe said. "Let's get you home safe and sound."

Together they walked east on Forty-second Street, passing the stately Commodore Hotel; the streetlamps, curved like shepherd's crooks; and the cabstand, where drivers were sleeping. Two streetcars rattled

40

past each other like tired old men.

When Joe and Nora turned north onto Lexington Avenue, the wind hit them hard.

"You must be freezing," she said.

"I'm not."

She stopped walking and turned to face him.

"What is it?" he asked.

Wordlessly, she reached up to tug the brim of his cap down, then took hold of his scarf and wrapped it twice around his neck.

"There, Joe Reynolds," she said to him tenderly. "Maybe that'll help."

They passed a dress shop and a cigar store, both closed up tight for the night. The traffic was thin. At this hour, there were usually only a few cars heading north to the Harlem nightclubs and a few horse-drawn carts heading south to the markets and warehouses.

"Do you always work this late?" Nora asked.

"Well, all the shifts are eight hours, but the BRT made it so we take turns on the late ones. That's the Brotherhood of Railroad Trainmen." Joe pointed to the red tin union pin on the lapel of his coat. "Been a member for twelve years," he said. Then he felt embarrassed for talking so much about himself.

"You're kind of a pip, you know," he said.

"A pip?"

He wondered if she was nervous to be out so late, even with him walking beside her. The streets were plenty menacing, as they'd been throughout the Depression. Just a few blocks from the terminal, two men were picking through a garbage can. Half a block down, a streetwalker was trying but failing to look proper. Somebody somewhere shouted, "Don't think I won't!" Next came the sound of glass breaking.

Nora stopped again. "Wait, Joe," she said. "I'm not sure I'm ready —"

"It's all right," he said. "Don't worry."

They had just crossed the street at Lexington and Forty-sixth when a young guy stumbled out of a doorway. At first Joe thought he was just a drunk, but the kid planted his feet firmly, waved his arms, and shouted, "Stop!"

By instinct — protective and swift — Joe stepped in front of Nora.

"I want your watch," the kid said.

"Yeah?" Joe said. "My watch is a piece of junk. But I want it too."

The guy smirked as if they were in a poker game and he had a fistful of aces, but he couldn't have been more than eighteen. Out came his switchblade, the steel catching the light and gleaming like an icicle. Joe's brother, Finn, was a cop, and even as kids, they had taught each other how to fight. Now, almost as if he were playing in the backyard in Queens, Joe hit the kid's wrist, and the knife fell easily from his hand. Joe kicked the knife to the gutter. When he looked up again, the kid looked scared.

"Get lost!" Joe shouted, then chased him for half a block. "Beat it!" he called after him.

It had all taken less than a minute.

Slightly winded, slightly proud, Joe watched until the guy was out of sight, and then he turned to go back to Nora. But Nora was gone.

The cold air whipped Joe's hair and made his shirt flap against his back. He looked in every direction, scanning the buildings and their empty shadows. He felt his throat tighten, but he called her name. Then he called it louder. Had someone gotten hold of her? Had she just run away?

"Nora!" he shouted. "Nora!"

Joe started back to the corner where the kid had come out of the doorway. He crossed Forty-sixth Street again, and then he saw it: his coat, lying on the sidewalk. He threw it on and started to run, but somehow, he was colder now than he'd been before.

44

5
GOT SOMETHING GOOD?

1938

No place could have been more convenient or better suited to Joe's life than the YMCA on East Forty-seventh Street. Just a short walk from the terminal, it was named the Railroad Branch because it had been built by the Vanderbilts as a home base for trainmen and engineers. The rooms upstairs were small and bare, but the common areas downstairs were lavish, decked out in the ornate Vanderbilt acorns and oak leaves, furnished in leather, paneled in wood.

Coming in chilled and unsettled by his search for Nora, Joe nodded hello to the half-dozen guys who were still awake in the club room, but he walked past them to the phone booth in back. Exhausted, he sat on the small wood seat, staring at the phone's dial, with its white petal tabs for the tiny red letters and black numbers. Then he picked up the receiver, took out the ticket

45

stub, and dialed Nora's number. When a man answered, Joe thought maybe Nora had given him a wrong number on purpose.

He leaned forward to speak into the phone's bell-shaped mouthpiece. "Can I talk to Nora Lansing?" he asked.

"Oh, God."

"Excuse me?"

"I've been wondering if I'd get another call," the man said.

"I'm looking for Nora Lansing," Joe said.

"I know."

"Are you her father?"

"No."

"Is she there?" Joe asked.

"No."

"When do you expect her?"

"I don't expect her. Not much, anyway. She doesn't live here," the man said.

"What do you mean, 'Not much'? She gave me this number."

"Right."

"Turtle Bay?"

"Right."

Joe took a moment. "I'm sorry," he said. "Can you tell me where I can find her?"

The man gave Joe his address and told him to come the next day after work.

"I don't understand," Joe said. "Can't you just tell me now?"

"I'm going to have to explain this in person," the man said.

"Why?" Joe asked.

"Because you're going to want a drink."

Joe couldn't sleep. He couldn't remember another night when his room had felt so empty. He kept imagining all the things that might have happened to Nora, kept trying to figure out what the man on the phone had meant.

At two A.M., he heard his neighbor Mitchell rattle and roar in from work.

"Joseph Damian Reynolds!" Mitchell shouted, gleefully drumming on Joe's door as he passed. Mitchell was a leverman who rarely ended a night shift without some kind of celebration. Joe chose to ignore him. The aroma of his cigar smoke lingered after the sound of his footsteps faded, but Joe imagined he could still smell Nora's perfume as well. Involuntarily, he played and replayed the scenes in his head. The Whispering Gallery. The red leather booth. The look on her face when she ate the grilled cheese. And then the kid with the knife.

At five o'clock, Joe got out of bed and glanced once more at the ticket stub, the only proof that any of what he remembered had actually happened. He dozed, but at seven he gave up trying to sleep. Though today's shift didn't start until ten, he had showered and left the Y by eight. He arrived at the terminal just in time for the crest of the morning rush hour, when commuters swarmed up from the platforms in sevens and eights instead of twos and threes.

Roughly three thousand people worked at Grand Central, and like most of them, Joe had long since stopped noticing the countless visitors who moved through it. To be more precise, he did notice them, but rarely as individuals. Instead, they belonged to a system: a swarm of bees, say, or a school of fish.

Grand Central Terminal was the destination, departure point for half a million travelers a day. For the thousands of people who worked there, though, it was really more like a hometown: beige, pink, and amber; cool in summer and warm in winter. Grand Central had a town square, which was the Main Concourse, and it had a main street, which was the lower concourse — also called the lower level, the commuter level, the dining concourse — with its coffee shops and restaurants, barbershop, bank, and shoeshine stands.

Grand Central had an art gallery and a newsreel theater, where Joe routinely went on breaks to learn about the wider world, the world he had never yet had the chance or the money to see for himself. The terminal had town tramps and town drunks, a drugstore and a bakery, a doctor's office, a police force, and even a small morgue. When Joe walked through the terminal in the mornings, he imagined it was the way his father had once strolled past the neighbors on his way to work in Queens. So Joe would nod his good mornings — to Patsy, at the florist, or to Jim, at the drugstore. "You need a haircut!" Charlotte might shout from the barbershop. "So do you!" he might shout back.

But this morning was different. Joe felt as if, for once, he was the rube — wide-eyed, gawking — as he stood in the concourse, scanning the ever-moving crowd, marveling at the variety of human beings, at the hope and dismay he felt in his unaccustomed search for just one person. He stayed for a long time, looking for Nora, and finally, a bit reluctantly, he went to buy his breakfast.

Big Sal, giving a customer change at Bond's Bakery, gestured for Joe to come over.

"Got something good?" he asked her, eyeing the rows of Danish and muffins that she always lined up with military precision.

"No, but I hear you did."

"Oh, Sal," he said. "Who's been telling you lies today?"

"Oh, Joseph," she said, and she winked at him. She was old, and her eyelids drooped, so at times her wink looked more like a tic.

"All right, Sal. What'd you hear?" he asked.

"You know what I heard. Quite a bombshell, this girl was, Mr. Movie Star. Alva said you couldn't take your eyes off her."

Joe sighed for effect, but the ribbing didn't really bother him. Sal was one of the old-timers who basically felt they'd watched him grow up.

"I was a perfect gentleman," Joe told Sally.

"No one is perfect, Joseph, except our Lord Jesus Christ."

"Black coffee and a cheese Danish, Sal."

"Come on, what's the story?" Sal asked.

"You want a story? Go buy yourself a magazine."

He used his breakfast as an excuse to return to the Main Concourse, where he leaned against the marble stairs, slowly eating his Danish and, once more, searching the crowd. Above him was the famous vaulted ceiling, an indoor heaven with a shining frame and 2,500 stars that twinkled against

50

an improbable blue-green sky.

Years before, the clock master, Jacob, had told Joe that the mural had been painted all wrong — with the constellations backward and from different parts of the sky. The Vanderbilts claimed this was not a mistake, that the mural had been intended to show how God saw the stars from heaven. According to Jake, the painters had just screwed up.

The reason didn't matter to Joe, who loved the ceiling the way it was — no matter if the color of the sky was even less realistic than its stars. Joe had memorized the names of its constellations: Leo, Orion, and all the rest, which stayed fixed in their places, predictable as the stations on a train line's route. If one of those stars had suddenly whirled off as a comet and crashed down from the ceiling, it would have been every bit as startling to Joe as meeting and losing Nora had been.

The locker rooms in the signal towers shook as the trains came in, but the shower stalls were clean, with oatmeal soap that felt like sandpaper and could scrape off a good work sweat. After his shift, Joe braced himself against the tiled wall as if he were trying to push it away. He let the water scald the back of his neck, his shoulders, his scalp. Staring into the steamed-up mirror over the sink, he waited until he could see his face. His eyes looked gray and questioning.

Snow had been falling all afternoon, and the winter sky was almost purple when Joe left the station at five. The snow had outlined the building's edges. High atop the entrance, the huge Mercury statue's outstretched hand looked as if it were armed with a giant snowball.

Joe made a second knot in his scarf, pulled the brim of his cap down, and raced off toward Turtle Bay.

Number 229 East Forty-eighth Street stood in the elegant row of Turtle Bay townhouses whose brass numbers and large door knockers gleamed in the dusk. The entrance was down a half flight of stairs, and Joe nearly slipped on the ice-slicked steps. He rang the doorbell and waited. The wind had picked up, and his cheeks were numb. He rang the bell again and was about to try the knocker when he heard an inside door open and close. A moment later, a heavyset man in a striped shirt, high-waisted tweed pants, and round black glasses opened the door.

"Arthur Fox," the man said, extending his hand. "Call me Artie."

"Joe Reynolds," Joe said. "Joe."

They shook hands.

"So, what wouldn't you tell me on the phone?" Joe asked. His eyes were tearing from the cold. A blast of wind lifted Artie's tie.

"Come in," Artie said. He put his hands on Joe's shoulders and steered him inside. The entranceway was warm and smelled of steam heat. It was dim, and Joe could just make out flowery wallpaper and a pair of gold wall lamps with flame-shaped bulbs that reminded him of Nora's earrings.

Artie's living room didn't look like Artie. He seemed tough and wise-guy sure, but the chairs were covered in silk or something shiny, and the heavy curtains, tied back with fringed ropes, looked like tall women in fancy robes.

Artie sat down in a deep-blue armchair but leaned forward enthusiastically. He gestured for Joe to sit too, but Joe kept standing.

"You met her in Grand Central, right?" Artie asked.

"How'd you know?"

"And she was wearing, what, no coat? Just a dress?"

Joe nodded.

"And she wanted to go home?"

53

Joe nodded again.

Artie offered an exaggerated shudder. "Sit down," he said, and now Joe did.

Artie reached over to a curved marble side table and flung open a polished wooden box. He took out a cigar, then rolled it appraisingly over his thumb.

"Mr. Fox," Joe said.

"Artie."

"Artie, I'm not here to make trouble. I'm just worried about her."

"You don't need to worry about her," he said, with an emphasis on the last word.

Artie struck the match, lit his cigar, and smiled behind the leaping flame.

Joe had never needed to be the smartest guy in the room, but he was damned if he was going to let someone make him feel stupid. "Let me ask you this," he said. "Did Nora *ever* live here?"

Artie tried to draw a first puff from the cigar, *pah-pah*ing until the tip glowed orange. "She grew up here," he said. "I never met her, but I bought the place from her mother. Her, I met. Elsie Lansing." He gestured around the room. "Most of this was her stuff. Not exactly my style, but the woman was in a hurry. And anyway, my wife liked it." Artie puffed on his cigar again. "Ex-wife," he added.

"Sorry."

Artie shrugged.

Joe asked, "And where is Mrs. Lansing now?"

"Connecticut," Artie said. "I called her a few times to tell her what I'd heard. That people had seen the daughter."

"And?"

"She didn't want to hear it. Cold as an Eskimo's nuts."

"So, what, Nora had a crack-up or something? She obviously thinks this is still her home. She wrote this phone number down for me."

Joe took out the ticket stub, which was already smudged and slightly worn. Artie put his cigar in an ashtray, leaned over, and looked at the ticket. "Yeah. About that," he said. "Notice anything strange about the number?"

Joe shook his head.

"Read it to me," Artie said.

Joe read "P-L-A-4-9-8-8."

"P-L-*A*," Artie said. He lifted the telephone from the side table and showed it, face-front, to Joe, so he could see the number printed in the middle of the dial.

"Now read that," Artie said.

"P-L-2-4-9-8-8."

"P-L-*2*," Artie said.

"I don't understand," Joe said.

"Remember? Before the thirties, the phone numbers used to start with three letters?"

Joe nodded slowly. "Not two."

"That's right."

"They changed the third letters to numbers when the city needed more phone lines."

"Exactly," Artie said. "No one would have written her telephone number that way after 1929."

"You're saying she gave me the wrong number?"

"I'm saying she gave you the right number — but for the wrong decade."

Joe merely stared back at Artie.

"So now," Artie said, "it's time for that drink."

He put the phone down, took three steps toward a large oak console, and opened a door to reveal a miniature bar. He reached for a bottle of bourbon, filled two glasses, and handed one to Joe.

"Look, none of this makes a damn bit of sense," Artie said. "I mean, none of it. You're confused? *I'm* confused. When other people tell me about her, *they're* confused. Drink."

Joe hesitated a moment, then tossed back

the bourbon. It was smooth, not at all like the Old Crow he sometimes had with his father or Finn.

"*When* have other people seen her?" Joe asked.

"First week of December," Artie said, sitting back down. "Whenever she comes, it's the first week of December. People see her, and then she disappears. Last year, she called here herself. Or anyway, someone pretending to be her. I hung up on her before I could stop myself. Wish I hadn't done that."

A chill jabbed at Joe's back.

"And how do you — what do you —"

"What do I do about it?" Artie asked. "I drink to the first week of December." He held up his glass in a vague toast, then took a long sip. "Do you know what happened that week in 1925?"

Joe knew all too well.

"There was a big crash at Grand Central," Artie said. "A subway accident. Lots of casualties."

"I was there," Joe said softly. He would never forget that day or its impact: the chaos, the panic, the smoke, the smells — and the way that it had changed him.

"You're still not getting it," Artie said.

"What?" Joe asked impatiently. "What am

I not getting?"

"Nora died in that crash. She's been dead for thirteen years."

6
SWIFTER, HIGHER, STRONGER

1924

Nora didn't know where she was.

She had the map that the hotel clerk had given her, but she must have taken a wrong turn somewhere. She had been walking for more than half an hour, and each street had led to a smaller one, the way tree trunks lead to branches, then twigs. I'm on a twig, she thought. *Je suis sur un . . .* But who knew the French word for it? *Je suis sur un twig?* Usually she had no trouble finding her way. But this was Paris, not New York, and she had arrived only the day before, and she was still a little unsteady from nearly a week on board the ship. Now she couldn't find her way back to any of the broad, open avenues, the ones where she'd seen the Métro signs on the way from Le Havre to her hotel.

She was wearing a new green-and-white-plaid dress with green shoes and a white

59

floppy hat, and she felt wonderfully stylish, despite her fatigue. It was only ten in the morning, but it was July, and even in the shade of the narrow streets, Nora could feel the stubbornness of the summer heat, the kind of heat that lurks between fevers.

A man with grayish cheeks and a white stubbly beard approached her.

"Pardon, mademoiselle," he said.

"Oui?"

"Vous êtes perdue?"

"No, I'm not lost," she said, as if the man had insulted her. *"Non,"* she said. *"Je sais où je suis."*

The man waved his hand as if pushing aside a cloud of smoke. *"Bon,"* he said, walking off. *"Ça va."*

Nora folded her too-conspicuous map and decided to trust her instincts. It was a summer morning in Paris. How bad would it be to be lost?

She was so glad to be on her own. Back at the hotel, she had left a note on Margaret's night table and tiptoed past her. She wanted to let Margaret sleep, but she also didn't want company on this first venture out. It wasn't that she didn't like Margaret, but she'd always believed she would fall in love with Paris when she finally saw it in person, and Nora thought it old-fashioned to need a chaperone, whether for meeting a man or a city.

Now she walked the sleepy streets, wondering where everyone was, until finally she started to hear horns honking, people shouting, and whistles blowing. Eventually, by trial and error, she found herself borne along with an eager crowd, back to a loud, vivid boulevard. All over the buildings and streetlamps, she could see Olympics posters: three men standing proudly before billowing blue, white, and red French flags, their pale torsos thrust out like doves' breasts and their arms raised high in salute below the bold capital letters:

Paris — 1924

Nora was now part of the group bobbing toward the Métro, then down the steps and onto the packed, hot platform, where visitors were vying for better positions as their hats collided and they held their purses close. An older woman on shipboard had warned her that there had been some sort of riot between Frenchmen and Italians at a boxing match, and once inside the Métro car, Nora could sense the tribal tension among the riders, their loud voices and languages crossing in the air like unseen swords. She found this tension less menacing than thrilling. She listened to the arguments, not saying a word even when a man took off his cap and — in Spanish or Italian, she wasn't sure which — stood up to offer her his seat. She merely nodded her thanks and sat, trying to ignore the annoyed looks of the women who'd been passed over.

"What are you, then, a duchess?" one of them asked in an Irish accent.

Nora pretended not to understand. As long as she didn't speak, she figured, she was free to be anyone here; she could have come from anywhere. On the event programs, in magazines, and in newspaper ads, she had seen the Olympic motto: *Citius, Altius, Fortius* — "Swifter, Higher, Stronger." She read it as a personal mandate.

The Olympic swimming pool had been built on the outskirts of Paris, the last stop on the Métro. The streets around it were nearly as crowded as the train had been, with people carrying small Olympic or national flags, clutching their tickets, glancing at their guidebooks, and trying to find their way around or between the people in front of them.

Inside the stadium, Nora managed to get a ticket, although her seat was high up in the stands. Above her, the sky was perfectly blue. Below her, the huge pool gleamed like a square-cut sapphire, with the timers and photographers inset around it like other gems, their white straw hats brilliant in the sun. How would it feel, Nora wondered as she watched the swimmers putting on their bathing caps and taking off their robes, to parade around the side of a pool with bare shoulders, bare legs, and a thousand people watching you? Even the American swimmers — who had presumably grown up wearing the same heavy wool bathing skirts and black tights that Nora had — seemed perfectly natural about it, maybe even a little bit proud.

In addition to the dress she was wearing, Nora had purchased two short flapper dresses at Saks Fifth Avenue the day before she sailed, and seeing the swimmers strutting, she couldn't wait to wear her new clothes.

"Which one do you fancy?" a red-cheeked, chubby young man to Nora's left asked his friend.

"I'll take the I-tie," the friend said, and Nora understood him to mean the girl with the Italian flag sewn onto the front of her swimsuit.

"Nah, Hugh, you're blind! You're blind!

Look at Sweden over there."

"Ohhhh," Hugh said, as if the Swedish swimmer had been delivered onto his lap to stroke his temples and twirl his hair. "Yeah, look at the diddies on that one. 'Course she floats."

They laughed loudly enough that a few people turned. Nora gave them the same look her mother would have given one of the servants if he'd dropped a silver tray.

"Shh, mate," the friend said, as if Nora couldn't hear him.

But Hugh didn't want to be quiet. "Guess *you* think they should be more covered up," he said to Nora. "Old-fashion-like."

Nora summoned her mother's frost. "Actually," she said, "if they were totally naked, they'd swim even faster." Then she turned away from the two of them, delighting in their shock. Every once in a while, she had to admit, it was fine to be Elsie Lansing's daughter. Elsie knew her power. By example, by conflict, or by both, she had taught Nora to know hers.

"*À vos marques,*" an announcer said, and with the rest of the crowd Nora leaned forward to watch the first five of the marvelous women line up at the edge of the pool.

"*Prêt,*" the announcer said, and the women crouched into dive positions.

"Partez!" he said, and the splashes came up from the water as the cheers came up from the crowd.

Nora stayed through the four heats and the semifinals of the women's 100-meter freestyle, cheering the Americans, who placed every time. The diving heats were next, but it was after one o'clock by then, and Nora suddenly felt unsteady. It was hot, and she hadn't eaten, and she could still feel the lilt of the ocean.

"*So* nice to have met you," she said drily as she slid past the two red-faced men.

Up the aisle and out the entry she went, then down staircase after staircase, which did nothing to steady her. Back on the ground floor, Nora heard the cheers from the arena sounding even louder, and she looked back with momentary regret.

At the exit, a bald, damp-looking man who smelled horribly of sweat held the door for her, then handed her a postcard of the arena.

"Merci," she said, and kept walking as she looked down at the card.

Citius, Altius, Fortius, it read. Just as she smiled, she felt a strong hand clutching her shoulder.

"Pardon," the bald man said.

"Oui?"

He gestured excitedly toward the postcard and spoke very fast, his words tumbling out and around her, as unpleasant as his smell. She tried to hand the postcard back.

"Non, non!" he cried. *"Non!"* and he pointed repeatedly at her purse.

"They do this," a starchy voice said, and there, quite unexpectedly, was a thin, tidily dressed older man with a sharp nose and blue-gray eyes, smoothly pressing a colorful bill into the man's hand. "Don't let it bother you," he said to Nora. "They're totally mad for their tips. You'll see. We foreigners get used to it."

He took off his straw hat and ran a hand through his thick salt-and-pepper hair, which was parted down the middle but wiry and wild despite what seemed to be a good deal of brilliantine. Nora guessed he was in his mid-forties.

"Thank you," she said, nodding in the direction of the bald man, who was already taking aim at another departing spectator.

"Don't mention it," the man said. His English accent was as crisp as his white shirt. He peered down at her. "You look a little parched," he said.

"I am, actually," Nora confessed.

66

"Then let me buy you something cold to drink."

She looked at him warily.

"Nothing with alcohol, I assure you," he said.

"I'd love something cold to drink," Nora said, and as the man walked off toward the nearest concession stand, she leaned gratefully against the stadium wall, taking off her hat to fan herself. There were the posters again, those three men with their chests bare, their thighs just covered by foliage, and their insignificant athletes' shorts painted flat and beige, an afterthought. A few yards away, several young women about Nora's age pointed at one of the posters, giggled, and turned around, apparently embarrassed. Nora would never be that kind of girl.

She stared at the poster and its many copies, which ribboned the stadium wall. Three mostly naked men, then six, then nine, then twelve — as far as she could see.

"You don't know one of them, do you?" the British man said, winking as he handed her a club-shaped green bottle with a label that said *Perrier.*

"I used to be married to that one," Nora declared without missing a beat. She pointed to the man on the right. "His name

67

is Eugene."

The man smiled. "How extraordinary," he said. "*My* name is Eugene."

His real name was Oliver Halliday, and he ran a small art gallery on the Left Bank. Ollie would be the first friend Nora made in Paris; her guide and advisor and eventually, once she'd run out of funds and begged him for a job, her employer. In her position as his assistant, Nora would get to spend three days a week prowling smaller galleries or the stalls of Montmartre, engaged in a constant treasure hunt for undiscovered talent — and sneaking away whenever she could, to do her own work.

Nora had taken drawing and painting classes all through high school and college; at her graduation from Barnard, she had even won the senior prize for achievement in the fine arts. Now, inspired by the art and the city around her, she drew or painted every day. At lunchtime, she would choose a café, order a croque-monsieur and nurse a lemonade or a café au lait while she studied and sketched the customers. Relentlessly Nora tried to capture the bustle and idleness, the roughness and restraint, of the people around her.

In Notre-Dame, she sketched the leaves

and scrolls on the capitals of the stone columns, the endless rows of towering organ pipes, the praying hands on the statue of Saint Joan. No matter the size of her purse, she always kept a sketchpad and a pencil tucked somewhere inside it. She allowed herself to dream that someday people might see what she'd drawn.

She and Margaret shared a small attic flat with red toile bedspreads and a copper-framed sky. At night, Nora would lie in bed and look up at the skylight, where, on clear nights, she could see subtle layers of darkness behind and around the stars. She would watch for the only constellations that, as a city girl, she had managed to learn: the Big Dipper, the Little Dipper, Leo. Enclosed by the skylight's copper frame, the stars were a painting that changed above her every night. Sometimes she could even see wisps of chimney smoke darting by like spirits.

7
I MET THIS GIRL

1938

For days Joe looked for ways to explain away
what Artie had said about Nora. At one
point, he even wondered if he was being
scammed in some way. Joe knew about all
sorts of con games. Especially during the
desperate thirties, you couldn't work in
Grand Central without seeing them come
and go. But neither Nora nor Artie had
asked him for a dime, and in any case, Artie
was the one with the money.

For three long weeks, ever since their talk,
Joe had spent almost all his free nights playing pool or poker at the Y. He drank a bit
more than usual, and he talked less. He told
no one about Nora — not about meeting
her, and not about what Artie had said she
was. And yet there, carved over the fireplace,
the YMCA motto had seemed haunting in
itself: *Spirit, Mind, Body.*

Joe was the son of two Irish Catholics. He

had grown up keeping most things to himself. He'd been told that whatever secrets he had should be revealed only in the confessional, but as a child, he'd feared that small wooden closet as soon as he'd found out what it was. He had imagined that there was a chute inside the booth, and that if Father Gregory didn't like what you said, he could pull a handle, the floor would open, and down you would slide into hell.

As a result, Joe had saved up most of his doubts and sins to tell his big brother, Finn. With Finn, the risk was of ridicule, not damnation. Finn was older than Joe by two years, still taller by nearly two inches, and had always been the one to start a scuffle or pull a prank. But after school, they had sat at the kitchen table, eating sponge cake or last night's leftovers, playing gin rummy, arguing about whose turn it was to do what chores, and letting their secrets travel back and forth along the same worn brother-to-brother path. At this table, with its white porcelain top and its faded pattern of red diamonds and squares, Finn had told Joe that he was making extra pocket money selling pinched cigarettes, and Joe had told Finn about his passionate longing for Mrs. Belknap, his eighth-grade history teacher.

The kitchen in those days had been a

warm but dark place, with cabinets made of sturdy wood, a black-and-white-checked linoleum floor, and a stained flowered skirt hiding the legs and pipes of the kitchen sink. Even in summer the kitchen had smelled of their mother's stews and soups: the constant, comforting aroma of boiled potatoes and slightly burned meat.

It had been sixteen years since their mother, Katherine, had died, and the kitchen was now presided over by Finn's wife, Faye, a neighborhood girl with hazel eyes and dark brown hair who knew how to flirt and fight. In her constant battle to wipe out the losses and sadness of the past, Faye's chief weapon was color. She dressed in the liveliest shades she could find, and she had brightened things up around the house. The scratched white porcelain table had long since been replaced by a round wooden one with Kelly-green trim; the cabinet doors had been painted yellow; and the treasured prints and maps of old Ireland that had lined the walls above them had been hidden by colorful bowls, pitchers, and vases. But the kitchen was still the kitchen, and on this Christmas Eve, Joe walked in with the intention of telling Finn about Nora.

First, though, Joe had to laugh. Finn was

on his hands and knees, gathering up stray cranberries that his and Faye's kids — Mike and Alice — had no doubt dropped while stringing garlands for the tree.

"Quit that cackling," Finn said. "Faye's going to kill these kids for making this mess. Or me, if I don't clean it up before she sees it. Come on. What are you waiting for?"

Joe took a heavy striped bowl from the table and joined Finn on the floor, collecting the cranberries while trying to decide exactly how to start the conversation.

So, listen, Finny. I met this girl. . . .

"Don't forget under the stove," Finn said.

"If I find any money, can I keep it?" Joe asked.

"If you find any money, it'll be a fucking miracle."

They were just standing up when Faye swung the kitchen door open — only enough for her voice to enter.

"Your pa wants his Old Crow," she said, and the door swung shut again.

Joe reached up for the bottle of bourbon, which was strategically kept on a high shelf, beyond the reach of their father, Damian, who had been in a wheelchair since the Great War.

Say, Finn. You ever had something happen to you that you couldn't explain?

73

Finn grabbed an ice tray from the freezer and cranked back the metal handle, popping up the cubes. Joe took down three of the good glasses, and Finn dropped in the ice. Then Joe poured two fingers of bourbon into the first glass and added a splash of water.

"Thin it down more," Finn said.

"It already looks like ginger ale."

"He won't notice. I don't want him tight. Did I tell you he pinched Faye's fanny last week?"

"Bet she loved that."

"Yeah. It'd be hard to say how much."

Finn poured a shot for himself and one for Joe.

"Happy Christmas," Joe said.

"Mud in your eye," Finn said.

"Dirt in your nails."

The brothers clinked glasses and drank.

I met this amazing girl, Finn, but there's one little problem. . . .

The swinging door flapped open again, and this time Faye stepped in. She was dressed for Christmas Eve mass in a smart striped dress, her hair tucked up into a bright green wool hat with a slightly droopy satin bow.

"Kids are ready now," she said. She squeezed Joe's shoulders from behind,

74

kissed the side of his neck, snatched the glass from his hand, took a sip of his drink, and put the glass down. "Merry Christmas, Joey," she said, and swung back out.

Joe followed her into the living room and handed Damian his drink.

"Happy Christmas, Pa," Joe said.

"Mud in your eye," said Damian.

At home and at the VFW, Damian always used his wheelchair, but at church — and especially for Christmas Eve mass — he didn't want so many people to see him being rolled in by his sons. So there were elaborate, unspoken rules about which cane to bring, which son to lean on, and which entrance to use. Wounded in France in 1918, Damian lacked his left leg from the knee down and all but two of the fingers on his left hand.

Mike and Alice were endlessly fascinated by the missing parts of their grandfather and often asked him to hike up his pant leg so they could see his false limb. Alice was only six, but Mike, at eleven, was almost tall enough for Damian to lean on now. Still, Faye followed the usual protocol and ushered the children in front of the men, zeroing in on a pew near the front.

Joe went to church now only on the big

holidays, or on a Sunday if for some reason Finn or Faye couldn't take Damian. Joe still remembered the rules, though, and the rules said that when you died, you went to heaven, hell, or purgatory, not to Grand Central Terminal. The rules said there were no such things as ghosts. Occasionally, you might cross paths with a soul in purgatory, someone God had made visible for the purpose of teaching a lesson or inspiring a prayer. But even if you happened to see such a soul, she would not, Joe clearly understood, be someone who stopped to chat, eat a grilled cheese sandwich, and leave your winter coat lying like a tar stain on Lexington Avenue.

Joe looked to his left, at the rows of earnest worshippers, their round, red, interchangeable faces lined up like apples in a fruit stand. Before them, flanked by choirboys in wide white collars, Father Gregory presided in his white-and-gold robe. He had shrunk quite a bit over the years since Joe and Finn's childhood, a fact that gave Joe continual, secret delight. The priest's hair and beard were yellow-white now, and his face was so colorless that he could have passed for a barely living version of one of the stone saints carved over the entrance to the church.

For the hundredth time, and without exactly wanting to, Joe thought about Nora's eyes, laugh, hair, hands — even the way she had said "Oh, Joe" and made it sound like a secret. He knew it was sacrilegious, but it hit him, as the mass droned on, that what he was feeling for Nora wasn't all that different from what the people around him were feeling. He was simply — if not as confidently — believing in the wrong miracle and hoping for the wrong person's return.

Joe knew dozens of girls at the terminal; he'd had sex for the first time back in his teens with one of the Century Girls, the secretaries on the 20th Century Limited who were usually as elegant and sleek as their train. Since then, he'd known all sorts of others. In Queens, as in the terminal, he was everyone's favorite bachelor catch. Finn had set him up with the sisters of half the cops in the precinct. Faye had made him meet the girls who'd gone to school with her. He had dated the pretty ones and gone to bed with some of the willing ones. He'd learned what they wanted and what they feared; what they were willing to take and willing to give. Not one of them had made him feel what Nora had — this dynamic, electric thrill: a hint that not only he, but the whole exhausted world, might jump up and dance, and want to look its best.

Thinking about this, Joe only half heard what the priest was saying. Meanwhile, little Alice, wearing brown leather lace-up shoes that looked too small, was kicking her legs back and forth. Mike pretended his foot was in the way. Alice kicked Mike. Mike kicked Alice. Faye managed, impressively, to grab each of them by an ear.

The priest continued mercilessly, extolling the coming of God's son and the mystery of his sacrifice. But for Joe it was the same way it had been in Ralston's prayer meeting the morning he'd first met Nora. All he could think about was the mystery of *her,* and about what Finn would say if Joe got up the nerve to tell him what had happened.

Back at home, Finn helped Damian up the stairs while Faye put the kids to bed. Joe waited alone in the living room. The tree, trimmed with old ornaments and the kids' strands of cranberries, looked just like the trees of Joe's childhood. He stood up to straighten the straw angel at the top. The smell of pine engulfed him, and he closed his eyes, finding his mother, his father, his brother, his younger self; the joy of an unopened present; the hopes of a Christmas morning.

The sound of Finn and Faye's laughter broke the moment, and Joe turned to see them coming down the stairs, Finn chasing Faye. As they reached the living room, he grabbed her around the waist and kissed her shoulder.

"Quit your fooling," she said. "There's work to be done."

Finn sighed but smiled as Faye went to the kitchen, and he moved the good crystal candlesticks from the center of the dining room table.

"Grab those scissors from the shelf, Joe," he said. "Where's the paper?"

Every Christmas since the Crash, Joe had talked Big Sal into giving him sheets of the bakery's brown waxed paper to use for wrapping the presents. He took it now from his canvas satchel and laid it out on the table. "Sal was stingy this year," he told Finn.

"Aw, we'll make it. We've always got newspaper if we run out."

Do you believe in an afterlife, Finny?

Can you promise not to make fun of me?

Faye emerged from the kitchen with a meager assortment of toys and clothes and two small balls of thick yarn. She put the gifts on the table and sighed. "Well, boys, it

79

isn't much, but it'll have to do," she said. "I've got to hit the hay now. Those two urchins are going to be up at dawn to see what Santa brought."

She kissed Joe good night on the lips, a flirty habit she enjoyed more than he did but that came from years of teasing Finn that she'd married the wrong brother. From the top of the stairs, she called down, "Don't forget — red yarn for Alice, green for Mike."

Joe laid out a sheet of waxed paper, and Finn took a pair of gloves from the pile of gifts Faye had left them.

"I'm guessing these are for you," Finn said. Joe laughed, opened the tin of Scotch tape, and scratched at the roll to find the edge. Finn did the wrapping and Joe did the taping, and they worked for a while without talking.

Hey, Finn, want to hear something funny?

But it was Finn who broke the silence. "Faye says she's got someone new for you."

"Faye always says that around this time of year."

"She says she's got a really great feeling about this one."

"She always says that too," Joe said.

"The girl's named Emma. Ella. Emma. One of those," Finn said. He shut his eyes, trying to remember, then counted off the items on his fingers, reciting. "Twenty-five. Irish. Catholic. Lives in Woodside —"

"Gee," Joe said. "An Irish Catholic girl from Queens. What were the odds?"

Smiling, Finn held up a small red steel box and shook it, rattling its contents.

"Did Pa actually pick that out?" Joe asked.

"Yeah, can you believe it? He made me take him to Puck's."

The Erector sets, in their tin boxes, were a Damian tradition dating back to Joe and Finn's childhood, when Katherine had also managed to knit each of them a new scarf every Christmas.

"Just one this year?" Joe asked.

"Had to be. He didn't want them to have to share, but I told him if we bought two, then we'd have to give up the Christmas ham."

"They'll understand," Joe said.

Finn nodded, then asked, "How can you be sure?"

"That they'll understand?"

"That Faye's friend might not turn out to be the one."

"I can't be," Joe said. "But I think I may have met the one."

"At the terminal?" Finn asked.

Joe nodded.

"Gee," Finn said. "Another Century Girl. What were the odds?"

"Not this time," Joe told Finn.

"Let me ask you this," Finn said, laughing. "Do you date them because they've gone all the way to Chicago or because they'll go all the way with you?"

"Do you know how many times you've used that line?"

"Do you know how many Century Girls you've dated?"

"This is different," Joe said softly. "Really different."

"Okay, so, who is she?" Finn asked.

Joe was silent, taping the present that Finn had just wrapped.

"Who is she?" Finn asked again.

"Look," Joe said, putting down the tape roll. "I've got to tell you something about her, Finny, and there's no one else I can tell."

"About this one you met?"

Joe nodded.

"What, is she married?" Finn asked.

"No. But Finny, this is a No-Matter-What."

It was something they'd had since childhood: A No-Matter-What was not just a secret, but the understanding that went with it — that some things would always transcend any fight, any bribe, any girl, any moment. A No-Matter-What was a secret sealed by the struggles and joys of their shared childhood.

"Give," Finn said.

So Joe told Finn about Nora: not just about how and when he had met her, or how she had looked or made him feel, but also about the way she'd disappeared, and how he'd gone to her house, and how Artie had told him that she had died in the subway accident.

"In 'twenty-five?" Finn asked.

Joe nodded.

"You were there for that," Finn said.

"I know."

Then Joe whispered, "Do you believe that people can come back from the dead?"

Joe could see Finn fighting the urge to laugh.

"A No-Matter-What, Finny," Joe repeated.

"All right," Finn said. He looked down at the pile of gifts again. He picked up one of Alice's presents: a doll from the coming World's Fair, decked out in New York orange and blue. "You mean do I believe in ghosts?" he asked, holding the doll in one hand as Joe smoothed out another piece of brown paper.

"Yes," Joe said, still whispering. "Do you?"

"Well, Pa would probably say she's a fairy. You know, the fairies, they can make themselves look any way they want, and he says no one can ever resist them."

"So, you believe in fairies," Joe said, and Finn laughed.

Finn placed the doll faceup and laid the wrapping paper over her, a move that suddenly struck Joe as creepy.

"This girl," Finn said. "She was probably just some floozy trying to pick you up."

"This was no floozy, Finn. And her earrings had real pearls in them."

"Oh, yeah? You're a jeweler all of a sudden?"

"Finny, they were real. And she grew up in Turtle Bay Gardens."

"And that proves she wasn't scamming you?"

"For what?" Joe asked. "What was the scam?"

"I don't know. How would I know?"

Joe took a breath. "Finny," he said. "Did you ever see something you couldn't explain?"

"You mean aside from your —"

"Don't," Joe said, heading off the inevitable insult: Joe's fat head, his ugly mug, his tiny dick, whatever.

Finn recognized Joe's tone of voice. He

84

peered into his younger brother's eyes and seemed to see both Joe's worry and his hope.

Finn sat in the desk chair now, and Joe leaned against the sofa.

"There's a guy at the precinct," Finn said. "He was on a case in Staten Island once. Some mob runner got bumped, and there was supposed to be cash in the guy's house. So, Frankie — that's my guy — he and his partner go to check out the place. It's late. They're tired. But they're sober, right? Frankie says he's looking through the upstairs bedroom, and he sees this thing, this shadow, walk right across in front of him. Frankie can tell it's a fireman, because he can see the shape of the guy's hat."

"Was there a fire?" Joe asked.

Finn shook his head. "No fire," he said. "So, a few minutes later, he feels a hand on his back. He turns around. No one there. Scares him down to his boots, but he decides not to say anything about it. Doesn't want the other cop to think he's cracked. They keep looking for the dough, but nothing turns up, and it's not till they're back in the squad car that Frankie's partner says, 'Did you see that fireman?' "

Joe said nothing.

Finn stood up. "No lie," he said, then

85

wordlessly went to the kitchen and returned with the bottle of bourbon and glasses. As he had hours before, Finn poured two shots, and the brothers drank.

"I don't know," Finn said. "Think of the mass we just went to. Wasn't it all about miracles?"

"Sure," Joe said. "But *this*?"

Finn leaned forward, big-brother protective.

"Were you scared when you were with her?" he asked Joe softly.

"Not even a little," Joe said, and as he said it, he realized both how odd and how thrilling that fact was.

8
NO MORE STRANGE WOMEN

1938–1939

The week between Christmas and New Year's was always a critical time at the terminal, with added trains, extra shifts, and double the number of travelers and lines at the markets and shops. In Tower A, as on most holidays, resentment was at its height because the levermen were denied the very leisure they were making possible for others. Joe, for his part, was relieved to have the distraction of the heavier workload, and he tried to summon Finn's attitude about Nora and about what Artie had said. Maybe there were such things as ghosts. Maybe there weren't. Maybe only God knew.

But the attitude didn't last. On a bleak, cloudy afternoon on the second-to-last day of 1938, Joe came up from Tower A to find Gus Bardello outside the Vanderbilt Avenue entrance, sweeping the pavement with a heavy, splayed push broom. Like Ralston,

Gus had been working at the terminal since its opening day in 1913. For years he had been an engineer's assistant, but his health had begun to fail around the start of Prohibition, and he'd been kept on as a jack-of-all-trades — at least of all trades that didn't require young legs or steady hands. He looked a bit like a marshmallow now: dusty, white, and soft; when he smiled, his mouth seemed to sink into the rest of his face, and his eyes nearly disappeared.

Gus barely glanced up when Joe said hello, hardly altering the rhythm of his sweeping. That was nothing personal. When you worked with a broom or mop in Grand Central, you usually looked down, not because you cared so much for the work, but because — never more than during Christmas week — you were always searching for the perfect prize: the dropped money clip or the lost diamond earring.

"Hey, Gus."

"Hey, Young America," Gus said.

"I've got to ask you a question."

"Shoot."

Gus stopped sweeping and knelt stiffly to pick up a scrap of paper, turning it over intently before tossing it back into the small pyramid of ticket stubs and cigarette butts he'd already created. He leaned on the broom, the tip of the handle pushing slightly into his pillowy face.

"What's the question?" he asked Joe.

"Have you ever heard of there being a ghost in Grand Central?"

Gus smiled merrily, but fortunately he didn't laugh. He formed a thumb and forefinger into the shape of a U and shakily wiped the corners of his mouth.

"Which ghost did you have in mind?" he said.

"*Which* ghost?"

"Crazy Mabel? Captain Beauregard? Or, wait, Maud S.? You have to have heard of Maud S."

"Who is Maud S.?"

Gus reached into his coat pocket for a pack of Luckies and tapped one out. *"Was,"* he said. *"Was.* She was a horse. A famous racehorse."

"No, Gus," Joe said. "I was asking you about ghosts."

Gus lit his cigarette and contentedly exhaled through enormous nostrils. Then he explained. Back in the days before they built the new terminal, William Henry Vanderbilt purchased one of the fastest racehorses in the country: a filly named Maud S. But instead of racing her, Vanderbilt hitched her to a carriage and built a

89

stable for her, right near the train shed. So whenever he came back from any trip, Maud S. would be waiting, and he'd get the fastest ride home that could be had.

"And?" Joe asked. "Did she kick someone in the head? Or trample someone to death?"

Gus dropped his cigarette butt on the pavement, ground it out with his heel, and swept it into the pile. "Naw, naw," he said. "It's the *horse.* The ghost is the horse."

"What?"

"Maud S. She's a ghost horse. People hear her hoofbeats in the Vanderbilt Passage. That's where the stables used to be."

Joe looked at Gus and gently took the broom from him.

"What're you doing?"

Joe led Gus indoors and laid the broom against the lobby wall. "I'm buying you a drink," Joe said.

They sat at the bar called the Junction, a dive in the lower concourse more popular with workers than with visitors. Joe ordered Gus a scotch and himself a beer and sat back to listen. The ghost horse wasn't Gus's only story. He also told Joe about the odd sounds that came from the north wall in the men's smoking room — the large public lounge off the main waiting room. It seemed

90

that Captain Beauregard, a Civil War veteran, had dressed in his Confederate uniform and thrown himself in front of a train on Track 9; sometimes at night you could swear there was the sound of a train screeching to a stop, and then a lot of worried shouts. And that wasn't all. In the catwalks that crossed the arched windows on the east wall — the passageways that looked like single windowpanes from a distance — that was where the old woman called Crazy Mabel was said to appear near dawn, shouting for someone to save her, although it was never clear from what.

Joe picked up his beer bottle, looked at it appraisingly, then swigged it high in the air. Gus took a sip of his scotch and, once again, wiped the corners of his mouth.

"Do you believe all this?" Joe asked Gus.

"What, do I believe in ghosts?"

"Yeah."

Gus lit another cigarette and shook his head. "I don't think God would want to make that kind of a mess."

"Have you ever seen or heard anything yourself?" Joe asked Gus.

Gus shook his head. "Only thing I've heard are the stories."

"Did you ever hear one about a young woman in a blue dress?" Joe asked.

"Sounds like a dime novel," Gus said.

"I heard she shows up the first week of December and she doesn't have a coat. She's got reddish hair, sort of curly, and she wears a long blue dress, kind of like a flapper."

"A flapper ghost?" Gus asked, amused.

"I guess," Joe said.

"Who told you that one?"

Joe shrugged. "Don't remember," he said, though there was nothing, not a single thing, about Nora Lansing that he'd been able to forget.

Joe woke up on the first day of 1939 with a blistering hangover and his clothes still on. He tugged off the tie he'd worn to the union party, but otherwise unchanged — unshowered, unshaved — he went downstairs to have breakfast in the Y's club room, where most of the guys seemed to be nursing their own pounding heads. The long narrow tables — usually covered in pleated white tablecloths — this morning looked as rumpled and used as the men, several of whom were either sleeping or still drunk, their heads resting heavily on their crossed forearms.

The guys spoke in single words:

"Blind."

"Blotto."

"Bent."

The resolutions came next: never again; no more booze.

"No more strange women," one of the guys said.

Joe had to smile grimly at that. Strange women. No fooling.

He put down his coffee cup, pushed back his chair, and walked off to the game room, where he settled into a worn brown leather sofa. A fire hissed in the fireplace, and he put his head back and closed his eyes, letting his fingers explore a winding crack on the side of the armrest. An old blues tune played on the radio, and it carried Joe back to December of 1925.

He had been just twenty on the day of the subway accident, still working for Damian's friend Mr. Brennan, who ran the Lost and Found. In fact, Joe had been with Mr. Brennan on the morning of December 5, having come in early to do the regular Saturday inventory. They had both been on their way to get coffee when all the regular early-morning sounds had been drowned out by shouts and urgent calls for help. Everyone had started running. Even the ticket sellers (who'd seen it all), even the information men (who knew it all) — almost everyone in the terminal had started rushing toward the subway tracks.

The accident had occurred about six hundred yards from the platform, and there was so much thick black smoke that at first it had been hard to see the train at all. Many of the men around Joe stopped short after rushing down the stairs, but Joe followed others straight into the darkness, where only a few flashlights and one of the subway car's dim emergency lights made navigation possible. The smell of burning insulation was putrid; the moans and cries of the victims were horrifying. Trainmen were yelling for passengers to wait until the power to the third rail was shut off, but once it had been, even the emergency lights went out, and then the true panic started. Along with the cries and shouts came the sounds of windows being smashed by passengers struggling to get out.

Joe hurried farther along the platform, then stopped and reached down to start pulling people up from the tracks. He took them by the elbows, the armpits, the hands — whatever he could find in the dark. Every time his eyes started to adjust, there came a fresh cloud of blinding, choking smoke. He didn't know how long he stayed or how many people he helped to safety. For weeks afterward he barely slept, coughing from the dense smoke that had filled his lungs. But what had happened that day changed the way people saw him and the way he saw himself.

Eyes closed, listening to the radio now, he was grateful that he had today off. He would spend the whole of it here, at the Railroad Branch, in some ways simply a smaller version of the terminal: a self-contained world providing most of what a man could need — food, showers, barbershop, library, gym, bowling lanes, card and billiard tables. Everything except women.

By noon, Joe had sweated it out in the gym, showered and shaved in the locker room, and glanced at the sports pages. Just before lunch, he went up to the roof. Looking out at the skyline, which was gray and yellow with a coming snow, he still had December 5 on his mind, and he wondered — not for the first time — how his life would have unfolded if the accident hadn't happened. There had been so much mayhem and terror that day, so much tragedy and grief. But it had also been the day when Joe was discovered by Steady Max Sullivan. Max, it turned out, had been standing next to Joe on the platform as they pulled people up from the tracks. Max had seen Joe's calmness, strength, and stamina, and that very afternoon had plucked him from his job at the Lost and Found, taken him under his wing, and started training him as a lever-man.

Was it possible — in any way possible — that the very day Joe thought of as the start of his real life was the day that Nora's had ended?

The main branch of the New York Public Library was a mere two blocks from Grand Central, but Joe had never once been inside. There had always been a quiet rivalry between the people who worked in one great building and those who worked in the other. They crossed paths sometimes at the neighborhood bars, but the trainmen thought the librarians kept their noses in their books or up in the air. Joe had dated one once, and she'd lived up to the reputa-tion. The few times he'd gone to pick her up, she had met him outside on the library steps, as if, like the big stone lions out front, she was there to guard the building.

What struck Joe when he walked through the doors this day was the relative barren-ness of the place. Like Grand Central, it had beautiful arches, marble floors, and sweeping staircases. But at the terminal, though there was always a sense of peace, there was a sense of life as well. There were layers of noise — every place, any hour. You could always hear carts rolling, people talking, the loudspeaker sputtering, trains arriving and leaving, and underneath it all there was a distant thrum, like the sound of the ocean in the big shell Joe's parents had brought back from their long-ago Newport honeymoon.

Here at the library, the quiet seemed flat, dead, and gray, and even in the entrance hall, where no one was reading or studying, Joe felt as if the walls themselves were telling him to be quiet. Upstairs, in a special room behind heavy wood-and-glass doors, the old newspapers were kept in huge bound volumes that were stored in huge flat drawers. A male attendant wearing prissy white gloves and looking vaguely annoyed was in charge of opening the drawers and taking out the books. Joe felt awkward being waited on, and the guy who brought him the volume for 1925 didn't seem thrilled about the arrangement either.

There was no mention of an accident on the front page of the afternoon *Times* for December 5, so Joe started turning the pages, recalling how everyone had been on edge for a while, and how all that next year, the New York Central had issued safety

97

notice after safety notice. As Joe searched for the stories in the paper, the ads brought back pleasanter memories: the licorice flavor of Black Jack gum, the tart fizz of orange soda pop, the cozy flannel of knickers. Finally, Joe reached a small item at the bottom of page eight:

TRAIN DELAYS

An accident causing numerous injuries and some fatalities on the Lexington Avenue subway line was to blame for delays throughout the borough for most of the day. Quick thinking on the part of an engineer who cut power to the third rail may have saved many lives. Read the *Times*'s full report, including lists of the injured, in tomorrow's morning edition.

Eagerly, Joe turned to the next day's paper. The article was on the front page, in the far-left column of the December 6 *Times.*

DOZENS DIE, 100 INJURED IN SUBWAY ACCIDENT

Smoke, Darkness, Add to Panic

According to eyewitnesses, women desperately used lunch boxes and shoes to

98

smash the car windows, literally flinging themselves and pulling each other through the jagged frames of glass and falling in heaps on the tracks on either side. Scores of patients were treated for cuts they admitted they had received in their wild efforts to smash their way out.

Joe's mother used to say there were two kinds of people in life: the kind who'd walk around a brick wall and the kind who'd try to knock it down. She thought the second kind were better. Joe remembered the spark in Nora's eyes, the energy in her step, and he wondered if she had been one of the women crashing her way through a window to get out. Had he crossed paths with her? Had he failed to help her?

Joe read that victims who couldn't walk had been carried upstairs from the smoky tracks and laid out on the floor of the Main Concourse, which had quickly been set up as a first-aid station.

In the confusion, it was difficult to keep track of all the victims, some of whom were deemed fit enough to leave, others of whom were taken to nearby hospitals, and still others of whom waited, many still in shock, to have their injuries tended to.

"It was chaos," said one witness. "Everyone running this way and that. People bleeding. Windows smashing. Women fainting, and even some of the men were crying."

The story didn't give the names of the dead, but the next day's paper included two lists: one of the known injured, the other of the known dead. Aware of his heartbeat, Joe searched both lists for the name *Lansing,* running his forefinger down the capital letters on the left margin of each list, finding Lackamore, Lawrence, Liberman, Ludden — until the librarian shot over and said, "Patrons may turn the pages but please do not smudge them —"

"Sorry," Joe said.

Nora was not listed among the injured. She was not listed among the dead. Joe felt simultaneously relieved and frustrated. He closed the enormous book, noticing the librarian's grimace at the slight creaking of the spine.

Joe had walked all the way to the elevators before a thought made him pivot and head back to the reading room. The attendant gave him the fish eye. "Is there something else?" the guy asked.

"I'd like to see that again," Joe said.

"What, the same volume?"

"Yeah. The same book." Joe said it with self-assurance, but he'd started sweating through his shirt.

He sat down as the attendant again placed the huge book before him. Joe had never liked studying. He wasn't what you'd call a book reader. And he usually only glanced at the front-page stories before turning to the sports section of the *World* or the *Journal*. But right now he seemed to have no choice but to pore over each page of the following days' papers, scanning for later stories about the accident. The items became shorter and placed farther back every few days, but the lists of the dead grew longer and the lists of the missing grew shorter. Nine days after the crash, in the *Times*'s morning edition for Monday, December 14, Joe found what he'd been looking for with hope and dread. He stood up quickly and instinctively pushed the book away, then took a breath and leaned back over. The list of dead was by now more than two dozen lines long, and roughly halfway down it, Joe read: *Lansing, Eleanora, 23 years old.*

9
WHERE WERE THE REAL STARS?

1925

It was Nora's last night in Paris, and she wasn't going to waste a minute of it. She had spent two whole days cleaning and packing so she would be free to enjoy herself. The drawers of her wardrobe trunk were crammed with the sketchpads she'd used up and the postcards, matchbooks, and menus she'd saved. The hangers along the top of the trunk held her fanciest dresses, though she had left out her favorite and most daring for tonight: a wine-colored satin masterpiece of shimmering sequins and beaded fringe.

Margaret had put out the word that Nora was sailing in the morning, and a host of their French and expatriate friends converged on the Caveau in the Latin Quarter. Nora's women friends wore dazzling dresses and haircuts tidy as helmets, and her men friends sported bold neckties and wanted a turn with her on the sticky dance floor. Every time she was spun around, Nora caught sight of herself in the mirror behind the bar, which also doubled the bottles and glasses and brass coffee urns. The whole place smelled wonderfully of coffee, spilled drinks, and cigarette smoke. Sometime during the evening, Nora kissed a young man from Cincinnati whom she'd never met before. And there was an artist named Jean-Paul who spoke not a word of English, but who led her from the dance floor to sit at one of the small tables. His hands, blue and gray with pastel dust, reached for Nora's across the table, a gesture more intimate than a kiss, though a kiss soon followed.

It was two in the morning, and Nora was more than a little tipsy by the time she and Margaret left. A few of their friends chipped in to treat them to a taxi, so Nora's last image of the evening was the Champs-Élysées, where the upswept chestnut trees were decorated with a thousand Christmas lights, as if the branches had put forth shining white buds.

Bellowing and raucous, the SS *Paris* pulled out of Le Havre nine hours later, and though it was the last day of November and well below freezing, Nora stayed on deck until Ollie insisted she come inside to get warm.

Ollie — suave and avuncular as always — had claimed to have some business with one of the galleries in New York, though Nora suspected he was really coming as a self-appointed chaperone. She didn't mind. It had been more than two weeks since she had found out that her father, Frederick, had cancer. Nora's mother had written to say he was probably dying, and that it was time for Nora to come home. At first, Nora had suspected Elsie of, at the very least, hyperbole. But as soon as the letters were replaced by phone calls, Nora booked passage on the *Paris.* For a year and a half, she had reveled in the jagged energy of the nightclubs, the consolation of the cafés, the profusion of flower carts and dress shops — and always the parks and boulevards, where in summer the leaves on the trees had waved her on like soft-gloved hands. And now it was time to go.

The crossing took five days, and Nora spent most of them on deck, sitting under two steamer blankets and reading a P. G. Wodehouse novel she'd found in the ship's library. In Paris, she'd read H. G. Wells, E. M. Forster, and F. Scott Fitzgerald. But now she didn't want to be inspired, only distracted.

The *Paris* was indeed Paris all over. Its grand double staircase, modeled on that of the opera house, flowed and flared out under high arched ceilings. Its marvelous café served pastries and coffee on an airy veranda. Its dance floor was famously made up of lighted glass squares. But Nora had already said her goodbyes to Paris at the Caveau.

It was common practice all over the world that when ocean liners came into port at any hour past sunset, passengers could stay on board and not disembark until morning. The laws of Prohibition dictated that liquor had to be locked up three miles from the pier, but whether people were still drunk or still secretly drinking, a lot of them seemed determined to stay until the last moment.

Nora wasn't tempted. She wanted to see her father as soon as she could, so the minute New York came into view, she donned her pale-blue day dress, her pearl earrings, and the gold charm bracelet Frederick had given her at her graduation. She brushed her hair, powdered her nose, and applied fresh dark lipstick in the bee-stung style of the times. She shut the last of her steamer trunks, tucked francs for tip money into her pockets, and, after one last glance at the mirror over her coat's silver-fox collar, stepped out of the cabin.

"It's still going to be hours," Ollie said when she knocked on his cabin door. "The trunks have to go down first, and then there's customs."

"I don't want to wait until morning," she said.

"All right, then. I'll have to come with you."

Up on deck, the three red-and-black smokestacks shone, jaunty as trumpet keys. Despite the hour, some people were clustered on the pier, waving hello, and reporters stood ready to take note — and, if possible, photographs — of whatever celebrities might be trying to sneak ashore. Among the crowd was William, the Lansings' sometime driver, who deftly hustled his way through the crowd once he spotted Nora descending the long gangplank.

"Your mother expects you to come right home," William said when Nora told him she planned to go straight to the hospital, leaving him to wait for the trunks. "She won't be at all pleased with you."

"My mother is never pleased with me," Nora said. "And I've come to see my father."

■ ■ ■ ■

It was past four A.M. by the time she and
Ollie flagged one of the taxis waiting at the
pier. Nora told the driver, "Lenox Hill
Hospital, Seventy-sixth and Lex," sat back,
and then straightened up again, stricken.

"What?" Ollie said.

"Money," Nora whispered. "I forgot to get
American dollars."

Ollie presented his wallet, which was tidily
lined with fresh U.S. currency.

"Oh, you're brilliant," Nora said.

"Oh, I know," he said.

"I can't believe you remembered."

"I've got less on my mind than you."

At the hospital Ollie took a seat in the
waiting room and refused Nora's entreaties
for him to go to his hotel. "It's my job to
see you get home safely," he said, and Nora
was in no mood to argue.

One of the nurses walked her down the
hall. There were scuff marks on the heavy
wood doors of Frederick Lansing's hospital
room, scars of who knew how many medical emergencies. Nervously — the only time
Nora had been in a hospital was when, at
ten, she'd had her tonsils out — she pulled
back a dingy plaid curtain. She had figured

she might find her father asleep. But for whatever reason — illness or insomnia — there he was in striped silk pajamas, reading, excessively thin, but well-shaven and alert, just as if he were sitting in the parlor at home, his feet on the ottoman by the fire. Meanwhile, a nurse — presumably a private nurse hired by Elsie — dozed, improbably, in a small wooden chair, her head against the white wall, her mouth open.

"What in heaven's name are *you* doing here?" Frederick asked, as if he had just caught his daughter sneaking in late from a date.

"What do you think I'm doing here?" Nora said. "Mother told me you weren't well, and I figured she must be driving you crazy."

Nora's father beamed. "Absolutely crackers," he said. "And so you've come to rescue me?"

Glass bottles of fluids hung from metal poles, dripping medicine into her father's arm. Heedless of them, he gestured for Nora to lean down, and he hugged her.

"What are you doing awake, Dad?"

"Waiting up for you, apparently." He smiled at her. "You beauty."

"Dad."

"I want to hear," he said, sitting up

straighter. "Tell me all about Paris."

Nora took off her coat and sat at the foot of his bed. "Well, what do you want to know?" she asked.

"Everything you didn't want to put in your letters home," he said conspiratorially. "Everything you didn't tell your mother." He took her hand. "Start with how long it took you to get that dandy haircut."

Nora laughed and ran her hands through her hair, which fell between her ears and her shoulders.

"It was a lot shorter when I first got it cut," she said, and she told Frederick about the day she and Margaret had gone to a salon on the rue de Bac.

"Margaret was furious," she said. "She got a coif with the ends flipped up, and she said she looked like a playing-card king."

Frederick laughed. "Did she?"

Nora nodded. "It took weeks for it to grow out."

"What else?" Frederick asked.

"Oh, Dad. The art. It's everywhere. It's every single place you go — not just the galleries and the museums, but even the smallest café on the narrowest street. There'll be a basket of bread that should be a painting, and it's inside a restaurant that should be a painting, on a street corner that should be a painting."

"And you?" Frederick asked. "Did you get to paint the way you wanted to? And draw?"

"Both," Nora said. "And I brought a bunch of my sketches home. I'll bring some tomorrow to brighten up this room."

Frederick smiled again and closed his eyes. His eyelids were honeycombed with tiny purple blood vessels, and for some reason he had no eyelashes.

"Dad?" Nora whispered.

"I'm right here," he said, and cleared his throat. "Keep talking. I'm just resting my eyes. Tell me about my daughter the artist."

He was asleep moments later, just in time for the nurse to rouse herself.

"Who are you?" she asked Nora sharply. "It's way past visiting hours."

"I'm his daughter," Nora said in as soft a voice as she could. "I've been away."

"Oh, I'm sorry, dear," the nurse said. The nurse's sympathy — coming so quickly after her brusqueness — was all Nora needed to realize that Elsie had not been exaggerating about Frederick's condition.

"Can I have a few moments alone with him?" Nora asked.

"Of course," the nurse said.

"And could you tell Mr. Halliday, the gentleman in the waiting room, that I'll be just a little while longer?"

Alone, Nora took the nurse's chair, studying Frederick through the white enamel bars of his footboard. Motionless in sleep, his face seemed to have deflated; his skin looked less like flesh than like pale-gray fabric.

The radiator in the room clanked noisily but didn't seem to disturb him. There was a small throw rug on the floor and drapes on the double windows. Nora wondered if this was commonplace in a private hospital room, or whether Elsie had brought these things uptown. She could imagine her mother's tone of voice as she told the nurse exactly what was needed, what was lacking. The nurse must have loved that, Nora thought. Elsie, as usual, getting her way. Nora suddenly realized that she herself was half asleep. She stood up, put on her coat, bent over carefully to kiss her father's forehead, then rushed to relieve Ollie of his post in the waiting room.

It was after six in the morning, and it was cold. Ollie and Nora stood on Lexington Avenue at the hospital's main entrance. A few automobiles slipped by, followed by half a dozen horse carts, but otherwise there was stillness. Across the street, a line of trees looked bare and tangled.

"Where are all the cabs?" Nora said.

"Isn't there a queue somewhere?" Ollie asked.

"No, it's not like that here, Ollie. They cruise, and you just flag one down."

They were quiet.

"He looked so thin," Nora said.

Ollie said, "I'm very sorry."

"I'm going to miss him so much," Nora said. "I could have been here this whole last year —" Tears came to her eyes.

"Don't do that," Ollie said.

"What?"

"Don't think that way."

Nora used her right hand to fiddle with her charm bracelet, remembering how it had looked in the narrow velvet box Frederick had handed her after graduation; remembering how he'd waited until they could be alone, without Elsie. The gold heart with her name engraved on it was the largest of the charms, but there had been others, representing things she loved: a ballerina, a pair of ice skates, an ice cream cone, a Coca-Cola bottle, a birthday cake, and a phonograph player with a top that actually opened. Best of all was the gold artist's palette with spots of bright paint made by colored enamel. She held that one now. *My daughter the artist.* No one had ever believed in her the way her father did.

"Why don't you wait back inside?" Ollie asked.

"I'm all right," Nora told him.

A few more minutes passed. "We'll have to take the subway," she said.

She was surprised to see how full the train was at this hour, especially given how empty the streets had been. But these were working-class men and women, riding to or from whatever jobs they had. In the double seats that faced forward, half a dozen washed-out riders were asleep with their heads against the windows. Unlike the Métro Nora had ridden so often in Paris, this car was nearly silent.

Ollie led them to a seat along the windows.

"It's always been your dad, then?" Ollie asked. "You and your mum —"

"Chalk and cheese," Nora said. "Isn't that what you Brits say? I know it's strange. She loves me, but I think I've scandalized her. She's not bad to me, but for some reason she just doesn't like me. Or understand me. Never has."

Ollie said nothing. Nora allowed herself to be lulled by the rhythm of the train, imagining she was still on the ship. But the image

113

of her father's face, tightened and narrowed by age and illness, was inescapable. She had called him Dad, but she'd kept thinking, Oh, Daddy.

Just as the train was slowing on its approach to the station at Grand Central, it came to a harsh stop, and every passenger who had been asleep woke up, many looking startled, some apparently annoyed by the delay. Several moments of stillness followed, and people checked their watches. Then the train lurched wildly, and the lights exploded in succession: flared, popped, and smoked, like a long line of firecrackers rimming the top of the subway car. Now the passengers, eyes up, were as spellbound as a circus crowd. Soon, however, enveloped in the growing darkness, they started to clamber and shout. Black smoke began to make some of them cough, and everything that had been too bright and silent was now too noisy and dark.

Ollie had been hurled out of his seat and violently slammed into a metal pole. Nora's body, thrown partly on top of him, had been cushioned by his, but something inside her felt twisted. Her whole chest and stomach hurt when she tried to catch her breath. As she struggled to her knees, men and women were yelling and hustling past her to find a

114

way out.

Ollie was lying facedown. Nora felt for his shoulders and shook him. His body was leaden. She shouted, "Ollie! Ollie! Come on, Ollie," but he didn't move. Nora looked up, desperate for someone who could help, but no one seemed to be helping anyone. Passengers were climbing up onto the seats, smashing windows, then crawling through the openings, so bent on saving themselves that the shards of broken glass didn't stop them.

Could one blow to the head kill a man in an instant? With all her strength, Nora managed to turn Ollie over, and when she bent down to his face, she could see in even this dimmest light that it was covered in blood. Another passenger tripped over her, trying to get out.

"Better move, miss," he said.

"Can you help me with my friend? Please?"

But already the man was gone. Nora put her fingers on Ollie's wrist but couldn't find his pulse; she leaned in close but couldn't feel his breath. Now there were waves of people rushing past her and over each other. She could smell burning rubber. She heard cries of "Fire!" Someone stepped on Ollie's arm. It was a stampede, and Nora under-

115

stood that there would be no way to save Ollie, even if he was still alive. She shook him once more, but he was lifeless.

One of the subway doors had been pried open by now, and Nora, standing up, was swept through it amid the crush of people. To her horror, she realized that some passengers were trapped underneath the throng, and at one point she stepped on someone's hand. Bent over in pain, she moved as quickly as she could. A few times she felt sure she was going to fall, but somehow she braced herself, and for a few minutes at least, she was able to keep going. Through the smoke, which was now so thick that it sickened her, she saw not too far ahead the lights and signs of the subway platform. Then someone rammed into her, hard, from the side, and she fell onto the tracks, her chest and stomach hitting one of the rails. She barely managed to stand up. She was trying to climb onto the platform, but she thought she must have broken her ribs, because it hurt just to lift her arms, and it hurt to breathe. She shook off her coat and dropped her purse.

By now people were scrambling up on either side of her, not stopping to look back or down, only desperate to leave the darkness behind them.

"Please!" Nora shouted, and, amazingly, a woman who'd just made it onto the platform turned back and knelt to reach for Nora's hands.

"Come, child," she said. "Grab hold. You must, or they'll trample you like the others."

Nora braced herself and took hold. She felt her charm bracelet digging into her wrist and snapping off. She put one foot on the wall and tried to help herself up, but the pain was stronger than the darkness or the fear. Half conscious now, she realized that the woman was pulling her up like a body over the side of a boat, but the boat was the edge of the platform, and that didn't make any sense, and the edge of the platform smacked her ribs, and she felt something break even deeper inside her, and when she tried to breathe she couldn't.

Someone must have carried her upstairs. The next thing she was aware of, she was lying on a cold floor, hearing cries, shouts, and orders. "Broken leg!" "Burns!" "Blunt trauma!" "Internal bleeding!" Now a man with a reassuring hand — maybe he was a doctor — knelt beside her and said, "Just lie still. We're going to take you to the hospital."

With victims on either side of her, and more being brought up from the tracks, Nora continued to hear curt instructions, shouts of alarm, moans and bleats of pain. For a few minutes, she was able to keep her eyes open, staring up at the twinkling ceiling, stars against a blue-green sky the color of ocean, not night. Where were the real stars, she wondered, the stars that her wonderful Paris skylight had framed? She searched for the Big Dipper, the Little Dipper, Leo.

"Ollie," she said. "Ollie."

Then, in a blaze, the pain in her chest and stomach overwhelmed her, and even as the pain dulled, Nora realized with a panicked precision that she was going to die. It was a specific understanding of death, gripping and clear in a way that, even minutes before, leaning over Ollie, and even an hour before, standing by her father's bed and looking at his wasted face, she hadn't been able to have. One of her last thoughts was whether her father felt the same way. She had been forced onto the threshold of a door that was seconds from closing behind her. The past and present ceased to exist, or rather, each of them pulled at her. But she wasn't able to turn back, and she wasn't able to go forward.

Nora died at 7:05 on the morning of December 5 on the marble floor of Grand Central's Main Concourse, frightened until the sunlight coursed in from the east windows and washed over the ceiling, seeming to turn it into a real sky. Then for a moment sunlight filled the room — colossal and shadowless — pushing into every gray corner and making Nora's last sensation one of vibrant, reassuring warmth.

PART TWO

1
THE WORLD OF TOMORROW

1939

The idea of hosting a World's Fair in 1939 had come from a group of retired New York City policemen who wanted to rejuvenate a broken city. This was a fact that Finn never failed to point out whenever he felt like bragging about the decency of his colleagues. "See, Joey, we have foresight," Finn would say. "Some call it wisdom. Maybe it has something to do with the fact that we don't work in tunnels all day long."

There was no denying the boost the fair had given the city. There were endless news stories, ads, posters, and talk. The Dodgers wore World's Fair patches on their sleeves, a new three-cent stamp had shown up, and a line of amber lights had been installed along Queens Boulevard, making the route to Flushing Meadows seem like a heavenly path. Practically everyone Joe and Finn had grown up with had helped build the fair,

123

were working at it now, or were profiting from it one way or another. It was the pride not only of Queens but of all New York City. Even weeks before the fair officially opened, Grand Central had been filled with ever more visitors, accents, and confusion. From all over the country, families were coming to see "the World of Tomorrow," trying to put the broken, barren decade behind them.

Opening day fell at the end of April, and Finn had wrangled tickets. Faye had called Joe at least three times to remind him where and when to meet. Joe was excited. He had teased Finn about how the Trylon and the Perisphere — the huge white cone and sphere that were on all the stamps and posters — looked like a giant golf ball and a huge, misshapen club. Yet when Joe started walking toward the actual structures in Flushing, he was awed by their size and brilliance.

Getting closer, he could see the familiar silhouettes of Faye, Finn, and the kids, along with Damian in his wheelchair, looking as if they'd been painted onto the big white globe. Then he noticed a sixth figure with them, a short, well-formed figure wearing a straw summer hat. So, this was it, Joe thought — the reason Faye had been nagging him: the fix-up he had resisted on

Christmas Eve. "Emma, this is Joe. Joe, this is Emma," Faye said abruptly.

"Have fun. We're taking the kids to the rides. Bye."

Joe didn't have time to hug the kids hello or bend down to Damian's chair before Finn shrugged helplessly and Faye whisked everyone away. Joe stood alone with Emma. She was a slightly round, lovely-looking girl who, refreshingly, seemed neither nervous nor shy — the two things he'd always liked least in the women Faye usually chose for him. "It's good to meet you, Joe," she said. She had a map, and they stood side by side for a while, studying it. Joe had heard that the fair was huge, but he'd had no idea how huge: He realized he was crowding Emma a little as he tried to make out all the buildings on the map labeled with names of foreign countries.

"What do you want to do first?" he asked her, hoping she wouldn't pick an exhibit about New York or textiles or Wonder Bread.

She didn't. "Let's go to Italy," she said decisively, and Joe was happy as they started the long walk down the Constitution Mall. France and Brazil were on their left, Belgium and Russia on their right. There was no country that Joe didn't want to visit, but Italy did look impressive, with a statue of a woman in a purple toga sitting high atop the pavilion. At her feet, a two-hundred-foot waterfall roared down a flight of aqua steps.

Inside, Joe and Emma heard opera music and saw exhibits about history, art, and engineering. Upstairs were fancy restaurants that they knew would be too expensive.

"Wouldn't it be wonderful, though," Emma said.

"What?"

"Wouldn't it be wonderful to go there someday?"

Joe thought about all the maps that years of teachers had pulled down like window shades over dozens of blackboards — shades that had opened the world up instead of shutting it out. Italy, shaped like a boot, had always been the easiest foreign country to identify, and Joe remembered that his fifth-grade teacher had said she had gone there once, and that hundreds of cats lived in the Colosseum.

"Yes," was all he said to Emma. "It would be wonderful to go there."

Once, when Joe was little — before the Great War, before Katherine's death — he had gone with his father and Finn to a cabin owned by one of the old man's buddies. Joe had been so excited about fishing or hiking

126

or doing whatever you did in the country. But it had rained, the men had gotten drunk, and Joe and Finn had ended up playing gin rummy with an incomplete, slightly mildewed deck. That weekend might just as well have been spent at the corner bar, listening to the men reminisce about their bachelor days. As a grown-up, Joe had never taken a vacation. He would have loved to know what swimming was like, or how it felt to climb a mountain or take a train to another city. In the twenties, though, he had gone to school and helped take care of his father, and in the thirties, you missed a day of work at your peril. These days, as far as Joe knew, no one except a millionaire could go somewhere just for pleasure.

Yet even during these bitter years, Joe had allowed himself to picture the travels he would take someday. There was a huge globe in the library at the Y, and once in a while — when no one else was around — he would spin it, close his eyes, and imagine what it would be like to go wherever his hand happened to land.

For now, the fair's travels would have to do. After Italy, Emma and Joe walked to the USSR pavilion, where there was an exact replica of a famous Moscow subway station. They passed Texas's Alamo and Philadelphia's Independence Hall, a Swedish pavilion and the Temple of Religion. They went to the Billy Rose Aquacade, where everything was shining: the instruments in the orchestra, the sequins on the swimmers' suits, the squiggles and stitches in the huge swimming pool where the sunlight hit the water. A row of fifty women wearing identical bathing suits and caps dove in one after the other, like a line of falling dominoes.

By eight o'clock the temperature was dropping, it had started to rain, and the crowd was thinning as visitors either ducked into exhibit halls or decided to call it a day. Emma's comments grew briefer and her smile more forced.

"Aw, Emma," Joe said. "I'm sorry. I should have realized. You're cold."

He unzipped his denim work coat and held it for her as she slipped her arms into the sleeves. Then, as if the whole fair had vanished, Joe's mind raced back to the moment in Grand Central when he'd given his coat to Nora, the night he'd spent six months trying to understand, when the strangest thing in his life had happened and left only one useless scrap of paper as proof that it had.

FDR had opened the fair with a speech first

thing in the morning, but Einstein was going to speak at the official illumination of the fair's lights this evening. Emma and Joe got to the Lagoon of Nations just as a light rain was starting. "I told the professor I was sorry about the weather," the master of ceremonies was saying, "but he told me it was only water."

That line, which was greeted with polite laughter, was one of the last things the audience understood. Einstein began: "If science, like art, is to perform its mission truly and fully, its achievements must enter not only superficially, but with their inner meaning, into the consciousness of people." It was straight downhill from there. His accent was so thick that it was almost funny, and the microphone crackled and buzzed in the rain. Joe knew enough about engineering and electricity to understand — more or less — that Einstein was trying to explain how scientists could harness energy from the sky.

The plan to demonstrate this was extremely complex: At the Hayden Planetarium, miles away in Manhattan, rays of electrically charged particles would be captured, modified, sorted, converted to audio signals, then sent by telephone to Flushing, where they would be converted back to electric current and used to switch on the lights of the fair.

The science wasn't the point, though; the spectacle was. "Give us ten cosmic rays!" a dramatic voice could be heard over the public address system, supposedly calling out to the planetarium.

"Here comes the first ray!" another voice exclaimed.

With each command, the Trylon was lit up one layer and color at a time, until Einstein threw the switch for the last layer — the tip — and the whole system overloaded and all the lights blacked out. To Joe, it made sense. On the way home he explained it to Emma: how, despite the fact that a surge of electricity had caused a short circuit, cosmic power had in fact been brought down to earth and made into something spectacular.

Joe knew there was a place for him in the world of Faye, Finn, and Emma. It was like an extra chair at the dinner table, a spot that had, in a sense, been set for him, been saved for him. Damian was always saying, "Who are you waiting for? A trout in the pot is better than a salmon in the sea." And yet the deepest part of Joe had always wondered why what was supposed to be so perfect had never felt right. Emma was a good sport. She looked nice. She *was* nice. But forty-five minutes later, Joe dropped her at her door in Woodside and didn't make a pass or a plan. They both knew he wouldn't be calling. She was too nice a girl to date twice.

Tonight, trying to sleep, Joe thought only of Nora. To want someone who was unavailable was not an entirely new experience for him. There had been unwilling girls in high school who had occupied his thoughts and the secret parts of his nights. Just a few years before, there had been a hairdresser named Sue at the terminal who had led him into the back room one day, made him take off his shirt, and rubbed his sore shoulders with witch hazel. But after that, for reasons he never understood, she would never go out on a date with him. Wanting Nora was entirely different. It was a constant, dominating ache that Joe knew could be soothed only by her actual touch.

When it came to women, it had never been possible for Joe to know where or when the right one might arrive. There was something more right about Nora than there had ever been about anyone else. What if Nora was the right one, but she never came back?

■ ■ ■ ■

What Joe needed was patience, and you had to have patience to be a leverman. Steady Max had taught him that when he was just starting out. You had to have patience the way a nun had faith or a singer had pitch. As a leverman, you were always waiting: for the next shift to begin, the next train to come in, the next switch to throw. But patience, real patience, meant more than simply waiting. Patience meant you had to honor the moments before things happened the same way you honored the moments when they did.

Joe knew that most people didn't do this. Most people — Finn, for example — always seemed to be rushing to get somewhere, something, or someone. Finn had starting dating Faye pretty much as soon as her parents had let her out of the house, and he'd married her when they were just twenty-one and twenty-two. Big Sal was always saying that someday her ship would come in. And Shoebox Lou, who ran the lower-level shoeshine booth and sat reading books in the leather chairs when he didn't have a customer, was always flipping to the back pages, unable to wait even long enough to see how a book would end.

Sometimes, just passing through the waiting room, Joe would be amazed by how few people managed to sit still. They checked their watches, paced, adjusted their hats, made their children miserable by fussing with them — all, it seemed, to avoid the simple pleasures that could come with being patient.

Joe felt sure that if he ever got to go somewhere, he would sit on one of those wooden benches, savoring the stillness of the moment, the moment between getting ready and going away. In a sense this was how he had lived a life that was weighted down by duty and bound to one place: He believed something was coming, and believing this gave him peace.

Even in his daily life, Joe had never been impatient. He had never tried to plot his rise in the ranks of the BRT or angle for higher pay or better hours. Like most men who'd managed to stay employed through the Depression, he was grateful to have work. And in the meantime, he was happy just aiming to be Steady Joe Reynolds.

All that had changed because of Nora.

Now Joe had begun to feel a subtle resentment about the slow passage of time. He had always been young enough that time hadn't mattered a damn to him. But he'd never wanted anything as much as he wanted Nora to come back, and he had no idea if or when that would happen. Patience was a lot harder when you threw in so much doubt.

2
UNFINISHED BUSINESS

1939

Madame Rosalita's real name was Esther
Tettleman. She was a Jewish divorcée who
wore gypsy skirts and told fortunes with a
crystal ball, a deck of cards, and sometimes
a scratched-up Ouija board. She sat most
days in the lower concourse at a small table
covered with a quilted floral cloth, her dark
hair roped into long fuzzy braids, her silver
bracelets jangling as she turned the pages of
the latest movie magazine. Beside her table
stood a crimson sign whose ornate yellow
letters spelled out:

HAVE YOUR FUTURE TOLD
by Madame Rosalita
Fortunologist

Joe didn't know how much she believed of
the stuff she peddled, and he knew he didn't
believe any of it. He had never truly trusted

135

anything he couldn't see. But in the last week of November, just days before what would be the fourteenth anniversary of Nora's death, he brought Esther a Coca-Cola, sat down at her table, and asked her what she knew about ghosts.

Esther turned a page of her magazine and didn't look up. "Are you asking me or asking Madame Rosalita?"

"What do you think?"

Esther let out an unrelated roar about the article she was reading. "Oh, sweet Jesus!" she said. "You'll never believe how many Munchkins they had in Culver City."

"Could you please put that down a minute?" Joe asked.

Esther sighed, closed the magazine, lit a Chesterfield, and blew out a stream of smoke that scooped around and clouded her crystal ball.

"Ghosts?" she said. "Jeez, Joe, didn't you ever go to Boy Scouts or something and listen around a campfire?"

Joe had to laugh, trying to imagine how in his life there could ever have been enough time or money for him to go anywhere but to school or work.

"No," he said. "No campfires for me. So tell me. Do you believe in ghosts?"

"Well, spirits of the dead are supposed to

136

talk to us through the Ouija board," she said. "Would you like to place a call?"

Joe sighed.

"Madame Rosalita," he said. "Do you know where I can find Esther Tettleman?"

Esther picked a flake of tobacco from her upper lip. "I have heard stories," she said. "Some woman in one of the big windows here."

"Crazy Mabel."

"Yeah. Who told you that?"

"Gus."

"Well, Gus has been around," she said.

"Have *you* ever seen Crazy Mabel?"

"No. But that doesn't mean she doesn't pop in."

"I can't tell if you're kidding or not."

Esther put out her cigarette in an iron ashtray shaped like a spider. "Honestly? I'm not sure," she said. "I do believe people have energy that has to go somewhere when they die."

"And?"

"And one thing I've heard is that some people get stuck being ghosts because they die in the middle of doing something, and they don't even know they're dead. Unfinished business, that's what people call it. That sort of makes sense to me. Their spirits are supposed to come back every year,

137

exactly at the same time and in the same place they died. Kind of like an echo."

"An echo?"

"Yeah. Kind of. Like an echo of the time they died."

An echo, Joe thought as he walked away. It certainly seemed that Nora had shown up on the anniversary of her death. But since when could an echo laugh at your jokes, give you her phone number, and gently wrap a scarf around your neck to keep you warm?

On the morning of December 5, Joe left the Y at six. It might as well have been midnight. The sky was blue-black, and the streets were icy and still. Only a few cars passed him, and then an old coal truck with wagon-type wheels and one of its front lights out. Once inside the terminal, Joe stole past the information booth, hurried down the ramp to the lower level and then to the subway platform. If Nora had really died here, and if Esther was right about ghosts coming back where and when they died — then, Joe figured, this would be where Nora would show up.

Not many people were waiting at this hour, a time of more arrivals than departures. But the place wasn't deserted, either.

Wearing his black wool coat, his cap jammed into his pocket, Joe paced beside the tiled wall.

The newspaper had said that the accident happened "around 6:30 in the morning." Nothing more specific. It was 6:20 when Joe felt the subway train before he heard or saw it: a buzzing under his feet. Next came the light, the roar, and the cars, which slowed to a shuddering stop. Terrified but excited, Joe studied the passengers who stepped off the subway, almost all of them working men and women by the look of it. Joe searched for Nora's dress, her hair, her signal-red lipstick. When the doors closed, embracing the new passengers, it simplified Joe's view and made it clearer that Nora hadn't come.

Joe waited, determined. Decades of Father Gregory's words about grace and damnation had left him unconvinced about either. Still, there seemed something sinful about believing that dead people could walk among the living. For a moment, he felt relieved that she hadn't come. He sighed and backed up to the wall, leaning against the cold tiles, watching the platform empty, seeing the tunnel darken, hearing the noise fade.

Joe wondered what exactly he had expected. Had he thought that Nora would just step like a regular passenger from a subway car onto the platform? Or if, as he feared, she had died on the tracks because no one had managed to help her up, what had Joe imagined — that she would rise from them now, like a mist?

Was that even what he wanted?

It was 6:40. Joe waited for a second train. Again, Nora wasn't anywhere to be seen, and whatever relief he'd felt disappeared. Waiting for a third train, he suddenly found it unbearable to think he might never see Nora again. Nora, who seemed to be the answer to a question he didn't even know he'd asked.

He told himself he would wait for just one more train, and as he did he started to relive the chaos of the accident. This subway platform had been dark, smoky, and loud, a scene of immense terror and pain. Joe remembered how exhausted his arms had become, pulling up one person after another from the tracks, some of them not in good enough shape to stand. What had happened to them? As he and Steady Max were pulling people up, other men must have been carrying them to the Main Concourse. Maybe Nora hadn't died here at all.

Now, driven by an urgency unlike anything

he usually felt, Joe ran back up the ramp to the Main Concourse, which had the hush of a day just beginning. In the quiet, he could hear the faint ringing of the rails from the tracks below. But the floor of the concourse was 38,000 square feet. If, as Esther Tettleman said, Nora might come back as a kind of echo, then what would be the source of her sound? Where had she died, exactly?

At which window of the information booth had she been standing that first morning when she'd asked about the bank? Doggedly, cautiously, Joe began to walk around the booth, a slow planet circling the sun. A few of the guys just coming up from their shifts waved energetic hellos. Joe, for his part, was exhausted.

Suddenly, he became aware that he was being watched. Turning around, hoping to see Nora, he found instead a cluster of the regulars coming down the staircase, bear-like in their winter coats, hats, and scarves. Of course, Joe thought. December 5 was the date of the accident. But it was also Manhattanhenge sunrise.

"Where the hell were you, Joseph?" Big Sal called down to him.

"Too cold out there!" he called back.

"You're getting soft!" Sal shouted, followed by a chorus of the others.

141

"Go on!" he shouted back at them. "Don't you people have jobs?"

They scattered, and for a moment Joe sat heavily on the marble steps, feeling the uniquely leaden emptiness that comes with lost hope. Obviously, Nora wasn't returning. It had been foolish of him to think she would. He contemplated the year behind him, which was a pastime every bit as unusual for him as contemplating a year ahead.

Eventually Joe remembered that his shift didn't start until 10 o'clock; he could go to Ralston's meeting and still get back to the Y for some sleep. He stood up to leave and was halfway toward Track 13 when Nora grabbed him from behind.

3
BITS OF MEMORY

1929

The marble of the Main Concourse floor was cool and smooth beneath Nora's back, and the first sight she had when she opened her eyes was the last one she'd seen at the moment of her death: the sun-washed sky and glittering stars of the Grand Central Terminal ceiling. But there were no people calling for help now, or shouting orders to each other. In fact, there was no one lying beside her anymore, no line of injured passengers, no doctors or other people scurrying about to help.

And there was no pain. Whatever had been twisting Nora's insides had stopped.

Panicked, confused, she got to her knees, scanning the nearly empty concourse. A Red Cap in a black uniform with shiny brass buttons was standing before her, extending his hand.

"Miss, can I help you?" he asked.

Tentatively, Nora reached up as he pulled her to her feet. Nearly a decade before Joe would have the same reaction, the Red Cap quickly let go of her hand.

"Beg pardon, miss," he said. "Are you feeling all right?"

She stared back at him.

"Did you faint, miss?"

"I don't know," she said. "I suppose I must have." She gestured to the ground. "But where did all the people go?" she asked.

"The people?"

"Porter!"

The Red Cap was being summoned by a woman near the ticket booths. He looked at Nora warily. "There's a doctor's office on the third floor," he said. "Maybe you should go have them take a look at you, miss." He tipped his hat as he left.

Nora stood still, fighting fear. She turned in every direction, trying to take in the scene. There were the ticket booths; there was the gold clock; there was the sunlight, coursing through the huge arched window, turning the pink floor orange and the blue-green ceiling lavender.

Bits of memory settled around her like ash. Her shoes were badly scuffed, and her dress was grimy in places, but this was definitely the same outfit she'd been wearing when she'd stepped off the ship, when she'd visited her father, when she'd gotten on the subway with Ollie to go home. *Ollie.* She remembered turning Ollie over and seeing the blood on his face. She remembered that Ollie was dead. Then she remembered the rest: the crash, the mayhem, being pulled up to the platform, her handbag falling, her charm bracelet being ripped away.

Feeling her empty left wrist with her right hand, Nora walked unsteadily toward the ticket booths and picked up a timetable for the New York Central Hudson River Line. On its cover were the month and year: December 1929. She struggled to take this in. Nora knew she had come home from Paris in December of 1925. How could four years have passed since then? Had she lost her memory in the accident?

More quickly now, she moved along the concourse to the Travelers Aid station and the tall wooden desk with its half-dozen heavy telephones. Not once in her life had she wanted this much to hear her mother's voice.

She dialed the number with a shaking finger. When Elsie answered, Nora started to cry.

"Hello?" Elsie said. "Who is this?"

145

Nora tried to keep her voice from shaking. "Mother," she said. "It's me."

A flat, hoarse voice said, "Pardon me." It sounded less like a question than an accusation.

"Mother!" Nora said again. "It's me. It's Nora!"

Two words ripped through the receiver like electric shocks. "It's who?"

"Mama!" That was a word Nora hadn't used since childhood. "It's Nora! I've been in an accident. I'm at Grand Central. I need to get home. Please, Mama, come and get me!"

For a dreadful moment Elsie said nothing, and then Nora heard her catch her breath.

"Whoever you are," Elsie said, emphasizing each syllable, "I don't know why you would ever think to be so cruel to me."

"But —"

The phone cut off as Elsie hung up.

Nora returned the receiver to its cradle with both hands and rested her forehead against them. Tears filled her eyes again. She lifted her head, wiped them away, and dialed the number a second time.

The phone rang once, twice, ten times, a useless pulse.

So although Nora had no coat, and although it was just past seven on a frigid winter morning, she stepped outside the terminal and started to walk home.

4
YOU READ ME *PETER RABBIT*

1931

When she was ten years old, Nora had had
her tonsils out, and for months and even
years afterward she had found herself shuddering at the memory. Her distress hadn't
come from recalling the pain, or even the
imperious way that Elsie had ordered the
nurses around. What Nora had never shaken
was the memory of fighting to come out of
the ether. One nurse and then another had
tried to coax her back into wakefulness, but
for what seemed like a very long time, Nora
had simply remained suspended. On one
side of her there had been the ether, which
was so much darker and more timeless than
sleep, and on the other side there had been
the nurses' voices, the sense of light and
movement. In the awful grayness that lay in
between, she had been unable to get free,
unable to speak, to move, even to open her
eyes.

This suspension, at dawn two years after her first reappearance in Grand Central, was exactly the feeling she recognized now. She sensed herself being pulled between darkness and light, tugged back and forth in some gray in-between place, until the bright force became so powerful that at last, to her relief, it drew her in.

Then, once again, she found herself lying on the marble floor inside a shaft of sunlight. This time, though, her most recent memory was not of the injured people on either side of her. This time, it was of calling her mother and walking out to the street to go home. But what had happened since then?

Nora hurried to her feet and grabbed another train schedule: 1931, it read. Not only a different year, but a different decade. And how could that be?

Today, the Travelers Aid desk was already busy. A young woman in a blue apron was handing a map to a small man who looked as lost as Nora felt. Several other people stood in a cluster, and Nora sensed all of them staring at her as she picked up the phone.

Avoiding their gaze, she brushed soot and dust from her pale-blue dress. She knew she must look awful.

"Please, please be there," she whispered to no one as, once again, she dialed her home number. The phone rang several times and Nora stiffened in panic, but finally she heard her mother's voice — proper and sharp as always.

"Hello?"

"Mother, don't hang up!" Nora shouted.

"Oh, no!" Elsie said. "No, no, no! Not again!"

"Don't hang up. Please, Mother, listen. Please." Nora gripped the receiver. "It's me. It really is. We live in Turtle Bay. I went to Paris. I came back in December. I saw Father in the hospital. It was 1925. My bedroom is on the second floor. There's a chandelier with flowers that are painted different colors."

Nora paused to catch her breath. There was silence on Elsie's end, but at least she hadn't hung up.

"I went to Barnard," Nora continued. "You read me *Peter Rabbit*." She was aware that the details she was choosing were scattered through time, but time was evidently ignoring the rules with her as well. "I was a debutante. You put my coming-out dress in a big purple box. We always had brunch at the Plaza on Easter Sunday. You didn't like people calling me Nora as much as —"

150

"Eleanora," her mother said, and at that, Nora felt her knees start to shake.

"Mama," she said quietly.

"How is this possible?" Elsie said. "We thought — We knew — Don't you see? The accident. Where have you *been* all this time? I thought — I thought it was you we buried. We *buried* you."

"That must have been someone else," Nora said. "Please, Mama. Please come and get me."

"Where? Where are you?"

"Grand Central."

"Grand Central?"

"Yes. Please come and get me," Nora said again. "Mama, I'm so scared."

Nora heard Elsie exhale a staccato breath. "I'll meet you at the gold clock," she said firmly. "For heaven's sake, don't go anywhere."

Nora held on to the phone for a few moments after Elsie had hung up. Home, which before Paris had stood for everything old-fashioned and confining, now seemed to be more than she could ever want.

She knew she would have at least half an hour before Elsie composed herself and got to the terminal, so she left the Travelers Aid station, walked through the waiting room, and slipped into the ladies' lounge, an

151

opulent place paneled in oak, with high ceilings and low chandeliers. Through the marble-framed doorway that led to the washroom, Nora approached a line of white porcelain sinks beneath a row of gilt-framed oval mirrors. Her hair was disheveled, her dress smudged at the elbows and waist, but she looked exactly the way she had when she'd glanced at the mirror just before leaving the *Paris* with Ollie. How could it be that nothing had changed except time? She splashed water on her face, patted it dry with a hand towel, and rushed back to stand at the gold clock. It was nearly eight o'clock now, and all she could do was wait.

Elsie Lansing was a perfectly assembled woman whose thin arms and slim frame had always, in Nora's experience, been less useful for embraces than for ornamentation. There was almost nothing soft, round, or warm about Elsie. Even now, as she strode toward the gold clock and scanned the crowd for Nora, her high heels clipped like tiny hammers against the marble floor. Nora waited only a moment before she ran to her mother and hugged her. The embrace was warmer than any Nora remembered from her childhood. Leaning her cheek into the exuberant white fur collar of Elsie's brocade

152

coat, Nora felt her mother's arms grip her tightly.

"Mama!" Nora said.

Elsie pulled away. "How can this be? How can this be?" she asked. She searched the huge room desperately, as if looking for someone who would tell her she wasn't asleep or insane.

Elsie studied her daughter — from scuffed ivory shoes to missing hat — exactly as she used to do before Nora went out on a date or to school. Then she reached out a hand, removed her glove, and awkwardly, shakily, stroked Nora's hair.

"Eleanora," she finally said.

Unlike Nora, Elsie had aged; what had previously been brittle now seemed fragile. Her skin, always fair, was gray and drawn against her white collar. She shook her head slowly, as if trying not to injure herself. Nora had never imagined that her mother could look so unsure.

"How did you get here?" Elsie finally asked.

"I don't know," Nora said.

"Where have you been all this time?"

"I don't know!"

Elsie tightened the belt of her coat, closing it up like armor. "Well, come," she said, either feigning or regaining her usual aura of command. "I have a taxi waiting. Where's your coat? Why aren't you carrying a purse? We'll have to call Dr. Lascher." Following her mother's voice up the steps to the street, Nora smiled a little. Elsie had always felt there was an expert to call, no matter what the problem was.

"You'll freeze," she told Nora, as if it had been Nora's plan to be without a coat. "But just for a moment." Elsie waved at one of the waiting taxis. "This is us," she said.

It had snowed, and the streets were as white as Elsie's collar, the perfect canvas for the colorful figures who were checking their watches, whether hurrying to or from the terminal.

Nora turned to look at her mother. "When did Daddy die?" she asked her gently.

Elsie gave the cabbie the address.

"Mother?"

"Just a few months after you —" Elsie stopped herself. "After we lost you."

The driver started the car.

"Oh, Mother," Nora said.

Elsie sat up a bit straighter.

Nora thought about the Turtle Bay house, which had always been so busy with guests and servants and plans. She mentally clicked off the lights in her bedroom, then gently closed the tall doors of her father's study.

"That must have been awful for you," Nora said.

Elsie seemed to teeter between emotion and restraint. "Yes," she finally said, and stoically lifted her chin.

The taxi started to move.

"And poor Daddy —"

It was excruciating for Nora to imagine Frederick, already so sick, learning that his daughter had died.

"Yes, poor Daddy," Elsie said — and then, more quietly: "But Daddy didn't have to be the only one left."

On the street, tradesmen were sweeping the snow from their storefronts, and a mother and two children, noses identically pink, were waiting at a bus stop.

"Well, I'll be home now," Nora said.

The last sight she had was a horrific one: her mother, as scared as anyone she'd ever seen, eyes open wide, shouting Nora's name. Then Nora felt herself being pulled into the grayness, after which she felt and saw nothing at all.

5
Is That Play Money?

1934

Each time Nora came back, she was a little less frightened. Three times now, she had fought through the awful gray in-between to appear at the same hour, on the same date, in the same spot, in the same clothes, and she had never left the terminal without disappearing. She still didn't have the vaguest idea how any of this was happening, and it would be a while before she would meet Joe and longer still before they would figure out why she appeared some years and not others.

But she knew that time was passing. The terminal seemed grimmer than before, and derelict. At the edges of the vast room, several dozen people stood, looking glazed, as if they were waiting for something to start. Nora was alarmed by the main waiting room, where she saw at least fifty people either sleeping or reluctantly waking up.

These didn't look like regular travelers. They looked like vagrants. On the heavy wooden benches that striped the room like church pews, some of them were using newspapers as blankets or pillows. Others had bundles of things beside them. Still others had children by their sides. Nora saw one little girl asleep on a large corner bench clutching a Raggedy Ann doll, which she dustily resembled. Everything in the room seemed colorless and terribly sad. There was an odor too: pungent, zoolike, shocking.

Even the ladies' lounge had an aura of neglect. Had it been like this last time? Maybe she hadn't noticed. There were abandoned coffee cups with lipstick half-kisses on the rims, used napkins, and old magazines and newspapers on the round wooden tables. Around these tables, and against the paneled walls, women slept in velvet chairs, adrift on an ocean of beat-up shopping bags.

Nora chose the nearest empty rocking chair and picked up a discarded *New York Times:* December 4, 1934. On the front page she read about a man who had killed himself by inhaling illuminating gas. "He had been out of a job," she read, "since shortly after the stock market crash." So that explained all the vagrants and the sad,

157

stifling air.

In the washroom Nora found no soap or fresh towels — but she did find herself in the mirror again. Her hair still fell against her neck in soft curls. Her lips were still a vivid red. She thought about her college friends, now in their thirties. She wondered if the market crash had hurt them, but also how their faces had changed. She tried not to think about Elsie's at all. The horror on her mother's face — like the blood on Ollie's — was simply too terrible to recall.

Back in the concourse, Nora stopped at a water fountain, with its elegant marble frame of carved acorns and oak leaves. The sink of the fountain was stopped up and filled with brackish water. Nearby was a woman with two little boys. Nora guessed them to be about four and eight, their faces pale as putty. The smaller of the two had his arms crossed inside a jacket that was at least two sizes too big for him. The larger boy had apparently wiped his nose on his sleeve.

"Can you help me?" the woman asked Nora.

Nora almost laughed: Who was she to help anyone? She looked at the woman more closely. She had on a dirty green wool coat that was missing two of its four front buttons. Even through the coat, Nora could smell the woman's body odor, and maybe a whiff of urine.

"What's your name?" Nora asked.

"Isabel," she said tentatively, as if it had been a long time since anyone had treated her with anything like civility. "Morton. Isabel Morton. Is there any way you can help me?"

Nora reached into her dress pocket but realized as she withdrew the folded bills that these were the same five-hundred-franc notes she'd grabbed for tips when she and Ollie got off the *Paris.* Damn, she thought. She still had no American money.

Together, she and Isabel stared down at the bills.

"Is that play money?" the older boy asked.

Nora shook her head. "Come with me," she said.

"Come where?" Isabel asked her.

"Just follow me," Nora said.

Isabel started to fuss with her children's hair but quickly gave up, instead gathering her bags and distributing them to the boys.

"Would you mind?" she asked Nora, handing her a blanket to carry — a mustard-colored wool blanket with what had once been a silk border now hanging from it like a large, hideous necklace.

Resolutely, Nora took the blanket and led

the way down the ramp to the lower level. She was first in line when the teller opened the window, and she had him change her francs for what came to about eighty dollars. She gave half to Isabel and watched the woman's face change from haggard and beaten to hopeful and beautiful. "Will you still have enough?" she asked Nora.

"I'll be fine," Nora said. "We'll go to my house, and they can help you and the boys get fixed up." Nora gathered up the blanket.

Isabel looked at Nora disbelievingly. "Oh, I wish I could find a way to thank you —"

"Eleanora?"

Nora snapped her head around, thinking for just a moment that it might be Elsie who'd said her name. Instead she realized with a start that she was only yards away from Margaret's mother, Ruth Ingram, one of the porcelain women who throughout Nora's teen years had come to play bridge with Elsie.

"Mrs. Ingram!" Nora said.

Now she watched the color drain from Mrs. Ingram's face, her lips faltering as she tried to speak.

"Eleanora?" she finally repeated, this time in a whisper.

Nora started forward eagerly, and just as quickly, Mrs. Ingram turned and ran, actually ran, in the opposite direction, slipping a little in her haste to exit the terminal. Nora dropped Isabel's blanket and called out the Turtle Bay address to her. Racing after Mrs. Ingram, she grabbed the heavy brass-and-glass door and pulled it open. Frigid wind was sucked in all around her, but she pushed through it and saw the older woman rushing off toward the corner.

"Mrs. Ingram!" Nora shouted. "Mrs. Ingram!"

Nora kept running, though the sidewalk was icy. And then, nothing again. Nothing.

6
LIFE

1936

Two years later, the terminal seemed even darker, despite the beam of light in which Nora once again found herself. The walls of the Main Concourse, which had always been warm and beige, were now so brown with grime that they looked as if they'd been singed. Many of the people Nora saw seemed even more lost and frightened than Isabel and her children had.

It was now December of 1936. Eleven years had passed since the accident, and still, when Nora looked at herself in the washroom mirror, she found a twenty-three-year-old woman with wavy copper hair, dark-red lipstick, and a 1920s day dress that was splotchy and gray with soot. She also found the same five hundred francs in her dress pocket that somehow reappeared each time she returned. What a boon this might be, Nora thought as she counted the bills

— if only she could figure out some way the money could help her. Failing that, she figured it might help someone else — perhaps another Isabel, she thought, with another couple of children.

On the lower level, just past the bank where she once again had her francs changed to dollars, she saw a tall, thin man nearly blending into the column against which he was leaning. There was a handwritten sign hanging from a frayed string around his neck:

WILL WORK FOR FOOD

He had one greasy hand on the top of the sign and the other outstretched, palm up.

"Miss! Miss!" the man said. "Spare some change?"

Nora remembered the bald man at the stadium in Paris who'd tried to make her buy postcards from him, and she pressed several dollars into this man's hand, then walked on and furtively doled out dollars to a few other people. She felt as if she had landed in some artist's crazy, dark painting. As if Max Beckmann or Picasso or Braque had splintered the beauty of this place into a black-and-gray nightmare.

It was past noon when she made her way back to the ladies' lounge. Around the tables, abandoned velvet rocking chairs were tipped in haphazard positions, as if they themselves were deep in conversation. Discarded newspapers were spread out on the tables. A large magazine, nearly the size of a desk blotter, caught her eye. The cover image was of a young cadet, but it was the title of the magazine that drew Nora's attention — four large white capital letters nearly filling a bright red rectangle: LIFE.

Nora had to smile at that. A magazine about life.

Was this life, after all? If she was alive, then why did she keep disappearing? If she was dead, then where were all the other dead people? Surely she couldn't be the only person who had died in this great building. Even during the accident, she knew, there had been other fatalities. Ollie, for a starter. Where was Ollie? Then, too, if she was dead, why did she feel so completely and restlessly alive?

Leaning back in her chair, Nora closed her eyes. The accident had been in 1925. She'd been back in '29, '31, '34. More than a decade had passed, but she'd really lived only a handful of days. She had never stayed longer than a few hours. She had never had coffee or a piece of cake. She had never exchanged more than a few words with

164

anyone. What might happen if she stayed? Could this *be* a life?

She picked up the magazine and started to turn the pages. She had never seen a magazine that was mostly photographs. Image by image, she tried for the first time to understand the world to which she'd been returned. There were pictures of a President Roosevelt whose first name was Franklin, not Theodore; a party to protest a gas tax; a human brain during an operation. In a story about a talent agent, twenty models were posed on a high-diving platform, wearing alternating white and black bathing suits, slim and straight as piano keys.

A middle-aged woman with badly dyed hair the color of salmon entered the lounge, glanced over at Nora, then grunted and looked down, twisting a thread around a loose button. Another woman, with runs in her stockings, was wearing a hat that must once have been jaunty but now looked as if it were part of her hair. Eventually a third woman came in, and Nora couldn't look away. This one was all eyes, cheekbones, and perfect posture. Her hair was mostly brown, but a patch of her scalp was showing. She was wearing a fur coat that, like her hair, had evidently thinned disastrously. Nora couldn't stop staring. Give the woman an appointment with a hairdresser, some makeup, and a new coat, and she could have been Elsie.

Two questions struck Nora in quick succession. The first: What if her mother had been hit by the Depression and was herself destitute and living in some broken place? The second, even worse: What if Elsie had died? Before Paris, the two of them had been so harsh with each other. And here in the terminal it had been so painful for Nora to see Elsie — and then to scare her — that Nora had concluded it would be cruel to try to get in touch with her mother again. Yet Nora felt hollowed out by the thought that she might be completely alone in the world now. She had almost accepted the notion that in order to get home she would have to build some sort of bridge. But it hadn't occurred to her till this moment that even if she succeeded in doing so, Elsie might not be there to greet her.

Meanwhile, she realized she was still staring at the balding woman, who shouted "What? What the hell do you want?"

Nora shoved a five-dollar bill into the woman's hand, then ran from the room and kept running until she reached the public telephone booths on the lower level. She closed the door of a booth and dialed home.

Maybe it would be enough just to hear her mother's voice, she thought. But nobody picked up. Nora could picture the empty living room, with the telephone ringing on the chinoiserie side table next to Elsie's prized statue of a sleek black Egyptian cat.

She began walking around the lower level. At a Salvation Army table near the subway entrance, a line of expressionless people waited in front of large iron kettles, and the steamy smells of chicken and vegetable soup were nearly conquering the more human and unpleasant odors of the people in line. At a bakery called Bond's, a round woman with droopy eyes was busily selling rolls, Danish, and coffee. Commuters approached her counter, the tops of the men's fedoras lightly dusted by snow, like alpine peaks. Once served, they hurried away looking guilty — perhaps because they could afford such treats.

Every hour, Nora called home. After a while she chose a small table and chair against one of the walls near the phone booths. Looking around for a clock, she found at least four in view. They were perfectly synchronized, down to the second hand. While she waited, she watched the clocks and eavesdropped on the conversations around her. Someone had a cousin who'd just gotten work. Someone else had an uncle with a factory that had just closed down. Everyone seemed to be in some kind of trouble. Their predicaments formed little tents around them, even as their words spilled out.

Still unable to get an answer at home, Nora realized that she was getting sleepy. She'd never stayed in the terminal long enough — or perhaps calmly enough — to risk falling asleep.

Wrapped up in thoughts of Elsie, she drifted back to a morning in 1921. She remembered lying across the foot of her mother's bed, tracing the raised chenille patterns on the Wedgwood-blue bedspread. It had been January, the morning after Nora's debut. Enamored of every suffragist who'd finally secured the women's vote, enthralled equally by Edna St. Vincent Millay and the Ziegfeld Girls, Nora had fought participating in this society milestone with every ounce of her budding flapper spirit. Nevertheless, Elsie Lansing had, as usual, prevailed, and so, the night before, wearing a white dress, white pearls, and a crown of tiny white roses, Nora had been escorted by Frederick, dressed in a morning suit and betraying a tender pride.

It had been warm in the bedroom. Little

flames had skittered across a log in the fireplace as Elsie carefully folded the dress, wrapped it in white tissue, and laid it in a large purple box.

"This isn't the last white dress you're ever going to need," her mother had said. Nora had rolled her eyes, the signature gesture of a generation that had no use for tradition. But a moment later, she had glanced at her mother's dresser, where framed family photographs were staggered like stadium seats, as if the people in the pictures were all watching her expectantly.

Too tired now to go back to the velvet chairs in the lounge, Nora rested her head on her arms and finally drifted to sleep.

She woke to the relief of realizing that no years had passed. There had been no tug of war, no gray in-between. She had slept a normal sleep. Not much else was normal, but the sleep had strengthened her hope that she could make something of her predicament. *Citius, Altius, Fortius.* Swifter, Higher, Stronger.

Determinedly, she went back to the phone booth and once again called home. This time a man with a deep voice answered.

"May I speak with Mrs. Lansing, please?" Nora asked evenly.

"Sorry," the man said brusquely.

"When do you expect her?"

"I do not expect her," he said, then ran through answers to questions that Nora hadn't yet asked. "No, she doesn't live here anymore. No, I don't have a phone number for her. No, I haven't seen her."

"Who is this?" Nora asked.

"Who's *this*?"

"This is Mrs. Lansing's daughter."

There was a silence, and when the man spoke again, the rudeness was gone.

"Eleanora?" he asked tentatively.

"Yes!" Nora said, thrilled to be known. "This is Nora Lansing!"

The man hung up.

If she could break the telephone, if she could smash the glass of the booth, if she could let out one long, piercing scream — and then she thought, Well, why not? Why not scream? What would happen? People would surround her. They'd call the police. The police would ask her where she lived. She'd say she didn't live anywhere. They'd ask to call her parents. She'd say she didn't know where her mother was. They'd ask her what had made her scream. She'd tell them she was pretty sure she'd died in a subway accident in 1925. And at that point, even if they could get her out of this place, it would be straight to an asylum.

As angry as she was, Nora knew one thing: If she was going to be trapped, it wasn't going to be with people who thought she was crazy. And so far, with the possible exception of Isabel, who didn't look all that balanced herself, Nora had met no one who seemed likely to believe her. Moving away from the phone booth, she did a quick accounting. She had walked out of the terminal the first time; had taken a cab with Elsie; had chased after Mrs. Ingram. But there were a few other things she hadn't tried. She had never had another person walk her home. And she had never left by subway or by train. Now, squaring her shoulders, she walked past the shops and the bank and straight to the sign that said SUBWAY. Taking a breath, she continued down the stairs to the platform, the scene of the mayhem, the screams, the smoke. She stood waiting on the now calm platform beside the tiled wall, where a huge mosaic of an old-fashioned steam engine seemed to be, like Nora, out of place and time.

I am a ghost, she thought as she stood against the mural, as far from the tracks as she could get. And yet people could see her. So, maybe not *ghost,* she thought as the train approached with a rattle and roar. *Spirit,* she thought gamely, more pleased with that word and its livelier implication.

She found a seat at the back of the subway car, picked up a newspaper that someone had left, and began to read. Most of the front page was filled with stories about the British king, who had been having a love affair with a woman named Wallis Simpson. It seemed the king was so in love with this divorced American that he was planning to give up his kingdom so he could marry her.

The subway car was filling up now, and other passengers were apparently reading the same stories.

Edward VIII Shows No Sign of Yielding

Nora heard riders speculating about whether the king would insist on marrying this woman or follow his cabinet's wishes and break off the affair. No one glanced up as the train began to pull out. And if anyone had noticed Nora in the first place, all they would have seen after emerging from the tunnel under Park Avenue was a newspaper lying across the seat where she had been.

7
I CAN'T BELIEVE
YOU'RE HERE!

1939
The next time Nora came back was the morning she first met Joe. The following year she had waited for him, they'd had dinner, and he'd tried to walk her home. And this time was the one she'd never really believed would happen: *He* had been waiting for *her.*

Eventually, Nora would tell Joe as much as she could recall about all her visits in the twenties and thirties and her attempts to leave. For the moment, the only thing that mattered was that he was here. He was wearing the same red wool scarf she'd tied around his neck the night she'd vanished from the street. The same shiny red union pin was fixed to his lapel.

"Joe Reynolds," she said as she came up behind him with her embrace.

"Nora Lansing," he said, his voice filled with wonder. He was right: She had not been in the subway station at all, but here, on the Main Concourse.

She was wearing exactly the same dress, and he remembered: Yes, this was how tall she was; this was her sharp, sweet smell; this was the top of her head, with its amazing jumble of reds and browns.

"I can't believe you're here!" she said to him.

"You can't believe *I'm* here? You've got to be joking," he said. "Where did you come from?"

For the moment, she ignored the question.

"That man with the knife," she said. "Did you get hurt?"

"No. No, he ran right off. He was just a kid. But when I looked back, you were gone," Joe said.

"Yes," she said. "I know."

Her voice was filled with a note of sadness he hadn't heard before.

"So, you," he said. "What happened to you? Where did you go that night?"

"It's hard to explain," she said.

"Try," Joe said.

"You might not believe me."

"I think I might," Joe said. "Oh, honey, please try."

" 'Honey'?" Nora asked.

Joe grinned. "Call a policeman," he said. "I called you 'honey.'"

Nora laughed with that deep, husky laugh he had spent the year alternately trying to remember and trying to forget. They embraced and then enveloped each other, and when Nora took a step back, she could see that there was no fear in Joe's eyes, only excitement.

"How long has it been?" she asked him.

"A year."

"Another year," she said, looking around for changes. As he'd seen her do before, Nora circled her bare left wrist with her fingers.

"Come with me," he said. He took her hand and again felt that burst of heat, as if she'd been outside in the sun.

He led her to the waiting room, which she noticed was emptier and cleaner this year. They sat side by side on one of the heavy wooden benches. They might have been in church, but the closest thing to an altar was the large clock hanging over the entranceway.

"Nora," Joe said, as if her name would make her more real. He took her by the shoulders and looked into her eyes.

She folded her hands in her lap, like a schoolgirl. "What?" she said.

"I don't want you to take this the wrong way," Joe said, and he shook his head at the sheer craziness of what he was going to say.

"You want to know if you can call me *honey*?"

"No. I want to know if you're —" He took a breath.

"If I'm *real*?" she said.

Joe looked around to make sure no one could hear him. There was no one immediately nearby, but he whispered anyway. "Well, I was going to ask if you were dead, but that's the basic idea."

She laughed lightly and looked down. She wasn't shocked or angry. If anything, she seemed sheepish. "I think I got caught somehow," she said.

"Caught?"

"Not all alive and not all dead," she said. "I mean, more than most people."

"Most people? Most people don't show up in the same place every year wearing the same clothes and not knowing how they got there."

"You never met my grandmother," Nora said, and despite the strangeness of the circumstances, they both had to laugh.

She was sitting there, talking to him, fully human. She'd made a joke. She looked happy. He could touch her.

In his childhood, Joe had imagined ghosts as bloodless, transparent, and chilling. But Nora was nothing like that, and the only thing that seemed scary to Joe was the thought that she might disappear again.

The seats in the waiting room were beginning to fill with men coming in from the suburbs. They were chatting, smoking, drinking coffee, checking their watches, and the buzz from their chatter was suddenly annoying. Joe wished that he and Nora could have the whole room to themselves.

"Listen, Joe," Nora said. "I've almost stopped trying to figure it out. All I know is I've shown up here at the same time, on the same day, for a lot of different years, and eventually I wind up disappearing."

"But where do you go?" he asked her.

"I don't know," she said.

"Is it like being asleep?"

"No. There's no dreaming. It's like there's nothing until I start coming back, and then it's absolutely horrible. It's like trying to wake up from ether. Did you ever have to have ether?"

Joe shook his head.

"Well, it's kind of like that. It's just, I don't know . . ." Her voice trailed off, but then she tossed her head. It was an attempt to seem casual, Joe thought, but to him it

177

seemed heartbreakingly brave.

"I'm just not anywhere when I'm not here," she said, "but I guess time must go by, and then I start getting this awful, awful feeling. It's hard to explain, but it's like I'm being tugged in two different directions, and I can barely breathe. Then I either get pulled back into the ether or I show up back here. Time has passed, and things have changed a little, but I'm always the same. I know it sounds crazy. Crazy," she repeated. "But I'm telling you the truth, Joe. Have you ever heard of anything like this happening before? I mean, what's happened to me?"

"Well, I know other people have died here. I know there was an accident —"

"In 1925," Nora said. "That's when I — That's when this started."

"I know."

"How do you know?"

"Well, for one thing, I was there," Joe said.

"You were there? You were on that train?"

"Not on the train," Joe said. "On the platform. I was pulling people up from the tracks."

It took a moment, and then Nora's eyes widened. "Do you think we *saw* each other?" she asked.

"I've been wondering that same thing,"

Joe said. "It was really dark, and I couldn't see faces. But I've been wondering if you were one of them — or if I missed you and that's how you —"

"Died?"

"Well, yeah."

Nora shook her head. "No," she said. "I did get pulled up from the tracks, but I remember it was a woman who helped me. She was another passenger."

Joe didn't want to overwhelm Nora with questions; he didn't want her to think he was doubting her. But there was so much else he wanted to know.

"Do you remember dying?" he asked.

"Not exactly."

"What do you remember?"

"All the lights went out on the train."

"Why were you on the train in the first place?"

She told him about how she'd come from Paris, disembarking before dawn, making the trip to the hospital from the pier, seeing her sick father, and getting on the subway because there were no taxis around. "I remember the smoke," she said. "I remember the screaming. And Ollie. Poor Ollie —"

Nora looked at the floor, as if she was searching for something she'd lost there.

"Who's Ollie?" Joe said.

"My friend," she said sadly. "Also my boss in Paris. He'd come to New York to meet art dealers. He came with me to the hospital to see my father so I wouldn't be all alone. Otherwise he'd be alive. He died that morning. His head got smashed into one of the metal poles, and I had to leave him there."

"Or *you* would have been trampled," Joe said.

"That's right."

Nora waved her hand through the air, as if to wave away her memories, but it didn't seem to work. She closed her eyes, and her eyelashes, grazing the tops of her pale cheeks, made Joe think of the sun's rays.

"But you made it up to the Main Concourse?" Joe asked.

"Someone must have carried me there."

"You're sure?" Joe asked.

"I think so," Nora said.

"Because if you'd been on the tracks and I'd missed you — I haven't been able to get that thought out of my head."

"Joe."

"You know, it's a Catholic thing — that ghosts are only sent to earth to teach humans a lesson. I thought maybe that's why you were here — to haunt me."

Nora bowed her head, and when she

looked back up, her eyes were wet.

"Are you crying?" Joe asked.

"I don't think I'm here to haunt you," she said.

He leaned forward to kiss her and felt, in that grave, freighted moment, almost scared that the kiss might unmoor him or make her disappear. He imagined himself being suddenly weightless, lifted above the crowd and looking down from the great vaulted ceiling. Perhaps he could disappear with her.

He hesitated just long enough so that Nora leaned in slightly before their lips finally met.

8
LOST AND FOUND

1939

The kiss drew instant attention from the men in the rows behind them.

"Ni-i-ice," one of them said.

"What else are you having for breakfast, buddy?" said another.

Joe turned to stare them down.

"What are all these people doing here?" Nora whispered to Joe.

"Oh, don't mind them. They're just waiting for the Lost and Found to open."

"Why?"

"We call them the Drop-and-Carries. On their way home at night, they'll leave their bowling balls on the train so their wives won't see what they've been up to, and then they pick them up at the Lost and Found when they've got another game."

Nora laughed. "And they do this all the time?"

"It's sort of a ritual."

"Don't the people at the Lost and Found get furious?"

"Not really. It's usually just Mr. Brennan at the counter, and he's used to it. Sometimes he holds them up for ransom."

She looked up, excited. "Joe!"

"What?"

"Joe, I had things with me!" she said.

"Yeah? What things? What things did you have with you?"

"When I — During the accident."

"What things?"

"My winter coat and hat. And a clutch. I had a clutch."

"A clutch?"

"A purse. But I had to drop it. And my bracelet too. This beautiful charm bracelet that my father gave me for graduation. I remember it being pulled off."

Once again, Nora circled her bare left wrist with her fingers, a gesture Joe now understood.

"Do you think there's any chance that the Lost and Found —" she began.

Joe had already stood up to start walking them there.

The Lost and Found was clearly labeled in the same wide black capital letters that spanned the broad stone arches throughout the terminal. Behind its graceful façade was a simple front counter made of thick, scratched dark wood, the kind you might find in any old Irish bar, and behind the counter, almost every day, stood the curmudgeonly Randall Brennan, also the kind you might find in any old Irish bar.

Mr. Brennan — Joe had grown up calling him that and, even when he'd worked for him, had never been tempted to try for something less formal — had a broken nose that had healed wrong and had given him a bruised, menacing look. From Joe's first years at the terminal, though, he knew Mr. Brennan was more rogue than ogre, as long as you gave him his due. He guarded a storage room so vast that people always joked there had to be bodies buried in it. But if there were, they would have been toe-tagged by Mr. Brennan himself. Every single item in the Lost and Found was meticulously labeled and sorted. There were separate bins for eyeglasses, keys, umbrellas, handbags, wallets, books, and toys. There were long clothing racks bowed by the weight of men's blazers and women's coats, all organized by color, so that whenever they were wheeled out to be looked over, it seemed as if dusty rainbows were rolling by. A lot of lost items, especially the truly valuable ones, had been

184

donated to the Salvation Army in recent years because of the Depression. But new stuff came in every day, and Joe was aware that there were boxes of things recovered from crimes and suspicious incidents, boxes that had been marked and tucked away separately by Grand Central's police.

Mr. Brennan was just taking off his coat when Joe and Nora approached the counter.

"Smile big, and don't mind anything he says," Joe whispered to her.

"Joseph," Mr. Brennan said as he leered at Nora unapologetically. "Where'dja find *this*? And who would've been careless enough to leave *it* lying around?"

Nora managed to keep smiling brightly as she faced forward, but she whispered to Joe, "He called me 'it.' "

"Mr. Brennan," Joe said. "This is Miss —"

"Nora Lansing," Nora said politely, but, apparently unable to resist, added, "and I am not an 'it.' "

"What's that you said?" Mr. Brennan asked.

Joe nudged Nora gently in the ribs.

She hesitated. "I am not — lost," she said.

Like Joe's father, Mr. Brennan was past sixty-five now. He had white hair and a bright red face, but his hands, speckled with gold liver spots, were so pale they looked as if they belonged on another body.

"What'd *you* lose, then, Miss Lansing?" he asked.

"It wasn't Miss Lansing," Joe said, before Nora could answer. "It was an aunt of hers. Passed away in the twenties. The subway fire. You know. There's still a police box or two, I'd wager."

"More like a dozen," Mr. Brennan said. "Maybe fifteen. Yes, Joseph. Steady Max hired you away from me that same day. Before you could help me handle them."

Nora nearly purred. "You wouldn't allow us to take a look, would you, Mr. Brennan?"

"What is it you're looking for, darlin'?"

"A gold bracelet. And a clutch," she said.

"Huh. That's a word I haven't heard for a while."

"A clutch," Nora repeated. "It's a woman's purse."

"I know what a clutch is, darlin'."

"Well, this one was about the size of a football. It was blue satin, with a little pattern sewn in, and the clasp had a little sapphire, and —"

"Wait, wait, hold your horses," Mr. Brennan said. "This'll take a while. Those boxes are way in the back by now."

■ ■ ■ ■

When Mr. Brennan had left the counter, Nora leaned over and kissed Joe's cheek, right next to his ear.

"Who have you kissed before me?" he asked her.

"Who have you kissed before *me?*"

Plucky, Joe thought. Maybe that was the word for her.

He looked at the clock a few yards behind her.

"What?" she said, following his gaze.

"You won't believe it," Joe said, "but —"

"But what?" Nora said.

Another kiss.

"I have to go to work," Joe said miserably.

"To work? *Now?*"

"I have a shift," he said.

"That's right, you told me last time," Nora said. "You work here in — in a tower, right?"

"Well, that makes it sound like there's princesses there. I work in a signal tower. Believe me, it's no castle. It's just a crowded couple of hot rooms, and they're underground."

"Can I come watch you work?"

Joe laughed, imagining it. "No!" he said. "Lord Jesus, no!"

"Why not?"

"Well, for one thing, you've got to wait for those boxes. And for another, there's only four or five guys allowed in the room at a time. It's hot as blazes, and I'm not sure any visitor's *ever* been in there, let alone a woman, let alone a looker like you. Who *knows* where the trains would end up. But —"

"But what?"

Joe lowered his voice and leaned in closer to Nora in case Mr. Brennan was within earshot. "But you've got to promise you won't disappear again," he said. "I've been waiting for you forever —"

"Forever!" she said, cutting him off. "Don't you think I know a little more about forever than you do?"

Their faces were inches apart when Mr. Brennan came back with a box — a dusty but undented corrugated box with a police label on top and TRACK FIRE #1 scrawled on each of its sides.

Nora was at the counter in a single eager step.

"There's a table over here," Mr. Brennan said. "You can have a look. But it's one box at a time, and" — he winked — "I'll have my eye on you."

Nora lifted the hinged part of the counter,

188

but Joe took her arm before she could step through.

"Please," he said. "Don't go anywhere."

Nora said, "I'll be right here."

"I'll get someone to split my shift if I can," Joe said. "Back in four hours."

"Yes, sir," she said, and she slid past the counter into the crowded but tagged and organized world of the Grand Central Lost and Found.

Joe did trade shifts and finished by two. He managed to keep the trains from colliding and to hide his fear and excitement. No one could have guessed that he was having the most extraordinary day of his life. He showered in record time, anxious to wash off the sweat but desperate to get back to Nora. His chest was tight and his teeth set as he made his way through the tunnel.

His hair was still wet when he returned to the Lost and Found, but, miraculously, Nora was still there as promised, sitting behind the counter, reading a newspaper, her legs elegantly crossed: all proper and poised. Joe felt his jaw unclenching, his whole body unwinding.

As soon as she saw him, she waved her purse. "Look!" she said triumphantly.

The purse barely resembled the one that

Nora had described. He would never have guessed that this brownish-black fabric had ever been blue satin; the gem in the clasp was obviously long gone; and the rest of the frame was so bent and twisted that it looked as if it had been banged with a hammer.

"Is that it?" Joe asked.

Nora nodded. "But I can't get it open."

"We can fix that," Joe said. "And what about the bracelet?"

Nora held up her left arm triumphantly, letting the gold charms jangle against her wrist.

"It was in a special sealed envelope," she said. "But Mr. B. let me open it."

Mr. B., Joe thought. Clearly, she had charmed him.

"Well, while we're at it, let's get you a coat," Joe said. "Mr. Brennan? Would you show us the merchandise? Miss Lansing here needs a coat."

"What happened to your coat?" Mr. Brennan asked gruffly.

"Oh, I left it in the ladies' lounge, and one of those biddies must have walked off with it," Nora said. Joe smiled, delighted by how quickly she'd come up with a story.

Mr. Brennan obliged them by rolling out the rack holding the women's coats.

Unless you counted the summer dresses

she had occasionally borrowed from Margaret in Paris, Nora had never worn a second-hand item of clothing in her life. But gamely, she chose the first wool coat that looked as if it would fit her, and she was still thanking "Mr. B." as Joe took her by the elbow. "Come with me," he said.

He led her up one ramp to the upper level and straight down another to the empty train on Track 13 where Ralston held his prayer meetings. They settled together into one of the double seats. This was not a luxurious train car — not like the 20th Century Limited, with those deep, crimson armchairs and swanky lighting fixtures, the train Joe had so often imagined hopping for a ride. But it was clean, and the seats were comfortable enough. Sitting there in the semidarkness of a train that had traveled thousands of miles, Nora held her own purse in her hands — the proof that she'd been stuck in one place for fourteen years.

Inside the train, the air had the papery smell of cigarettes and newsprint. The only light came from the platform lamps, so Joe and Nora had to lean slightly toward the window in order to see her purse. Using both his hands and his strongest grip, Joe bent the metal of the purse's frame straight enough for it to open.

191

"I feel like Superman," he said.

"Like who?"

This was the first of countless times Joe would be reminded how many things Nora had missed. Superman. FDR. Father Coughlin. Amelia Earhart. Talking pictures. Radios you could lift in one hand.

"Doesn't matter," Joe said, and he handed back her open purse. If Joe had had any lingering doubts about her story, this was where they ended.

She took out her passport first. It had a red cover — the old kind, like his father's, instead of the olive-green covers that were issued now. Nora handed it to Joe, and he opened it. The photograph showed her wearing a shirt with a high, stiff white collar. Her hair was swept up in a bun, and her expression was one of distraction, almost annoyance. The photograph wasn't black and white, but brown and beige — the colors of tea and cream.

"Look at you," Joe said, marveling.

"Oh, I hated that picture," she said. "I got it before my hair was bobbed."

Next she took out a small sketchpad and eagerly flipped through the pages, showing Joe street scenes, landscapes, sketches of people, buildings, fruit.

"An artist in Paris," Joe said, wonderingly.

"Just like you told me."

"Here," Nora said as she tried to trade the sketchpad for the passport.

"No, wait," Joe said. He focused on her date of birth: January 7, 1902. Joe's father had been born in 1879, Joe in 1905. He stared at the faint typed letters. "Nora," he said, "you were born three years before me."

"I've never been courted by a younger man," she said.

"But I'm thirty-four and you're, what —"

"Twenty-three, pal."

They were both speechless for a moment.

"Always twenty-three," she added softly.

Next she pulled out a large stack of traveler's checks and some French money. After that came a small rectangular silver box — about the size of her thumb — with an intricate pattern etched on its sides. Nora pulled on one of the ends, extracting a raspberry-red lipstick and freeing a lid to pop up and reveal a tiny mirror.

"Presto," she said, and, squinting into the mirror, used the lipstick to make an *X* in the center of her already red lips. Her whole face brightened, though whether it was from the excitement or the cosmetics Joe couldn't tell.

"I hope this stuff doesn't grow mold or something," she said.

"Why, what if it did?" Joe asked, and they were both suddenly confounded by all they didn't know. "Could you get a rash? Or get sick in some way?"

"I never have," Nora said.

"If someone hit you, would you bruise?"

"Let's not find out."

"I mean it, though. If you're dead, can you die?"

"Apparently not," Nora said. "Or get older, I think. Every time I come back, I always look exactly the same."

"But what's the longest you've stayed?"

"A couple of days."

"So it's not like you disappear after twenty-four hours."

"I'm not Cinderella's pumpkin," she said.

"So do you think you'd get older if you stayed any longer?" he asked.

"Joe," Nora said, "I just don't know."

He stood and paced the entire length of the train car, as if distance from Nora could give him some better understanding.

"Can you see me?" he asked.

"You're right in front of me, Joe."

"No, I mean can you see me when I can't see you?"

"No. I told you. When I'm not here I don't see anything."

"How many times have you come back?"

194

"Five, I think. Maybe four."

"So it hasn't been every year."

"No," she said. "Definitely not."

Joe stopped at the seat opposite hers, putting his arms around the backrest.

"Can you *do* anything?" he asked her.

"What do you mean, like work?" she asked.

Joe released the backrest and started to pace again. "No. I mean like . . . walk through things. Or get invisible. Or fly. I don't know."

"Oh, you mean like ghost things."

"Yeah."

She grinned. "What, you don't think I'm amazing enough?"

Joe shook his head.

"I think you are amazing in every possible way."

He was tempted to kiss her again, but two tracks over, the lights in another train were being turned on, and Joe could see one of the gatemen reaching for his keys.

"We've got to go," Joe said.

"Why?"

"Against the rules for us to be here."

Nora closed her purse and stood up.

"Where can we go?" she asked. "I've already tried to get to Turtle Bay, and even if I could, there's some rude man living there now."

"I know. His name is Artie Fox. He's the one who first told me you were —"

"Pretty much dead," Nora said.

She stepped out of the train car. She was so beautiful, a sliver of energy amid all the shadows.

"We could try to get to my place," he said.

"In Queens?"

"No. That's where I grew up," he said. "I live at the Railroad Branch of the Y."

"The YMCA?" she said.

"Yes."

"The Young Men's Christian Association?" She emphasized every word, smiling.

"Sure."

"Joe, I'm young, and I'm Christian, but I am not a man."

"Of this," Joe said, "I am well aware."

"So what would I be doing there? Do I wear a disguise?"

She looked almost hopeful that he'd say yes.

"Guys smuggle girls in all the time."

"You would do that?"

"I would," Joe said.

"It's your face, isn't it?" Nora asked.

"What about my face?"

"It's just that kind of face," Nora said.

"People trust you." She touched his cheek.

He walked her across the platform toward the ramp that led back up to the commuter level and the brightness, noise, and bustle of real people doing real things that they were able to take completely for granted.

They headed for the Forty-second Street exit, just as they had the year before, although they both now felt they had more to lose.

Nora put on the Lost and Found coat.

"How many blocks?" she asked.

"Forty-seventh between Third and Second," he said.

"That's closer than Turtle Bay! That's great!"

Joe put his hands on her shoulders. "I'm not worried about getting you into the Y, but I can't let you disappear again."

"Hold on to me this time. Maybe that'll keep me —"

"Grounded," Joe said. "Like grounding a wire. When you ground an electric current, you tie it to the earth."

"Right! Like I'm an electrical current!" Nora said, and laughing that deep laugh of hers, she added, "I'm a live wire!"

Joe pushed the heavy glass door open with his shoulder. They reached for each other simultaneously, their arms turning their bodies into one M-shaped entity. Together they stepped outside into the cold air.

"You should have gotten a hat too," Joe said.

"I'm not cold," she declared, and in fact the warmth of her hand was barely diminished. "Just don't let go," she said. "Hold on to me."

"You hold on to me too."

"And have a little faith," Nora said.

"My ma always said you can either have a lot of faith or no faith at all."

Neither of them could speak as they started the walk down Forty-second Street — the same way they'd walked the year before.

"So far, so good," Joe said.

They reached the corner of Lexington and crossed the street, heading toward Third.

"So, what's this Y place like?" Nora asked, but Joe could tell she was nervous, and he didn't have it in him to pretend he wasn't.

"Joe?" she said.

"You'll see when we get there," he murmured.

They had nearly reached Third Avenue. "Joe, you're hurting my hand!" Nora said.

He loosened his grip, but just a little. "Remember, I'm your ground," he said.

Her ground, Nora thought. Down to earth

in every way. Solid. Firm. Joe.

But just a few steps farther, Joe felt the warmth draining from Nora's hand. He held tighter, but the loss was unmistakable.

"Joe!" Nora shouted.

"Don't let go!" they both said.

Joe desperately tried to pull her toward him, but he couldn't hold on.

"December fifth!" she shouted, her face yearning and helpless. Then her whole body flickered, exactly like a lightbulb just before it burns out: a few quick shimmers of heat and light, then darkness.

Alone, bereft, and angry, Joe bent to pick up Nora's clutch, coat, and bracelet — the things she hadn't had with her when she died; the things she apparently couldn't keep with her when she left — and he hugged the coat to his chest until every last trace of its warmth was gone.

9
TIME

1940

In the first month of the new decade, Joe Reynolds, like every other employee of the New York Central, was handed the debut issue of a four-page newsletter called the *Central Headlight.* At Alva's on a Tuesday morning, he sat across from Mitchell, his neighbor from the Y, drinking coffee and scanning the pages. There were items about traffic, profits, employees' resignations, marriages, and new babies. There were updates on the bowling league and the camera club. But front and center was the news that one of the chief New York Central big wheels, the general passenger traffic manager, was retiring after more than a half-century of service.

"Fifty-three years," Mitchell said. "Do me a favor. If I'm still working here in fifty-three years, just tie me to the third rail, okay?"

Joe didn't answer. He was studying the drawing at the top of the first page. It was a sketch of the streamlined 20th Century Limited, with its famous bullet nose and its headlamp casting a cone of light around the newsletter's title. "Hey," Mitchell said to him. "I'm talking to you. Third rail. Promise."

Joe looked up. "What makes you think *I'm* going to be here?" he asked.

Mitchell shrugged. "You'll probably be running the place."

Joe laughed as he tried to picture wearing a suit every day, working at a desk, making the guys in shirtsleeves feel as uncomfortable as Mr. Walters from Ralston Young's prayer group made him feel. The article in the newsletter said that Louis Landsman had been born on a farm and started as a night telegrapher in Indiana when he was eighteen. He had made his way to Chicago, then New York, where he'd climbed the ranks and married and had two children who were now grown. Unlike Joe, Landsman had gotten to see at least a bit of the country. But since settling here, had Louis Landsman ever traveled the vast, sprawling routes of the system he'd overseen? Had Louis Landsman, Joe wondered, ever been to another country? Was the man only now, at seventy, free to begin his adventures?

Joe did a quick calculation. He would be sixty-nine, one year away from his own mandatory retirement, if he ended up working for the Central as long as Louis Landsman had. Joe shook his head, putting the newsletter down. It would be 1975, a year impossible to imagine, especially because of Nora. It was hard enough these days to imagine getting to the next December 5.

The new girlie calendar in the shower room at Tower A was already puckered by steam, and January boasted a voluptuous brunette clothed only in the sheerest dressing gown. Joe had basically grown into manhood staring at such pictures, and like the other guys in the place, he had always looked forward to the first of each month, when a mock ceremony was conducted by whoever happened to be around to unveil the next month's girl. That was practically meaningless to Joe now; the only thing that mattered was the speed with which those months could pass.

"God makes time. Only man makes haste" was one of Damian's favorite sayings.

As far as Joe was concerned, man could be doing a better job.

On a June day off, Joe set out for Turtle Bay

Gardens. For months, not knowing how Nora would feel about it, he had resisted the impulse to try to find her mother. But gradually he had convinced himself that finding Elsie Lansing was his best, if not his only, way of staying connected to Nora.

Rain had brought out the competing smells of a New York afternoon in early summer: the sour garbage in the alleys and the too-sweet hyacinths at the flower stand, the steam vapor rising from an open manhole, the tarry pavement along Third Avenue. Turtle Bay Gardens in summer, though, was fragrant. Red, orange, and purple flowers — bright as kids' crayons — smelled as if they'd just been planted in the painted green boxes that underlined most of the windows. The streets were tidy and quiet, and sunlight zigzagged across the shiny black hoods of the cars parked along the way.

"So. You're back?" Artie asked. He stood in the doorway, wearing a plaid short-sleeved shirt and a pair of rumpled black pants. He looked at his watch, comically. "It's June, for Christ's sake. Where've you been all year?"

Joe smiled, relieved that Artie was still here and that he didn't seem annoyed by another visit. But from behind the ritzy entryway came the sounds of men working and the smell of plaster and paint.

"I'd ask you in," Artie said, "but I'm finally having the place done over. Enough with the chintz and silk, you know?"

Joe nodded. He didn't know what chintz was.

Confidentially — though with the noise behind him there was no chance he'd be heard — Artie asked, "So, did you see her again? First week of December?"

Joe nodded.

"And she disappeared again?"

"Right in front of me."

Artie didn't have Nora's mother's address. The occasional piece of mail he had previously forwarded to Connecticut was now being bounced back with the words RETURNED TO WRITER UNCLAIMED and the red stamp of a hand pointing to his address.

"You gotta realize," Artie said. "Elsie was spooked as hell. Thought she was going crazy. Not sure I blame her."

"Is Elsie even alive?" Joe asked, realizing that his definition of the word was no longer as fixed as it had once been.

"No idea," Artie said.

Joe groaned inwardly, imagining himself

back at the library, looking for Elsie's death notice.

But Artie said he did have the phone number of one of Elsie's friends. "Ruth something," he told Joe. "I met her the same year this other woman showed up with a couple of kids, looking for a handout, saying Nora gave her this address. But Ruth, that was someone who knew her. She saw Nora in Grand Central too. Scared her senseless. She told me to call her if I ever got this figured out. Not much chance of that, I don't think."

Joe asked for Ruth's number.

Unlike the formal downstairs rooms that Joe had seen back in 1937, the rooms upstairs were a jumbled mess. They reminded him of some arts-and-crafts project Mike and Alice might have started and dropped. Some trappings of the Lansings' former life remained — the fancy wallpaper, the heavy rugs, the huge mirrors framed by gold leaves and shells. But over and around these was the life Artie was living — a stack of newspapers on a marble hall table; a bright modern painting between fussy light fixtures.

"Must be in my study," Artie said, and he led the way across the landing to a flight of worn carpeted stairs. The study was a small room, and Joe knew immediately that it had to have been Nora's bedroom. The wall-paper had a delicate pattern of vines and birds, and the arms of the white iron ceiling fixture ended in flowers and leaves painted yellow, orange, and pink. A massive wooden desk stood where the bed must have been. A telephone, a bust of someone like George Washington, and what looked like a month's worth of mail sat on top of it. Joe wondered casually what Artie did but had a vague sense that it wasn't entirely on the up-and-up. Other mysteries were far more important.

Joe scanned the room for traces of Nora. She had stared up at this flowery light fixture when she had gone to sleep each night. She had hung her clothes in this closet, doorless now to accommodate Artie's file cabinets. She had looked at herself in this mirror hanging on this wall, looked at herself, probably, at every age. Joe wished that her reflections had been left behind.

A ceiling-high bookcase painted a girlish butter yellow held *The Maltese Falcon, The Big Sleep,* and a bunch of dime novels: *The Wolves of New York, Spicy New York.* There was something wrong, almost twisted, Joe thought, about having this grown man's fantasies shelved in what had been a young

206

girl's room. He looked over his shoulder and saw that Artie was busy searching through his desk drawers. Then Joe turned back and found, on the top shelf, *The Tale of Peter Rabbit, Alice in Wonderland.*

Keeping his back to Artie, Joe tried to sound casual. "These Nora's books?"

"Hmm," Artie said, still shuffling through the things in his desk. "I guess. Elsie left a lot of books. I never really sorted them."

"Any clothes?" Joe asked, turning around.

Artie squinted. "What? Clothes?"

"Just curious," Joe said. He smiled faintly but guiltily: the smile of a man a bit ashamed of who or what he loves.

"Salvation Army," Artie said. "They got the clothes."

Joe turned back to the bookshelf. *Pollyanna, The Magic Pudding.* These were the books of Joe's childhood too. *Peter Pan, Dr. Dolittle,* and next to that one, a book about half its size. The cover was also red but made of leather, and the only writing on the spine were two words in faint gold capital letters:

MY DIARY

Joe had never stolen anything in his life, but he left Artie Fox's house and walked down the dappled streets of Turtle Bay with Ruth Ingram's phone number in one pants pocket and Nora's diary in the other. He had made a date to meet Finn at the Polo Grounds, but with practically no hesitation he turned east instead of west and continued down to the river. There was a small area of grass there — not big enough to call a park — and several benches by the water. Joe took the diary from his pocket and sat in the sun, feeling the breeze whip his bangs against his forehead. He already knew he wouldn't make it to the game today.

Examining the book, Joe saw that the page edges had been dyed in a wavy pattern of red and gold. The gold was mustard yellow now, but in a few spots it still shone where it caught the sunlight. The book was kept closed by a cracked, tongue-shaped flap slipped into a worn, thin loop. Gently, Joe pulled the tongue through and even more gently opened the book. The paper on the inside covers had a pale-plaid design, and Nora's name, in a flowery schoolgirl script, was written in the upper right-hand corner.

He turned one page.

Five-Year Diary, 1919–1923

This book, if Nora had used it, would

contain the record of her life from the time she was seventeen until she was twenty-one, just two years before her death.

It had been six months since Joe had seen this young woman who had died in 1925 and yet was undeniably alive in Grand Central, according to laws neither of them understood. Whatever qualms he might have had about reading someone else's diary were overcome by the mystery of who she was and by the wish — which now felt like a crushing need — to be with her in any way he could.

He fanned the thin pages, which crackled a little, unstiffening, and bent over to read. The book was arranged by the days of the year, each day given two pages, with a section for each year. The earliest entries were written in a large but careful script. Some were just a line or two from a saying or song. Others recorded grades Nora had gotten — lots of A's but, Joe was somehow relieved to see, plenty of B's and some C's too. There were also many days she had left blank. Occasionally Joe found two pages on which Nora had written something in every year, and he could see how her handwriting had gotten smaller and neater as her thoughts had gotten larger and bolder.

May 7, 1919

I don't think I like Roxanne anymore. Is that because she didn't pick me in field hockey? Do I even care about field hockey? Do I even care about Roxanne? Do I only like people who like me?

May 7, 1920

Tonight Mother and Father took me to see the Follies! I saw Fanny Brice, W. C. Fields, Vanda Hoff, Sybil Carmen, and the Ziegfeld Girls. It was divine!

May 7, 1921

Mother always tells me never to use the word "hate" unless I really mean it. She says: "Hate is a very strong word." But right now I hate her! She thinks she knows everything, but I think all she knows is what it was like to be young when she was young!

May 7, 1922

I hate how Mother treats Father. She acts as if all he's ever doing when he's home is just waiting to see what he can do for her.

She says his name even when she doesn't need anything. "Fred? Fred?" She sounds like a parrot. And Father just says, "Yes, Elsie?" Sometimes she doesn't even answer. She just has to know he's there. I will never be like that with Jenks.

Nora had drawn a heart next to the name Jenks.

Joe put down the book for a moment and looked out at the river. To his left was the Queensboro Bridge, with its double-pointed towers that always reminded him of bats' ears. To his right, much farther away, was the solid Williamsburg Bridge, which led to Brooklyn.

The sun leapt over the water, and he could smell the brine. Aside from the backyard of the house in Queens, the East River was as close to nature as Joe usually managed to get. For a few minutes he watched its traffic: a red-and-white fireboat gliding along; a green tug steering a huge tanker; a steamer veering so close to shore that Joe could see the captain's beard. So many different lives and destinations.

He went back to reading:

May 7, 1923

Just because I want to get my hair bobbed, Mother says she's not sure I'm the girl she thought I was. Well, maybe I'm not. And maybe that's one of the best things I can say! After that, there were only occasional entries for the year 1923. A fight with Jenks, whoever that had been. A kiss from some guy named Sebastian. Joe was about to close the book when he found the last entry:

Thanksgiving, 1923
Thanksgiving Day? Here is what I'm most thankful for: It didn't hurt. I didn't bleed. Sebastian swears he's not going to tell anyone we did it. And I'm never going to have to wonder again what the big deal is. And P.S. Thanks to wonderful Father, I am going to go to Paris after graduation next summer, no matter what Mother says!

Joe closed the book and held it to his chest, the way he had held Nora's coat after she disappeared and the way he was determined to hold her again, when she came back on the next anniversary of her death.

Joe went to Paris in September — or, rather, went as near as he could, which was France's pavilion at the World's Fair. The fair was scheduled to close for good at the end of October, and by now Joe had already been back six or seven times. He had visited Greece, Belgium, Brazil, Japan, and Norway, and he had seen almost all the United States buildings. He had saved France — what he'd assumed would be the best — for last.

Even before he'd met Nora, Joe had been curious about Paris. During the war, Damian had landed in a rehabilitation hospital there, and he had always talked about the city with uncharacteristic enthusiasm. The beauty of the Eiffel Tower, the beauty of Notre-Dame, and — when Katherine wasn't listening — the beauty of the French nurse who had wheeled him outside daily. "Bee-you-tiful," he would whisper to Finn and Joe, using jittery hands to sketch an hour-glass in the air. "And believe me, when a man's just lost a limb and half a hand, he needs some warmth and kindness."

At the fair's French pavilion, though, there seemed to be not much of either. However cheerful the hostesses tried to be, they were forcing their smiles. Despite the high picture windows, with their views of the fountains and bright avenues, the mood here was dark and hushed. The Germans had taken Paris in June. I HAVE SEEN THE FUTURE, read the pins given to visitors at the World of Tomorrow. Worn in this pavilion, these buttons seemed less like proud declarations and more like a grim prophecy.

Nevertheless, Joe settled at a café table and, without a moment's hesitation, ordered a croque-monsieur. He wasn't even that hungry, but he remembered the joy with which Nora had held up her sandwich at Alva's that first night. It didn't take long before a tired, somber waitress put a plate in front of him with a honey-colored sandwich and a cluster of tiny pickles. With faithful anticipation, Joe took a first bite, but really it was just a sandwich, special only because it represented a slim connection to Nora.

After the French pavilion, Joe made sure to visit some of the nongeographic exhibits he had heard or read about. He saw a building-sized cash register that toted up the day's attendance and a see-through Plexiglas Pontiac that was, strangely enough, called "The Ghost Car." At the Westinghouse pavilion he saw Elektro, the gleaming metal robot who could walk, talk, and smoke a cigar, and right outside that building there were copies of the objects that had been placed inside a time capsule and buried fifty feet underground: a woman's hat, a man's razor, a can opener, phonograph records, things like that. The capsule wasn't supposed to be opened for five thousand years; the engraving on the tip read "1939 A.D. to 6939 A.D." Joe had to smile at that, thinking back to the start of the year, when Mr. Landsman's retirement had made 1975 seem hard to imagine.

Joe's last destination was the Elgin Time Observatory, where Jacob the clock master had insisted Joe stop. Jake himself had gotten to go only once: With a sash of tools across his chest that made him look like a bandit, he tended nearly a thousand clocks that he hated to leave for long. As Jake had promised, though, Joe enjoyed looking at the many clock faces, gears, and telescopes, and he stopped at a machine that could show you in thirty seconds how much time your watch gained or lost in a day. Finally, he joined a small crowd that had gathered around an ugly twelve-foot-high statue. With massive muscles, a hunched back, and a club in its hands, this figure was meant to represent Time as a slave, striking a gong every hour. Checking their watches, the visitors waited at the base of the statue. At five o'clock exactly, like a great beast, the statue moved to swing its club against the gong. Instinctively, Joe turned away. In his life at this moment, time wasn't the slave, but the master.

10
M42

Joe had been working at the Piano in Tower A for eight hours, following the lights on the board, bringing the trains in, pulling and pushing the worn brass handles. He needed more than ever to be busy today. One thought kept getting in his way, and it felt like a physical tap on the shoulder each time he worked a lever. A year before, he had almost been scared that Nora would appear, and now he was terrified that she wouldn't.

By six A.M., he was famished, but after cleaning up and trudging through the tunnel to the concourse, he had lost his appetite. He picked up a newspaper so he would look busy, and he sat under the west balcony on the marble steps, perfectly positioned in front of the spot on the east side of the concourse where Nora had told him she had died. Flexing his sore hands,

217

Joe was grateful for the sparseness of the hall at this hour.

Joe stared up at the three arched east windows, which were wide enough to drive a train through. He'd heard once that that had been the architects' plan, in case New York got so big that the windows had to be taken out and new tracks laid right through the concourse. If that ever happened, Joe thought, he would have to look elsewhere for work. These windows were more holy to him than the stained-glass ones in St. Anthony's. In churches, light lit up pictures of what was supposed to be sacred. In Grand Central Terminal, the light itself seemed sacred. This morning, though, before dawn, Joe felt no special grace, only a murky, thick exhaustion.

At 6:15, the New Haven came in, and a few woozy travelers came up from the commuter tracks, blinking like mice. A couple of teenagers followed them, drunk and noisy and carrying on until one of them bent almost double and puked into his cap.

Fifteen minutes later, despite himself, Joe had almost dozed off, but he was brought to attention by the *squeech-squeech* sound of Butch Becker's heavy black galoshes. The new shoeshine kid was standing at the bottom of the stairs, taking off his dripping slicker.

"Still raining, I guess," Joe said.

"They said it was going to stop," Butch said.

"You're making a puddle."

Butch stared down at Joe awkwardly. "Hey, Joe?"

"Huh?"

"Is something wrong?"

"Something like what?"

"You look sort of worried."

"Nah," Joe said. "I'm just meeting someone."

"It's still dark out," Butch said. "Who —"

Joe cut him off. "You'd better get dried off and go open up, or Shoebox Lou's going to have your hide."

Joe watched, nearly hypnotized, as Butch turned to walk back down the long length of the concourse, the pink floor and the high stone walls gradually absorbing him.

Old and new photographs of Grand Central looked practically identical, and people often spoke about the place being timeless — like a mountain or a monument, unchanged by the years. But to anyone who knew it well, the terminal was filled with time: not just with scars and history, but

219

with time you could sense all around you, as if the many people who'd come and gone had left something real behind them, had *spent* their time, like money.

Joe felt adrift in this time as he waited, studying the long rectangular slabs of the marble floor, trying to find a pattern in the veins — some gray, some white, some black. It was nearly seven, the hour of the accident, the hour of Nora's arrival. Joe opened the newspaper and stared at the words but wasn't able to read them. What if she didn't come? He wished there were a lever he could use to push the thought away.

It was just past seven when the Manhattanhenge sunrise blasted through the window. Joe leapt to his feet. The sunlight seemed to wipe away all the details of the room and change every color. Seemingly at the same instant, Nora appeared, lying on the floor and bathed in the light. Joe shot down the steps and reached her just as she was standing up. At that moment, her image flickered — exactly as it had when she'd disappeared on the street the year before. Joe lunged for her, arms out, trying to hold and tether her. For a split second their eyes met — in joy, followed by helplessness. He felt her warmth run through his body, but then he fell, facedown, arms empty. He hit the now dull floor. Dumbfounded, he looked out the window toward the clouds that had passed in front of the sun.

"Is there a problem, Joseph?" Joe heard someone say.

Steady Max was walking past him. It took Joe a moment to realize that Max hadn't seen Nora, though he'd seen Joe fall. It had all happened so quickly. Joe himself wouldn't have seen her unless he had known where to look.

"Drunk again?" Max asked, which was a joke.

Joe scrambled to his feet. "I just slipped," he said. "The rain —"

He bent down to untie and retie first one shoelace, then the other, biding his time.

Come back, come back, come back.

Joe hadn't cried when his mother died, not even on the rainy warm morning when she was buried in Calvary Cemetery. But now, half-way down the ramp to the lower concourse, he was fighting tears. Blinking them back, he passed under the enormous egg-shaped chandeliers, whose naked lightbulbs, stuck on gold-plated bands, still shone as a celebration of the terminal's once revolutionary electric power. There was nothing to celebrate today. The morning greetings that usually gave Joe such comfort — that made him feel so welcome and neighborly — were all at once an intrusion. If hope could make you drunk, then this was its hangover, and Joe had to be alone to nurse it.

Moving swiftly now, cap slanted over his eyes, he walked down one ramp after another, into the terminal's depths, where staircases replaced the ramps designed to ease travelers' ways. It had taken Joe a few years before he'd felt comfortable in the depths of Grand Central. The farther down you went, the fewer people you saw, and in the barely lit tunnels and passageways, it became harder and harder to separate shadows from the objects that cast them. There were black corners, peeling pipes, damp smells, the oil and sweat of machines and men. The concourse — with its signs and stars and windows and light — was easy for anyone to know. Even the platforms offered the comfort of math and motion, purpose and straight lines. But the layers below the track levels held the power and secrets, and the men who could navigate those levels knew the building the way doctors knew bodies.

Today Joe's destination was the deepest and most deserted level of all, carved out to hold an enormous secret room known only as M42. Located ten stories belowground, M42 appeared on no blue-print and was drawn on no map. Even some of the old-timers didn't know how to get there, but in both power and sound, it provided Grand Central's heartbeat. The room was as large as the concourse itself, and it housed the roaring rotary converters that changed the city's alternating current — which powered the terminal's lights and loudspeakers, fans and clocks — into direct current, which powered the tracks up and down the whole East Coast.

Outside this room were catwalks, metal staircases, and one long stretch of rock, barely lit, the rock from which the space for the whole terminal had been blasted, carved, and cut. A band of stray cats — Joe imagined the Colosseum had nothing on Grand Central — had grown surprisingly fat on the scraps that probably ten different guys were feeding them. Other than the cats, and some legendarily enormous rats, the place had no life.

Today Joe hadn't come with scraps, but that didn't stop the cats from converging on him, slinking up to his pant legs, mewing in the dim light. He had named only one of them: Dillinger — after the gangster — for the balls-out way he always got to Joe before the others, then stole away at any hint of trouble. Sitting in the darkness — a hole cut into the earth that smelled of rotting food and cat piss — Joe used his thumb to rub the spot between Dillinger's shoulders, feeling the reassurance of the animal's warmth. A few moments passed, and Joe realized he was rubbing the cat's chest in time to the rhythm of the converters. He replayed what had just happened in the concourse, how he had lunged like an idiot into the light beam and how everything had seemed all right until the clouds covered the sun.

"The fucking clouds," he whispered fiercely to Dillinger.

Dillinger must have felt something change in Joe, because now the cat butted his head into him as if he were trying to stroke Joe's chest. Joe sat up straighter.

It was the clouds. The clouds had blocked the sunrise. Today was Manhattanhenge sunrise. Nora must have died in this special sunlight of the winter solstice, and somehow, every December 5, the sunlight tried to bring her back.

No matter what your means of transportation, Joe thought — car, train, or sunbeam — if something blocks its path, you're not going to get where you want to go. Forget the looks, the love, the fear, and the faith. If the weather hadn't been clear last year, Nora would not have come through. There would have been no purse or coat or kiss. And Joe would never have learned since then — from Artie, the papers, from Nora herself — where and when to expect her appearance this morning. The desolation Joe felt at missing her was almost matched by the grim pride of believing he had figured out something that no else knew. Yes, he thought. It wasn't God or magic that brought Nora back to life. Or rather, if it was magic, then it was magic with a pattern, magic with rules, a calendar, some calculation that Joe just might be able to make.

He stood up, practically throwing Dillinger off his lap. Hurriedly, he climbed back up to the track level and, removing his cap, hustled into the train on Track 13 just in time to hear Ralston Young intone, "Let us say a prayer on that."

Joe stood panting in the doorway as members of the prayer group lifted their bowed heads expectantly. He must have looked as if he were about to announce that the Savior had returned. The hope on their faces reflected the excitement on his, yet he instantly regretted that he'd come here. He believed he had just found the answer to a question, but he remembered that it was a question no one else was asking.

"I'm sorry," Joe managed to say. Then he raced along the platform, barely nodding at the gateman and the conductor on the next train over, both of whom he knew.

He hadn't eaten since before his shift the previous day. He still wasn't hungry, but he needed a cup of coffee. He was on his way back from Bond's Bakery when Ralston caught up with him on the lower level. Ralston was wearing his porter's hat, which meant he was heading back to work, but he stopped Joe anyway.

"You came to tell us something," Ralston said.

"Well, yes, but I realized it was the wrong moment."

"Is this the right moment?" Ralston asked.

"I don't think so," Joe said.

"If you don't mind my saying so, you look like you could use some sleep."

"I could," Joe admitted.

"Proverbs 3:24."

"Excuse me?"

" 'When you lie down, you will not be afraid; yes, when you lie down, your sleep will be sweet.' "

The rain had stopped by the time Joe left the terminal. Exhausted, he walked north to the Y under skies that were now maddeningly clear, the sun over his shoulder like a kid's balloon.

He could tell Artie what he'd figured out, but what good would that do? Joe knew that the person he needed to tell — the only one who might want the answer as much as he did — was Nora's mother. Back at the Y, he retrieved her friend's phone number from his desk drawer and used the phone in the downstairs study to make the call. But it was a call that led to the day's second empty embrace. In a tight, clipped voice, with almost no emotion, Ruth Ingram told Joe that Nora's mother had died three years before.

11
WAITING FOR THE SUN TO SET

1941

Joe had never noticed how much time the guys at the Y spent talking about women. Whether it was over a round of pool or a round of drinks, there was constant chatter about who was pairing up. There were the elegant, prized Century Girls, the chatty waitresses from Alva's, the grateful laundresses from one of the subfloors, and the kitchen workers from the Oyster Bar, who never quite shook the shellfish smell.

In the first months after Nora flickered through his arms, even though Joe had spent a few nights with some of these women, the last thing he wanted to do was sit around and talk about them. He went more often than usual to the newsreel theater under Grand Central's east balcony, where the plush seats beneath the low ceiling had always made a comfortable nest, a place to take a break or a nap. These days

228

the cartoons and human-interest stories were still going strong, but everything was being overshadowed by news of the war in Europe. In the almost empty theater, tucked into one of the back rows, Joe watched footage showing America's preparations, and everything revolved around tanks, guns, airplanes, and training. Soldiers drilled, assembly-line workers built, and planes took off, group after group, in perfect formation.

The war made a constant noise, even when that noise was a mere whisper. The threat — the question and worry about whether the United States should get involved — was always there, just like the rumble in the terminal that, even at its quietest, pulsed with potential force.

In some ways, the war noise was loudest in Queens, where conversations held on the church steps were now more often about *when* than *if.* The isolationists who called themselves America Firsters were given cold shoulders or icy glares, especially by Damian, who these days rarely talked about anything but war. He didn't understand why the United States was waiting.

"The damn Huns," he said after lunch one cold Sunday in March. "The damn Huns should know their place." Alice and Mike,

Faye and Finn, and Damian and Joe were gathered in the living room, sipping hot cider from mismatched mugs. Like a lot of his friends who'd seen action in the Great War, Damian thought that taking on Germany was the only way to justify all the awful things they'd seen and the great things they'd lost: time and innocence, comrades and limbs.

"You can step on a cockroach and think it's dead," Damian said, "but it can show up an hour later and you'll have to step on it again." He stamped his real leg, hard, on the floor.

"There's a cockroach?" an alarmed nine-year-old Alice asked, tucking her feet beneath her on the couch.

Mike wiggled his fingers in her face.

"Germany!" Damian shouted. "I'm talking about goddamned Germany!"

The kids froze, eyes wide, united in their surprise. At fourteen, Mike certainly understood what his grandfather was talking about, but even so, the volume of Damian's voice was a shock.

He turned to his sons and bellowed, "And when are you two signing up?" This was hardly the first time he'd asked the question. Damian frequently mentioned Faye's brother, Ron Jr., who had joined the navy in the fall of 1939. Junie had grown up as the skinny kid in the neighborhood, the one who was always tagging along with the older, braver boys. Most people thought Junie had joined up only to get away from the other kids' teasing, but that didn't stop Damian from holding him up as the perfect young patriot.

"We'll sign up as soon as they need us, Pa," Finn said.

Finn's answer was not new either. It was the one both he and Joe had been giving Damian since the war in Europe started. The answer was an evasion. Joe and the other levermen had already been told that if it came to war, they would be classified as "essential personnel" and not allowed to enlist — "Even if the Nazis land in New York Harbor," the stationmaster had said. The New York Central Line would never risk losing anyone it had trained to stand at a Piano, especially when the trains would be overloaded with soldiers and supplies. Finn, likewise, had been informed that if America actually got into the war, the city would need more cops to protect it.

Still, Joe and Finn heard the drumbeat, and not only from Damian. Just this morning, Father Gregory had slipped some Bible verses about battle and bravery into his sermon, though his ever-shrinking body was a reminder that physical strength had its limits.

"If I had two good legs, I'd lose one again, to get at those bastards," Damian said now.

Faye said, "Pa! Language," and she motioned Finn into the kitchen.

The minute the door swished shut, Mike's questions spilled out: What was it like in battle? Had Damian ever killed anyone? How many? Had any of his friends been killed? Had he used a bayonet? Had he carried a hand grenade? Had he been afraid it would go off? Did he still have his uniform?

"Joseph," Damian said, "go up to the attic. Find my helmet and bring it down. I want Mike to see it."

"Don't you think we should check with Finn and Faye?" Joe asked.

"I'm the boy's grandfather," Damian growled, which was not an answer but served the same purpose.

Reluctantly, Joe climbed upstairs, passing the master bedroom — where Damian still slept — and the bedrooms that had once been his and Joe's and were now crowded by the kids in one and by Finn and Faye in the other. In the hallway, Joe tugged on the thick, frayed rope and pulled down the attic stairs. The earthy smell of mold and trapped

232

moisture hit him as soon as he started up. Boxes and old furniture, a sewing machine and broken lamps, were all coated in a layer of dust.

Joe had intended only to find Damian's helmet — and perhaps the Purple Heart he'd been awarded but always said would make him seem to be boasting if he displayed it. In a box marked "1918," however — a box just like the ones Nora had sifted through at the Lost and Found — Joe uncovered a small bundle of sepia photographs and a stack of letters in faded blue envelopes addressed to Katherine in Damian's handwriting. There were French stamps in the upper right-hand corners and, in the lower left, round purple marks that read PASSED AS CENSORED. Gently, Joe slid the top letter from its envelope. "My darling Pretty Kitty," it began. "How I miss your sweet smile and your soft warm —" That was all Joe read. Swiftly, he put the letter back, as if closing a door on a conversation he knew he shouldn't be hearing.

He thought about how his mother and father had been kept apart by the war. Sure, that must have been rough, he thought. But Damian had made it through. The romantic soldier had come home to become the husband who bickered, teased, and bitched.

True, he'd come home in a wheelchair, but he'd been gone only a year. Maybe it had been a year in hell, but Damian had known where Katherine was, and Katherine had known what Damian was doing. Joe would gladly have sacrificed a limb and some fingers for the chance to write a letter to Nora that he could be certain she'd read.

"What's taking you so damn long?" Damian shouted from downstairs, and after a quick search of two more boxes, Joe found his father's turtle-shaped steel helmet and climbed back down the ladder.

"What took you so long?" Damian asked again as Mike jumped up to look at his grandfather's gear.

"There's a lot of junk up there," Joe said.

"That's what attics are for," Damian said.

"Don't you think we should clean it out someday?"

"Your mother's things are up there," Damian said gruffly. "You can clean it out when I die."

Without warning, that happened just four months later.

Unlike the man himself, Damian's death was neither noisy nor demanding. On the first Wednesday in a hot July, with the kids already away at 4H summer camp, Faye

234

dropped Damian at his usual VFW meeting. A poll was being taken that night about America's entry into the war. Most of the veterans, like Damian, were firmly in favor of joining the fight. So when the votes were tallied and turned out to be strongly against entry, there was a squall of confusion and complaints. It soon became clear that a group of America Firsters had infiltrated the meeting. When the VFW members found out that these isolationists were not even veterans, a brawl broke out.

Damian's heart attack pitched him out of his wheelchair. Later, his buddy Elbert said he'd gotten to him just in time to hear Damian's last words.

"Tell them I died —"

Elbert was sure Damian had meant to say, "Tell them I died fighting."

"*Was* he fighting?" Joe asked Elbert.

Elbert hesitated. "I know he was wanting to," he said.

Father Gregory came to the house on the eve of Damian's burial to lead the vigil and help welcome guests. There were several dozen: a few neighbors, some cops from Finn's precinct, some people from the church and the VFW. Many of them talked about heaven as if it were some neighborhood restaurant they went to often. Joe wished he could believe it was a real place like that. But even with the little he had learned about Nora, Joe was sure of only one thing: Neither death nor life could possibly be that simple.

At the funeral home Joe had slipped the stack of war letters into Damian's coffin, trying to convince himself that Damian and Katherine might — as so many of the guests kept saying — be reunited. As he lifted Damian's head to place the letters beneath it, Joe felt the rubbery coldness of his father's neck — a coldness that made his heart ache. Though he couldn't yet explain it all, Joe knew that Nora's afterlife had something to do with where and how she had died; it was something specific to her, to Manhattanhenge, perhaps to the terminal itself. Touching his father for the last time, Joe didn't think it possible that Damian could ever be alive again, in any place or form.

On the morning of July 8, a Tuesday, they buried Damian next to Katherine in the ancient Calvary Cemetery, not far from home. Graves were festooned with fresh wreaths and small American flags, the evidence of recent July Fourth visits to other veterans' graves. Katherine's red granite headstone, which Joe remembered had cost

Damian two months' pay, was despite that fact as simple as any in sight. Engraved capital letters spelled out her name and the dates of her birth and death; a small cross carved at the top was the only decoration. Like the rest of the graves in this and most cemeteries, Katherine's faced east. When they'd buried her years before, Damian had told Joe and Finn that graves faced east so that when Christ returned and the dead rose, they would already be facing him. Facing the east, Joe thought today, would also mean facing the power of the rising sun.

Both Joe and Finn had shifts that afternoon. Faye went back home to write to the children at camp and to begin the task of sorting through Damian's things.

On the subway, returning to Manhattan, Joe closed his eyes and considered his father's life. It hadn't been an easy one. Damian had struggled and been all but broken by the war. But Joe found himself once again envying the normality of what Damian had experienced. Damian had believed in God, America, Ireland, the pope, and heaven, in roughly that order, and nothing had ever happened to him to challenge any of those beliefs.

The last time Joe had prayed — had actually put his head down and his hands together and tried to talk to God — it had been when his mother was dying. That had been in 1919, and he, Finn, and Damian had taken turns sitting beside her as her fever soared, her energy waned, and the Spanish flu ran its swift, terrifying course. When she died — her mouth grotesquely open, and her sheets soiled, even down to the bottom of the mattress — the fourteen-year-old Joe had stopped believing that God was listening.

Standing by Damian's open casket last night, Joe had not prayed. Watching the coffin being lowered into the ground today, he had not prayed. But as it happened, today fell just a few days after a summer Manhattanhenge. Back in the city, waiting for the sun to set — it wouldn't be that far off-center — Joe tried to talk to God. Outside the terminal, he stared west at the sun as it passed between the buildings on Forty-third Street, and he prayed that the winter solstice would bring equally clear skies. He prayed for a sunrise to let in the light that would carry Nora back to him.

■ ■ ■ ■

PART THREE

■ ■ ■ ■

PART THREE

1
EVER HEARD OF STONEHENGE?

1941

Joe was used to waiting minutes between trains, days between shifts, weeks between visits to Queens. Months — assuming you didn't count the calendar in the tower's shower room — were a different matter. Yet this had been the way he'd told time in 1941. How many months since the last December 5. How many months till the next one. The present was less and less vivid to him.

The promise of love, the way Joe had heard it growing up, was that it might be plenty hard to find but much easier to recognize. You'd know the right moment. She'd be the right girl. And the rightness — implied, sometimes even spoken, so clear in Irish working-class Queens — was that she would be one of us. Like Faye with Finn, she would be like your sisters, cousins, and mother: freckled and strong-willed, God-fearing and sassy.

Yet even beyond the strange details of Nora's existence — or nonexistence — she didn't seem to be anything like Faye or Katherine. She didn't even seem to be anything like Joe. He knew that what should have stunned him — even scared him — was the apparent fact of her death. But *she* was what stunned him. Something about that laugh, those lips, that toss of her head. Maybe it was her energy, and the way she was trying so fiercely to take what had happened to her in stride. Or maybe it was the thrill she gave him of knowing that, after all the shocks of the Depression, a life could change course in an instant — not for the worse but for the better.

Joe had been listening to weather reports since Thanksgiving. Starting the first day of December, the forecast was for clear skies and unusually warm temperatures. On December 4, Big Sal scared him by saying her rheumatism was acting up, a usually reliable predictor of rain or snow. Yet as Joe walked to the terminal just before dawn on December 5, the sky was clear and filled with stars, and his mind was filled with something he had heard Ralston Young say more than once: "Miracles are the children of the Earth and the Everlasting."

When Nora appeared, it was at precisely 7:05, just as the rising sun swept through the center east window, clear and bold as a beacon. Aside from its brief appearance the year before, Joe had never seen Manhattan-henge from inside the terminal. It looked like the light on the bullet nose of the 20th Century Limited, something you knew would hurt your eyes if you stared at it straight on, but something you nonetheless couldn't avoid.

When Joe moved out of the sun's path, he could see Nora lying on the marble floor and scrambling to her feet. He saw her shake off her fear the way a dog shakes off water, then start running toward him.

"You're here again!" she said, and nearly knocked him over with her embrace. It was all she could say before he kissed her. No matter who might be watching, he had to kiss her. He had to feel how real she was. And Nora, having broken through that gray, paralyzing in-between, seemed to melt into Joe, her warmth radiating around them both.

Maybe, Joe thought, the one good thing about Nora's uncommon comings and goings was that so many of their kisses had the urgency of a first one.

The Biltmore Hotel had opened in 1913 and had been designed by some of the same architects who had created the terminal and envisioned what they called Terminal City: a cluster of modern, related structures — hotels, apartment houses, office towers — all of which were physically connected to one another. Thus buildings had grown up around Grand Central every few years, like younger siblings. You could get to the lobby of the Commodore Hotel from the Main Concourse, and you could reach the Biltmore lobby from an elevator in the terminal's so-called Kissing Room, where people waited to greet their friends and loved ones as they arrived.

Today, three weeks before Christmas, there was mistletoe hanging above that elevator's door, though Joe, having led Nora there, didn't need any excuse to kiss her again.

"Where are we going?" she asked as he fumbled to ring for the elevator.

Joe reached into his pants pocket and withdrew a hotel room key. Nora was beautifully, spectacularly unshocked.

■ ■ ■ ■

Just as many of the buildings around Grand Central were connected to one another, so were the people who worked in them. Especially during the worst of the Depression, when everyone with a job had three relatives without one, a casual system of barter had evolved: this loaf of bread for those magazines; this pair of shoes for that manicure or haircut. The day before Nora's arrival, Joe had traded a pair of Giants tickets for a Floating Key. Between the Biltmore's nearly one thousand rooms and the Commodore's two thousand, there were always — even in the best of economies — several dozen empty rooms on any given night. Each hotel had a source for the keys, but for Joe the most reliable was the Biltmore's daytime doorman. Max Colton was a sweet, tall guy from the Midwest who unfailingly watched the street, rapt, as if it were a Broadway stage and the pedestrians were the performers.

"Just leave the room how you found it," he'd said to Joe the day before while handing him the key.

"Hoping I'll need it more than one night," Joe had said.

"Special lady?"

"Very special."

"Well, no rush. I'll let you know if you need to move."

Now, waiting for the elevator with Nora and more nervous than he wanted to be, Joe used his thumb to trace the ornate raised Biltmore *B* on the heavy oval key fob in his palm.

When he and Nora stepped into the elevator, she seemed to shine amid the fine walnut interior. One short floor later, he took her hot hand as they entered the soaring, carpeted lobby of the Biltmore's Palm Court, with its feathery potted plants and huge chandeliers. They walked over the vast Oriental carpets, each one like a separate country, with clusters of chairs and tables graced by people from all over the world. Wearing honeymoon smiles, Joe and Nora moved closer to each other and strolled through the lobby single-mindedly. Whatever looks they got — because of her flapper dress, his working clothes, their obvious intimacy — bounced off them as if their feelings had created a physical shield. Pressing her face against Joe's shoulder, Nora allowed herself to revel in the scent of fresh laundry and in the simple, steady strength of him.

Room 809 was the first of countless hotel rooms that Joe and Nora would share by the grace of Max Colton and the Floating Key. The room was so large that Joe's single at the Y could have fit neatly inside it twice. Aside from the bed, there were brocade curtains and two small couches covered in muted tapestry fabrics, a small dressing table with a mirror, a large wooden desk that reminded Joe of Artie's, and a wooden side table with a top shaped like a shamrock. The room was silent and musty, with the slight scent of furniture polish. Nora's purse — the one they had recovered from the Lost and Found — was waiting for her on the dresser, her bracelet tucked inside it.

"You brought my things!" she exclaimed. She fished the bracelet from the bag and expertly rolled it over her left hand. She hurried to the window, where she gazed out, excited, on the streets just starting to fill with the day. Then she turned and ran back to Joe, her eyes gleaming.

Finding approval there, he reached for the back of her dress. Four years of knowing her, three of constant imagining, two of thinking he understood, a week of fretting about the weather — all powered his movements. He fumbled with the long row of small black silk buttons on the back of her

247

dress, but after a moment he gave up all pretense of skill and said: "You're just going to have to turn around."

Laughing, she obeyed him. His worker's fingers tackled the buttons methodically, efficiently. Just before he undid the last one, Nora reached down to the hem of her dress and pulled it up over her head.

She was wearing a peach-colored silk slip, which she peeled off boldly, revealing garters and the ivory stockings they held up. Joe stared, amazed, at her beauty, her youth, her confidence. He let out an unintelligible sound, locked the door, and stripped off his clothes. Diving with her onto the bed, he managed only to say her name.

"So tell me," Nora said, when they finally allowed themselves to catch their breath and were lying side by side. Calmly, almost casually: "If I'm dead, how could I have felt all *that*?"

How do you explain the inexplicable? Joe had already tried, with Finn, and learned just how hard it would be to tell anyone else. Nora herself was the mystery, though, and she had more reason than anyone to want to find a solution. It had been sixteen years since she had begun bouncing through different states of being, different moments in time, none of which she had gotten to choose, none of which she had quite understood.

"I think it's the way you said it the last time you were here," Joe said. "You said you thought you got stuck. I think I know how that happened. I think I know what brings you here. But I don't know what keeps you here."

Nora put her slip back on. "Tell me," she said simply. She walked to the sofa and sat expectantly, playing with the tassel on one of the silk throw pillows, tangling the fine gold threads around her forefinger.

Joe pulled on his pants, took a pencil and a piece of Biltmore stationery from the desk drawer, and sat down beside her.

"So, words aren't going to be enough?" Nora asked.

Joe drew the rectangle of Grand Central Terminal, centered on Forty-third Street and embraced by the split roadways of Park Avenue. He sketched lines for the East Side and West Side avenues that ran perpendicular to Forty-third Street, and wavy lines on either side of the page to represent the two rivers that cradled Manhattan Island in their arms.

"Joe," Nora said. "I was born in Manhattan. I know it's got a river on either side of it."

"Just wait."

Next he drew three arches on the right and left sides of the terminal. "These are the big windows, okay?" he said. "The ones that face east and west?"

"Okay," she said. She touched his shoulder.

He drew a dot in the center of the rectangle.

"That's the clock at the information booth, right?" she asked, and he nodded.

Next, all the way over on the right side of the page, above where the East River was, Joe drew a smiling sun, like the kind Alice and Mike had always put on their kindergarten drawings.

Nora laughed.

Joe handed her the beat-up purse. "Can I borrow your lipstick?" he asked.

Nora squinted slightly but reached into the bag for the little silver box and handed it to him.

Using the tip of the lipstick, Joe drew a red line from the sun past each avenue — First, Second, Third, Lex — until it entered the middle of the terminal's arched windows, passed through the clock, and continued out the window on the other side, all the way to the Hudson River.

"Have you ever heard of Stonehenge?" he asked.

"I went there!" she said.

"You did?"

"The summer before I came home. My flatmate and I drove half the night so we could get there in time for the sunrise."

"Did you make it?"

Nora nodded. "It was so beautiful," she said. "The sun came up dead center between the stones."

Joe ran his finger along the lipstick line he'd drawn. "So that's what happens at sunrise here too. Only we call it Manhattanhenge. It isn't stones. It's buildings. And the sunrise isn't in the summer. It's in the winter."

"On December fifth."

"That's right."

"The day of the accident."

Joe nodded. "Somehow," he said, "the sunrise must have hit you just at the exact minute when you were —"

"Dying," Nora said. "It's all right, Joe. You can say it."

"Dying," he repeated, his voice just a bit shaky. "I don't know. It must have given you some kind of special energy."

"Just me?"

"I think you were the only one lying in just the right spot and dying at just the right moment."

Nora stared down at the page and took her lipstick back from Joe, meditatively sliding it into its box. Joe said nothing while he gave her time to take in what he'd said.

"Special energy," she repeated.

"That's the best I've been able to figure it," he said.

"So I come back on Manhattanhenge."

"When the weather's clear."

"And when it's not, that's why I can't get through."

"That's how I figure it."

"So I really am kind of alive," Nora said.

"Well," Joe said, "I think we've just proved that."

"Which is why I can eat and drink and kiss you and —"

"Yes," Joe said.

"But naturally everyone thinks I'm dead."

"Yes."

"My poor mother. You should have seen her face when she saw me."

Nora told Joe what had happened with the phone calls and then with the taxi.

Joe's look was all Nora needed in order to know what he was going to say.

"When did she die?" Nora asked before

he could say it.

"Five years ago."

Nora sighed and pulled one of the pillows onto her lap. She hugged it as if it could hug back, buried her face in it as if such a childlike gesture could bring her childhood back. After a few minutes, she looked up.

"How did you find out?" Nora asked.

"The guy who lives there now gave me the phone number of a friend of hers. I called."

"Ruth Ingram," Nora said.

"You saw her too?"

"She saw me. Then she ran."

Joe nodded.

A single tear traveled over Nora's round, smooth cheek. "*You* never ran," she said.

"I couldn't," Joe said. "It was you."

Gently, Joe eased the pillow from her grasp and tucked Nora into his arms.

He had known she would be sad, but nothing could diminish the joy he felt at being able to hold her, the uncommon elation of knowing that somehow they were both exactly where they were meant to be.

For Nora's part, she could not recall a moment in her life — either the real one or this *after* one — when she'd felt both so powerful and so powerless. Somehow, she had been given a second kind of life. The sun, as if it were capable of choice — as if it actually possessed the smiling face that Joe had drawn on it — had tapped her on the shoulder with a finger of light.

She thought back to Stonehenge, how she and Margaret had paid for admission at the gate, just like at a fair. On the grounds around the huge stones, there had been hundreds of people who'd come with picnic blankets and tents. They'd called themselves modern Druids, and they'd spent the morning praying and chanting, believing in the mystical power of the rising sun.

Nora looked at Joe. He was smiling like a doctor who, with a great bedside manner, has just given a complicated diagnosis.

"It's all right," he said, which was needless, because everything about him was reassuring to her.

"You make it *seem* all right," she said.

"Well, that's how it's going to be."

She nestled beside him, and he stroked her hair.

"Do you understand?" she asked.

"What?"

"When I was in high school and college, my mother was always nagging me to tell her what I was doing and where I was going and when I'd be back. It was one of the reasons I went to Paris. 'When are you going to be home?' 'Don't forget to call me.' I used to hate that so much. But now —"

Nora's eyes filled with tears again, and Joe took her hand and kissed it.

"Now what?" he asked.

"Now," she said, "I love that you want to know where I am."

"Good," Joe said softly. "Get used to it."

2
NO ONE'S WINNING

1941

There was a flowery padded headboard on the bed in Room 809, the kind that climbed, like a wedding cake, into a high rounded peak. Two mornings after Nora's arrival, she lay with her feet up on this headboard, her legs lithe and smooth and not much wider than Joe's arms. The only garment she had on was her peach-colored slip, the hem of which had risen to her waist while she and Joe had been making love. Her forefingers fell over her lips, as if she was trying to hide her smile.

"Why are you hiding?" Joe asked.

"Hiding!" she said. She pointed her toes and stretched and laughed. "In what way am I hiding?" she asked.

Joe's head lay against a stack of pillows, but now he leaned forward on one elbow, raised Nora's slip another inch, and kissed her stomach, which wrinkled when she laughed.

Sighing, eyes up, she had the luxury of wondering how she would sketch the rosette surrounding the ceiling fixture. She looked past Joe to the window, where sunlight split open the dark brocade curtains. A terrible framed watercolor hung beside them, an old-fashioned painting of a train beside a river, steam rising from its engine like the plume of a fancy hat.

"I'm getting pretty good at this lovemaking, aren't I?" Nora asked.

"You've been good at it from the start," Joe said. "Too good, I'm thinking."

"It was the twenties, Joe. The twenties. Things were . . . freer."

"You mean women were looser."

Joe bent over Nora, combing her hair with his fingers. "I knew all about you flapper girls."

"Oh, did you?"

"Our priest said you'd all lost your way."

Nora laughed, unfolding her arms with a flourish. "Boy did he get *that* right."

"So, you danced, and you smoked and —"

"I never smoked. Well, that's not exactly true. I did try a pipe once."

"You're kidding."

"On a dare."

Joe laughed. "Okay, so you didn't smoke.

But you went out dancing and you drank and you cut your hair short —"

"It used to be even shorter than this," Nora said.

"And you didn't want to get married?"

Nora sat up and looked at him quizzically. "Well, I might have," she said. "Eventually. But I wanted to be an artist first."

"What kind of artist?" he asked.

Nora pointed to the watercolor. "Like whoever did that. But much better."

Joe tried to imagine any of the women he'd ever known wanting to be an artist before being a wife, let alone announcing it. He shook his head.

"Say something," Nora said.

"All the girls I grew up with — all the young women I know now — I think they all just want to get married and have babies."

"My friends and I just wanted to live our own lives."

Nora reached across Joe to grab the pencil and notepad that he'd used to draw Manhattanhenge the day she arrived.

"Sit up," she told him.

He did so, looking wary.

"And don't move for just a few minutes," she said.

Cross-legged at the foot of the bed, still in

her slip, she started to sketch Joe's face.

"Are you drawing me?" he asked her.

"Shush. Hold still."

"I —"

"Shush," she said again.

Three minutes passed in complete silence, and as Nora drew, she rediscovered the particular joy of making something out of nothing.

"Do you realize your ears don't match?" she asked Joe.

"I thought you told me not to talk."

She laughed. "That's all right. I'm done," she said.

She turned around the pad so he could see what she'd drawn.

"It's me!" he said, as if she'd performed a magic act.

Nora laughed. "Who did you think it was going to be?"

"I don't know. It's just — It's so good," he said. "I mean, I don't know what's good. But I know the guy I see in the mirror every morning, and this looks a whole lot like him."

For two days now, they had done little except devote themselves to learning each other's bodies, preferences, and pasts. They teased each other about their differences, even as they marveled at how little those differences seemed to matter. Nora told Joe about the Art Deco show in Paris; the women artists she'd sought out while scouting for Ollie's gallery; the pastries, nightclubs, and jazz. Joe told Nora about FDR, Japan, and Germany; about Bugs Bunny, Ritz Crackers, and Joe DiMaggio's hitting streak.

Joe had brought their meals and drinks from shops and restaurants all over the terminal, as well as magazines for Nora to study.

"Homework," he'd said. "You've got to catch up."

He'd snagged a few blouses and skirts for her from the Lost and Found. Both of them understood that she would need to change her appearance in order to leave the room without looking out of place. There was not a doubt in either of their minds that their challenge was no longer for Nora to get to Turtle Bay or even to the Y: She was going to have to stay here, until or unless they could figure out a safe way for her to leave.

She had given Joe all her French money and the traveler's checks that had been tucked into her clutch. He'd taken them to the bank and come back with an impressive stack of cash, as well as a few essentials:

toothbrush, hairbrush, comb, shampoo.

Meanwhile, Nora had curled up with an issue of *Life* — the same publication she'd first seen back in 1936 — and paged past stories about the war heating up in Europe, defense preparations in the U.S., and ads for liquor, stockings, playing cards, cigarettes, and new cars that were longer, lower, and sleeker than the tall black boxes of the twenties and early thirties.

Halfway through the issue, she'd seen an ad for a clothing company:

FOR WOMEN WHO WANT
THAT NEW YORK LOOK

Mrs. Donald Lofink, national defense housewife, plans a 5-dress wardrobe of New York Creations for $40.00.

Nora had no idea what a "national defense housewife" was, but she'd studied the styles of the five dresses, noting pleated skirts, belted waists, jeweled buttons, wide collars, and bell-shaped or puffed-out sleeves. The straight, slim look of the twenties was completely out; the boyish haircuts and tight helmet hats were gone. Now the hats had slouchy flaps or bows, and the haircuts had more waves and curlier bangs. Standing

261

before the bathroom mirror, Nora had already figured out how to tease her hair up and away from her forehead, wiggling the comb up and down to make her curls fuller. Eventually, with a pair of tweezers, she would shape her eyebrows into whispery arcs and use an apple-red lipstick to update her darker twenties pout.

In the meantime, there was this room and this bed. Stretched out again, her head on a pillow at the foot of the bed, Nora studied Joe's face as he studied the drawing she'd made of it. Beside him on the night table there was a Philco radio — a nifty, small wooden job with dials for the tuner and volume — and also a built-in clock. After two days and nights, Nora already knew Joe well enough to understand the language of his glance at it.

It was 2:15, and his shift didn't start until five.

"There's a game today, isn't there?" she said. "You want to listen to a game, am I right?"

"It's the Giants and the Dodgers," he said. "Uptown at the Polo Grounds."

"You know what I'm going to do?" Nora said. "I'm going to take a bath. Do you know how they make these bubble baths?"

"These what?"

"I don't know. I saw a picture of a woman covered up to her neck in suds."

"Well, I guess we'll just have to figure that out," Joe said.

"Yet another mystery," Nora said.

She grinned and, like a ballerina, extended a slender right calf toward the side table. Clutching one knob between her big and second toes, she just managed to turn the radio on. Joe and she both laughed.

"You have talented toes," he said.

"I know," she said. "It's a gift, pal."

Joe watched, his arms around her. The dial started warming up, its color deepening from dark brown to yellow to nearly white as the scratch and static of sound began to fill the room.

Nora switched to the second dial and, still with her toes, began to turn it, rolling past a burst of music and a spray of talk to find the station airing the football game.

"I still can't get over how small this radio is," she said.

The announcer's voice came over the crowd noise and into the room, staccato and enthusiastic.

Nora slipped out from under Joe's embrace, kissed him, and glided into the bathroom.

Joe leaned back on the pillows, his arms

behind his head. He listened for a few minutes, as perfectly content as he could remember ever having been. He knew this could not be a real life. He understood how a real life was supposed to be. A husband, a wife, a job, a home, children. Not some accident with the sunrise. Not some magical gift of power and light. But this gift had been given, and he could hear the water running in the bathroom and hear Nora singing in a sweet, surprisingly delicate voice.

Joe turned up the volume slightly and lay back again to listen to the game.

> Dodgers are ready to kick off now. They just scored. Ace Parker did it. Jock Sutherland's boys lead the Giants seven to nothing. Here's the whistle. . . .

He checked the clock. It was only 2:30 — still more than two hours before he had to report to Tower A. But he couldn't remember a time when the thought of work had been less appealing. Whatever Joe usually liked about the Piano — the sense of power and order it gave him — seemed completely humdrum now. How could that feeling, how could anything, compete with the woman who was singing in the bathroom now, the woman he'd been waiting for all year and, in another sense, all his life?

Ward Cuff takes it. Cutting up to his left and over to ten. Nice block there by Lee-mans. Cuff still going. . . .

Suddenly the sounds of the crowd disappeared, and the familiar shout of the game's play-by-play was replaced by a lone, insistent voice:

We interrupt this broadcast to bring you this important bulletin from the United Press. Flash, Washington. The White House announces Japanese attack on Pearl Harbor. Stay tuned to WOR for further developments which will be broadcast immediately as received.

Joe sat up straight, swung his legs over the side of the bed, and stood up with primal urgency. Faye's brother, Junie, was stationed at Pearl. It was Hawaii. It was America.

In the bathroom, Nora was still singing.

Joe could hear horns honking and people shouting in the street. Weirdly, the radio went back to broadcasting the game. Strong, young New York men were chasing each other up and down the green-gray turf, but now Americans were going to be fighting on a map instead of a football field, fighting for kills and countries instead of points and yards.

Joe started to get dressed. Your country gets attacked by the Japanese Empire, you don't want to be naked. You feel naked enough. He walked around to the other side of the bed and began to turn the radio dial, searching for any station that might be broadcasting more news.

When Nora emerged from the bathroom, she had one white terrycloth towel wrapped around her body and was drying her hair with another.

"Why are you dressed?" she asked. "Who's winning?"

Joe didn't answer at first. He looked stricken.

Nora was at his side in a moment.

"What is it?" she asked him.

"No one's winning," Joe answered, and he told her what had happened.

He had expected the terminal to be in chaos, but it was in shock. People were either standing completely still or moving unusually slowly, as if they were all trying to keep their balance. For two years, while Americans had debated what their role in Europe's war should be, the noise had been growing, as had the propaganda and the production of weapons. Now all debate would be silenced.

On the Main Concourse, normal speech was hushed, perhaps in an instinctive tribute to however many men had just been killed — or perhaps in the hope that some sort of announcements might be made or instructions given.

Joe knew Faye and Finn would be frantic about Junie, but the pay phones were swarmed. He rushed over to the baggage room, and the guys let him join the shorter line there.

Faye answered on the first ring.

"Oh, my Lord, Joey," she said. "Do you know anything?"

"Just what I heard on the radio."

"There's no way to find out how bad it was," Faye said.

"Or if it's over," Joe added. "Where's Finn?"

"They wanted more men on the Queensboro Bridge."

"How're the kids?"

"Well, Alice doesn't know anything yet. But Mike's up in the attic, looking to see if your pa had a bayonet," she said.

"Really?"

"No, stupid. We cleaned out the attic. I

just mean he's excited."

She was quiet for a moment. When she spoke again, it was in a whisper. "Joey," she said. "You know, Finn's going to want to sign up, no matter whether Junie's alive or —" Joe heard Faye stifle a sob.

"Don't think the worst, Faye," he said. "Let's take this as it comes."

Bill Keogh, the daytime caller at the arrival station, had a box of yellow chalk and a loudspeaker, and with these, he usually announced the trains' arrival and departure times. Today, people were looking to him, hoping for more information, but there was nothing official. Bits of news circulated through the crowd the way rumors traveled when a celebrity came in on the 20th Century Limited and the red carpet was rolled out on the platform. Today's rumors were grim: first that Manila had also been bombed, then that a lumber transport had been torpedoed, then that the number of fatalities was in the hundreds but was expected to rise. Already the terminal was filling with servicemen: Guys who'd already enlisted seemed eager to show that they were prepared. There would be tens of thousands more in the days, weeks, and months to come, and it would become stranger to see young men out of uniform than in.

Gradually the noise of the crowd deepened. Calls and curses rose above the rumble. Then Mary Lee Read, who had been playing concerts on the electric Hammond organ in the north balcony since the late 1920s, appeared, and the mood changed again. Her fingers touched the keys even before she sat down, and she launched into a string of patriotic tunes: "Over There," "Anchors Aweigh," "You're a Grand Old Flag." The songs were intended to galvanize, but when she played "The Star-Spangled Banner," the travelers, the ticket agents, the soldiers, and the Red Caps froze, humbled, their hands over their hearts.

After the national anthem, Joe started back toward the Biltmore. On the lower level he passed Bond's, where, through the glass case of the bakery counter, the tears on Big Sal's cheeks seemed to catch the light twice.

Upstairs he found Nora still listening to the radio, though she turned it off when he came in, reporting that she'd heard nothing new.

"I've got to go to work," he told her dejectedly.

"Eight hours?"

He nodded. "I'll come back as soon as I can."

"I just got here," she said, shaking her head.

"I know."

Her face did a dozen different beautiful things. The last was to mask whatever fear or unfairness she felt.

"Are you going to enlist?" she asked. She put the question in such a careful tone that it almost didn't seem like a question.

Joe shook his head. "They're not going to let us. Levermen, I mean. No. They told us a year ago. Took too long to train us."

She didn't try to hide her relief. She hugged Joe tightly around the waist and put her head against his chest.

Joe pressed the Floating Key into her hand.

"Leave the room if you have to, but don't you dare leave this building while I'm gone," he said.

Down in Tower A, some of the men were just hearing about the attack as they came off their shifts. Others were waiting outside, near the showers. Steady Max, it turned out, had ordered an extra crew, just in case.

"In case of what?" Joe asked, folding his shirtsleeves up, precisely, as if he were folding an American flag.

"Attack," Max said. "Spies. I don't know. How can you know?"

Like Damian, Steady Max had been bitterly spoiling for America to get into the war, and he seemed almost buoyant amid the shock and confusion.

"What's going on out there?" he asked as Joe took his place at the Piano. "Does it feel like the end of the world?"

"Damn close," Joe said. "But no one's heard anything new yet."

Once the guys from the previous shift were gone, the work became blessedly unexceptional. The trains ran as usual, the lights blinked as usual, the engines roared, the sweat poured down Joe's back. Years ago, Max had told Joe that the best levermen didn't think about the trains at all, and certainly not the passengers on the trains. The best levermen worked solely by reflex — "thinking with your arms," as Steady Max put it. Today was like that for Joe.

The director would call "Y-143 to Track I," and Joe would answer: "Y-143 to Track I."

"Track I to Ladder W."

"Track I to W."

On it went, the trains rolling in like parts

on an assembly line, and Joe's only job not to drop a single one.

As soon as his shift was over, Joe hurried back through the tunnel to the terminal. He hadn't taken the time to shower, and as he walked he could feel the sweat drying on his back. For the first time in his life, he understood rage; he understood vengeance and the violence it seemed to demand. He understood why what his father had lost in the war hadn't made him feel less like a man, but more.

The blessing of Nora's return had collided with the horror of the Japanese bombing. Either event would have dazed him. To-gether they threw off questions the way that wheels on the rails could throw off sparks. Still, there was nothing for Joe to do except return to the Biltmore and make sure Nora understood that, in the coming weeks, no matter how badly he wanted to be with her, he would need to turn his attention to his family in Queens. Later, it would seem almost funny that he had ever imagined this need could be measured in weeks, not months or years.

Joe found Nora sitting stiffly on one of their room's small couches. She had made the bed. She had folded the towels. She had put away Joe's few clothes, her flapper dress, and what there was of her Lost and Found wardrobe. In their two days and nights together, Nora had done none of these things, and Joe had even teased her about whether she was expecting Housekeeping to pick up after them. She had laughed — they had done so much laughing already — but now here she was, with all the laughter, the silk slip, and the terrycloth towels tucked away.

Through the long, cold night, they held each other, wordless. There was the insistence of desire; the ache of guilt for feeling it; the fear that they might lose what they'd found, even as they knew there would be so many greater, less personal losses in the time to come. Joe knew the president would ask Congress to declare war. But as long as he stayed in this room with Nora, there was still peace, however private a peace.

3
ESSENTIAL PERSONNEL

In 1941, the largest room in New York City was the grand ballroom of the Commodore Hotel. The place was so big that back in 1922 it had been the site of a one-night circus, when horses, camels, an elephant, and a lady riding a motorcycle inside a steel cage had all been brought in to entertain hotel workers from around the country. On this morning, December 8, it was the only room large enough to hold the employees of the New York Central System, and nothing glittered.

The velvet ballroom chairs had been arranged in hundreds of rows, with benches and chairs from other rooms lined up behind them. Most of the seats were already taken when Joe arrived on time at eight, and it was strange to see such a fancy room filled with so many men from all parts of the terminal — Red Caps and ticket takers, engineers and executives, levermen and plumbers. Though sitting, they already appeared to be at attention. Neither Joe nor the men around him looked inclined to talk to anyone. Their only interactions were the kind of tight smiles people exchanged at funerals. Joe thought about Damian, knowing he would have relished the prospect of the United States finally stepping in.

The president of the New York Central System — an owl-faced and always impeccable man — stepped up to the podium at the front of the room and adjusted his glasses. A loudspeaker had been placed before him, and it crackled from time to time, which didn't matter at all, because his message could not have been clearer.

"As we all know," he began, "the United States was brutally attacked yesterday, with absolutely no warning. President Roosevelt will be making his speech at twelve-thirty today. He is going to declare war against the Japanese Empire. And I want us to be ready, because all hell is about to break loose for the Central." The president went on to say what anyone in the room with half a brain already knew and no one wanted to hear: that with virtually no exceptions, every trainman — working in, on, or around the New York Central System — had just been deemed "essential personnel." Enlisting would not be an option. Even the young and less skilled would be discouraged from joining up.

"Think of it this way," he said. "All of you men — from our conductors to our Red Caps to our signalmen to our guys who clean the floors — if you leave, you'll just have to be replaced by a new man. And why shouldn't Uncle Sam be able to count on you doing the job you've already been trained for?"

"Aw, bullshit!" someone a few chairs away from Joe shouted.

That lone voice almost immediately became a duet, then a quartet, then a chorus of shouts and curses. "Not fair!" "Screw that!" "Damn the Japs to hell!"

Joe looked up at the men calling down from the ballroom's balconies, which were decorated with delicate carvings of garlands and birds. Despite himself, he thought of the lace that trimmed the hem of Nora's peach-colored slip, and he felt grateful for the New York Central's orders. Still — in the midst of the hullabaloo — he was also ashamed of his gratitude.

"Men! Men!" the president kept shouting, and eventually his authority won out. "You will all still be soldiers! You will all still be soldiers and marines and sailors and pilots! You'll be just as damned important as any of the fighting men." He paused, rotating his owl head like a searchlight, trying to address every part of the room. "You just won't be wearing khaki," he said.

The shifts were shortened in length but tripled in number. The volume in the first week alone made it seem as if the heavy traffic for the World's Fair had been a mere dress rehearsal. Grand Central went from being a bustling destination for tourists, commuters, goods, and services to being all that plus a vital hub for the war effort. The New York Central System moved raw materials bound for munitions plants, food bound for training camps, weapons bound for ships, and, above all, men bound for basic training and likely battle. In the first seven weeks after Pearl Harbor, more than half a million men would cross the country by train, along with their uniforms, duffel bags, books, and sundries. And in the months to come, Grand Central Terminal would become a legendary place from which men would leave, looking young, scared, and fierce, and to which hospital trains and morgue trains would inevitably return many of the very same men.

■ ■ ■ ■

At mid-morning on December 9, an enormous American flag was hung from the north balcony. Mary Lee Read kept playing patriotic songs, but since her first few renditions of "The Star-Spangled Banner," she'd been forbidden to play the national anthem again. It was clear to the stationmaster that Americans were unable to hear it without stopping traffic on the Main Concourse to sing along, their hands on their hearts. Amid these shows of patriotism, starting on the morning of the ninth, all the terminal's windows — like those in the most obvious bomb targets all over the city — were being coated with paint and tar.

"Wait, that's my window!" Nora whispered as she and Joe stood watching as the east windows' panes were being blackened, oddly enough, by window washers. There were more than a dozen men on each of the three windows, silhouetted against the light.

"What?"

"Isn't that my window they're blacking out? You know, the one you drew the lipstick through? The one Manhattanhenge light comes through?"

Other than a few brisk circuits of the

Biltmore's Palm Court, this was the first time Nora had ventured out of the room since her arrival four days before. Today she had insisted that it was time for her to stretch her legs, see some strangers, buy a sketchpad, and find better clothes at the Lost and Found.

"You just want to go flirt with Mr. Brennan, don't you?" Joe had said.

"Of course."

Now Joe stared at Nora's window, which was being turned into a heavy, dark door.

"Aw," Nora said when she saw his face, "don't worry, Joe. It's only a problem if I leave."

He shook his head, doubting.

She touched his elbow. "I think," she said with mock solemnity, "that somebody needs some pancakes."

But next, as if the black tar on the east windows was not enough, there came the Farm Security Administration mural, creating another barrier to Nora's return, should she disappear again. For months a group in Washington had been assembling a mammoth photomontage of American scenes designed to cover the entire east wall of the terminal with an urgent appeal:

In short order, the word DEFENSE was emphatically replaced by the word WAR, and throughout the week, people stopped to look up as the enormous panels were affixed to a special scaffold. On Sunday, exactly a week after the bombing of Pearl Harbor, the head of the Treasury Department's defense bonds committee presided over the dedication ceremony, urging the crowds to buy. An actor read a poem. A schoolgirl said a prayer. A public school chorus and a Ladies' Garment Workers' Union glee club sang. Nothing felt normal, sounded normal, looked normal. No one had yet learned how to laugh again, or smile.

Nora and Joe, standing at the west end of the Main Concourse, shared in the universal feeling, the almost palpable mixture of shock and resolve. But they also clung to each other for a different reason.

"As long as it's up, it'll be like there *is* no December fifth," Joe said. "Manhattanhenge will happen, but the light won't be able to get in *here.*"

"Joe," Nora said. She straightened the collar on his blue cotton shirt and lightly kissed his shoulder. "I have no intention of leav-

280

ing. So you don't have to worry about how I'm going to get back."

Nora meant it. Even beyond the effects of Manhattanhenge, she felt spellbound. Joe was a Catholic working guy from Queens who owned one coat and one scarf and took his tie off over his head. But he was strong and straight, and from the start he had seen her — not just her predicament — as no one before him ever had. She had never known it was possible to feel both safe and excited at the same time, and that was how she felt with Joe.

A dozen days after Nora's arrival, Joe moved his things over from the Y and gave Nora her old diary. Reading it only confirmed her feelings. How different it had been with Christopher Jenkins — Jenks — the object of her high school crush. Or with Sebastian, who had introduced her to sex, however perfunctorily. Not even counting the frolics of her last night in Paris, there had been one or two expat friends with whom she had necked and sometimes done more. But with every one of them, a part of her had always been watching, comparing, thinking. With Joe, everything was a feeling — exquisite, almost painful, a sense of some deep thing being unfolded that needed to be unfolded again. Even in their brief time together, Nora had come to understand the difference between infatuation and love. Infatuation was weather. Love was climate.

In that climate — bizarre though it was at the outset of a war — Joe had made Nora feel at peace. She was here. She had died. By an extraordinary confluence of events, she'd been granted more life. Now what she needed was to understand its limits, and the sooner she did, the sooner she could experience all its pleasures. Already she'd learned that — not even counting the exquisite delights of sex — there would be clean sheets, sleep, and dreams. There would be magazines and newspapers, books and art supplies. There would be food: the powdered sugar on the doughnuts from Bond's; the sour cold beer she and Joe drank from bottles he nabbed from the Oyster Bar; the best coffee, from the Biltmore's kitchen.

"But Joe," she said as they lay close to each other one night. "I'm going to have to learn how far I *can* go, or how long I *can* be outside."

He kissed her. "Why do you need to go outside?" he said, and he kissed her again.

"Joe," she said, breaking off the kiss. "I'm going to have to learn what's keeping me here."

His hands on her wrists, he pulled her up forcefully to lie on top of him, and he kissed her deeply, straining his neck to reach up to her.

"*Me,*" he said to Nora. "Me. *I'm* keeping you here."

Whatever thoughts they had of solving the puzzle were in any case halted a few days before Christmas, when Faye and her mother finally learned that Junie was safe at Pearl Harbor. It had taken nearly three weeks for his letter to reach home. It would take longer than that before many families found out what had happened to their sons, husbands, and brothers on December 7.

At St. Anthony's, the members of the congregation, several of whom had brothers or sons in the Pacific, were naturally more somber than usual, though what Joe sensed wasn't mourning, at least not yet. What he sensed was more like a bewildered anger. In every pew, the parishioners looked like passengers who'd missed their train and were wondering if there was something or someone to blame. Meanwhile, Father Gregory, now gnomelike, tried in his sermon to inspire the courage and faith that his parish would need. "Make us strong, O God, in our hearts and bodies," he prayed.

"Amen," the congregation seemed almost to whisper.

"God of all goodness, look with love on those who wait for the safe return of their loved ones."

"Amen," they all whispered again.

Outside the church, Faye seemed in no mood to whisper, and she didn't seem somber as much as gamely determined. Usually after a Sunday service, it would take nearly an hour to pry her from the church steps, where she would stand, collecting and dispensing gossip like coins, kids tugging at her sleeves. Today there was none of that. Faye grabbed Alice's hand and briskly pulled her down the steps.

"Mama!" Alice shouted as her blue beret dropped behind her.

"Saints alive!" Faye groaned as she lunged back up the steps to grab the hat.

During the long days of waiting to hear about her brother, Faye's worry had turned into anger at the Japanese, and now that she knew Junie was alive, her anger had turned into rage. She had already told Finn that she no longer had a single objection to his signing up. But police were needed now more than ever, they'd been told: The harbors, the airfields, the train terminals, the subways, the great buildings of New

York — all would need extra protection. In the past two weeks, there had already been air raid drills, the rounding up of Japanese people in and around the city, and word that there were enemy ships in the waters off both coasts. Nightly blackouts and brownouts were creating ever more shadows in the city, and a sense of menace and lawlessness seemed to darken them further.

"There are cops three deep just guarding the terminal," Joe said as he and Finn walked up the front steps of the house. "Everyone's saying you're more important now than ever. Same as us on the job."

Faye swept the children past the men. "Not in front of the kids," she hissed. Mike, who was fifteen now, bitter and brusque, said: "Guess what, Ma? I've got two ears, and they both work."

Lunch was cold leftover meatloaf sandwiches bleeding ketchup through Wonder Bread. Faye popped open cans of potato sticks and distractedly shook them, like seasoning, onto the plates. Then she unfolded the kitchen stepstool, sat on it, lit a Lucky Strike, and tugged her orange cardigan to crisscross her thin frame.

"Not hungry?" Joe asked her.

Faye shook her head.

"Mike, turn on the radio," she said with a

forced smile that everyone knew was for Alice's benefit. "Let's see if we can't get some Christmas music."

Grimacing, Mike pushed and then tilted his chair far back, reaching the kitchen radio with one long arm. The twisting noise of the signal came in, and then some lilting dance music.

"Jimmy Dorsey," Faye said appreciatively.

"I want to find the news," Mike said, turning the knob again.

"Later," Finn said firmly, with a glance at Alice. "We don't need to hear the news now."

"Turn back to that music," Faye said, and Mike sulkily obeyed.

Faye took a drag of her cigarette and, exhaling, said: "Sit up straight, Mike. And eat up, both of you."

"Ma! We just started!" Alice said.

"The grown-ups need to talk in private."

Alice, now nine, with the days of her childhood numbered, looked suspicious. "What do the grown-ups need to talk about?" she asked.

With perfect older brother coordination, Mike swiped some of the potato sticks from Alice's plate, popped them into his mouth, crunched them noisily in front of her, and

286

said, "They have to talk about Santa, nit-wit."

"Don't call your sister 'nitwit,' " Finn and Faye said in unison.

"You *know* I don't believe in Santa anymore!" Alice exclaimed.

"Well, you weren't so sure last year!" Mike said.

"Ma!"

"Well, she wasn't!" Mike said.

Faye stubbed out her cigarette in an old Highland Queen ashtray.

"Go eat in the dining room, kids."

They each took a silent bite of sandwich.

"I mean it!" Faye said, and that was that.

Reluctantly, they left the kitchen with their plates, the door swinging shut behind them.

Joe waited until the creaking of the hinge stopped. He leaned forward. "You can't just quit the force," he said to Finn.

"The hell he can't," Faye said.

"The hell I can't," Finn said. "I heard about a couple of guys in Jersey who already did. You know it's what Pa would have expected me to do."

"You're essential personnel," Joe said. "Just like me."

Finn shrugged. "Not like you, Joe. Took what, three or four years to train you?" Finn said. "Took just a year for me."

"You're too old," Joe said. "Christ, Finny. You're going to have to lie about your age. *And* about your kids."

"You think any of that would have stopped Pa?"

To utter the next sentence, Joe had to will Nora out of his mind — pushing her, pushing her, as if trying to shut the door on the sun. "If either of us should sign up," he finally said, "you know it should be me."

"I'm the one who knows how to use a gun," Finn said.

"You're the one with the family."

"So you're the one who'll look after them."

It was only a little past four when Joe walked to the subway to go back to the city, but the sun was already about to set. With clouds and snow moving in, the sky was pea green and the river was violet.

The train was crowded with holiday shoppers, and Joe found it comforting to see that whatever their thoughts and fears, people were going to continue to give each other gifts; they were not going to deny themselves the possibility of joy. For the first time since that morning, Joe let himself linger on his thoughts about Nora. He relished the way she'd been neatening things up when he'd left, and he loved the thought that she would be waiting for him in their room. Nora's presence had turned that room into more of a home than any he'd had as a grown man.

The tunnel under the East River flew by, with only a few dim lights along the way. Lulled by the rhythm of the train, Joe closed his eyes, remembering all the war games he and Finn had played as kids. In those days, the backyard had seemed enormous: sometimes a battlefield, sometimes a bunker. As the older brother, Finn had almost always gotten to choose the scene and cast it, and he was almost always the German, because that meant he got to die the most gruesome deaths. Joe remembered that those games had seemed to delight Damian as much as they had upset Katherine.

"Look at your pa!" Joe remembered his mother shouting once. "Look at him! Don't you apes realize what's happened to him? Do you think he lost that leg in a game?"

Finn never told Joe what people he had bribed or what lies he'd had to tell in order to enlist. Soon enough, Joe would learn that there were lots of guys who fudged or forged their information, claiming to be older, younger, healthier, or less essential to their jobs or families than they actually were. Especially if you were known by your local draft board — either directly or through family and friends — rules could be bent and already had been. Joe suspected that Finn had asked one of Damian's old VFW buddies to help grease the wheels, but Finn told Joe it would be best if he stayed in the dark about it.

"People *are* going to notice you're not here, Finny," Joe said when Finn came down to the terminal to show him his enlistment card. "They *are* going to ask me where you went."

"And you'll be able to tell them I got in, but you don't know how. All you need to know is that if something happens to me, the army will know how to find Faye."

Joe looked at his older brother, both envious and proud.

"I guess Pa would have been buying you a drink right about now," he said.

"Something stopping you?" Finn asked.

They went to the Junction and drank. With a flourish, as if he were putting a winning hand down in a game of gin rummy, Finn dealt his enlistment card onto the pockmarked bar top. Joe picked up the card. Name, address, date of birth, marital status, blood type, religion, date of enlistment, signature, rank, serial number. As far as the army knew, Finnegan Reynolds was twenty-six, married, and had no children.

"You're going to have to practice saying how old you are, Finny."

"I think I can manage that."

"And what year you were born. You're not that bright, you know."

Finn laughed, took the card back from Joe, and carefully returned it to his wallet.

Joe motioned the bartender for another round. When their glasses were refilled, Joe lifted his to Finn. "Here's to you finally getting that hair mowed," he said.

They toasted their father, their mother, their childhood, Mike, Alice, and Faye.

"And here's to Nora," Finn said, "and all the other women of your sweaty dreams."

"Not a dream," Joe said, and then whispered, "She came back, Finny. She's here."

Finn looked over his shoulder. "She's where?"

"Here. In the Biltmore Hotel."

Finn downed the rest of his drink in one motion and placed his glass emphatically on the bar. He said, "Joe. Talk some sense."

So, just as he had with Nora, Joe explained Manhattanhenge, the coincidence of Nora's death, and the way the special sunrise seemed to bring her back to life.

Finn took Joe's glass and drained what was left of it too.

"And I want you to meet her before you go," Joe said.

"Nora," Finn said. "The ghost." He started to smile.

"Remember, Finny," Joe said, before his brother could get another word out. "This is a No-Matter-What."

The smile left Finn's lips immediately. "Honor bound," he said.

"I know it's weird. I know it's crazy," Joe said.

"You know Faye would go out of her mind if she thought you'd thrown all those great girls over for a —"

"A spirit," Joe said. "Or call her a ghost. I don't care what you call her. But sure, Faye would go nuts. Which is why I'll kill you if you breathe a word of it to her."

"Jesus."

"A No-Matter-What. Will you do it?" Joe asked. "Will you meet her before you go?"

"Jesus, Joey."

But he promised he would.

"Before you go?"

"Before I go."

4
OH, BUDDY

1942

"He's a lot like me," Joe said to Nora.

"No one's like you," she answered.

It was a Tuesday morning in April — the Tuesday of Finn's departure for basic training — and Nora had taken Joe along to one of the high-class shops on the Biltmore's third floor. She'd said she was determined to find something lovely to wear for meeting Finn.

"No," Joe said, "what I mean is, he's not fancy. He won't care a hoot what you're wearing."

"*I'll* care," she said.

She was whisking the dresses along a rack with dazzling speed and certainty, each hanger making a confident jangle and click as she slid it from right to left. After only a few racks, she stopped and promptly pulled out a dark-green dress. Folding the hanger back, she held the dress up to her shoulders and turned to face Joe.

"What do you think?" she asked him.

"Beautiful," he said.

"You'd say that about anything."

"Can't blame me for that," he said. "What do you want me to do, lie?"

In the four months that she and Joe had used Floating Keys for a succession of free rooms at the Biltmore, Nora had learned how to be frugal with her own money and with Joe's. She had made frequent use of the Lost and Found, where Mr. Brennan — who softened like warm tar whenever Nora stopped by — helped her find basic items and, with uncharacteristic gallantry, never once asked why she needed them.

A purchased dress, never worn, was therefore a rediscovered joy, and Nora turned toward the mirror now, holding the dress in front of her.

"It needs something," she said.

"Something like what?"

"I don't know. Something to give it a little sparkle."

Joe watched as Nora's eyes expertly roamed the store and brightened as she strode toward a rack of belts. She held a number of them against the dress in turn, tilting her head slightly, just as Joe had seen her do when she'd assessed anything she

was making — from an arrangement of pillows on the couch to the petals on the
daisies in a charcoal sketch.

Joe loved the way she made things beautiful, but today, as she chose a shiny black
belt, he was also touched by the effort she
was making for his brother.

With just a half hour left, Nora told Joe
she'd see them both at Alva's, and, shopping bag in hand, she went back up to their
room to change.

A product of Turtle Bay Gardens, Elsie
Lansing, and the fashion-crazed 1920s,
Nora had been, like practically every girl
she'd known at Barnard or in Paris, con-
sumed during her life with questions of appearance: the length of her hair and her
dresses, the fullness of her eyebrows,
whether or not to use rouge. Nora remembered how much all that had mattered to
her. But when she spent time in front of a
mirror now, what concerned her had nothing to do with vanity: If anything, it was the
opposite. While most women might check
their mirrors nervously for unwanted
changes, Nora longed to find them. A blem-
ish here, a wrinkle there — even the smallest alteration — would have made her feel
more normal: closer to Joe, closer to every-

one alive. Joe woke up every morning with such a heavy beard that it looked as if someone had come during the night to draw it on with the rough stub of an oil pastel.

In her more than four months here, Nora realized that her hair hadn't grown. Her nails hadn't grown. She'd never had her time of the month. She hadn't lost or gained any weight. The few little scrapes or bruises she'd gotten had healed in hours, not days. Each week, behind a closed bathroom door, she had smoothed her bangs down over her forehead with a wet comb, hoping to find that they had reached below her eyebrows. In Paris, she was always trimming her bangs or asking Margaret to do so. Here, they remained exactly the same length, and Nora was starting to think she might as well have been a statue, unaffected by the passage of time. Had Joe noticed yet? He hadn't said anything about it, but looking at her unchanged face in the mirror, she shuddered at the evidence that even as she and Joe might grow closer, the gap between their ages was only going to widen.

Joe would age. She would not.

Finn walked into the restaurant carrying the small duffel bag that Joe recognized as Damian's dusty World War I issue.

"For good luck?" Joe asked as Finn took a seat in the booth across from him.

"What, the bag? You mean because Pa made it back?"

Joe nodded.

"Nah. It was the only bag I could find in the house besides the kids' camp bags. When did we ever go anywhere?"

"I never did," Joe said. "You had a honeymoon."

"Ancient history," Finn said. "Anyway, I think Faye borrowed her ma's suitcase for that."

Joe had never owned a suitcase, though he had been surrounded for most of his life by people carrying them around like little billboards. During the past decade, the decade of the Depression, Joe had spent any free time he had either helping Damian, playing handyman for the house, or babysitting Finn's kids. Joe's only trips beyond Manhattan or Queens had been on the Harlem or Hudson lines — just a few stops up — to salute some conductor's work anniversary or toast a retirement. Those celebrations, by tradition, had always been confined to the train cars themselves. Whatever other travels Joe had taken had been in his imagination, inspired by the routes in New York Central fliers or by images in newspapers, magazines, and newsreels.

"So?" Finn said. "Where's Nora?"

"She'll be here any minute."

Finn nodded and picked up a menu. "You buying?" he asked.

"No, Finny, I'm sending you off to fight in a war, but I'm making you buy me lunch first."

"Sounds like you."

Alva came over, poured them coffee, and took their orders. Finn grasped the cream-colored diner mug with his left hand, clinking his wedding ring against its handle. After a sip, he squinted at Joe.

"Where is she?" he asked again, just as Joe stood up to greet her. She looked dazzling in the new dress, which in fact did sparkle a little more because of the shiny belt.

Finn watched warily as Nora slid into the booth beside Joe.

"I got us some pancakes," Joe told her. "I thought we'd share."

Finn kept staring at Nora.

"Yes. I'm *Nora,*" she finally said, which broke the tension and made them all laugh. She extended her hand, and Finn took it in his, startled by its warmth and seemingly hypnotized by its solidity. He glanced back and forth between it and Nora's face.

"Finn, say something," said Joe. "You're being rude."

Finn dropped Nora's hand and shook his head slightly. "Well," he said a bit helplessly, "I'll say this, Joe. She sure is a looker."

Nora ignored the awkwardness. "That's so kind of you," she said in what Joe thought of as her best society voice. Then it was her turn to stare. "But you, Finn. Joe never told me how much you two look alike."

"Wait, Nora," Joe said, "those are fighting words."

Neither of them seemed to hear him.

"Your nose," Nora said. "It's got that same slope."

"Irish nose," Joe said. "A dime a dozen."

"And your mouth, it's kind of crooked, the same as Joe's," Nora continued. "And your hair —"

"Stop right there," Joe said. "Finn's hair is like a push broom."

Again, they didn't seem to hear. All this time, Joe had been imagining how amazed Finn would be to find that Nora was real. He hadn't figured on Nora's amazement. For the first time, she was encountering the evidence — not stories, memories, or reports on some visit, errand, or phone call — of Joe's life beyond Grand Central. Joe had expected Finn to grill Nora in an attempt to confirm or dismiss her story. But whether it was because Finn had simply chosen to believe, or because — more likely, Joe thought — Finn's mind was focused on leaving, it was Nora who asked most of the questions: How old were Mike and Alice now? What had Joe been like as a kid? How and when had Finn met Faye? Where had they gone on their honeymoon?

Nora's continuing existence in Grand Central was uncertain at best; Finn was about to leave for who knew how long. And yet, through the whole conversation, Joe felt that he was the one who was least present. Only when they stood up to go did the two of them seem to remember that he was there at all. And they left him to pay the bill.

Passing the entrance to Alva's together, Finn said to Nora: "Just one question."

"Just one?"

"I know he's got it bad for you. He's walking on air. But what do you think is going to happen?"

Nora looked back toward Joe and then at Finn.

"I don't know, Finn," she finally said. "But whatever happens, it'll happen to both of us."

The terminal had grown busier than ever since the U.S. had entered the war. Additional ticket booths took up space in the concourse. Increased numbers of travelers made navigation harder than usual. The whole place seemed in shadow: The walls, which had already been brown from decades of cigarette smoke, were darker now with the windows blacked out and the mural covering the east windows. The room that to Joe had so often seemed to be all sky now seemed to be all earth.

Standing by the ramp that led to the Kissing Room, Nora hugged Finn goodbye, wished him good luck, and gracefully left the brothers alone. Gamely, they walked through the crowds in the concourse, where friends and family members were forming little clusters around their young men, hands reaching in to touch them, arms like spokes on wheels.

Finn had insisted that Faye stay home. He didn't want tears or scenes. "A no-waterworks goodbye," he had ordered.

Now he threw one question after another at Joe: How did he know that Nora had really died? Didn't she have any family or friends? If it was Manhattanhenge that had brought her here, then what was it that kept her here? Could he actually, um, do *everything* with her that he'd do with a real woman? And finally: Was Joe really in love with someone who couldn't make a home with him? Joe answered as many of the questions as he could but was reminded how much more the feelings mattered than the facts.

They had reached the track platform for Finn's train, and Joe changed the subject back to Finn.

"How did the kids take it?" he asked.

"Troupers. You shoulda seen Mike, actually," Finn said. "He stood up and saluted me."

"And Alice?"

"She cried. I guess I knew that would happen. But I gave Mike the 'man of the house now' talk. And I told him not to torture Alice."

Saying the name of his little girl brought out the pain in Finn's eyes, but he spent the next few minutes giving Joe distracting if unnecessary instructions about how to help Faye take care of the house. By the time his train was ready to leave, he had talked to Joe about everything from the furnace to the attic. It wasn't until Finn actually hopped across the little space between the platform and the car that Joe felt the first shudder, the first hint, of loss.

Like the dozens of other civilians standing on the platform, Joe was unable to turn away until the tunnel had swallowed the train, and its sound had faded. He had a crazy impulse to follow, to shout — some part of him, the heart of him, traveling down the tracks, the little brother running to keep up with the older one. The fact that for the next few weeks Finn would still be stateside at basic training did nothing to keep Joe from feeling the panic in his chest.

A few yards away, a young mother with stocky legs and a chubby toddler in her arms tucked her head into the little boy's neck, trying to wipe her tears on his collar. "Oh, Buddy. Oh, Buddy," she said. "I'm sorry, I'm sorry. Oh, Buddy."

For a moment her sad eyes met Joe's, and her distress turned to embarrassment: a grown woman seeking comfort in the crook of her little boy's neck. Joe smiled at her with as much reassurance as he could muster, and then, walking up the track ramp, across the concourse, and down to the local level, he waited for the subway that would take him out to Queens.

Back in their hotel room, Nora carefully stepped out of her new green dress and hung it in the closet beside Joe's work shirts and trousers and her own few blouses and skirts. Then she leaned into the closet, her hands clasping the wooden pole. She put her cheek against the collar of one of Joe's shirts. It had shaken her to see him with Finn. It had never been clearer to her that he had a life beyond his job and whatever hotel room she shared with him.

Still in her slip and stockings, she settled onto the couch and picked up the morning's paper. The war in Europe filled the pages with headlines about bombings and troop movements, photographs of tanks and generals, maps of places she'd never heard of: Tobruk, Salonika, Rostock. Nora turned the pages slowly, and eventually — the way shards of blue can overtake a gray sky — these images and stories were brightened by the glimpses of the everyday life she still felt she needed to study: an ad for men's shoes, another for women's dresses; reviews of books, restaurants, and plays. A small item about Mussolini looked inconsequential next to an enormous ad for a hat called the

Ferris-Wheel Milan. Two different Italys, Nora thought. With the kind of pang she would have felt if she were still living in the youthful who-cares moment of 1925, she realized she would never see Rome. In the next moment, back in the present, she had to wonder what would be left of Europe when the war was over. And finally, war notwithstanding, if Joe would ever get to go there.

Turning more pages, she came to the society section, where it seemed the world was still at peace. There were the everyday announcements of brides-to-be and preparations for an Easter luncheon for debutantes. Just as they had been during the Great War, the debs were more inclined to be doing volunteer work. But still, there were the dresses, and then there was this item:

A son, their third, was born to Mr. and Mrs. Thomas F. Raymond of 21 East Ninetieth Street on Monday in the Harkness Pavilion, Columbia-Presbyterian Medical Center. Mrs. Raymond is the former Miss Margaret Ingram, daughter of Mrs. Ruth Ingram and the late Mr. Alfred Ingram of this city. The child will be named for his grandfather.

With a suddenness that nearly frightened her, Nora felt jolted, dislodged by memories. She closed her eyes, seeing the attic room she and Margaret had shared in the four-story house with the peeling green door and the dark wooden staircase worn down enough to be slippery. Margaret would be in her late thirties now, exactly as old as Nora would have been if her life had continued as she'd always imagined it would. Briefly, she considered trying to call Margaret, but she knew that would only terrify her — and might even threaten the equilibrium she and Joe had just found.

Nora remembered how joyously she and Margaret had tackled the sights: Versailles and Montmartre, Mont Saint-Michel and the Tuileries. Margaret had flagged occasionally, but Nora had been intrepid. There hadn't been a food she didn't want to try, a cabaret she didn't want to attend, or a neighborhood she didn't want to explore. What more would she have tasted or seen or done if she had lived to be Margaret's age? She could imagine all sorts of answers to that question, but she knew it made no sense to dwell on what and who she would have been or would never be. She had landed in a life both absurdly lucky and unlucky: She had infinite love in a finite space.

One thought, however, was unavoidable: In that life, her former life, Nora would never have been pacing a hotel room waiting for someone to return and provide her happiness. She would have been making something, buying something, going somewhere, seeing someone. She would not have been caught dead just waiting, she thought, and chuckled to herself. That was it, she thought. *Not caught dead.*

She took a deep breath, stepped back to the closet, and pulled on the plain skirt and blouse she'd been wearing this morning when she and Joe had bought the green dress. At the bureau she picked up her comb, teased her hair back from her forehead, and ruffled it a bit with her hands. Satisfied, she dabbed her lips with a fashionably matte red lipstick and used a tissue to blot them. She grabbed the room key, tucked it into a handbag, and without a backward glance firmly closed the door behind her.

It was after three by the time Joe returned from Queens. He was sad about Finn and felt helpless about the family. But he was also desperate to see Nora, if only for a moment, before his half shift at four. Their room in the Biltmore was dark and empty, though, and Joe, for the second time that day, felt almost breathless with loss. For good measure, he turned on the light, hoping to find a note, but there was nothing, and the bed was made, the clothes put away.

Hadn't they specifically agreed to meet back in the room? He felt sure they had, though maybe not. The goodbye with Finn and the visit with Faye and the kids were filling up his head. He dove back into the hallway but, not wanting to wait for the elevator, vaulted down the steps. He headed to the concourse, scanning the clusters of visitors who as usual were squinting up at the mural, the families surrounding yet more departing men, the dotted lines of the Red Caps winding through the crowd. Nora was nowhere to be seen, and there was no time left for finding her before his shift began.

At the Piano, the mechanical world of levers and lights did little to calm Joe this time. The green lights on the board — the manmade markers of manmade machines — blinked on and off as usual, tracing the trains' progress along the numbered sections of each track. Joe wished there was a board of lights that could help him follow

Nora. The trains kept arriving with their usual glare and noise, but the hours dragged. By the time Joe's shift was over, he was, as always, drenched in sweat. He was tempted to skip his shower, but superstitiously, he decided that if he acted as though everything was normal, everything would be normal. In the ringing silence of the shower stall, he made the water as hot as he could stand it, letting it pound down on his shoulders and flatten his dark hair into bangs. He kept his shower time to three minutes, then used one of the stiff, nearly gray towels to dry himself. He felt unnerved, almost panicky.

He hurried through the tunnel from Fiftieth Street, and once he reached the concourse he tried to be systematic in his search: ticket booths, no; gold clock, no; marble steps, no; track entrances, no. Down on the lower level, he tried to get past Bond's without being spotted by Big Sal, but she called to him, and he went over.

"That was your brother this morning, Joseph?"

"That's right, Sal."

"Aww, kid. Don't look so worried. It's just basic training for now. For all you know, he could get assigned to some desk stateside."

"That's not why I'm worried. Have you

seen Nora?"

"Not since this morning with you. Where does that girl work, anyway? What's her story?"

"You want a story, Sal —"

"I know, 'Go buy yourself a magazine.' "

He passed Alva's and the Lost and Found, the Whispering Gallery and the Oyster Bar. How many times over the four years since he'd first seen Nora had he lost and then found her again? And how could he be expected to face losing Finn and Nora on the same day?

Dejectedly, he returned to the Main Concourse, where he saw Mary Lee Read at the organ, accompanying today's choir, some young women's group. Their faces were the brightest thing in the room, and suddenly he found Nora's among them. For the moment, anyway, his anger turned to awe. She stood out, not because of anything she was doing, but because her face was so filled with pride and glee, you'd have thought she was singing a solo on opening day of the World Series. She smiled as if she had a private joke with the whole world, and Joe was fairly sure he'd never seen anyone look as happy.

5
I Was Thinking
It Looked Like Fun

1942

It hadn't been difficult for Nora to get a place in the choir. The Salvation Singers was a group made up of young women from Salvation Army branches all across the country. Most of them had never met each other anyway, and all of them had needed to introduce themselves to the choir director. So, just like that, Nora had a place in the north gallery, where she could stand that much closer to the wondrous aqua sky, the dotted line of lightbulbs that surrounded it, and the six cap-shaped windows adorned with acorns and birds.

Joe had seemed proud of her — or at least glad to see her — for about a minute. But as the choir kept singing, he paced the marble floor, stopping only occasionally to glare up at her. After the concert was over, he was silent as they crossed the Biltmore lobby, rode upstairs in the elevator, and walked down the hallway to their room.

As soon as he closed the door behind them, he tore off his coat and windmilled it onto the desk. Coins burst from the pockets, some bouncing off the desk, most of them raining down noiselessly on the carpet.

"Joe!" Nora said.

He started to bend to pick up the coins but kicked the desk chair instead.

"Joe!"

He glanced at her, just barely, almost suspiciously.

"What is it?" she asked. "Was it Finn? Or Faye? Was it me?"

Agitated, he tugged at his tie knot, sliding it back and forth until it was low enough that he could lift the tie over his head.

"What'd I do?" Nora asked him.

Unbuttoning his shirt with one hand, he let the other swing free, the set of his mouth almost flattening his crooked smile away.

"The choir," he said at last. "What were you thinking?"

"I was thinking it looked like fun."

"Like fun?"

"Yes."

"How did you get in?"

"It was easy," Nora said. "I just told the choir director I was from Wisconsin."

"Why Wisconsin?"

312

"I don't know. Why not?"

Joe shook his head, fuming.

"What *is* it?" she asked again.

"I couldn't find you," Joe said. "I thought maybe you'd flickered out."

"Oh, Joe," Nora said slowly, understanding for the first time.

"I expected you to be here, and when you weren't —"

She apologized. "I didn't think I'd be gone that long."

Joe, usually so even and deliberate in his actions and words — so much the leverman incapable of being surprised — paced the length of their room, up and down the plush maroon carpet. Just two days before, Nora had accidentally spilled some red wine on it, and while she'd been frantic about leaving a stain, Joe had calmly gone to the bathroom, soaked a washcloth with warm water, and used it to clean the rug. You could barely see any trace of it now, but the way Joe kept walking up and down, Nora wondered if he would leave his tracks there instead. She stood up. "Stop," she said. She put her hands on Joe's shoulders and kept them there until she felt him starting to relax.

"Stay," she said, and he grasped her so tightly that she could feel his fear along with his need. She broke away and went to the dresser, where she poured a shot of bourbon into a New York souvenir glass that she'd pinched from the ladies' lounge. "Your big brother left to become a soldier and fight in a war today. Then you went to Queens to buck up his family. Then you worked a shift. Then you thought I'd disappeared. Drink up."

Joe smiled. Angry as he was, he did have to admire Nora's gutsiness. How many women did he know — how many people — who would saunter their way into a choir, pretending to belong?

"Come on," Nora said. "Throw it back."

"Throw it back?" he said. "Where'd you learn that expression?"

"I get around," she said.

He sighed and took the glass from her.

"Maybe that'll warm you up," she said.

"Aw," Joe said, cocking his head to one side. "Honey," he added, and now it was her turn to pull him close, their mouths tilting around each other's until they locked at just the right angle.

6

WHAT A WIFE DID

1942

For the next few days, while Joe came and went from his shifts, Nora reveled in the choir, feeling an old kind of happiness. Surrounded by other women, she sensed the music as a warm embrace: her voice a part of something; *herself* a part of something. As a choir, the singers were only fair, but people stopped to listen — old couples leaning against each other, women arriving from out of town, even terminal workers pausing to sing along or just watch. Occasionally a soldier or sailor, seeming to notice Nora's exuberance, would catch her eye and smile or wink. She hadn't realized how accustomed she'd become to trying to avoid attention, and she'd forgotten how much she enjoyed getting it.

By Sunday the stint was over, and a different choir was beaming down from the balcony where the Salvation Singers had performed. That was that, Nora understood, and envy seemed to be her chief emotion now. Trying to read *The New York Times* in the ladies' lounge, she was transfixed instead by the luggage of a tidy woman sitting nearby. The suitcase's leather was old and battered, but it served as the perfect canvas for colorful stickers from hotels all over the world: Venezia, Dubrovnik, Napoli, Barcelona, Cairo. As the woman left, Nora caught a glimpse of one more sticker: PARIS, HÔTEL DES DEUX MONDES. Two worlds indeed.

In her Paris world, Nora had lived like a true child of the twenties, rocked by the losses of the Great War and determined to waste not a moment of life. As enthralling as it was now to lie in Joe's arms — shadows stirring the darkness at midnight or later — Nora had been here for five months now, and she couldn't help feeling confined.

In May, she visited the Biltmore's library, a room with the hush of a vault and an unexpectedly old-woman smell of lavender and mothballs. Hundreds of the books left by decades of visitors were haphazardly shelved here without any consideration of subject or author. On one end of a high oak table sat an enormous globe the color of cornbread, encircled by iron bands bearing figurines of bare-breasted women.

A few weeks later, Nora went to the Biltmore's Turkish baths — known as the "salt-water plunge" — but was disappointed to find that they had been closed because of the war. For a long while she lay back in one of the striped canvas reclining chairs on the tiled deck, pondering the empty shallow pool. It was impossible not to think of the glorious Olympic swimmers under that perfect blue sky in 1924.

On the sixth floor of the terminal building, tucked right under the roof, were the Grand Central Art Galleries. Founded by John Singer Sargent and filled with the works of other famous artists, the place seemed a similarly pale echo of Paris. Nora had seen signs for the Grand Central School of Art, and some of the classes offered were for abstract painting and mixed media. But the works on display here seemed staid, old-fashioned. There were fifteen exhibition rooms, but none held the excitement of the twenties' cubism, expressionism, and surrealism. Most were traditional portraits or landscapes. Only a few were by women. Still, stopping on one of the large crimson rugs that added a homey touch to the place, Nora stared for a long time at one painting, in which a mitten-shaped cloud hung grace-

317

fully behind a confusion of alpine rocks. She took a deep breath, and when she exhaled, she imagined herself standing in that landscape. For a moment she thought she could feel the spiky, icy air, even smell the moss and heather. She had almost forgotten how entering a work of art could be an effective way to travel.

That same day, Nora treated herself to a large tin of colored pencils and a large sketchpad at the stationery store on the lower level. Thereafter she would sit in the waiting room or in the Biltmore's Palm Court or in any one of the hotel and terminal's coffee shops and, just as she had in Paris, draw the people she saw. She noticed how the veins at one man's temple abutted the heavy stubble on his carved-out cheeks, a miniature landscape of river and valley. How a shock of ice-white hair crowned another man's head. How a third man — with his companion seeming not to care — walked with his arm not around her waist or shoulders but hooked tightly around her neck like a scarf.

Sometimes in the terminal Nora studied the details *in* the details. Sketching the terminal's logo, she noticed how the *T,* turned upside down, looked like an anchor. On the elevator indicator in the lobby of the

New York Central building, she found lightning bolts, a hammer, stars, ribbons, and a winged helmet. The staircase in the concourse was, like the one on the SS *Paris,* modeled after the original in the Paris Opera House. The carvings over the windows included symbols of transportation — wheels, ships, and wings. She was living inside a masterwork whose vast size and constant motion sometimes obscured its magnificence, but Nora was determined not to take any part of it for granted.

Drawing made Nora feel tied to the part of herself that had been planted in high school and had bloomed in Paris, dependent on no one's presence or praise. Drawing was the piece of her that didn't so much transcend her situation — transcendence, right now, was the last thing she needed — as much as anchor it. She might be a witness, but that didn't mean she couldn't be an active witness. Having landed in this vibrant Terminal City, she felt compelled to become as much a part of it as any other element was.

Throughout that spring, Nora heard on the radio about clothing drives, Victory Gardens, women being mobilized to work in factories. In Joe's *Central Headlight* newsletter, she read that there had been a national call for twenty-five thousand women to serve as volunteers or be trained as nurses' aides. On top of that, the Central itself was planning to hire fourteen young women as the first female ticket sellers in the terminal's history. Nora ached to be one of them, or at least to find a useful place for herself.

On a Tuesday morning in June, quite by chance, she discovered that place. She was standing on the Main Concourse amid a buzzing crowd, watching as the war bonds mural was being dismantled to make way for an even grander patriotic project. Panel by panel, the pieces were handed down the scaffolding, carefully wrapped, and stacked on large carts.

"Well, hallelujah," Nora heard someone say as the panel displaying the face of the forty-foot-high sailor was taken from the scaffolding. Nora turned toward the voice to find a tall, solid woman with tapered cheekbones, shockingly blue eyes, and ebony hair that formed a slightly off-center widow's peak. "Good riddance, sailor boy," the woman said to Nora.

Nora laughed, grateful for this minor bit of treason. " 'Sailor boy'?" she asked.

"I always thought he was undressing me with his eyes."

320

Nora pointed to the other tall figure on the opposite side of the mural. "And what about his army friend?"

The woman shook her head. "Apparently I'm not his type," she said.

That was how their friendship began, the first of many friendships Nora would make in time. Paige Barrow was twenty-nine, or, as she preferred to put it, "not yet thirty." She was about a head taller than Nora, and though she pushed away compliments as if they were brambles, she was darkly, richly beautiful. Despite her marriage, her three children, and their apartment on the West Side, Paige had become a Travelers Aid volunteer the week of the Pearl Harbor attack, and she told Nora that it was the Travelers Aid Society that was assembling the replacement for the mural — not another advertisement filling the east windows, but a servicemen's lounge filling the whole east balcony in front of them.

Paige grabbed Nora by the elbow and pulled her back to the western side of the concourse, the better to take in the east wall.

"Picture this, sweetie," she said dramatically, waving her arm in a large semicircle as if in doing so she could conjure the future. The lounge, she explained, was going to be divided into three sections and

321

decorated in red, white, and blue. The red section was where the men would check their belongings and play pool, cards, or board games. The white section would have a five-hundred-book library, as well as couches, chairs, magazines, newspapers, stationery, stamps, and art supplies. And in the blue section, Paige said, there would be a snack bar, telephones, and — best of all — a Panoram, which was part jukebox and part miniature movie screen.

Nora tried to picture it all, but what inspired her most was when Paige reported that Travelers Aid would need four hundred volunteers to run the place.

"Do you think they'd let me be one of them?" Nora asked.

Paige let out a startled "Ha!" and followed it with a warm embrace. "*Let* you!" she said.

7
FROM THAT MOMENT ON

1942

On October 1, Nora proudly donned the blue garrison cap and apron of her fellow Travelers Aid volunteers, and from that moment on, she belonged. At the servicemen's lounge, she had a husband in the navy, she lived in Queens, she was an amateur painter, she didn't have children, and she was here to help. Other than occasionally humming an outdated tune or having to pretend to get a joke or a reference to a movie, she had become a completely convincing citizen of Grand Central's Terminal City.

A month before the lounge's official opening, painters and construction crews applied the finishing touches to each of the three sections while the volunteers organized the library's books, set up the baggage and coat checks, hung patriotic and informational posters, and sorted out donated games and supplies. Paige was everywhere — maybe it was the widow's peak, or maybe just her speed, that made her seem like a bright, quick bird. For her part, Nora spent most of the time in the art section, unpacking and arranging the art supplies on a couple of large wooden tables. There were sketchpads, colored pencils, boxes of crayons, and a dozen sets of children's watercolors.

Throughout the first day, to her delight, volunteers of all ages started asking her advice. In her former life, Nora had often been a ringleader, with classmates at Barnard and with Margaret and other expatriate friends in Paris. She was thrilled to realize that she could still give the impression of someone who knew the answers. Where do we put the extra paper? Should we cover the art tables or let them get splashed with paint? The answers didn't exactly require wisdom, but to be asked was invigorating.

Late in the afternoon, Nora painted a sign to hang above the art supplies:

PRAISE THE LORD AND
PASS THE PAINTBRUSH

It was a play on a song she'd been hearing on the radio (*ammunition* instead of *paintbrush*), and she figured it might attract the men. A lot of the girls stopped to admire

Nora's artful lettering, and Hattie Pope, who was in charge of the whole lounge enterprise, went out of her way to applaud the effort.

That first day didn't end until after seven in the evening. Nora had worked for ten hours straight, and she was elated, taking off her apron and cap reluctantly. She shared warm goodbyes with the women she'd met and, best of all, with Mrs. Pope, who already knew her by name and made a point of asking when she'd return.

"I'll be here as much as you need me," Nora said.

"That's the spirit," Mrs. Pope said, and although Nora hadn't needed an extra blessing, there it was.

Smoothing her skirt, fluffing up her hair, Nora hurried through the Biltmore's Palm Court and up to their current room. Flinging open the door, she exclaimed "I did it!" But Joe, unmoving, looking like part of the armchair in which he was sitting, gave Nora only the tightest smile, barely meeting her eyes.

"Joe?"

He looked down at a sports page she guessed he'd either already read or had no interest in reading.

"Where've you been?" he asked.

"You know where. The servicemen's lounge. Don't tell me you didn't see my note. I know I left you a note this time."

"You've been there all *day*?" he asked suspiciously.

"Since nine this morning," she said proudly. "What do you think? That I'm seeing someone else?"

He smiled faintly.

"It was so wonderful, Joe," she said. "You should have seen me! I was setting out supplies and organizing books and figuring out the bag check system. These girls are so slow! Except Paige. I told you about Paige, didn't I? She's the one who signed me up in the first place. I think we could really be friends."

This had all come out in a burst, and Joe didn't respond to any of it.

Nora sat down, trying to tame her own enthusiasm.

"I don't like you being out there," Joe said at last.

"What do you mean, 'out there'?"

"Out there. In the terminal. Working like that around so many people. Who knows what might happen?"

Nora's eyes narrowed slightly. "What do you *think* might happen?" she asked.

"I don't know. That's the point. *You* don't know." Joe folded his newspaper and stood up to pace. "Don't you realize? If anyone found out about you, they'd never let you alone again. People would think you were crazy. The minute they'd start asking questions, we'd never have any peace again."

Nora sighed. "Why can't I just be volunteering, like a regular girl?"

"Because you're *not* a regular girl!"

Nora winced, then locked eyes with him.

"Why don't you *see* that?" he said angrily.

"You're saying I don't understand my own situation?"

"I'm saying I want to keep you *safe!*"

"Safe!" Nora said. "When I was in Paris, I never thought about 'safe.' I went places. I did things. I had a job. A paycheck. Friends. When I was in Paris —"

"But, you're *not* in Paris, goddamnit!" Joe shouted.

"Joseph!" she shouted back.

They had never raised their voices at each other. She had never used his full name. They both looked shocked.

Then they both started laughing. Laughter turned into an embrace, the embrace into kisses.

"You're a feisty one, all right," Joe said. She

327

was lying in his arms.

"It's so odd," she said.

"What?"

"I'm more than a decade behind you, but you're so much more old-fashioned than I am."

"Not old-fashioned," he said. "Just realistic."

"If you say so, pal."

She had found in Joe the irrefutable center of her inexplicable life. He clearly bristled at her independence and didn't know the first thing about her art. But unlike Nora, he had never known the giddy freedoms she had, and it made sense that he would want to protect what he had. That now included her.

"Joe," Nora said nonetheless, "it's not like I can cook dinner for you every night."

She fell asleep before he did that night, and for a long time he watched her. He had seen her sleep in the semidarkness many times, marveling at the fact that, unlike any woman he'd ever spent the night with, she somehow looked as beautiful asleep as she did when she was awake. Her mouth was closed, her cheeks pearly, and her hair fell across her forehead in a tumble of curls. She seemed to be barely breathing.

After a while he closed his eyes and

thought back. It was 1914 or '15, and his mother was standing by the stove in the kitchen in Queens, stirring one of her soups or stews. Her favorite apron was tied around her waist, several of its stitched-on shamrocks hanging by threads. It was February, and it was so cold that she was wearing a cardigan over her housedress; so cold that Finn and Joe, eleven and nine, didn't want to play outside. They sat at the white enamel kitchen table, playing gin rummy instead. Finn had recently learned this game from the older boys at school, but he changed the rules to suit his hand every time he had the chance.

Katherine Reynolds alternated between looking at her watch and stopping her stirring to listen for the sound of the front door.

Joe pulled a ten of diamonds from the deck and discarded it.

"So you don't have any tens," Finn said.

"What?"

"If you had tens, you would have kept that. You're supposed to put whatever card you pick up into your hand so I can't know what you don't have."

Joe shook his head, not understanding. "But I don't need the card," he said.

"It doesn't matter. You're supposed to pretend you *might* need the card."

Katherine was humming one of her folk tunes — all of them sounded the same — and checking her watch.

"Clear that table and set it," she told the boys.

"Okay, Ma," they said in unison, but went on playing in silence, the snap of the cards like the ticking of a clock.

Joe had three fours in his hand and a run of three spades, and his extra cards totaled fifteen, so he needed only one low card to complete his hand, but at that point Finn declared "Gin!"

"Show me."

Finn laid out his cards. He had twos, fives, and a run of jack, queen, king, and ace.

"No!" Joe said. "You told me ace is never high."

"I never told you that."

"Cheater!"

"Brat!"

Katherine knocked her wooden spoon twice against the side of the pot and whirled around, the spoon nonetheless dripping a few gray-brown spots on the floor.

"Do you think I have time for your bickering?" she asked. "Don't you apes realize your pa is going to be home any minute?"

She made a point of straightening her apron and pinching her cheeks. She'd been married to Pa for twelve years, and she still pinched her cheeks for him. She was there, waiting for him, every single night, no exception. If he was five minutes late, she worried something had happened to him. If he was five minutes early, it was the same. This, Joe had always thought, was what a wife did. And Faye too. It was what Faye had done for Finn — even when they were first married; even when the kids were babies; even when his beat kept him out till all hours.

But Nora was not Faye, though they both made him worry. Joe worried that Nora might fly away, and he worried that, in Finn's absence, Faye might weigh him down.

Joe felt that full weight on an October morning when Faye left a message with the tower director to call her as soon as possible. Joe moved slowly through the tunnel from Tower A to the concourse, dread about Finn making it hard for him to swallow.

When Faye picked up the phone, he could tell she was frightened.

"Finn's fine," she said, before Joe could ask, and he exhaled. "It's Mike. He wants to enlist."

"Are you crazy?"

"I said *he* wants to enlist."

"Well, you've got to tell him he can't," Joe said.

"Gee, Joey, I never thought of that."

"Sorry."

"But I swear, Joey, he's going to do it if you don't talk to him," she said.

Joe cursed inwardly. He realized that his teeth were set so tightly that his jaw ached.

"Want me to come out this afternoon?" he asked.

"No, I'm on the line this week." For the past few months, Faye had been making ninety cents an hour working part time at the watch factory in Woodside.

They agreed on a Sunday visit, and when Joe hung up, he went to look for Nora. The servicemen's lounge was a muddle of uniforms: sailors in blue and white, soldiers in khaki and brown, marines in olive, and Travelers Aid girls in light-blue smocks. But Nora — as she had in the choir — stood out. She was bending over a sailor who was sacked out in one of the armchairs. With a gentle, nurselike smile, she pinned a card to his jacket lapel. A few yards farther on, she placed a reassuring hand on the arm of a soldier who seemed frozen before one of the bookshelves. They talked briefly, and Nora pointed him toward another shelf.

Despite all Joe's worries, he couldn't help feeling proud. Nora was kind. She was confident. She was doing her part. And she loved him.

When Joe got to Queens on Sunday, a speechless Faye offered no greeting, merely pointing to the kitchen. Walking in, Joe could see through the screen of the back door that Mike was standing in the tiny backyard, his skinny arms crossed against his just-broadening chest. The expression on his face was basically identical to the one he'd had as a crabby baby.

"What are you doing out here?" Joe asked him.

"Ma said she didn't want to look at my face."

The screen door hissed shut behind Joe. It was a cloudy day, and the sky was the color of paste.

"You are fifteen years old," Joe said.

"Almost sixteen."

"Fine. Almost sixteen. That's old enough to know that you can't leave your ma and sister without a man around the house. Not to mention school. You've got to finish school."

"Pete Sullivan already shipped out last month."

"Pete Sullivan doesn't have a father in the service."

"That's only because Pete Sullivan's old man isn't as brave as Pa!"

Joe sighed. "Go ahead," he said. "Get it off your chest."

Joe listened as Mike plunged into the speech he had obviously been preparing for months. What the Japs had done. What the Jerries were doing. The shame of sitting on his duff when Uncle Sam needed him. Joe had heard it all before. There was barely a trainman under forty who hadn't bitched about having to stay behind. Back on the Fourth of July, the Central had had the nerve to hang an enormous service flag — a blue star on a field of white — in honor of the employees who'd enlisted. This was salt in the wounds of every railman who'd followed orders and bought the line about being too essential to serve.

"And don't tell me it's wrong to fake my age," Mike was saying. "Because I know Pa had to have lied to get in, and if he could do it, I should be able to do it too."

The sun moved out from behind a cloud. Several bees flew over the fence and left quickly, having found no place to work. Around the sides of the yard, where Joe's mother had long ago tended a small but vibrant garden of black-eyed Susans, peonies, and wisteria, there were only the remnants of dead vines, twisted like dusty cables in what once had been soil and was now just dirt.

"Have you gotten a letter from your pa lately?" Joe asked Mike.

"Just at the beginning. He writes to Ma. And it's always gooey sweet stuff."

"Well, he wrote this to me," Joe said, removing an airmail letter from his shirt pocket. "I don't know if he'd want you to read it, but here it is."

He handed Mike the most recent letter he'd gotten from Finn.

Dear Meatball:

Yes, I know I never called you Meatball before, but here everyone gets nicknames. There's Noodle and Timber and Legs and Crab and Dubble Bubble and Snickers. Come to think on it, a lot of them are food names.

There's not much I can tell you about where I am or what I'm doing. I'll just say it's hard work and Uncle Sam needs us to be doing it. I know you're wondering if I killed anyone. I haven't. But Snickers did, a few weeks back, and so it's hard to call him Snickers anymore.

At night, he gets buggy. Doesn't matter where we are or what we've done that day. You always know he's going to scream out in his sleep, if he sleeps. A couple times I heard him crying. This guy's almost seven feet tall. Curses and carries on. A total cut-up when we started. Now he's got blood on his hands.

Actually, I saw the guy he killed. Not just blood. Blood and guts.

It isn't anything like I thought it would be. But then I guess, like Ma always said, "War isn't a game."

Well, that's all for now. I'm not sure you and I have ever been apart long enough for me to write you any kind of letter. Hope this one's OK. Give my two girls a kiss and a hug from me. And make sure Mike keeps busy. And don't think I forgot. Tell Nora hi from me too — that is, if she hasn't disappeared again.

Your brother,
Pvt. Finnegan Damian Reynolds

Mike folded the letter and handed it back to Joe.

"Who's Nora?" he asked.

Joe shook his head. "*That's* all you got

from this?"

"Well, no. But who's Nora?"

"Nora is none of your business," Joe said, just as Faye stepped out into the yard. She blinked in the sunlight. She was wearing a bright-pink shirt and dungarees, and the freckles on her fair arms seemed to be darkening before Joe's eyes. Joe didn't know if she'd heard Mike say Nora's name, but if she had, it obviously wasn't her chief concern.

"Has your uncle explained the facts of life to you?" Faye asked Mike.

Mike crossed his arms again, sullen. He nodded and walked to the back door.

Faye put a hand around his upper arm, and her voice got husky as she said, "Mike-tyke. Don't you understand? I wouldn't know how to get by without you."

Mike glared at his mother from under his bowed head and threw open the door.

"Hey," Joe said after him.

"What."

"Don't be rude to your ma."

"Sorry."

"Have you been helping her around the house?"

Mike shrugged. "I guess," he said. "I take out the garbage. I make Alice's lunch."

"What about the marketing?" Joe asked.

"Ma does the marketing," Mike said.

Joe reached into his wallet and pulled out a ten-dollar bill. He handed it to Mike.

"What's this for?"

"Groceries," Joe said. "So you can help. Think you can hold on to that and not spend it on a girl?"

Mike, disbelieving, looked toward Faye.

"Can you?" she asked Mike.

"I guess," Mike said. He stuffed the bill into his pants pocket, clearly trying as hard as he could not to look pleased.

"Go check the cupboards," Faye said, "and see what we need."

The screen door bounced shut behind him.

As he started to follow Mike, Joe suddenly felt Faye's hand clasping his upper arm. He stopped and turned to look back at her. She had always been a lively tease, but it seemed to Joe that today there was more need than playfulness in her eyes.

"And you, Joey," Faye said. "I wouldn't know how to get by without you either."

8
REAL STARS

1942

"Will you pose for me?" the soldier asked. "I could carry your portrait with me overseas." He said *portrait* like "portrate." This was not an uncommon kind of request in the servicemen's lounge; asking for things to take with them was just one of the many ways the boys flirted. Nora was almost always too busy to oblige, but the lounge wasn't very crowded on this early November evening, and the soldier added: "You're probably the last woman I'm going to see before I ship out."

His face was the shape of a lightbulb — a pointed chin, a broad forehead that was covered with acne scars. He was wearing a Timex watch that was too big for his wrist. There was something particularly endearing about him, and after Nora made certain that the other men had what they needed, she sat for him while he sketched.

"Just for a few minutes," he said.

It wound up taking longer, and yet his drawing bore absolutely no resemblance to Nora — and barely to any human. She was lavish in her praise. With delicate care, the soldier tore the page from the sketchpad. "I'm taking this with me," he said. He folded it into a perfect half, halved it twice more, and tucked it into his breast pocket. "*You're* coming with me," he said. "You're going to bring me luck."

Naturally, Nora would never know what became of him. But it was an unexpected pleasure to think that some part of her could exist — if only on paper — in the outside world.

As the soldier left, Nora ducked a questioning glance from Hattie Pope, whose many rules for the volunteers included a phrase she repeated almost weekly: "No favorites." A longtime veteran of the Travelers Aid Society, Mrs. Pope had previously overseen a rotating team of at most forty women. Now, with the war on and the lounge open, she'd been given hundreds to command and had in effect become a general, issuing orders and deploying her troops as she saw fit.

It was not a small challenge. The men came in at all hours, in all numbers and states of mind. Some of them used the pool tables or the art supplies. A lot of them just sacked out as soon as they arrived, able neither to be greeted nor fed. They would settle into the armchairs or couches or even, when the place was full, the folding beach chairs. Books, magazines, or newspapers would be draped unread across their chests, as effective as DO NOT DISTURB signs. No one was allowed to miss a train, however, which is why Mrs. Pope instructed the girls to hand a "WAKE ME AT _____" card to every man who looked sleepy.

The servicemen rarely stayed longer than six hours and sometimes as few as two, but they brought all kinds of things to check at the baggage counter. Nora hadn't been on duty the legendary day when one soldier's pet monkey and another's dozen chicks provided most of the concourse with an hour's worth of unintended entertainment. Occasionally a sailor would bring a white mouse or two in a shoebox — mice were said to be good luck on shipboard — and a few times Nora had found herself trying in vain to chase one down.

But once a day, no matter how busy things got, Nora slipped out of the lounge and wove her way across the concourse and up the stairs to the Vanderbilt Avenue doors.

341

There, she would stand for a while, pretending to be waiting for someone. It was easy to go unnoticed. Nora had long ago realized that people in Grand Central Terminal were far more focused on signs, clocks, and bags than they were on other people. Every time one of the terminal doors swung open, the inrushing air seemed like an invitation — the wide world reaching out its arms and asking Nora to come away with it. However brief, the breeze carried with it the outdoor smells that to Nora were by now exotic: gasoline from a passing taxi, chestnuts from a nearby vendor, beer spilled on the pavement. Nora knew that to step outside would be to tempt fate — or physics — or whatever had kept her here since she had arrived on the Manhattanhenge morning that was almost a year ago now. She still didn't know what had made her disappear when she left the realm of the terminal. Was it the time she spent outside? Or was it the distance she walked? If it was time, then how long could she stay safe? If it was distance, how far could she go? How many blocks had she run that day back in the Depression when she'd chased after Mrs. Ingram? With Joe on that first frosty night, how long had they been walking before the kid with the knife had shown up? Had it been five minutes?

Ten? How far had they gotten? A block, for sure. Maybe two? Three? What was it about the terminal that kept her alive? What was it about the world outside that made her flicker out — that threatened to send her not only into that dreadful in-between, but now, just as important, away from Joe?

She'd not once felt tired of being with him, had never been unmoved by making love with him. All the things she might once have thought would trouble her in a man — lack of sophistication, education, worldly experience — not only didn't bother her, but were part of what she loved in Joe. She loved his strength and stillness, and the honest way he wanted her: the innocent side of this regular guy with a prized skill that moved machinery that moved whole parts of the world.

And yet, standing near the terminal's exit, watching the women walk by wearing their autumn coats and hats, she kept thinking about how close she was to St. Patrick's Cathedral, Bryant Park, the Morgan Library. She wanted to reclaim the city, the whole city that had once been hers. She wanted to go uptown to Barnard, where her girlfriends and she had run to classes through a fresh snow; staged a scandalous dance in bare feet and scarves; holed up in the library, waiting — she had to laugh now — for the ghost everyone said haunted the stacks. If she couldn't walk by the Seine again, perhaps she could walk by the East River. If she couldn't stroll through the Tuileries, perhaps she could stroll through Central Park.

Without exactly realizing it, Nora inched a little bit closer to the street each day.

It was a Sunday afternoon in mid-November when Nora decided to bring it up with Joe. They were sitting in the deep leather shoe-shine chairs where Joe had gotten a brush-up from the kid, Butch Becker. The smell of the polish was crisp and warm at the same time, and there was something comforting about it.

"We should, don't you think?" Nora asked.

"Should?"

"Should try to figure it out."

"You mean about you."

"Is there anyone we can ask?"

Joe looked over his shoulder to make sure Butch wasn't within earshot. "You mean, ask 'What is it about this place that keeps my dead girlfriend alive?' "

"Well, maybe not when you put it that way."

"There's no one."

344

"What about Madame Rosalita?" Nora asked, gesturing toward the fortune-teller's FUTURE sign.

Joe laughed. "Hate to break it to you, but Madame Rosalita is really Esther Tettleman," he said. "I did ask her about ghosts once, though. Before I understood Manhattanhenge."

"And?"

"And, trust me, her answers did not help explain *you.*"

A man with an accordion started playing nearby. It took a moment for Nora to realize he was playing "Over There," which seemed the wrong choice for the instrument. But oddly, the music made the moment seem more pressing.

"We have to do some experiments," Nora said. "We have to find out what my limits are."

Joe stared down at his newly buffed shoes.

"Don't look so grim," Nora said.

"I can't afford to lose you again," he whispered.

That night she and Joe lay in bed, so tired from their workdays that they were speaking with their eyes closed. Nora started to talk about the girls she'd known at Barnard and, later, in Paris. About the parts of

England she'd seen on the way to Stonehenge, and the cities she'd planned to visit:
Rome, Athens, Vienna. "It was going to be
such a big life," she said.

"I went to Italy once," Joe said. "And
Belgium and Russia too."

"Really?"

"Well, no. They were just pavilions at the
World's Fair. But they were swell."

In the dark, Nora reached out her left
palm to find his right one. Her hand was so
small against his that the tips of her fingers
barely reached the top joints of his.

"You should go to those places for real,
Joe," she said. "You should see the world."

"Someday."

For a moment, they seesawed their hands
back and forth.

"If you could go anywhere," she said,
"where would it be?"

In an instant, Joe traveled in his own mind
from place to place: all the countries represented by the pavilions at the World's Fair,
the newsreel pictures of the Atlantic City
boardwalk, the bustle of Chicago, the wheat
fields of the Midwest, the Rocky Mountains,
the Pacific Coast. He had never been to an
ocean, a mountain, or a desert. Images
rushed through his head along with the train
routes he'd travel to get to them, the routes

he knew by heart, even though he had never taken them. What he said was: "If I could go anywhere, I'd stay right here with you."

He held his palm still and flat against hers, as if joining her in a prayer.

In the darkness, tears slipped from Nora's eyes and made their way down her cheeks to her ears.

It was Nora who devised their first experiment, a nighttime trip to the eighth-floor roof, the one that connected the two matching towers of the Biltmore Hotel. Nora hadn't been outside for ages. The icy air, which would have driven most women back indoors amid white puffs of protest, seemed to elate her.

In the summers this roof was planted with greenery in formal patterns, lined by benches, and strolled by well-dressed tourists. In the winters it was transformed into a small but festive ice-skating rink. Since the war had started, however, there had been no time for that kind of thing. For Nora and Joe, that was all the better. On this bitterly cold November night, they had the rooftop entirely to themselves. Being alone together was hardly new, but being alone together in the open air was exceptional. For months, their only shared sky had been the blue-green ceiling of the Main Concourse.

For a long time, Nora and Joe just stood, holding hands on the threshold of the terrace, as if they were waiting to dive into a pool. They had agreed that, given Nora's previous disappearances — on foot and in a taxi — somewhere between five and ten minutes was the most time she had spent outside the terminal before flickering out. So when they stepped gingerly onto the roof, they stayed close to the door.

Joe checked his watch. It was 9:15 exactly. He cupped his hands and blew into them. Nora took his hands in hers and warmed them. Together, and tunelessly, they sang three choruses of "Over There." It wasn't a patriotic moment, just a way to make the time pass. At 9:20, Nora said, "Come on, let's go out farther."

They took a dozen steps, and nothing happened.

"A little farther," Nora said.

They settled onto one of the stone benches, which felt as cold as steel, even through their wool coats. An airplane flew by, close and noisy, its wings tipped at an angle. Nora jumped up.

"It's just an air patrol," Joe said, standing up beside her.

"Does that happen a lot?" Nora asked.

"Every night," Joe said. "I guess you've never seen an airplane."

"Just in pictures," she said. She stared after the twin white taillights until they were out of sight.

Joe circled her with his arms from behind, kissing the part of her cheek he could reach, reveling in the strong, powdery smell of her neck. They looked out over the Manhattan skyline, so many of its lights dimmed because of the war. Perhaps that was why the stars seemed so bright.

"Real sky!" Nora said. "Real stars!"

Joe hugged her tighter.

"Which one's the one to wish on?" Nora asked.

"Wish on any one you want," Joe said. "Wish on them all."

"No, I mean, do you know — what is it? The morning star? The evening star?"

Joe laughed. "I could tell you I knew, but if I did, I'd be lying," he said.

Nora turned, like a gear, still inside his arms. She smiled, brushing a strand of hair from his forehead. They kissed, the city before them and the unpainted sky above. And then, to be safe, they hurried back inside.

■ ■ ■ ■

The next test came a week later — twenty minutes on the terrace, in daylight this time, and on a warmer day. Joe and Nora walked hand in hand to the edge of the roof.

"So it isn't time," Nora said. "I'm sure we've been out here longer than I've ever been."

"I really don't think we were out more than ten minutes before you disappeared that night with me."

"So it has to be distance, not time," Nora said.

"A bigger distance from the terminal than we are right now."

Together they stared down from the roof, mesmerized by the everyday things: the arguments, the embraces, the cab rides, the skyscrapers, the man selling hot chestnuts — all the big, small, and tempting freedoms of the streets.

9
THE CASCADES

1942

Before the war, the Grand Central Palace, just blocks from the terminal, had been a famous exhibition hall, hosting car and boat shows, fashion and flower shows, even the Westminster Dog Show. In mid-November, it was turned into the largest army induction center in the United States. So now, in addition to the clusters of men who were already set to ship out, there was a river of potential recruits flowing through the terminal, following the signs to the center or wandering back from it, heartsick that they'd been rejected for one reason or another.

At the end of the month, the terminal was also busy preparing for a series of ceremonies on the anniversary of Pearl Harbor. The goal was to honor the sacrifices Americans had made thus far in the war effort and, naturally, to urge civilians to buy more bonds. New bunting was draped from the north balcony. Larger choirs than usual were engaged, and several famous singers had been lined up for December 7.

For Nora and Joe, there would be a private anniversary two days earlier. It had been an entire year since the December 5 when Nora's light had come through the east window, bringing her back to Joe's embrace. They had decided to celebrate, and Nora knew exactly how she wanted to do it. She had seen the signs in the Biltmore's lobby and in magazine and newspaper ads: The Biltmore's grand ballroom was on the twenty-second floor, and its restaurant there was called the Cascades. Even with the war going on, it remained famous for its twenty-eight-foot waterfall, as well as its wall of roses, its clientele, its orchestra, and its oval dance floor.

Joe, slightly uncomfortable in the one suit he owned, nevertheless beamed as he saw Nora slip into the sparkly black dress she had borrowed from her friend Paige. He watched over her shoulder as she bent toward the mirror, applying her lipstick the way he'd seen her use paintbrushes, pursing her lips and then laughing as he grabbed her, kissed her, and thereby made it necessary for her to reapply the lipstick he'd smeared.

They rode the elevator up to the twenty-second floor. Nora stopped talking as they approached the restaurant's entrance. Inside, the crystal glittered, the tables were arranged around the polished dance floor, and a swing band was providing the music. Joe and Nora had nearly reached the maître d' station when Joe saw Nora begin to waver, her normally sure footsteps slowing.

"What is it?" he asked.

She didn't answer, or even look at him. She listed to one side, as if the floor had suddenly slanted, and as the smile left her face, her hand grew colder.

"Nora," Joe said, immediately feeling the hollow horror of those two nights when they'd been out on the street and he'd lost her.

Before he could even turn her around, she flickered for just a second. If anyone saw it, Joe would never know, because he was already pulling her away, back down the hall toward the nearest staircase, as quickly as he could. He scooped her up over his shoulder. Fireman's carry. He'd learned that from Finn years before. With each step he descended, she seemed to grow warmer.

They were back down on the nineteenth floor when she said, "You can put me down

353

now, Joe."

Despite her protests, he carried her all the way to their room.

It had obviously exhausted her, that loss of energy, and when they were back in their room, Joe helped Nora off with her dress and tucked her into bed. He watched her as she fell asleep and for a long time after. Every once in a while, he reached out to touch her hand, needing to feel its warmth.

When, eventually, he tried to sleep, Joe struggled to understand what had happened. They had already proved that Nora's limits were ruled by distance, not time. Why had she flickered at the Cascades? It hadn't occurred to either of them that her limits could be related to floors as well as streets, could be vertical as well as horizontal. On the street that first night, she had vanished at the corner of Forty-sixth and Lex. The next year, she'd gotten as far as Third Avenue. How far were those places from the spot where she had died? Joe did a rough calculation. Eight hundred, maybe 900 feet? She should have been safe at the Cascades. Twenty-two floors, even in a grand building, couldn't cover those city blocks. Yes, she should have been safe, with several hundred more feet above her.

Joe sat up, wide awake. Unless. Unless she had several hundred more below.

He crept out of bed, grabbed a notepad and pencil from the desk, and stepped into the bathroom, blinking at the bright light. He knelt on the tiled floor, leaned the notepad against his thighs, and did the math. Yes, if he was right, those feet below should take them all the way down to the converters in M42. From there to the Cascades, it was roughly the same distance to the spots where she'd flickered out.

Back in the room, Joe stared at Nora in the darkness. Those converters created the current that powered the rails that powered the trains all up and down the East Coast. And apparently, in Nora's strange magic, they were powering her life as well. Stealthily, for the rest of the night, Joe watched Nora sleeping, every once in a while rethinking his calculations, just as he had checked the warmth of her hand. It had been terrifying, that moment of almost losing her again. He wanted to put his arms around her, but he didn't want to disturb her. He figured she had been through more than enough.

Nora woke at around eight to find Joe holding a silver hotel tray laid out with a cup of coffee, a glass of orange juice, and a basket of pastries that shone like fine leather.

"Breakfast in bed?" she asked Joe, smiling.

"I didn't know how you'd be feeling," he said.

"Starved," she said, and bit into a roll. "Tired, I guess," she added reluctantly.

"Well, that's no wonder," Joe said. He gestured to her coffee cup. "Drink up. I want to show you something."

She knew he was worried about her. Even if he hadn't asked how she was feeling, she would have known by the extra-casual attitude he was putting on. And she actually wasn't that steady. In the bathroom, she soaked a washcloth in steaming water and pressed it against her cheeks and eyelids, a simple luxury. Brushing her curls, she met her eyes in the mirror and saw Joe's reflection behind her.

"What is it?" she asked.

"I've got this idea," he said.

"An idea for what?" she asked.

"For a little experiment of my own."

"Right now?"

"If you're game," he said. "If you're up to it."

She took a breath, but after a second she said, "When am I not game?"

■ ■ ■ ■

Since the beginning of the war, the mammoth converters in M42 had been guarded by armed soldiers twenty-four hours a day. For all their power and size, the machines were weirdly vulnerable. All an enemy would have to do was pour a bucket of sand into one, and the third rail would instantly be compromised: The communications and transportation systems along the entire Eastern Seaboard would grind — literally grind — to a halt. As a consequence, the soldiers stationed at the entrance to M42 had been ordered to shoot to kill any person who approached carrying anything at all.

Joe had no intention of risking any misunderstandings, but he wanted to get Nora as close to the converters as he could, as close to what he now believed was the power that kept her going.

"You have any particular place in mind?" she asked as they made their way down to the tracks.

"Down," Joe said.

She was skeptical. "Is this going to be like last night?" she asked.

"If I'm right," he said, "it'll be just the opposite."

■ ■ ■ ■

Nora had never seen any level of the terminal below the subway, and she took the first set of metal stairs cautiously. It wasn't just that she feared a repeat of the previous night. The world she was entering was murky and dank. Here, beneath the terminal's glamour and its celebration of light, it was so dim that it was almost impossible to see more than a few feet beyond the stairwells. The first two subfloors were used for maintenance, filled with all the essential supplies, equipment, and men to keep the place in running order. On the third floor down, Nora could just make out three heavyset men apparently taking a break to have a smoke.

Down another flight, they passed rows of recently built bomb shelters, empty and closed for now but seemingly ready for disaster. Two more floors, and Joe realized that Nora had started speeding up, holding the yellow metal stair railing while she hopped over each bottom step.

"Wait up!" Joe said, but he was loving the way her strength was returning.

Four more floors down, Joe was out of breath, but Nora seemed elated.

When they finally stopped, it was because they could go no farther. They were standing in the dank carved-out hollow beside M42. There were three or four bare bulbs casting shadows, enough light so that Nora could see the wall of rock from which the space for the terminal had been blasted.

"How far does it go on?" she asked.

"A long way," Joe said. "You see those holes? That's where they crammed in the dynamite sticks when they blasted out the rock. This is what was left."

"What happened to the rest?" she asked.

"Did you ever go to Riverside Park?"

"Sure," she said.

"Down to the water's edge?"

"I think so."

"Well, the rocks that came from here are what they used to line the banks."

"Of the Hudson River?"

Joe nodded. "I once heard all the way up to Albany."

"That's a lot of rocks."

Joe sat on an overturned milk crate and motioned Nora over to sit beside him. Within moments, Dillinger had sprung onto Joe's lap, and perhaps a dozen other cats had come out as well.

"Oh, these poor kitties," Nora said. "All alone down here. Nowhere to go. And who feeds them?"

"*Everybody* feeds them," Joe said. "Everybody thinks no one else does. These are the fattest cats in creation. Look at them!"

Nora stood again and scooped up a gray kitten that had enormous white paws. "I wonder if the boys in the lounge would want to have a kitten around to cuddle."

"I'm guessing that wouldn't be their first choice for cuddling," Joe said.

Smiling, Nora put the kitten down and bent to pet some of the others. She seemed to have brightened this place.

"Nora," Joe said. "Come here."

"What?"

"Come back over here."

He reached out to take her hand, then pulled her down to sit next to him again. He kissed her on the lips, which were warm and soft.

"How do you feel?" he asked her.

"I feel terrific!" she said. "What's that smile for?"

He explained it to her. Sitting in the barely yellow light of this level far below the bustling world, Joe told her how he believed the energy from the converters in M42 had somehow captured and mingled with the energy of the Manhattanhenge sun. It was that special sunrise that had brought her

360

here, but it was the power of the terminal that kept her.

"So this is what keeps me going?" she asked.

Holding her nearly electric hands, Joe said that, as far as he could tell, the terminal's heartbeat had become her own.

■ ■ ■ ■

PART FOUR

■ ■ ■ ■

PART FOUR

1
700 FEET

1942

Eight hundred feet was just a measurement, but as the length of the radius that could keep Nora safe, it immediately became the most significant of the many significant numbers in Nora's and Joe's lives. More meaningful than the years 1925, '38, '39, or '41. More important than Track 13 or any room number they had. Even more weighty than twenty-three, the age Nora would always be — as long as Grand Central had electric power and she stayed within 800 feet of it.

That "as long as" might have frightened her. But climbing up from the subbasement with Joe this morning, back to the public levels of the terminal, Nora actually felt safer than she had in recent memory. An invisible sphere now existed, defining and containing her world. She was still trapped in a single place, but the simple number

365

800 had made the place feel less like a cage and more like a nest.

Back in the concourse, Joe walked Nora to the servicemen's lounge. It was just before ten o'clock, time for her shift. He squeezed her hand and said tenderly, "Don't work too hard. And no testing that number until I've measured it out."

But she had to test it a little. On her lunch break, Nora strode down to the lower level and bought herself a Hershey bar, went back up the ramp to the exit, opened the door, and stepped outside. If 800 feet was the limit of her freedom, it was still freedom. Standing for once across the street from the terminal's corner entrance, she watched a trio of charcoal-gray pigeons swoop onto the railing of the building's overhang. She tried to enjoy their flapping and bobbing without envying their chance to fly. Inhaling deeply, she broke off a piece of chocolate, popped it into her mouth, and stared straight up at the splendid white winter sky.

Like so many people all over the world in 1942, Nora and Joe were in the habit of beginning a lot of sentences with the phrase *After the war.* But since the morning of M42, their most exciting conversations had been starting with a different, private *after:*

"After we get our own place."

Their goal would be to find a way to live a settled life: to find an apartment, however modest, that would lie within Nora's safety zone. Joe figured that Ralston Young could marry them. They would be Mr. and Mrs. Joseph Damian Reynolds. They would have a home with a front-door key that wasn't constantly changing. For now, every extra dime Joe made was being used to help Faye and the kids, but when Finn came back, that would change. And who knew? The war had meant that women were doing men's work all over the country. Maybe Nora could get a paying job in the terminal to help with the rent. Even better — and Joe knew she dreamed of this — she might have the space in a place of their own to make her art and then sell it in the Vanderbilt Passage stalls or at the Christmas market. One way or another they would have a real address, and they would have their own furniture, plates, blankets, and stove.

Before any of that could happen, though, Joe would need to make sure about the 800 feet. So in that second week of December, he borrowed a 100-foot surveyor's tape from one of the engineers and got some yellow chalk from Bill Keogh. Joe knew where M42 was in relation to the Main Concourse.

Starting at that spot, he pinned down the tape end with a piece of brick and unwound the tape from the reel. Methodically measuring in 100-foot increments, he reached the corner where Nora had disappeared. Even being as conservative as possible, Joe calculated that the limit turned out to be closer to 850 feet than 800; 850 feet from Nora's presence to her absence; 800 feet from safety to danger. Surely they could eventually find some little place that was close enough. But for now, there was yet another *after:* "After the holidays." Because the Christmas rush came first.

"There were marines sleeping in beach chairs here last night," Nora told Joe as he walked her to the crowded lounge one morning when they each had an early shift.

"That doesn't sound too comfortable."

"It's not," Nora said. "Could you do me a favor, pal? Would you mind rerouting just a few of those trains today? Send some boys somewhere else for once?"

Joe laughed, gave her a see-you-tonight-honey kiss, and walked on toward the track entrances.

In the lounge, putting on her apron, Nora was practically accosted by Paige, who seized her by the elbow and pulled her back to the small space behind the baggage-check shelves.

"Okay," Paige said. "Enough. Who's the guy?"

"Shh. The girls will hear you!"

Paige lowered her voice. "Who's the guy who's always dropping you off looking like he wants a coat check ticket for *you*?"

Nora weighed her answer quickly. If she denied there was anything going on with Joe, that would pretty much be it for her friendship with Paige. Paige knew how to spot hooey as well as anyone Nora had ever known. On the other hand, if she didn't deny it, then in Paige's eyes Nora would automatically become a married woman who was cheating on "Danny," the patriotic husband she'd previously invented. Nora wasn't crazy about the second option, but — liking Paige as much as she did — she couldn't bear to risk the first.

She took a breath, looked over her shoulder, and said: "His name is Joe."

"Joe. Joe what?"

"Joe Reynolds."

"And he works here?"

"In the signal tower."

"And you and he — ?"

Nora nodded, trying to look guilty.

"How long has it been going on?" Paige asked.

"Do you really need to know the details?" Nora asked.

"Absolutely," Paige said.

"Why?"

"Because I thought I was the only one."

Paige, it turned out, had been having an affair of her own even before her husband joined the army. George, Paige was quick to explain, had cheated on her first.

"And your husband?" she asked. "It's Danny, right? Is he a bastard too?"

Nora shook her head. "No," she said. "With Danny, *I'm* the bastard."

They laughed hard enough that the girls at the coat check looked back at them. When they stopped laughing, Paige smiled with genuine warmth. "I'm so glad we're both so rotten," she said.

"Me too."

"Are you spending Christmas with him?"

"Can't. He'll be with his family," Nora said.

"Is he married too?"

"No."

It was refreshing to say something true. "Joe's brother is in the army, so he's going out to Queens to be with his sister-in-law and niece and nephew. And anyway, these guys —" Nora said, and together she and Paige looked out over the armchairs, couches, and beach chairs that were filled with the men. Even if Joe hadn't needed to go out to Queens on Christmas Eve, Nora would have felt it her duty to help take care of the men. Still, as she started to prepare the Christmas decorations, she couldn't help thinking what it would be like after they got their own place, to hang baubles on their own Christmas tree or sit with Joe in front of their own fire. Was that *after* really possible?

2
PRESENTS IN THE MORNING

1942

The railroad office had warned that there would be a huge increase in traffic for the holidays; all the trains were sold out through the first week of January. Joe and the other levermen had been told to prepare for additional shifts. But by Christmas Eve, it seemed that civilians had heeded the requests to stay home if they could. For the most part, the trains were filled with servicemen, and the extra shifts were canceled.

In the shower after his regular stint, Joe found himself singing "God Rest Ye Merry, Gentlemen." Smiling, he remembered how Alice, thinking the words *God rest* were actually *get dressed,* had long ago asked him why the merry gentlemen were not wearing clothes.

As he walked back from the tower, Joe felt his wet hair stiffening in the cold. Jamming his hands deep into his coat pockets, he thought about his parents and Finn, the years of Erector sets and his mother's knitted scarves. He sighed, his breath white and puffy. This would be the family's first Christmas without Damian. Knowing that Finn would have done the same, Joe had bought Mike and Alice the traditional Erector sets. Though he was sure the only additional gift Mike would have wanted was an enlistment card stamped *1A,* he had bought him an electric phonograph that came in its own carrying case. He'd found a Shirley Temple paper-doll book for Alice.

Somehow, though, he had forgotten Faye. They hadn't usually exchanged presents. But now, gathering the kids' gifts from the hotel room, he knew he couldn't show up empty-handed. Faye would either get feisty and curse him out, or she'd get that hollow, orphaned look she got when she was too hurt to bother acting tough.

The major department stores were always closed the day before Christmas, but the small shops in Grand Central stayed open until seven, and there was the holiday market too, with extra stalls set up in the Vanderbilt Passage. So, with the kids' presents in a shopping bag, Joe hustled down to the lower level and combed the stalls for something neither too personal nor too impersonal for Faye. He pondered a pair of gloves and a handbag, wishing he could steal Nora away from the lounge just long enough to get her advice, but then he saw it: a Kelly-green sweater with a white collar embroidered with red berries. He wasn't sure if the size would be right, but he knew Faye would love the bright colors.

As the saleswoman wrapped it, he felt a presence beside him and turned to see Big Sal, looking odd without a counter and pastries in front of her.

"That for your Nora, Joseph?" she asked.

"Sister-in-law," Joe said.

"Is that right? And what'd you get for your Nora?"

"What's that to you, Sal?"

"Just wondering when you're planning to put a ring on her finger. She seems to treat you awful nice."

"Sal? I promise you'll be the first to know," Joe said.

Sal chucked him on the arm, hard, but he walked away wondering how Nora would feel about Ralston performing their wedding ceremony in the empty train on Track 13. *After they got their own place.* There would be no reason why Steady Max and Gus, Shoebox Lou and Butch, Big Sal and

Alva — even Nora's friend Paige — couldn't attend.

Joe was humming as he headed back to the Main Concourse, where Mary Lee Read seemed to be pummeling the organ with extra enthusiasm. There were wreaths and holly draped across the balconies, and several dozen Christmas stockings hung from the marble railing of the servicemen's lounge. Behind the railing, three women on tall ladders were decorating a large Christmas tree, draping it with small presents for the men: neckties, pocket combs, handkerchiefs, and chocolate candy canes from Barton's wrapped in striped foil. Nora's back was to Joe, but he spotted her right away: She was the shortest, most petite of the women, but she was standing on the tallest of the three ladders, reaching up to the highest branches. Naturally, Joe thought proudly. Naturally she would be on the tallest ladder; that was who she was.

"They canceled my second shift!" he called up to her once he was in the lounge.

"That's great!" she said, and tossing a few neckties over her shoulder, climbed down the ladder as he held it steady for her.

"Does that mean we get to open Christmas presents before you go?" she asked.

Joe laughed. "Not a chance," he said. He

put his arms around her neck and kissed her, their lips hidden by the flannel-lined collar of his winter coat.

"Presents in the morning," he said. "Don't wait up for me."

Nora watched Joe leave, and for the next two hours she served the boys eggnog, lost to them at pool, and made sure they reached for presents from the tree. At around eight, Paige came by, her arms filled with Christmas packages. "I just wanted to say Merry Christmas," she said. "I've got to get these home. When are you knocking off?"

"Soon."

"Sorry you can't be with your sweetie," Paige said. She leaned over her packages and kissed Nora's cheek. "You know, this is the price of being a bastard."

Gradually most of the men left on their trains, and the lounge emptied out and quieted down. By midnight, only a few soldiers were left, sacked out in the armchairs and on the library couches. Nora picked up a sketchpad and a thick black pencil and settled contentedly into one of the leather armchairs, which smelled of rum. There was a soldier sleeping across from her on one of the couches. He was lying on his side with his back to the world.

Pad on her lap, pencil in hand, Nora studied him for a long time. Then slowly, gently, she drew the contour of his boots, his legs, his head and neck, pulling her pencil over his shoulder as if covering him with a blanket.

Out in Queens, Joe arrived just before Faye and the kids came home from church. He had to hand it to his sister-in-law: However lonely or sad she was feeling, she had done a swell job in decking out the place. The mantel held branches of juniper and mistletoe as well as the kids' stockings and bright red candles. The tree, in its customary place, was decorated with the usual cranberries and ornaments, though the kids had hung the glass balls from the ends of the branches; the effect, with the tips drooping, was to make the tree look sparser than it really was. Joe was tempted to adjust the ornaments, but he didn't want to correct Mike in anything that wasn't essential, so Joe just put his presents under the tree and slipped a silver dollar into each of the stockings.

He couldn't recall the last time he'd been alone in the house. Wandering past the living and dining rooms, he swung into the kitchen, which smelled of lemons and was, miraculously, spotless. Joe reached above the cabinets for the bottle of Old Crow that was now kept above Mike's sightline rather than Damian's reach. Sitting at the kitchen table, Joe poured himself a drink and silently raised his glass to the absent members of his family.

The noise at the front door was louder than he'd expected. This was not only the kids and Faye coming home from church. It sounded as if she'd brought half the congregation with her. Joe quickly took the last few sips of his drink and poured himself another. He tried to identify the voices, but Faye's was the only distinct one, instructing Alice and Mike to ask for people's coats and hats and bring them up to her bed.

When Joe swung open the kitchen door, he was greeted with cries of delight. Within moments he was engulfed in the competing perfumes of perhaps six churchwomen, all of whom were chattering, handing their hats and coats to the kids, talking about the Christmas choir and Father Gregory.

"Folks," Faye said. "Let's all settle in the living room. I'll get us some Christmas cheer."

Joe was relieved to see not one young single woman. Faye had either run out of candidates for him, or patience. In the living room, two of Damian's old VFW buddies had already taken one end of the

378

couch. A few others milled near the door. It was nice, Joe thought, to see people who had known his parents, however distant or unexpressed their memories might be. As for men of fighting age, other than Joe there were only two. The first, an old grade school classmate named Aidan Burke, had been classified 4F because he'd been born with a curved spine. The second, a cop from Finn's precinct named Steve Brady, had been badly wounded in the Solomon Islands a month or so after he'd joined up. One of his legs was still in a cast, and his face was so beaten up from shrapnel that it looked like broken bricks. Joe made sure Brady got a comfortable armchair and asked him if he wanted something stronger than eggnog. It took Joe a moment to realize that the woman who'd followed them into the room and was placing a hand on Brady's shoulder was Emma. Joe hadn't seen her since their date at the World's Fair in 1939. She looked older, she had changed hairstyles, and she was pregnant.

"Congratulations," he managed to say, looking from Emma to Brady and back. "When did you two —"

"Well," Emma said with a madonna smile. "More than nine months ago."

Someone had already put Bing Crosby on

the record player, singing the inevitable "White Christmas."

"Faye didn't tell me," Joe said.

Brady spoke for the first time: "She didn't want you to be jealous." There was more than a little pride in his voice.

Joe ladled out some eggnog for them. He didn't feel jealous, exactly. He was happy for Emma, who was still a peach, and happy for Brady, who'd plainly been through hell. It was more that Joe envied the seeming simplicity of what they would get to have: *treetops glistening; children listening.* Along with his dreams of travel, he had always assumed he would have that someday. Now having it would be meaningless without Nora.

Faye followed Joe into the kitchen with the nearly empty eggnog bowl.

"She looks great, doesn't she?"

"Who, Emma?"

"No, Joe, Mrs. Claus. Yes, Emma."

"She does," he agreed.

Faye put the empty eggnog bowl in the sink and said, "But Emma wasn't good enough for you."

"Actually, Faye, she was probably too good for me."

Faye turned around, her eyes narrowed. "That's it," she said. "You've got some girl in the city, right?"

Joe had known this question would come at some point, and now he nodded.

"It's that Laura from Finn's letter that Mike asked about, right?"

"Not Laura. Nora. I didn't know you'd heard that."

"Nora what?"

"Nora Lansing."

"That's not an Irish name, is it?"

"She's not an Irish girl."

Faye opened the refrigerator and bent to get a second bowl of eggnog. "They're putting this stuff away like water," she muttered. "Bunch of lushes."

"Faye," Joe said. "Emma was great. Emma *is* great. But Nora's the one I fell for."

"In love?"

"In love," Joe said.

"So why don't you bring her by?"

"Maybe I will sometime," he said, wishing he could.

"What are you hiding, Joey?"

"Come on," he said, taking the bowl of eggnog from Faye. "Let's get these people their booze."

Joe left by ten, just as Faye was organizing the crowd to go out caroling. At the front door he called for Faye and the kids to come over, and he hugged all three the way Finn did: an Irish-knot, four-way embrace invented by Damian and Katherine, adopted by Finn and Faye, and now carried out by Joe.

On the train ride back, the rattling of the car was soothing. Joe was glad Finn hadn't told Faye about Nora, had honored the No-Matter-What. Joe closed his eyes, and much to his surprise he felt Queens lifting away from him like steam. He was going back to Nora.

3
DID SANTA BRING ME COFFEE?

1942
Nora had stayed late in the lounge, finishing up what the girls now called the owl shift. By the time she got back to the room, Joe was fast asleep and didn't stir when she washed up and wrapped his present. In the morning he was awake before she was.

"Merry Christmas!" he said.

Nora ducked her head under her pillow. "Too early!" she said.

"Christmas morning!" he said.

She picked up a corner of the pillow and looked at him. "Are you eight years old?" she asked.

"Let's see if Santa brought you anything."

"Did Santa bring me coffee?"

"Why, yes he did!"

At that, Nora sat up.

Joe had brought them not only a pot of coffee from the hotel kitchen but a pot of thick, creamy hot chocolate as well.

"Coffee? Chocolate? Or a little of each?" he asked her.

"Oh, well, *now* it's Christmas," she said.

An hour later, they were wearing bathrobes and ready to exchange their presents. Nora's for Joe had come from the bookshop on the third floor of the Biltmore. She relished his lack of pretense as he unwrapped the package with one bear-paw swipe. She had bought him a Matthews-Northrup *Atlas of the World at War.* The cover read:

FOLLOW the Global War on
These Global Maps
COVER the battle fronts on
Dynamic Chronological Maps
REVIEW the entire background of
World War II
LEARN to recognize the planes of the
Allies and the Axis

Joe held the book, staring at the cover with its orange-and-blue globe and its illustrations of tanks, planes, and ships.

"Hey," he said, "this is really something."

"Open it," Nora said.

"I will, I will. Just give me a minute."

He stroked the cover.

"This is brand-new," he said.

"You bet it's brand-new. And it's got all the places where we're fighting."

He turned at random to a page with a diagram of combat planes silhouetted and stacked in columns. They looked more like toys than war machines.

The last letter Joe had gotten from Finn had been sent from somewhere in North Africa, a region about which Joe knew next to nothing. He found the page with the map of that part of the continent, where incursions and retreats were signified by tangles of arrows.

"I figured this could help you keep up with that big brother of yours," Nora said.

Joe closed the book and tapped its cover with his fist. "I've heard of these books," he said. "They're almost up-to-the-minute, right?" She saw his eyes gleam, and she put her hand on top of his fist.

He took a deep breath. "Your turn," he said. He reached underneath the bed and pulled out a box about the size of a brick.

"Merry Christmas," he said.

He was smiling so intently now that it looked as if his crooked mouth had been drawn on.

"What is it?" Nora asked.

"You expect me to tell you? Who *raised* you? Where I come from, that's why we *wrap* presents," he said.

She smiled and looked down at the box, which was covered in lovely Christmas paper: a painted pattern of holly and candles, in many shades of red and green.

"It's beautiful," Nora said.

"You still have to open it."

Smiling, Nora slipped her fingers under one of the end flaps. Careful not to tear the paper, she slid the box out. Inside was a plain business envelope, and inside that a letter on heavy ivory paper:

The Grand Central School of Art
ENROLLMENT

"Joe!" Nora exclaimed.

This is to certify that
Nora Lansing

She didn't have to read the rest. She jumped up and fell onto Joe's lap.

"You like?"

"Joe! Joe! Joe!"

"I did good?"

She kissed his cheek, his nose, his chin.

"And it's for the whole year," he said.

She stopped and looked down at the contract. It was true. He had paid for an entire year's tuition. For her. At one of the finest art schools in the country.

Tears in her eyes, she asked, "How did you know how much I've wanted to do this?"

"I get around," he said.

"And you won't mind —" They both knew the rest: mind that there would be yet another place where she would be going to do something on her own.

His answer was to take her in his arms.

4
VOILÀ

1943

Even though there were female ticket sellers on the Main Concourse now, there were no women in the art school. In fact, most of the students in Intermediate Painting were extremely old, extremely serious men, and they seemed absolutely flummoxed by the prospect of a young woman joining them as an artist.

But the teacher, Alphonse Fournier, took care of that handily. "No, messieurs, she is not here to model," he said, handing her a long blue smock like the ones he and the other men were wearing. Nora beamed as she put it on, and she felt at home immediately. The studio was warm and cozy and filled with wonderful smells: oil paints and acetone, turpentine and soap, pencil shavings and some sort of sandwich that sat, unwrapped and pungent, on the teacher's desk. Easels of varying heights and vintages stood in irregular rows, like untrained soldiers.

Mr. Fournier was an artist himself: talented, kind, and direct. He had white hair that was slightly yellow at the temples, and he stood bent a bit to his right. He had an almost comical French accent, and there was a twinkle in his eye that reminded Nora of Ollie.

Pale wood palette in one hand, Nora followed his instructions and squeezed out a dime-sized dot of each color from the several dozen tubes of watercolor paints arranged in a generous rainbow on a center table. He handed her a paintbrush as if it were a sorcerer's wand.

"You will take good care of that, will you, Miss Lansing?"

She nodded.

"Well, voilà, get to it," he said.

He walked over to his desk, clapped his hands, and held up his arms like a conductor. "Messieurs, mademoiselle," he said. "Today we start. Today we paint freely. No fruit. No bottles. No flowers. Today we do not paint what we see. We paint what we know."

The handle of the paintbrush he'd given Nora was cherry red, the bristles soft and, for a moment more, bright white. She dipped the brush into her cup of water, chose the darkest green on her palette, and let herself drive one stroke across the middle of the page from left to right. The color sank into the heavy, rough paper, a single fuzzy stripe across the page that she could turn into anything: the sash of an evening dress, the top of a kitchen table, the surface of a swimming pool — even the rich landscape that a person might have seen, say, on the way back from Stonehenge in 1925.

Walking around the room, Mr. Fournier kept up an intriguing monologue that sometimes sounded like wisdom and sometimes like pure bunk: "Let your pictures be a by-product of your life. Do not expect them to furnish life for you." "Try to find a motive for your picture that is universal in the hearts of men." "Love never loses sight of loveliness."

All that faded as Nora started to work. She remembered the hours after the Stonehenge sunrise, when she and Margaret, in a rented Citroën, had driven west to Bath. They had stopped by the side of the road so Margaret could have a turn at the wheel. The fields around them had been every shade of green, from velvet teal to scratchy yellow. Now Nora recalled those fields and painted them; then the sky and the gray wooden fence that had stumbled along the side of the road. She could smell the air, slightly salty. She could feel the breeze as the white cotton blouse she'd been wearing billowed warmly against her back.

She suddenly realized that Mr. Fournier must have said her name at least twice. She put her brush back into the water and apologized.

"This is nothing to be sorry for," he said. "This is what art can do."

"Excuse me?"

"Art," he said grandly. "It can shut out the war. It can even shut out the world."

For Nora, art was all the more wonderful because of the world it let in.

After class, Nora thanked Mr. Fournier profusely and walked through the gallery to get to the elevators. At the front desk, a stack of exhibition catalogues nearly obscured the chubby young man sitting behind them. Nora paused to look at the catalogue's cover: an impressive reproduction of a reclining nude.

"Can I help you?" the man asked.

"Just looking," Nora said, and realized that sounded odd, given the object of her gaze.

"That didn't sound the way you wanted it

to, did it?" the man asked.

Nora laughed. "You read my mind," she said. She introduced herself. His name was Leon Forrester, and it was clear that not a lot of people stopped to talk to him. He was pale and nearly bald, and the shape of his body — from his large belly to his small shoulders — formed an almost perfect triangle. Loneliness and *4F* seemed stamped onto his forehead. Nora would make a point of stopping to say hello after every class, and eventually that small kindness would lead to greater kindnesses from him.

For now, back in the hotel room, she changed her clothes, washed her face, and met her own smile in the mirror. No, nothing else had changed about her appearance. She had given up thinking she would ever age, but she took a bit of artistic pride in the bits of paint that speckled her hair.

Where was Joe? She knew there'd been a union meeting earlier in the day, but she was sure he would have mentioned it if he had a shift as well. She didn't understand why he wasn't here. Was it possible he had forgotten that they'd had to change rooms the day before? As she waited, she sang along with the radio, tidied things up, and tried not to let her excitement turn to impatience.

By ten o'clock, Nora had traveled from impatience to anger. Why was *she* supposed to leave a note every time she stepped out of her normal routine, yet Joe saw no such requirement for himself? By eleven, she was seething.

When Joe walked in and bent down to hug her, she could smell the sharp, sour odor of whiskey, and she pulled back. He looked embarrassed. He had come in holding a shopping bag, which he now put in the closet as he hung up his coat.

"How *are* you?" he said a little too loudly. Then he saw the look on her face. "Oh," he said. "You're steamed up. Really steamed up. Really, really steamed up."

She had seen him tipsy before, but she had never seen him in quite this state.

"What's in the bag?" she asked him, standing, arms crossed.

Joe was unbuttoning his shirt. He sighed.

"Do you not want to show me?" Nora asked. "I'm sorry if you think I'm prying. I know *you'd* be just fine with it if *I'd* walked in here, drunk, with no explanation and a big shopping bag —"

"All right," Joe said. He went back to the closet and retrieved the bag. He sat heavily on the couch and started to pull things out: a plaid cap, a red plastic shoehorn, a deck of Coca-Cola playing cards with a smiling blue-eyed stewardess in front of a winged bottle, and finally a stack of birthday cards that he dropped on the coffee table.

He was thirty-eight years old. He had turned thirty-eight today, under Nora's nose. Led by Big Sal at Bond's Bakery, his best friends from all over the terminal had thrown him a birthday party. Nora stared at him, letting this sink in.

Joe looked sheepish, and Nora didn't know whether she was more hurt or more angry.

He walked into the bathroom but didn't close the door, so she followed. He turned on the hot water and used his hands to splash his face and the back of his neck, then to sweep the usual stray bangs from his forehead.

"Why wasn't I at your birthday party?" she asked.

Joe said nothing as he reached for a hand towel.

"Didn't Big Sal or Alva or anyone wonder where I was?"

Joe dried his hands. "You were taking a painting class," he said.

"For God's sake, Joe, why didn't you even *tell* me it was your birthday?"

"Because," he said, trying to refold the

towel, finally balling it up and throwing it onto the sink, "I know you don't like to think about our ages."

Looking at him from the side, she noticed what she could swear were new lines beneath and beside his eyes.

"You turned thirty-eight," she said.

Joe saw how Nora was looking at him.

"See, I knew it," he said.

"Knew what?"

"Knew not to tell you it was my birthday. You hate this."

"Of course I do. I hate this. Don't you? There's fifteen years between us, Joe."

"I've done the math, Nora."

Nora stared back at him with genuine distaste. "You're really drunk," she said.

He started to put his shirt back on. "Come on," he said. "I've got an idea. Let's forget about all this birthday stuff. Put your coat on. Let's go find an apartment."

"It's too late to go apartment hunting," she said.

"It's never too late!" Joe said, flinging his scarf around his neck and throwing his coat on as the door shut behind him.

Whatever joy was left from Nora's painting class dissolved. Or rather, like one of the cats in M42, it scampered off, out of sight. No matter what time had done to her, no matter how hard she tried, she wouldn't be able to escape what time would do to Joe.

Joe wasn't really serious about looking for an apartment at this time of night. He walked north — past the Commodore Hotel, the Graybar Building, the post office. He had to admit that he was drunk, and he decided to keep walking, just trying to clear his head — of the booze, the fight, and the huge twin traps of time and place. Eventually he walked all the way to the East River. He found a bench and sat. He was sober now, sober enough to berate himself for thinking that hiding his birthday from Nora could come close to hiding the truth.

"But you'll see, honey," he whispered to her when, hours later, he came back to their room. "You'll see what it'll be like, after we get our own place."

Not bothering to undress, he climbed into bed beside her.

"The years won't matter," he said, wanting to believe it, and then he fell asleep.

5

LEXINGTON AVENUE
AND FORTY-FIRST

1943

The search for an apartment began in earnest the next day, when Joe started exploring different routes and destinations, using a surveyor's map he'd gotten from one of the engineers. Systematically, he marked off each path he tried.

Joe's reports on his searches seemed to overcome, or at least to balance, Nora's worries about the growing gap between their ages. On the nights when neither of them had a shift, they would eat dinner at one of their regular spots or pick up soup and sandwiches to have in their room. They might listen to a radio show, and after Joe checked the evening sports pages, the two of them would stretch out, end to end on the couch, and study the real estate ads in all the New York papers. As the evening wore on, they would take part in what became an almost nightly routine.

"It'd be nice if the dream apartment had a fireplace," Nora would say.

"I don't care about a fireplace."

"It'd be nice if it had a view."

"I don't care about a view. But you'll have to have light," Joe would say. "Light for your painting."

And Nora would snuggle her feet up beside him, allowing herself to be enthralled by his understanding and by the future it seemed to make possible.

They called each other "pal" and "honey." They looked back at each other — sometimes two or three times — whenever they parted in the concourse. They teased each other and played. Alone with her, Joe sometimes did a silly walk or spoke in a bad foreign accent. She learned to appreciate the subtleties of a football game. He posed for her — once even nude. She knew when his shoulders were hurting. He knew when she needed to stand outdoors. They took their coffee the same way — and never at Alva's.

On a warm, purple evening in the last week of April, Joe went south instead of north on Lexington and found himself standing before a six-story brick building with a coffee shop on the ground floor and what looked — from the windows he could see — like a mix of offices and apartments.

He was between Fortieth and Forty-first streets, just a block and a half down Lexington. Remembering the awful night at the Cascades, when Nora had started to flicker out, he was conservative with his estimate of the building's height: eighty feet tall, if that. The next morning, he borrowed the surveyor's tape again and measured the route. About 650 feet from M42. Nora could make it here easily, with yards to spare. All he would need would be a vacancy in the apartment house, a rent he could afford, and an absolute promise from Nora that a two-block taste of freedom wouldn't make a three-block or four-block taste become irresistible.

"Lexington Avenue and Forty-first!" Joe shouted when he got back to their hotel room. His arms were spread wide; his bangs were falling on his forehead like swipes of paint.

"You found it?"

"I found it!"

"How far away?"

"One block over and one and a half blocks down. And it's only six floors. So even if you stood on the roof on your tiptoes, you'd still be safe."

"Are you serious?"

"Don't I look serious?"

"Well, actually, you look kind of goofy," she said, but the way he really looked was handsome and proud. He lifted her in his arms the way he would have if there had been a threshold to cross. With one finger she scooped the bangs from his forehead and kissed him there, then on his cheek, then on his lips.

"And there's an apartment for rent there?" she asked.

"Oh, that I don't know yet," Joe said. He put her back down. "But it just looks right. And it's even got a coffee shop on the ground floor."

"So I'll have room to paint, and we'll have our own furniture, and you won't have to keep hunting down a Floating Key?"

"That's right."

"But what do *you* want?" she asked him for the umpteenth time. "What do *you* really want to have in the dream apartment? Other than me?"

"Hmm," Joe said. "How about running water?"

"Really."

"Or maybe electric light."

"You *do* dream big, Joe Reynolds."

He took her in his arms again. "Yes I do," he said.

They were agreed, and they were giddy. Two evenings later, never mind that they'd each worked long hours on their separate shifts, Joe and Nora decided to take the walk to Lexington Avenue.

It was the last week of May. Nora reached for Joe's hand, looking up at the cloudless sky, inhaling deeply, as if what she was hoping to smell was cut grass and roses.

"Come on," they said at the same moment.

On her own, Nora had already made several short trips outside, but this was the first time she'd be going farther than one block. As she looked down the street, Joe saw on her lovely face an uncharacteristic pallor. He knew that she was scared, and he was too, and they were both struggling to hide it.

With Nora's window still doubly blocked — by tar and by the servicemen's lounge — they both knew that any misstep might keep her out of the terminal for years. They passed a woman walking a poodle, another with a little boy. When they reached the corner of Forty-first, they looked up at the building across the street.

"This is it?" Nora asked.

"This is it."

"It's wonderful!"

"I've counted out the steps," Joe said. "But if it turns out I counted wrong —"

Nora said: "If it's too far, you'll pull me back, just like you did at the Cascades."

Joe braced himself exactly the way he did in the tower on the busiest days, the days when the trains came in three a minute and his whole body was on alert.

"Walk behind me," Nora told him, "so that way you can grab me."

He nodded.

She took a deep breath. "Here I go," she said.

It felt much the way it had during their first experiment, the one on the Biltmore's low roof. Holding Joe's hand, Nora went forward, taking each new step with her left foot, then bringing the right up behind it, as if she were leading him onto a narrow ledge. But she crossed the street without a hint of a flicker, and her hand never lost a bit of its warmth.

The building was red brick, with an entrance that sat under a high arched doorway.

"Another arch!" Nora said.

"I thought you'd like that."

"Just like my window."

She leaned against his shoulder and squeezed his arm.

It was too late to try to ring any bells or knock on any doors, so Nora and Joe just wandered slowly back to the terminal. The walk was magnificent: slow but not too timid, cautious but not too fearful. The sun had set, and the sky was turning pink. On Forty-first Street, defying Nora's proper upbringing and Joe's manly code, they kissed, right out in the open, as if they were any lovestruck couple out on a dizzy spring night.

After an owl shift, Nora would usually come back to the room to sleep, and if Joe wasn't around when she woke, she would either sketch at the window or pore over a stack of magazines. That was nothing new, but whereas before she had read the articles to catch up on the past she had missed and the styles, movies, and plays that were current, now she turned the pages imagining the world she would build with Joe. After all, a dream apartment would need to be furnished.

In *Cosmopolitan,* she found an ad for electric clocks: twenty-five models in all different styles. In *Harper's Bazaar,* she contemplated the colors and patterns of linens and linoleum tiles. Between those magazines and *Life, Look,* and *Collier's,* she weighed the pros and cons of different paint colors, toasters, glasses, tablecloths, and lamps. She saw other things they would need as well: soaps and floor waxes, whisk brooms and mops, and, most appealing of all somehow, an upright Hoover vacuum cleaner "for every woman who is proud of her home."

Home. Even in Nora's childhood, even in Paris, even in the first years of Manhattanhenge bringing her back, the word *home* had never meant so much to her.

6
YOU CAN'T MEASURE WORRY

1943

Home had a different, unavoidably worrisome, meaning for Joe. Out in Queens, *home* was still a bundle of obligations and memories, comforts and burdens. By mid-March, more than a month had gone by without a word from Finn, and Faye had summoned Joe to go to church and then help the kids plant a Victory Garden in the backyard. Sitting beside her in St. Anthony's, he could feel how frightened she was. There was fear in the way she sat — straight and stiff — and even in the way her flat eyes only pretended to focus on Father Gregory. Meanwhile Mike, on Faye's other side, slumped sullenly, jiggling his left leg on a restless foot, a habit of Finn's that Joe had never noticed in Mike.

In the pews, the congregation's many losses had become strikingly plain. Some of the worshippers wore black armbands. Others wore short black lace veils. Still others simply had the empty look Joe recognized as secret pain. Outside, the usual Lenten display had been set up beside the steps: the old jars of rocks, the purple cloth, and the just-cut pussy willows shuddering stiffly in the breeze. Joe looked on as the kids and Faye took out the small stones they had brought to add to the arrangement. Everyone was hushed. Standing in the church's wide doorway, Father Gregory seemed to be depending on the frame for support.

At home, as soon as the kids went upstairs to change out of their church clothes, Faye put her elbows on the table and her cheeks in her hands.

"So tell me, Joey," she said. "Did you give up this Nora for Lent?"

Joe glanced at the backyard. "I need to borrow a pair of Finn's work pants," he said.

"What are you hiding?" Faye asked. "Is she way too old? Is she way too young? She's married, right? Just tell me that."

"We've got a whole garden to plant," Joe said.

Joe could remember one long-ago spring — Finn must have been nearing his teens — when Katherine had insisted both boys help her with the flower garden that rimmed the brick-laid backyard. Joe realized now that their mother must have been hoping that the novelty would distract Finn from the rowdies down the block, the ones she always called "them maggots."

Joe could recall Katherine showing them how to test the soil in their palms, how it had to be moist enough to hold together but not so moist that it couldn't still crumble a bit when you opened your fist. And Joe could remember realizing, when the earth smelled like the potato drawer and the onion bin, that really it was the potato drawer and the onion bin that smelled like the earth.

Joe hadn't planted a single thing since then, nor could he remember having had a chance to spend a whole day working outside. But the Department of Agriculture had issued a call for Americans to create Victory Gardens, and all up and down the residential streets of Queens, little patches of green were being coaxed up and along. The idea was that if people grew and ate their own food, then more farm-grown food could get to the boys overseas.

Showing the flag was only part of the point today, Joe understood. The rest was to distract Mike, just as Katherine had done with Finn so many years before. Faye had

407

made Mike get the official garden planning booklet from the local home demonstration agent and had made him haul all the necessary supplies to the backyard. So when Joe, now dressed in work clothes with his sleeves rolled up, stepped outside, he found bags of soil and compost, a box of seed packets, some rusty trowels, a rake, a shovel, and a watering can.

Alice, herself in coveralls, squinted up at Joe. "Ma told us we're going to have to use the smelly stuff," she said.

Joe laughed and patted her head. Her short blond hair was already warm from the sun. "That's right."

"But then how do the flowers end up smelling nice?"

"They just do, peewee," Joe said.

Mike, wearing dungarees, was perched on an ancient iron bench whose sunburst back had once been white but was now brown and red with rust. He held up the instruction book. "Anyway, nitwit," he said, "we're not planting flowers. You can't eat flowers."

"Don't call your sister *nitwit,*" Joe and Faye said in unison. Their eyes met, connected by instinct — and by Finn.

For the first hour all four of them worked in near silence, alternately bending over to yank up what was left of the dusty roots and vines, then throwing them into a pile in the middle of the yard. Joe was enjoying the feeling of the sun on his head and neck. He wondered, as he had many times before meeting Nora, what it would be like to work outside — as a railman on a country line, say. In a small town, he could work in the fresh air, moving levers that were above-ground — for trains that came every three or four hours, not three or four to a minute — and he'd smell the steel and take the time to chat with the men unloading the freight. Having worked all these years in the famous towers of Grand Central, Joe would have the reputation to get a job anywhere. But maybe a small town would be too slow. Or maybe he wouldn't even work with trains. Maybe he'd be some kind of guide or scout in a place where nothing would be man-made except his clothes and the tools in his hands.

The sun climbed higher, and it got hot enough that he took off his shirt and worked in his undershirt.

"Jeez, Joey, your shoulders are broad," Faye said, a remark so intimate and out of place that it made both Joe and Mike stop working and look up at her. Uncharacteristi-cally embarrassed, she went inside, put the kitchen radio on the window ledge, and turned it around so the speaker faced the yard. She dialed up the volume on a station with musical-theater tunes. A few minutes later, standing at the screen door, she called above the music: "Who wants lemonade?"

No one helped Joe spread the compost, but Mike stepped up to shovel the fresh soil on top of it, and then Alice, a serious expression on her face, followed her older brother around the U-shaped bed, holding her nose with one hand and using the other to pat down the soil with a trowel.

By the time they were ready for the actual planting, it was already two in the afternoon, and everyone was ravenous.

In the kitchen they took turns washing their hands. Faye made them tuna sandwiches with her signature touch of cut-up pickles.

"Let's see those muscles," Joe said to Mike when they'd sat at the table.

"What?"

"Flex those arms."

Mike grinned and flexed his arm muscles, which bumped up like round apricots from his pink freckled skin.

"All right, then," Joe said. "You'll be doing the raking, and Alice and your ma will plant."

"And what will you be doing, Uncle Joe?"

Alice asked.

"I'll be watching you," he said, "just sitting in the sun."

They were finished by five and let Alice do the watering. It was what she'd been looking forward to all day, but she seemed disappointed when it was done. She stared at the darkened patches of soil as if expecting carrots, potatoes, and peas to appear at any moment.

"Give it time, peewee," Joe said.

By now the day had cooled, and Joe put his shirt back on.

Faye had brought out a hammer and nails and now pulled a heavy piece of paper from the seed box.

"Mike," she said, "let's go around front, and you put up the sign."

Joe could tell that his nephew was pleased. They all walked around to the front of the house to watch Mike proudly nail the government-issued sign to a fence post.

FOOD FOR FREEDOM
Our family will grow a Victory Garden.
Realizing the importance of reserve food
supplies, we will produce and conserve
food for home use.

It wasn't until the kids went inside that Faye, probably just too tired to fight it anymore, let her worry show.

"Do you think we'd know anything?" she asked Joe as they stood by the front door.

"Sure we would," Joe said. "You know. The mail just gets tied up. We'll probably get a month's worth of letters all on one day."

"I wish that day had been last week."

"I know."

Faye lit a cigarette and exhaled. "Are you worried? I mean, I know you're worried. But how worried are you?"

"You can't measure worry," Joe said.

"I just —" Faye took another puff of her cigarette. "I just don't know."

"Stay busy," Joe said.

"I just don't know," Faye said. "I keep thinking —"

"Don't."

Faye sighed. "But anyway, thank you for today." She said it without irony or teasing. Joe wasn't sure he'd ever seen her quite so incapable of either.

He put his hand on her shoulder. "Just keep doing what you're doing," he said.

"You really lifted their spirits today," Faye told him.

"It was nothing."

"You're good to me too," she said, and Joe again sensed the need in her, but also the exhaustion — not only from the day's work, but from the months of worry.

The sun lit up her hair, and for a shocking, illicit moment he wanted to touch it.

He kissed her on the forehead, but after that, as usual, she kissed him on the mouth. He felt, for the first time, the pull not just of attraction — that was easy to fight down — but the threat of something deeper, almost magnetic, as if Queens, if he wasn't careful, would draw him back into its orbit, and away from Nora's.

He found her in the servicemen's lounge, which was relatively quiet. She was drawing in an armchair, and she looked up, distracted, when she saw him.

"You look sunburned," she said.

"It was hot out there."

"How was Faye?"

"Worried about Finn but faking it."

"And the kids?"

"Well, we planted the garden. They were good. Pretty good, anyway."

Nora looked back at her sketchpad and started shading in one of the cornices she had drawn.

"How much do the kids know about me?"

413

she asked.

"Mike saw your name in a letter, that's all."

"And Faye? What does she think, that you're just this lonely guy who's never gotten a girl?"

"She thinks I'm in love with some girl in the city named Nora," Joe said, "and that I don't want to talk about it."

"You told her you're in love?"

Joe nodded.

"That's quite a coincidence," Nora said, finally looking up. "I happen to be in love myself."

A letter from Finn came the next day, and before Joe had read the first line, *no matter what,* underlined twice, jumped out at him.

Dear Squashface:

Here's all I can tell you. We started out rough and green, and the Panzers ate us alive. We lost a lot of men, dead, wounded, walked away. I didn't walk away but I caught shrapnel in my right ankle and my left knee. PLEASE don't tell Faye. This is the realest no matter what of all. Ever.

She doesn't need to know about this. I healed up pretty good, and so they let

414

me go out again.

It's weird but the hardest parts are when you're not fighting. Don't get me wrong. You piss your pants when the shelling starts. But at least you know what you're supposed to be doing. Anyway, I'm OK now.

You know I can't tell you much more than that, or it'll just be censored. But I can say I thought that being on the force in Queens meant I'd seen the bravest of the brave. Not to knock any of the guys back home. But these guys I'm with. They give courage a whole new ring.

I know this much. I'll never be sorry I came. You don't want to be born, live, and die in one place, like you leave just one dot on a map. I've seen the ocean and some hills and some towns and the desert. A lot of desert. Look up Tunis and Bizerte. Have you heard our theme song?

Dirty Gertie from Bizerte
Mattress cover for a shirty
Put a mouse trap up her skirty
Made her boyfriends quite alerty.

Come to think of it, that's another

thing Faye could probably do without seeing.

Sending you love and prayers for now,

Your brother,

Finn

PS How's that girl of yours? Still hanging around HA HA

"That's quite a ditty," Nora said that night, after he'd shown her the letter.

"Yeah, I know. But he's just trying to sound tough."

"Like brother, like brother," Nora said. "That 'one dot on a map,' though."

"What about it?"

"That got to you, didn't it?"

Joe was silent, folding up the letter.

They were sitting on the couch, and Nora moved a bit closer to him.

"Joe," she said softly.

"Sure," he answered at last. "But getting shot? Watching your buddies die? That's not how I want to see the world."

"How *do* you want to see it?"

Nora knew the real answer: Joe wanted to see it freely, happily, fiercely. And she knew he wouldn't say that, because to say it would mean reminding them both that he couldn't see the world and keep her safe at the same time.

"Someday" was all he said.

Nora waited another moment and then, with a flawless instinct for what could soothe him, she said: "Bizerte. Let's find out where that is."

As if giving him the present all over again, she handed him his atlas, and he took it from her eagerly. Running his fingers over the Bible-thin pages, he found the city on the map of North Africa, a true dot on a map, specifically a map of Tunisia. Tunis was south of Bizerte. Joe put circles around the cities, drew a line between them, and figured Finn's next letter might give him a new location and allow him to draw a new line.

7
MANHATTANHENGE SUNSET

1943

It turned out that there were no vacancies in the Forty-first Street apartment building, but even as Joe and Nora continued to comb the want ads, they made frequent pilgrimages to the spot. The war rolled and sparked beneath everything, like the trains. But it was a stellar spring. There was very little rain, and there were lots of cool breezes and the kind of light that seems so much more special than that of any other season, light that's emerged from darkness. On this Saturday evening, the last weekend in May, Joe and Nora were heading out of the terminal for a walk when they saw a crowd surging up the marble stairs to the front entrance.

"What's the fuss?" Nora asked.

"Don't know," Joe said, trying to see over the people.

"Maybe some movie star?" Nora asked.

"Maybe," Joe said. "Wanna see?"

They made their way up the staircase and found the source of the excitement: five fancy horses, with jaunty open carriages behind them and the word Saks emblazoned on their doors.

For a moment Nora was utterly confused, thrown back in time to the teens and twenties, when carriage rides were not a tourist novelty but a frequent means of transport. Feeling nostalgic, she walked straight up to the first horse in line. His mane and tail were braided with ribbons that matched the colors of the cart.

"May I?" she asked the driver. He was perched up on the seat, riding crop in hand and stovepipe hat on his head.

"Be my guest, miss," he said.

Joe stepped up behind Nora, intrigued as he watched her confidently show her hand to one of the horse's blinkered eyes and begin to stroke the bottom of its nose.

"How do you know how to do that?" Joe asked.

"I learned to ride when I was little," she said distractedly.

Nora slowly moved her hand from the horse's nose to its jaw and then its neck. With a little shudder of pleasure, the horse turned its head away from her, exposing more of its neck to her hand.

"Did you ever go riding, Joe?" she asked, dreamily petting the horse.

"Oh, sure," Joe said. "On all those family vacations we took out west."

"Sorry," Nora said.

"That's okay. In Queens the horses mainly pulled things, like fire wagons and wood and scrap."

"A lot better use for a horse than having its hair braided," the carriage driver said just as a gangly blonde in a WAAC uniform waved to him and approached with two shorter companions.

"It goes right to Saks?" the tall one asked.

"Right up to the door," said the driver.

"And you bring us back?" she asked while the other women looked on, excited.

"We do," the driver said. "Might not be me, but we've got crews coming and going."

"How much?"

"Free for anyone in uniform."

"That's it. Hop in, gals," the woman said.

As the driver helped them into the carriage, Nora looked on enviously.

The driver clucked and touched the horse's back with the crop. Nora started to follow along.

"Don't even think about it," Joe said.

"Isn't he beautiful?" she asked, still following.

"Slow down," Joe warned. "Not too far."

"I know," she answered testily.

Out on Vanderbilt Avenue, they turned left and came upon another small crowd, all looking in one direction as if they were listening to a speaker. There was no soapbox, though, and no speech. Only a bunch of regular people in light spring clothes, talking among themselves, checking their watches, and facing west. Right, Joe thought. Manhattanhenge sunset. It always drew more of a crowd than the sunrise did. You didn't have to get out at dawn in the freezing cold to see it.

Nora had never seen a Manhattanhenge sunset. She had only spent one spring in the terminal before now. Joe was amazed that he had been so caught up in their lives that he hadn't been thinking about it, but May 29 was a New York summer solstice, half a year after Nora's winter sunrise.

She stopped, spellbound, looking west toward New Jersey as a second Saks horse and carriage trotted on. The path down Forty-third Street was as holy and straight as a church aisle. Buildings framed the distant sky, pale yellow with a creamy line of clouds on top and a gaudy streak of neon yellow along the horizon.

"Looks like a slice of lemon meringue pie," Nora said, and Joe laughed.

"Well, this is Manhattanhenge sunset," he said.

"And look at all these people," she said.

"Yeah, a lot more than when you come, because then it's sunrise in winter, and it's pitch-black and bone cold."

With the other onlookers, Joe and Nora watched in wonder as a bright red sun slowly appeared from behind the most distant building on the left. A few seconds later, it sent forth two beams of bright red light that reached like elegant fingers around the building's corner. Next, on the opposite side of the street, more red light shimmered off the windows and streetlamps. Standing behind her, Joe locked his arms around Nora, feeling her warmth, sensing her excitement.

"Quite a sight, isn't it?" he whispered to her.

The crowd around them buzzed and chattered.

"It's a blessing," one woman declared.

"A blessing?" a man asked.

"It's a sign from God."

"It's just astronomy," the man told her.

"Well, who do you think made the stars?"

Gradually, over several exuberant moments, the sun made its progress toward the center of Forty-third Street. As it did, Nora unwrapped Joe's arms as if she were removing a shawl, and then she stepped forward.

At first Joe didn't notice. Like everyone else in that small congregation, he was spellbound as the sun gradually claimed its place on the altar of the city's horizon. But just before it filled the entire space — dead center — between the buildings, Nora let out a cry and lunged forward.

"Nora!" Joe shouted.

She dropped to the ground a few yards ahead of him and doubled up on her side in pain.

Like a soldier looking for a sniper, he spun around to find the perpetrator: the sun, the blazing light of the Manhattanhenge sun.

"Ollie," she said, her eyes shut tight.

Joe was terrified. Ollie?

He dragged Nora out of the crowd — springing backward, away from the sun and into the shade on the sidewalk, his hands under her armpits, no time for anything more gallant.

"Ollie," Nora repeated.

Even before Joe had touched her, he'd felt the heat coming from her. This was no fever, no natural heat. This was like machine heat: searing, explosive, dangerous. Nora's cheeks looked as if they'd been painted scarlet. Her eyes were still squeezed shut.

"Nora!"

She didn't respond. Sweat dotted her forehead. Joe had never seen her like this, never. Over the noise of the street and the horses, he was horrified to hear her moan.

Holding her was like holding a lightbulb that's just been removed from its socket. But Joe didn't let go until he felt her starting to cool. It wasn't until she opened her eyes that he pulled her to her feet, steered her gently into the terminal waiting room, and sat her down on one of the benches.

Hands on the worn wood of the bench, feet finding the subtle dips in the marble floor, Nora felt the pain ease, along with the heat and light that had overwhelmed her. Yet she was still caught up in the memory of the subway crash, the horror of Ollie dying, the panic of getting out, the smoke and darkness, the pain in her gut, the woman who'd pulled her to safety, and the burst of light on the concourse floor.

Gus the sweeper, who'd seen Joe bring Nora inside, had run to Mendel's for a loaf of bread and a cup of tea. Joe thanked him and handed them to Nora. Gratefully, she had a bite of the first and a sip of the second.

"I didn't flicker this time, did I?" she said. "It wasn't like the Cascades."

"No," Joe said. "It was more like you were burning, like you were going to explode. You were all lit up. And you called for Ollie."

"I was dying."

"Because of the sunset," Joe said. "It was burning you up."

"The opposite of sunrise," Nora said.

"Instead of bringing you here . . ."

"It was killing me."

They both understood. This wasn't what happened when Nora got too far away from M42; no trip to the in-between that could end when the weather and windows were clear. Nora would have been dead, for good, if Joe hadn't pulled her away from the sun in time.

They bent toward each other, their foreheads just touching. They hadn't expected to be in peril, so they hadn't expected to feel such relief.

"So that's how I could die," Nora said. "Could really die, I mean," she said.

"But you're alive, Nora," Joe said. "You're alive."

In her next painting class, Nora took a new

canvas and placed it on the easel vertically instead of horizontally. For a while she stared at it, trying to impose a mental image on it. With the lightest charcoal pencil, she traced a rectangle within the rectangle and perspective lines stretching to the four corners of the canvas, so that what she had sketched looked like the inside of a box. Then she put the pencil down and, for the first time, filled her palette with dollops of heavy oil paint rather than watercolors.

She started with thin dark-blue lines — the frame of the Manhattanhenge sunset. Thicker strokes of blue and purple followed — the suggestion of a canyon that could have been natural or man-made, could have been sides of buildings or sides of mountains. As the lines approached the left and right edges of the canvas, she let the blues and purples darken into browns and blacks. She wanted a perfect symmetry between the left and right sides because she understood that, just as at Stonehenge, the Manhattanhenge sun, so perfectly aligned, had cast no shadow on either side.

Mr. Fournier came by. "This looks as if it wants to be dark and bold," he said to her.

"Yes," she said.

"Something menacing."

"Yes," she said again. "Very menacing."

426

"I will leave you, then," he said. "But I will say one thing. If you are going to be dark and bold, be dark and bold in every way. In your idea. In your execution. In your heart. In your brush. Be dark and bold with your very soul."

Nora nodded, half inspired, half amused.

Between the horizon line and the bottom edge of the canvas, she created a collection of small rounded shapes in mottled colors — a suggestion of the heads and shoulders of the spectators. After that came the sky. But how could she paint the sun? How could she paint the light? Tentatively, then vigorously, Nora started, adding coat upon coat of white paint, filling the sky to the edge of the buildings, the bright canyon shimmering before her and obliterating everything else.

8
BRAT DAY

1943

Joe had only been out to Queens a few times in June. Ever since Nora's near death at Manhattanhenge sunset, he'd been finding it harder to leave her side. But Faye had made it clear that on July 3, his presence would be nonnegotiable — not in Queens, but in the terminal, for the annual circus that the old-timers called Brat Day. Every first Saturday morning in July, about ten thousand of the city's kids squeezed into the terminal — along with their shouts, tears, suitcases, and mothers — and went off to summer camp. The noise in the concourse — almost always a low, pleasant hum — rose and fell on these mornings with spikes of drama. The younger children cried, the mothers nagged and fussed, the older children played tag and tripped over the younger ones. Usually this was the worst day of the year, but the servicemen's depar-

428

tures for war had made the rowdiness of Brat Day seem a little more festive than annoying.

Most summers, Joe had made a point of helping to see Mike and Alice off, usually grabbing lunch with Finn afterward. This summer, in addition to Finn's absence, the difference was that both kids — now sixteen and eleven — were dead-set against going. Standing on the north balcony, Joe searched the concourse for the three of them. Signs bobbed above the buzzing crowd. CAMP WAH-NEE MEET HERE. ECHO CAMP MEET HERE. WABIGOON. BRIAR LAKE. There were so many bodies and signs that it looked like a union protest.

The loudspeaker faltered and hissed with static. "North Shore Limited! Departing Track Thirty-nine! Departing ten minutes for Harlem! Yonkers! Poughkeepsie! Albany . . ."

Eventually Joe spotted a bright pink dress: unmistakably Faye's. She and the kids were standing near the ticket booths, grimly looking around for him. He called their names and got their attention. "Stay where you are!" he shouted.

He ran down the ramp and staggered his way through the crowd until he reached them. Alice — wearing a pale-green gingham dress whose straps had fallen off her shoulders — was clinging damply to Faye's side, but when she saw Joe she ran to him, and he lifted her off her feet. Mike, in slacks and a short-sleeved button-down shirt, stood apart, arms crossed, wanting to make it clear that he was going as a counselor's helper, not as a camper.

"There it is, 4-H," Faye said, pointing toward the west side of the hall. "Come on, kids," she said. "Mike, help Uncle Joe with the bags."

"You take the big one," Joe told Mike.

Joe followed Mike as he followed Faye and Alice, the kid carrying the bag first with one hand, then two, then — embarrassed but determined — dragging it over the marble floor. It was comforting, in a way, to see Mike struggle. Since January, when the draft age had been lowered to eighteen, Mike had been agitating ever more passionately for the chance to sign up. Watching him now, Joe was secretly delighted to think that even if Mike tried to enlist, he wouldn't be physically strong enough to make the grade.

When they reached the placard for their camp, the kids had to pose for a group picture.

"Mike looks like he could actually hurt somebody," Faye whispered to Joe, her hand on his shoulder.

"He wants to be going to boot camp, not summer camp."

"He'll be fine unless he sees someone he knows."

The announcement came again: "North Shore Limited! Departing Track Thirty-nine!"

"Mama, no!" Alice cried, as if it were one word, and ran back to Faye.

Joe hesitated, seeing her face. "Are you sure this was such a good idea?" he asked Faye. He had tried to say it quietly, but Alice and Mike had both heard him.

"Can I stay, Ma?"

"Yeah, Ma, can we?" Mike asked.

Annoyed, Faye cocked her head at Joe and tightened her lips. Alice squeezed Faye's waist with both arms, nearly knocking her over. Faye mouthed the word *thanks* to Joe above Alice's head.

He shouldn't have said anything. They had talked this through on the phone several times. When he'd asked whether camp was too expensive, she'd said the 4-H was practically free. When he'd asked whether they'd be extra homesick with Finn overseas, she'd said they could use some fresh air. And when he'd asked whether she'd be too lonely, she'd told him she couldn't wait

431

to get a moment to herself. Joe didn't realize till later how much he wanted the kids to stay — not just because they wanted to, but because they served as a kind of buffer to what he sensed was Faye's growing dependence — and the temptation and confusion he sometimes felt with it.

Down on the platform, the North Shore Limited loomed. Staring up at it, the kids looked as if they were standing at the foot of a giant's castle. When a woman with a clipboard jammed against her waist called Alice's and Mike's names for a second time, Joe had to fight the urge to hold them back. But in one motion, clipboard still in hand, the woman slung an arm over each of their shoulders, keeping them clinched to her sides so that they couldn't look around.

"Bye, kids!" Faye shouted. She pivoted decisively to walk up to the concourse. Joe didn't follow immediately; on board the train now, Alice sat by the window, her large sweet eyes meeting Joe's. Faye reached back to grab Joe by the shirtsleeve and pull him along with her.

In the concourse, the crowd had thinned only slightly. There were still shouts from group leaders, scoldings from mothers, tears from children.

"She already looked homesick," Joe said to Faye.

"Let's go, Joey," Faye said.

"No, I've got to get to work."

"Didn't you tell me your shift wasn't till later? And I'm free. Come on. Let's go."

"I'm not sure I like that look in your eye. Where is it we're supposed to be going?"

"Just to the movies, Josephine," she said. "Don't get your panties in a bunch."

"Extra shift," he told her, and when she looked doubtful, he pointed to the crowd and said, "Have you ever seen a mess like this? They need me right now."

"Come by for dinner?"

"Some night this week, for sure," he said.

After her usual kiss on the lips, she slung her purse over her arm and strode off toward the street.

Joe hadn't told Nora that Faye and the kids were coming. He'd figured Nora would insist on meeting them, and the last thing he wanted was for either of the women to bombard him with questions about the other. But as Joe started back down the ramp on his way to Tower A, he glanced by habit toward the east end of the terminal and saw that Nora was standing there, waving at him from the edge of the servicemen's lounge. How long had she been watching?

Having waved her casual goodbye to Joe, Nora turned back to the lounge, where several sailors, just waking from their naps, were trying to figure out whose cap was whose. After she'd helped them sort that out, she needlessly rearranged the art supplies on the table.

She had seen how the little girl had scooted into Joe's arms, how he had picked her up, how he had let the boy carry the big bag, though obviously it was too heavy for him. Nora had seen in Joe an incredible tenderness. It was unmistakably a fatherly sort of affection: protective, supporting.

As for Faye, it was clear that no matter how Joe saw her, she clearly had plenty of feelings for him that were more than sisterly. And Faye was beautiful, there was no denying that. Even from a distance, Nora could see that Faye was tall and fair, with dark brown hair that wispily escaped the bun at the back of her neck. She'd looked worried and worn, but somehow no less lovely for that. It seemed momentarily unfair to Nora that whatever experiences she might have would never deepen her face into anything that showed endurance, let alone wisdom, let alone the kind of beauty those things could create. Even if Nora didn't exactly envy the lines and wrinkles that would eventually appear on Faye's face, she did yearn to be, like Faye, the same age as Joe. Watching him with Faye and the kids had made Nora's heart hurt. How much was he choosing to give up by loving her?

9
GESSO

1943

Waking the next morning to an already steamy July room, Nora dressed quietly so as not to disturb Joe. She had rubbed his neck the night before until her own neck and hands were cramped from the effort. He had been so worn out. She looked at him now from the hotel room door. His face, unshaven, was relaxed in sleep, though his cheeks had their usual scribbled-on look. His breathing was just audible: a warm, moist sound, perfectly even, steady, sure.

She stepped back into the room and dashed off a cartoon of the two of them, lying next to each other in bed. "Loving you," she wrote beneath it, left it on the pillow, and slipped out the door. She wanted him to feel that she was with him today. But with the images of Faye and the kids in her mind, she also needed to feel that she could be on her own.

She had started another landscape in painting class the week before, and as she set up her palette and brushes, Mr. Fournier walked over and stood behind her.

"Interesting," he said.

" 'Interesting,' Mr. Fournier?" Nora asked, smiling. "When you say 'Interesting,' why do I always think you mean 'What a shame!'?"

Mr. Fournier laughed. "No, no. It is just I observe something about your painting," he said with his wonderful French accent.

"And what is that?" Nora asked.

"Why do you never paint the people?"

Nora laughed. "I don't know."

"Or chairs? Or cats? Or bowls of fruit?"

"I can see people and chairs and cats and bowls of fruit whenever I want," she said.

"But not landscapes?"

She hesitated. "A lot less often. Anyway, I like landscapes."

"*Évidemment,*" Mr. Fournier said. "But someday, I must put a vase of flowers in front of you, there, *là,* and you will have no choice. You will have to live in those flowers."

"Yes. Someday," Nora said.

Mr. Fournier nodded and began his customary tour of the room, stopping to talk to each of the old men before settling at his

437

desk to eat his customary sandwich and turn on the radio.

As she worked, Nora thought again about Faye, the kids, and Joe, trying to fight her quiet, guilty resentment of them and even of Finn. The burden Finn's absence had placed on Joe — the need to be the perfect uncle, the perfect brother-in-law — was becoming more real to Nora, no matter how much Joe insisted on taking it in stride.

Nearly an hour later, Mr. Fournier was hovering behind her again. Palette and brush still in her hands, Nora stepped back to join him and survey the scene she had painted. She knew immediately that something was off. There was a line of trees clustered on the left side of the canvas that was deep and engaging, warm and inviting. Nora had painted these trees the week before, and she had layered on different hues of green and blue, able to imagine them from a distance but also up close. Today, on the right side of the canvas, she had added two trees that, by contrast, seemed flat and lifeless.

"These two," Mr. Fournier said in a confidential tone. *"Les deux."*

Nora laid her brush against her palette, as if she were putting a sword down. "Tell me," she said.

438

"I do not feel your sympathy with this picture," he said.

"My sympathy?"

He pointed to the trees. "You have had a little trouble with these two, I can tell. The more you worked on them, the more trouble they gave you, until finally you got angry with these trees and you left them to fend for themselves. But you cannot walk away from these trees. You see? You need to embrace these trees."

Nora smiled and nodded, as if she had just heard the deepest wisdom the world had to offer. It didn't matter that what Mr. Fournier had said was essentially gibberish. What was clear to Nora was that the picture didn't work. With only a bit of hesitation, and only a few minutes left in the day's class, she used a damp rag to wipe away as much of the scene as she could.

In one of her first classes, Mr. Fournier had shown Nora how to reuse a canvas by coating it with gesso. Now, racing the clock, she used a large flat brush to spread out the white chalky mixture, in effect creating a blank page. When the gesso dried by the next class, there would be only a wan green tint on the canvas, and she would be able to start anew.

"I made a mess in class today," Nora told Joe that evening.

He had asked her how the class had gone, but she wasn't sure he was listening. They were waiting on line at Bert's, on the lower level. Bert sold hand-cranked ice cream in spring and summer, soup and bread in winter and fall.

"What kind of mess?" Joe asked.

"A *real* mess. With my painting."

"I don't believe that."

A little boy who couldn't have been more than six was jumping and spinning with excitement, waiting for his ice cream cone.

"It's true. I was working on a new landscape," she said. She paused, aware that Joe was distracted. "It's hard to explain," she said.

"I know what a landscape is, Nora."

Nora raised an eyebrow at him. "It was about the kids," she said.

Joe braced himself.

"Faye's kids," Nora added.

"So you did see them."

"On Brat Day? Of course. Did you actually think I wouldn't look?"

Joe smiled faintly. "But I thought you told

me the painting was a landscape," he said.

"It was. But in a way it was also about you and me and Faye and the kids."

"How's that?"

"Well, I painted a whole group of trees together. A family of trees, you might say."

"Yes?"

"And then, on the other side of the canvas, I painted these two other trees, and, I don't know. They didn't look like they belonged."

"And you thought the two trees were like us?"

Nora nodded.

"Well, you were wrong," Joe said. "*We* belong."

He brought one of her hands to his lips to kiss, realizing that it was speckled with paint.

"Nice little rainbow you're collecting there," he said.

"I think you're missing the point," Nora said.

"What's the point?"

"The point is, we looked out of place. We didn't look right in that landscape."

He kissed her hand again, unwilling to be swayed from his own vision.

"We're making our own landscape," he said.

10
LONGING

1943

Joe thought he saw Finn. For just a moment, with Mike striding toward him across the concourse, Joe was nearly overwhelmed with joy. Next came the letdown of recognizing Mike as Mike. And after that was fury, because Joe thought that Mike, ignoring all prohibitions, had come down to enlist. Joe started toward him, intending to tackle him to the ground if necessary to keep him from the recruitment center. But as they approached each other, Mike didn't look at all like a rebel kid; he didn't look guilty or caught, and so Joe stopped walking and allowed Mike to come to him.

Their eyes met, and neither of them spoke. Mike reached into his jacket pocket for the telegram. Joe read it through tears. He didn't have time to look up before Mike flung his arms around him, and Joe realized that each of them needed the other in order

442

to stay upright.

Moments later, Joe felt himself almost physically grow older and more weighted down by the people he would now need to comfort, the decisions he would now need to make.

The telegram had come on a Tuesday in early August, the kind of day so sultry and oppressive that, everywhere but in the terminal, it seemed that all actions, even all thoughts, might just be crushed by the airless heat. That weather continued all week, which only added to Nora's sense that Finn's death had brought the world to a halt.

And she could not help Joe. She couldn't help him when he told the news to Alice, or held a sobbing Faye in his arms, or prayed side by side with the family and Father Gregory at St. Anthony's. She couldn't help him when he learned that Finn's body had already been buried in African soil, or when he found out that it might take months before Finn's personal effects were sent home — assuming they could ever be recovered.

Above all, Nora couldn't help Joe absorb the loss.

It was Friday before he returned to the

Biltmore and told her all he'd been doing. Nora had expected him to look haggard and sunken, but though the expression on his face seemed fixed into a grimace, his shoulders were back, and he was standing tall. Some combination of Irish stoicism and family pride, Nora thought. Then, too, this was just *Joe:* It was hard to imagine him breaking, no matter what the weight.

Nora put her arms firmly around his waist. His shirt was wrinkled and damp. She wanted him to understand that she had no needs. She wanted him to know that she could simply be a set of arms, unquestioning, untaking. But she could tell from the way he held himself that he didn't want sympathy.

She took a step back and asked, "Is there anything I can do for you?"

He sighed. "Just let me sleep, honey," he said.

She folded back a corner of the bedcover, making a perfect triangle, as if she were marking a page in a book.

"Come on," she said. "Get in."

Nora gathered her things and went for a walk. The air was motionless, humid, carrying the rancid scent of New York in summer, no different than it had ever been, even in Nora's privileged youth. She walked a few blocks anyway, noting, as she always had, the colors of the street: the cars, the billboards, the ribbons on women's hats. Later she would make a sketch of the man who had walked toward her carrying a shadeless lamp in a pack on his back, its tall metal harp seeming to form a halo above him.

Back in the lounge, she teamed up with Paige to tidy the bookshelves.

"Is he back yet?" Paige asked.

"Just now," Nora said.

"How is he?"

"He's tough," Nora said.

"Did he get more time off?"

Nora nodded. "His sister-in-law really needs him," she said, "and his niece and nephew too."

Paige put down the two thick books she was holding. "You must feel so helpless," she said, giving Nora the kind of hug that Nora had not been able to give Joe.

Nora straightened her cap, took a breath, and, with extra respect for the peril the servicemen were facing, went to see what they needed. She offered them coffee, food, books, games. What she wanted to say to them was: "Don't worry. Even if the worst happens, there might be life after death."

445

Despite her own situation, though, Nora didn't think she was proof of that. Even if she wasn't entirely alive, she had never been entirely dead.

Six hours later, she opened the door to the Biltmore room as quietly as possible but found Joe awake. He was sitting on the couch, still in his shirt and undershorts, his atlas before him on the coffee table. He shut the book quickly, as if he'd been caught at something, then crossed the room to place it at the back of the closet's top shelf. It seemed to Nora that he was putting the world as far away from himself as he could.

"Isn't there anything I can do for you?" Nora asked him.

He shook his head. "Nothing to do."

"How about a shower? A neck rub? A back rub?"

He shook his head again.

"But no shift today, right?"

"Not till next Monday."

"When do you go back out?"

"This evening," he said.

"So soon?"

"Faye's having some more friends over, and I told her I'd help out."

Nora walked over to the dresser drawer where Joe kept his odds and ends and pulled

446

out the deck of Coca-Cola playing cards he'd gotten on his birthday. She tried to mimic the smiling face of the stewardess in front of the winged Coke bottle.

"Care to play a hand or two?"

He sighed. "What's your game?" he asked.

"My game," she said, "is gin rummy."

Joe looked startled. "You know that's what I always played with Finn."

"That's sort of the point," Nora said. "I thought it might make you feel closer to him."

Joe stared at the deck of cards, then back at Nora. "I don't suppose you have some way you could get in touch with Finn and ask if he'd mind?"

"If you want to talk to Finn," Nora said, "I think you'll have to consult Madame Rosalita."

He smiled. She had made him smile.

"I should warn you," Nora said. "The rummy gods love me."

"You're going to regret this," Joe said. "I've been playing gin rummy since before you were born."

"Let me remind you, I was born before you."

"Don't get technical," Joe said. "I've *lived* a lot longer."

She tossed the pack of cards to him.

"Shuffle," she said.

He chuckled. She had made him chuckle. He sat back on the couch and started to deal the cards, the sweep of each one leaving the deck like the rhythm for a new song.

Though there was rarely anyone else in the oak-paneled Biltmore library, Nora found it a less lonely place than their hotel room to spend her off hours. Feet tucked under her in one of the deep floral armchairs, she decided to take on *Gone with the Wind.* Naturally, she had never seen the movie — no movie house existed within 850 feet of M42 — but she'd certainly heard about it. The book was 947 pages long. Paige had told her that a friend had fallen asleep while reading it, and that the book had slammed against her face and broken her nose. Nora figured it would keep her busy.

And it did — not only because of its steaminess and the suspenseful sentence that ended every chapter — but also because Nora couldn't help finding echoes of her own life in the pages she turned. In Scarlett O'Hara's background, she found Joe's stubborn stoicism. In the frivolity of Scarlett and her sisters before the war, Nora recognized herself and her friends from the 1920s. There was something else familiar about Scarlett too. Scarlett had grown up rich and pampered, adored by her father, courted by men. Then the war had come, and she'd had to face reality: death, loss, despair.

From time to time as she read, Nora would close the book and look up at the library's domed ceiling, a warm white field embroidered with intricate plaster patterns and brightened by six large, low-hanging chandeliers. Scarlett had been raised amid similar splendors, Nora thought, and so had she.

Given Scarlett's circumstances, would Nora have had the gumption to rescue Melanie, fight for Tara, shoot a Yankee soldier? Would she have ridden through the burning of Atlanta to get home? And by the same token, what if Scarlett had been in Nora's shoes? What if home could never be reached or rebuilt? What would Scarlett have done then? Would she have made a home in Grand Central? Would she have found Joe?

It had been three weeks since they'd learned of Finn's death, and when Joe came to the Biltmore now, it was only on nights when he'd worked a shift. He spent the rest of his free time in Queens. He was losing weight and looking exhausted, and half the time when he showed up, he was wearing clothes he'd put on two days before — or sometimes unfamiliar clothes that Nora assumed were Finn's.

Whenever Nora tried to embrace him, she could feel him struggling to stand still.

One night he let her curl up next to him in bed, and even though they were lying together, she felt only his absence.

"Tell me, Joseph," she said, gently lifting the wayward bangs from his forehead. "Do you think you'll ever want us to make love again?"

Joe closed his eyes and needlessly combed his fingers through the hair she'd just touched.

"I can't explain it," he said, his eyes still closed. "I feel like he's watching."

"If there's a heaven," Nora said, "I guarantee he's got better things to do than watch us."

Joe opened his eyes. "It's a feeling," he said flatly. "I can't let myself yet."

Nora knew that in her youth — her actual youth — she would have been hurt by Joe's absence. That wasn't what she felt now. The truth was that she had her art classes, her work at the lounge, her friendship with Paige, and her growing coziness with Big

Sal and Mr. Brennan, Alva and Leon. Naturally, she was missing Joe. But what she felt most strongly was the piercing rage of being powerless to help the person she loved.

"Come pray with me," Ralston Young said to Joe one evening as he was rushing through the terminal on his way to a shift. But Joe didn't have time for that. Or for drinks with the guys. Or for anything, it seemed, that wasn't an obligation. In Queens there were closets to be cleaned out, clothes from dresser drawers to be folded into boxes, supposedly awaiting the day when Mike would want them. There was paperwork involved in getting Finn's veteran's benefits to Faye, and it would be a while before that pension freed her from depending on Joe and on her own job for money. There were the kids — looking to him more than ever to be reassured that things would be all right, knowing that they never could be. And back in Manhattan, there was Nora. Unlike Faye, whose need was so vast that it seemed to lie in every corner of the house, Nora tried to keep hers hidden, but somehow that was only making it harder for Joe to be with her.

451

■ ■ ■ ■

Autumn came in, chilly and bright. Nora bought herself a modest but modern fall coat. Not counting her previous life, she had never had a coat that hadn't come from the Lost and Found — and, with the collar turned up and the belt fashionably knotted, she set out in early October for a visit to the apartment house. Today she intended to do more than look. At Lexington and Forty-first, it took several rings and at least five minutes before the super came to the front door. He opened it just enough for Nora to see half his face and a large, flesh-colored hearing aid. The device didn't seem to be much help; with his hand cupped behind it, he kept asking Nora to repeat herself.

"I'm interested in renting," Nora said a few times before the man seemed to understand. Eventually he led Nora into an overheated vestibule, the floor of which was a broken checkerboard of old black and white mosaic tiles.

"I'm interested in renting," Nora said one more time.

"I heard you," the super said.

"I don't need anything large," Nora said. "It's just my husband and me."

452

He looked her up and down. "Your husband not in the service? Why isn't *he* doing the asking?"

"He's a leverman at Grand Central," Nora said proudly.

"How's that?" Again, the hand behind his ear. Was he waiting to have his palm greased? Or maybe his hearing was really that bad.

"I might have something," he finally said.

"You might?"

"In a month or so, maybe."

"We don't need more than one bedroom," Nora said, still wondering if she was getting through to him.

He took her hand in his, yanking her forward a bit.

"Tell you what," he said, patting her hand condescendingly. "You bring your husband by next time, and we'll see what we can do."

"I think he wanted a bribe," Nora told Joe when they met at Alva's the next afternoon.

"Probably," he said.

"Apparently, women never rent apartments, at least not women with their husbands stateside. But he said to bring you by and he might have something."

Joe looked at her across the table.

"I can't now, Nora."

"I know. Because of Faye."

"Yes."

"And the kids."

"Yes. And all the things I need to put in order."

"But Joe, what if the dream apartment is just waiting for us?" she asked.

He sighed. "Then it'll have to keep waiting."

Nora felt her eyes fill with tears, and she didn't want them to show. It was the first time since she'd met Joe that she felt she was causing him pain — not annoyance, not worry, but actual pain.

Two days later Nora saw Faye crossing the concourse. She was wearing the same pink dress she had worn on Brat Day, but today it was mostly covered by a shabby coat. It stood out anyway, as did Faye's beauty. She was so tall, and her neck was so long and graceful. She reminded Nora of Alice in Wonderland after she's eaten the cake that makes her grow.

Nora had no reason to suspect that Faye had come to find her — not that Nora would have hidden if she'd known. She might have been subtler about the way she was sizing Faye up, though. Suddenly, she realized that Faye was staring back at her.

"You're the one, aren't you?" Faye asked, looking up at the balcony. "You're the one who's in love with Joey?"

Joey, Nora thought. That was new.

Nora could tell Faye was trying to sound warm and sisterly, but something hard and cold came through, as sharp as a blast of winter.

Nora wanted to say, *No, I'm the one he's in love with,* but she didn't.

"There's a place in back of the coat check," Nora told Faye. "Come on up."

She waved to get Paige's attention, and by a gesture across the heads of the men, she indicated that she was going to take a break. She led Faye behind the coat-check counter and back to the chairs where Paige and Nora sometimes took their breaks.

"How did you know it was me?" Nora asked Faye.

"He's described you. Red hair. Pretty. Short and perky. Servicemen's lounge. Also I thought I saw you watching us on Brat Day."

"I was."

"So, you work here, right? This is where Joey met you?"

"Well, we met in the terminal, yes."

"He said it's been more than a year."

"I imagine that's true."

455

"You *imagine.*"

"Yes. I suppose that's true."

"You *suppose.*"

Faye's repetition was mocking. Nora couldn't tell whether the target was what Nora was saying or how she was saying it. Nora realized she didn't want Faye to think she sounded stuck-up. Then she realized she didn't want to care what Faye thought.

"And you're married," Faye said.

"I'm what?"

"You're married."

"Why would you say that?"

"Because why else would he be keeping you such a secret? Why else hasn't he brought you out to the house? Since Finn died, we've had people there we haven't seen since we were kids. A couple of Joey's buddies from the tower even came. But not you. You've got to be hiding something."

Faye needlessly untied her ponytail, smoothed her hair out, and tied it back again. "Or maybe you think Queens isn't your kind of place?"

Nora shook her head, looking down, feeling trapped. She knew that Faye was in agony, but she was also being a bully. She studied Faye's hands, which were red and dry. She was still wearing her wedding band, and a man's watch with a clouded face that

456

Nora assumed was an old one of Finn's.

"You don't know him the way I know him," Faye said.

"Why is that important?" Nora asked.

"You probably think you make him happy," Faye said.

"I do make him happy."

"I'm sure you do. In some ways."

She didn't say it meanly. Their eyes connected for the first time — both of them loving him, both of them wanting him.

"We need him right now. His family. We're depending on him right now. But he keeps having to spend time with you."

"He doesn't have to do anything he doesn't want to do."

"Nora," Faye said softly, and hearing the softness was as surprising to Nora as hearing her own name. "Here's what I know. God wanted Joey to stay stateside and not go to war. Joey feels bad he couldn't do his duty. And now God wants him to take care of his family. And that's what he has to do. So whatever you're doing with him or for him, it's only tying him up in knots, and it's time for you to stop."

After Faye left, Nora's trip back to the Biltmore room was slow and sad. She made the rounds of both the Main Concourse and

457

the lower level. She spent fifteen or twenty minutes in one of the velvet rocking chairs in the ladies' lounge, just thinking. She sat for another ten minutes on one of the wooden benches in the waiting room, remembering how she and Joe had been here when they'd kissed for the first time. In one of the passageways, she ran her fingers lovingly along the majestic brass grille that covered a heating vent but was itself a work of art. For a while, she even watched Bill Keogh announcing the arrivals and departures. And then she stared up at the ceiling with its impossible, glorious, blue-green sky. She knew what she had to do.

At the Lost and Found, she traded five minutes of small talk with Mr. B. for a few fresh storage boxes. Up in the art school, she chose her two favorite canvases, wrapped them in brown paper, then took everything back to the Biltmore room. Packing up was easy. Nora and Joe had changed rooms every month or so, and she'd gotten used to traveling light — not that she owned much to begin with. It was strange to remember her trip home from Paris, the trunks she'd left for William to collect from the dock that winter night so long ago. She shuddered a little, wondering how long it had taken for Elsie to open them, what she had done with the clothing, whether she'd kept any of the drawings.

Nora packed up shirts and sweaters; dresses and skirts; shoes, hats, gloves, coat — all her clothes, new and borrowed. In a separate box she organized her books, sketchpads, pencils, and charcoals. Down in the hotel basement, she discarded her flapper dress — as well as other items that by now were torn or stained with paint. Back upstairs, she rolled her charm bracelet off her wrist, tucked it back into her old clutch along with all the cash she had, and left it on the dresser for Joe.

It wasn't until she had run out of tasks that she started to cry, circling the room helplessly, knowing that he might return at any moment.

Finally, nose red, she sat down at the desk and picked up a pen to write.

October 10, 1943

My dearest Joe:
I'm writing you this because I don't want you to spend even a minute looking for me or wondering why I'm leaving. I'm leaving because you have to be with your family now, because Faye and those kids need you to be their rock. It's

459

what Finn would have expected of you, and these last weeks have shown me that, even if you don't want to admit it, it's what you expect of yourself.

I know you'll be so mad at first, and you'll think I had no right to go without telling you. But I know that as mad as you are, it's going to be better this way. Not just better for Faye and the kids, but most of all, better for you. You can't keep trying to divide your heart between two homes.

I love you, Joe. And I know you love me.

Obviously, there is no way to know if I'll be back, or when. So please, please, live your life. It won't matter if that life ends up being in Queens or Grand Central or anywhere in the world.

Wherever you are, you'll know I love you.

Your
Nora

She left the letter on the dresser, took the elevator down to the lobby, and marched out into the street. If it had been a Manhattanhenge evening, would she have walked into the sunset to die? She was glad not to have to make that choice tonight. She was heading instead for the in-between. She knew her limit was 850 feet, and, crying, she made it three blocks, no more. Then, after a moment of looking back and a last ache of longing for Joe, she flickered out.

PART FIVE

1
SURRENDER

1945

On August 14, at 7:03 in the evening, the news began to glide across the zipper on the Times building in Manhattan:

TRUMAN ANNOUNCES
JAPANESE SURRENDER

Within minutes, more than two million people jammed the streets from Times Square to Grand Central Terminal, their joy and disbelief mingling with their shouts, songs, and prayers. Flags and servicemen's hats flew up; confetti, streamers, paper cups, and strips of newspaper fluttered down. Before an hour had passed, Broadway's usually flat charcoal pavement had been turned into a rippling paper sea.

Joe was at the Y on his way down to dinner when he heard the car horns honking. On the ground floor, he saw the men run-

465

ning out to join the crowds, and he followed them. He wasn't aware of having an actual destination until he had pushed his way into the terminal, through the concourse, and down to the subway platform, where people were standing fifteen deep. Joe managed to squeeze past the cops just before they started blocking the entrances so no one would get pushed onto the tracks. He had to get to Queens.

Train after train came, each one packed and raucous. It took nearly two hours for Joe to press his way into a subway car, and it had to be ninety degrees inside, and people were jammed against each other, smelling of booze, beer, and sweat. But no one minded a damn bit. At one point the subway car shuddered to a stop, and in the startled moment of quiet, someone started singing "Auld Lang Syne." Even as the train restarted, dozens of reverent voices joined in:

Should old acquaintance be forgot
And never brought to mind . . .

What was the last thing Finn had thought? What was the last thing Finn had seen? And why couldn't some magical trick of nature have brought him back to life too? The bodies around Joe were so close that he couldn't actually raise a hand to wipe the tears from his face.

In Queens, someone had hanged Hirohito in effigy from a lamppost. The taverns Joe passed had dragged their jukeboxes out into the street, so every few blocks, Joe encountered groups of people jitterbugging to a different tune.

Faye greeted Joe at the door with the hug of a lifetime. They both seemed to find it hard to let go.

He felt her tears against his neck. "Oh Joey!" she said. "He's not going to have to go!"

Joe looked over her shoulder to see Mike, frozen on the staircase, caught painfully between relief and regret. The kid had longed to be a hero, and Joe knew he should try to console him. But standing there solemnly, in a short-sleeved white shirt and dark pants, Mike looked more than ever like a young Finn, and by instinct all Joe really wanted to do was make him laugh and keep him safe. Stepping inside the house, Joe reached up the stairs to shake Mike's hand.

"Tonight," he said, "we'll drink Old Crow together and toast your pa."

That coaxed a faint smile.

Alice, now thirteen, came running through

467

the front door and had almost reached the kitchen before she noticed Joe.

"Where've you been?" Joe asked her. He doubted he would ever get used to this flighty, teenage version of his niece, let alone to the freedoms Faye granted her. He could still see the little-girl softness beneath the angles that were starting to shape her face, but now she was nearly as tall as Faye.

"Up the street," she said, slightly out of breath. She smoothed her crimson skirt with one hand and tried to straighten her blouse with the other. "It's so wonderful! Everyone's out dancing! I just came in to ask Ma if I can stay out!"

"Not unless Mike goes with you," Faye said.

"Aw, Ma," they said in unison, then simultaneously turned to Joe, wordlessly seeking a different verdict.

"Maybe let her go for an hour?" Joe asked Faye.

"The two of you, or neither," Faye said. "That's my final offer."

They were out the door a few minutes later.

"You know," Joe said, "there's nothing to stop them from going their separate ways once they're out there."

"Of course they will," Faye said. "But I

wanted to make sure they both got out of here."

Together they walked into the kitchen.

"What's to eat?" Joe asked, settling at the table.

"I almost gave up on you," she said.

"I would have called," Joe said, "but it's a nuthouse out there."

"What's in your hair?" she asked him.

"What?"

"All this garbage."

Joe bent over and shook his head. Faye ruffled his hair, and bits of paper spilled onto the black-and-white-checked floor.

Faye bent over to pick one up. "Is this a *gum* wrapper?" she asked.

"Probably," Joe said with a laugh. "People were making confetti out of anything they could find."

Faye opened the refrigerator. "I've got tuna salad, American cheese, a little leftover meatloaf, some Victory Garden carrots, and a whole lot of beer."

"Beer," Joe said. Faye handed him two bottles. "And some of everything else," he added.

He was ravenous. "Lord, but you know your way around a meatloaf," he said, clinking bottles with Faye.

They polished off three bottles of beer

469

each in no time at all, toasting every few minutes. "To Finn, the best brother." "To Finn, the best husband." "To Finn, the best father." "To the kids." "The men." "Roosevelt." "Truman."

"To you, Joe," Faye said, "for getting me through."

"And the same to you," Joe said.

That was what had happened. They had gotten each other through. In those first months after Finn's death, Joe had practically lived in Queens, helping Faye with the house, the bills, the army paperwork — even the groceries and the gutters. Faye had been endlessly grateful to him, but the truth was that Joe wouldn't have known how to mourn Finn without being able to help his family.

When Joe discovered Nora's goodbye letter, he had been furious at first. He had reread it so many times that its words had become as fixed in his mind as the Pledge of Allegiance or the Lord's Prayer. He had moved back to the Y just days afterward, bitterly taking all Nora's things with him. He had stashed her paintings in his closet and stacked her boxes in a corner. Sometimes he had loved the reminders of her, and sometimes he had resented them. Even outside his room, though they had been everywhere: the Whispering Gallery, Alva's, the Biltmore, the east balcony, the north balcony, the gold clock itself. The terminal, which had once been his, had at some point become theirs. One night he had balled up her letter and thrown it into the fire at the Y. Eventually, though, he had come to feel that what Nora had written to him was right. It had been a relief, as she had suggested, not to try to divide his heart between two homes.

Joe had gone to church with the family on Sundays and knelt beside Alice when, at eleven, she had her first communion. He had eaten Faye's meatloaf and casseroles at the old house weekly, encouraged her to speak up for a raise, and — when Mike announced that he'd decided to train as a cop — reminded her that Finn hadn't been any older when he'd joined the force. Joe felt for Faye, left with a war widow's pension and the boxes of Finn's clothes that she still claimed to be saving for Mike. Joe sensed that she just couldn't let the things go. She was thirty-nine. Everything about her — from her once-youthful body to the look in her eyes — had gone flat.

But right now, with a beer in one hand, a pencil stuck in the bun on her head, and wisps of hair tattooing her neck, she looked

471

at Joe with a vibrant smile, and he couldn't recall the last time he had seen her this happy. Maybe the day she and Finn had gotten married, or maybe on the Sunday when they'd baptized Mike.

In all this time, grief had bound Joe and Faye together, even as it had kept them sheltered from other people. In their two-some, they had often been tempted to soothe their loneliness with sex, but they had always managed to pull back. Tonight, however, lubricated by booze, relief, and joy, they both seemed to be feeling something deeper than need or loneliness, and Joe had no interest in resisting it.

At around nine, he and Faye drained the last of their beers, put the bottles down, flashed each other a look, and leaned in. Her customary kiss had always been an invitation, her lips just parted, available. Tonight, finding Joe willing, her kiss had force and purpose. Trying not to separate, they stood up on either side of the table, stepped awkwardly beside it, and locked into a kiss that felt neither entirely right nor entirely wrong. They broke it off after a few minutes. Alice and Mike would be coming home soon, and Finn, in a sense, had never left. Even on this night of celebration, kissing was as far as Joe and Faye could comfortably go.

Joe slept that night for what seemed like the thousandth time on the living room couch, which smelled — not unpleasantly — of the sawdust that occasionally leaked from its cushions. There was no point in trying to get back to the Y. The festivities would still be going strong, and however strange it had been to kiss Faye, Joe was certain it would be even stranger if he seemed to be slinking away.

"Get the blankets for Uncle Joe," Faye said around eleven, when Mike and Alice came home.

Uncle Joe, he thought as he rode the subway back to the city the next morning. Wasn't that who he was supposed to be?

Throughout the rest of that summer and fall — through the formal surrender of Japan, the formation of the United Nations, the Tigers winning the World Series — Joe took turns being Steady Joe Reynolds at the terminal, Uncle Joe with Mike and Alice, and, for Faye, just Joey, every few weeks, when they had enough time to be alone.

They had gone no further than kissing and cuddling, but Joe no longer cared if he was betraying one person, two, or neither. Finn

473

was dead. Nora had left, and who knew, who really knew, if she would ever come back? Though the servicemen's lounge was slowly being dismantled, the windows were still blocked by tar.

In the first months after Japan's surrender, most of the country was still rediscovering itself, peacetime only gradually becoming the trusted state of affairs. In the terminal, the hospital trains continued to come in, usually a dozen cars long, each of them completely filled. The cars had been configured with lower and upper sleeping berths, with lower and upper windows, so that all the patients could have light. But when the trains arrived, it was still miserable to see the wounded men peering out from their separate berths, finally home but looking so lost. There were war brides arriving almost daily too, women who'd crossed the Atlantic, often with babies, to board trains bound for homes they'd been promised by soldiers they hardly knew. In the continuing chaos of the terminal's traffic, Joe's dreams of travel were once again tethered to the Piano and to the railroad tracks.

Yet bit by bit, a new world was emerging. The wartime rationing ended; the price controls were loosened. Women were dressed a bit better, with longer skirts, cinched waists, and shiny shoes, and the soldiers and sailors who hadn't been wounded were camouflaged now by civilian clothes. Bright colors bloomed, making everything seem more blessed and triumphant.

"You know, Joe," Faye said on Christmas Eve after the kids had gone up to bed. "We could go somewhere."

"Somewhere like where?"

"Like, I don't know. Like the Jersey Shore. Like Connecticut. Upstate New York. A weekend away, you know?"

He knew what she was asking for, and he had mixed feelings about it, but he said, "I'll make the plans."

"Good."

"But what'll we tell Mike and Alice?" he asked.

"We'll tell them we're going away for a weekend," Faye said. "You think by now they haven't figured things out?"

2
ONE NIGHT

1946

The newspapers were calling it "Victory Vacation Year," and ads were showing up everywhere for resorts in Cuba, Bermuda, Florida, New Hampshire, and, closer to home, Atlantic City. Joe had promised Faye, with a hint of mystery, that he would plan their trip, but there were so many choices that he ended up with the most obvious one: Atlantic City. He had heard a lot about the place long before the war: the ocean, the boardwalk, the games, the girls. Atlantic City existed as one of the fixed destinations on Joe's mental map of the country, one of the places he'd always imagined going. Studying the leisure ads in the *Herald* and the *Times,* he chose — in the end, just because he liked the name — a hotel called the President that was right on the board-walk.

He made the reservations for a long

weekend starting March 21: not so cold that they couldn't walk on the beach, but not so warm that the best rooms would already be booked. For the occasion, he bought himself a couple of short-sleeved plaid shirts, a pair of gray twill trousers, and the first suitcase he'd ever owned. He allowed himself to get excited about it. Maybe, he thought as he made these purchases, they were the wardrobe of the life he was intended to start living.

Trains to Atlantic City left from Pennsylvania Station, not from Grand Central. Waiting for Faye beneath the dark steel framework of a ceiling that rose even higher than Grand Central's, Joe couldn't help feeling he was in the wrong place, which was hard to separate from worrying that he was doing the wrong thing. Faye didn't seem too certain, either. She greeted him wearing a pale hat and a nervous look, neither of which was typical for her.

On the train, she took out a pack of cigarettes and a pack of cards and suggested they play gin, but Joe had bought a newspaper and said he'd rather read it. Shrugging, Faye lit a cigarette and leaned back in her seat. Joe figured she would think the cards reminded him too much of Finn, and they did, but it was the banter with Nora that he didn't want to remember right now. He could hear her saying "That's how you shuffle?" and "Nice going, pal."

If he didn't want to play cards with Faye, how did he think he'd be able to make love with her?

Faye was knocked out by the room. It had two small beds, a low dresser, and an easy chair. For Joe, it couldn't hold a candle to the smallest, least tended of the Biltmore rooms, and that was not just about Nora. There was something pale and worn about this room in the President, as if not only the drapes but the bedspreads, the rug, and the very walls had been faded by too many seasons of sun. Joe was happy that after a quick freshening up, Faye seemed as eager as he was to leave their bags unpacked and go see the sights.

They stepped out of the hotel onto the boardwalk, and for possibly the first moment in his life, Joe didn't just recognize but truly felt the bigness of the world. The boardwalk was almost as wide as the beach, and the two stretched together, in both directions, into the shimmering distance. It was thrilling. The breeze was filled with moisture, and the sky went on forever. Just for that moment the past receded, and anything seemed possible.

It wasn't close to being warm enough for swimming, but the beach was crowded and busy anyway, dotted with folding chairs, striped canopies, umbrellas of every color, signs for food, women in bright spring dresses, men in light-colored jackets. Faye and Joe kept to the boardwalk and followed it to the Steel Pier, with its loud and crowded attractions: Ferris wheel and merry-go-round, fairground games and puppet shows, acrobats on high wires, and an enormous seal named Jumbo whose barks nearly drowned out the swing band. Like the other visitors, Joe and Faye stopped here and there, listening, watching, occasionally laughing. The smells were nearly overwhelming: hamburgers, fried chicken, funnel cakes, popcorn. Everyone seemed so happy, and though plenty of men were still in uniform, this was a country no longer at war.

The big draw — and the reason Faye had insisted they visit the Steel Pier before any of the others — was the so-called High Diving Horse, a large brown mare that, with a woman rider holding on for dear life, was said to jump from a forty-foot-high platform into a fifteen-foot-deep pool of water. Faye was the one who had told Joe about this.

He had thought she was pulling his leg, but a girlfriend of hers had sworn she'd seen it on a visit before the war. So they stood in a line for quite a while until they could buy their tickets, settle into their seats, and wait with the rest of the crowd. Finally, at exactly one o'clock, after a dramatic buildup by an announcer, a huge horse started trotting up the ramp to a towering platform, and Faye buried her face in Joe's shoulder.

"Faye!"

"I can't look!"

"Faye! You'll miss it!"

"Tell me when it's over!"

One moment the horse was on the platform, a girl in a sparkly blue bathing suit straddling its back, and the next moment it went falling nose first, almost parallel to the tower. Straight down, like a locomotive plunging over a cliff.

On the way back to the boardwalk, Joe gave Faye the kind of grief that she would have given him if the roles had been reversed.

"I can't believe you chickened out. Brought us all this way —"

A little farther on, Faye insisted they stop at a booth where birds were chirping and fortunes were being told.

"Don't you want to know the future,

Joey?" she said, flirting, and he realized at that moment that the only future he was interested in was the night ahead of them. All other futures were tied up with larger doubts. But Joe smiled and paid a dime so Faye could have her fortune told, and then a bright yellow parakeet hopped up a narrow plank into a dollhouse, where it pecked a slip of yellow paper from a pile and delivered it, by beak, into Faye's waiting hand.

"Well?" Joe asked. "What's it say?"

Faye lit a cigarette and exhaled, unfolding the yellow paper.

"Hah!" she said. "Perfect!"

"Yes?"

She read it to him: " 'Elegant surroundings will soon be yours.' "

"Has the bird seen the drapes upstairs?"

Faye laughed. "Your turn," she said.

"Nothing doing."

"Come on, Joey. Let's see what's in store for you."

With exaggerated grumpiness, he put down another dime and watched the yellow bird do its work, hopping up the little ramp, bringing back another folded note.

"Well?" Faye asked.

"I don't know," Joe said. "Some people say you shouldn't know the future."

481

"Now who's chicken?" Faye asked, and grabbed the paper from him, shielding it from his grasp. " 'You will have quarrels, lawsuits, and family disagreements,' " she read.

She crumpled up the paper and tossed it, comically, over her shoulder. "I don't see a family disagreement right now," she said. She pushed up the brim of her hat, leaned forward, and kissed him.

By early evening, it seemed the families had disappeared and there were mostly couples left on the boardwalk. Joe and Faye headed back to the President, somewhat awkwardly hand in hand, and although Joe was certain that they wanted the same thing, he wasn't sure they wanted it for the same reason.

In the end, they spent only one night in Atlantic City. It seemed clear to each of them that they had confused need with desire.

Joe woke in the morning to find Faye already showering. Maybe she was trying to wash him away. Maybe she was a better person than he was — certainly she was a better Catholic — and maybe she was more wracked by guilt about Finn than he was. He didn't actually feel guilty as much as he felt a quiet disappointment that Faye had turned out to be a station, not a terminal.

Before they left, they stopped at the legendary saltwater taffy place. They each chose a flavor for the other to try, and they bought a box to take back, the souvenir of a trip that neither of them would end up wanting to remember.

They rode the train home as brother- and sister-in-law. In Grand Central Terminal, Joe walked Faye to the Queens line. For the first time since he had met her, back when they were teenagers, she kissed him on the cheek instead of the mouth.

3

UP IN THE AIR

1946

After Atlantic City, Joe let himself want
Nora again. For more than three years, he
had kept her tucked into the back of his
mind, along with other things he'd lost: his
brother's laughter, his mother's voice, his
faith in Damian's heaven. Until now, he had
left Nora's boxes unopened, thinking that
might help keep his thoughts about her
locked up as well. But on a spring evening
close to Manhattanhenge sunset, he opened
one of her boxes and found, near the top,
the green dress they'd bought together the
morning she'd met Finn. Gathering it up in
his large hands, bringing it to his face, he
inhaled as deeply as he could, longing for
the sense and the powdery smell of her,
finding or imagining it — despite the years
that had gone by — still deep in the threads
of the cloth.

Among her things, too, Joe found stacks

of sketches, many of them with Nora's initials in the lower right-hand corner. Some were views of the terminal done from different angles and distances: details he knew like the back of his hand but had never quite noticed. Others were drawings of Joe that Nora had done without his knowledge. He saw himself as she'd seen him: serious, sleeping, laughing — and always a little more handsome than he'd ever thought he was. He wished she had left him a self-portrait. But especially at night, in the gray and brown shadows that came before sleep, he had no trouble remembering her body and her face.

With the servicemen's lounge now dismantled, the question was whether the east windows could be cleaned in time for Nora's sunrise. The one remaining barrier was the layer of black paint and tar that still coated the hundreds of windowpanes. But in May, as in buildings throughout the city, teams of window washers had finally been hired to rub and scrape the stuff away, and Joe no longer passed through the concourse without checking on their progress. To him it seemed that these workers lacked the urgency so many men had shown during the war. He would look up on his way to or

485

from a shift and see them taking what seemed like far too many breaks. No matter the time of day, some of them would always be sitting in the catwalks between the outer and inner windows, drinking coffee, having a smoke, chatting among themselves.

Toward the end of May, the entire country's railroad unions — including the BRT — went on strike, and Joe, waiting for a settlement, volunteered to pitch in on the windows. At the rate the window washers were going, who knew how long they would take, and until there was a chance of another Manhattanhenge bringing Nora back, Joe felt as suspended in his life as the men were in the windows.

He had never been wild about heights. Once, Jake had invited him up to see the works of the thirteen-foot-tall Tiffany clock that adorned the terminal's main entrance, the clock Jake called the Big Fellow. Its famous face was made of stained glass: a petal-like yellow sun on a turquoise field, with white Roman numerals set into deep-crimson circles. The circle holding the numeral VI was hinged, which allowed it to open so a narrow platform could be guided outside when maintenance was needed. Jake's was a prized invitation, the clock room a hallowed spot, and Joe had been thrilled to stand there beside Jake. Yet even climbing up the worn iron ladders to the room, he had felt as if the world were shifting beneath him. So, despite whatever temptation he had to see the view from that special perch, he had laughed when Jake offered to slide him outside on the platform.

Today, a Wednesday at the end of May, Joe took his first steps onto the lowest of the four east window catwalks. To his right were the blacked-out windows facing the street; to his left were the clear ones facing the concourse. Beneath him was a floor of thick, opaque glass. Before him were a bunch of guys accustomed to dangling like spiders at all heights of the terminal, outside and in. Joe knew they'd see he was edgy, and he tried his best to hide it. The view of the concourse, even from this lowest level, made him catch his breath. Every person crossing the floor below looked like a toy soldier; the gold clock seemed small enough to strap onto a wrist. Joe was grateful that the windows needing to be cleaned were the ones on the street-facing side of the catwalk, so he could turn away from this dizzying view of his daily world.

Doug Cafferty was the head of the work detail, and he must have sensed Joe's discomfort, because he strode toward him on the catwalk and clapped him on the shoulder warmly. "Grateful for the help," Cafferty said. "These are some big fucking windows."

Joe nodded and, careful not to look down, followed him back along the narrow passageway, past a dozen or so men, to a small supply room.

"Don't be a hero," Doug said, handing Joe the necessary tools. "If you can do one pane in a day, that's going to be plenty. This stuff was slapped on fast, but it comes off slow."

"Got it."

"And watch out for Crazy Mabel," Doug added.

"Crazy Mabel," Joe repeated. He had forgotten the bunch of Grand Central's ghostly characters that Gus had once described.

"They say this is where she shows up," Doug said, winking. "So far we haven't seen her."

Joe's arms were strong from years of pulling the levers, but scraping and wiping the windows, sometimes a square inch at a time, demanded a slightly different set of muscles. Also a different kind of patience. Despite those requirements — and despite the prickly fumes of the turpentine — Joe did manage, on this first day, to clear one whole pane of glass. The simplicity of this work was surprisingly satisfying: After the right combination of solvent, scrubbing, and scraping, a whole chip of tar or paint might pop clean off.

Sipping a cup of coffee — Joe now understood why the men seemed to take so many breaks — he realized he was closer to the concourse's painted sky than he had ever been. Whether it was the height or the turpentine or something else, he found himself envisioning Finn. What part of heaven had been above Finn's head when his unit had been shelled into dust? Was there a heaven after all? Was it like the dark ether on the other side of Nora's in-between? Or was there something beyond that: the heaven Damian and Katherine and Father Greg had always tried to sell him, a heaven where Finn and his parents might be watching over him?

The rail strike was settled within a week, but Joe continued on the catwalks on his days off from the Piano. As the weeks went by he became used to the height. Even on the top catwalk, where the windows formed the arches, he had no trouble looking down at the concourse now. But most of his focus remained on the world outside the terminal, and as the tar fell away, his view of Forty-third Street grew from keyhole to knothole to porthole. While the work progressed and the view widened, buildings rose behind shop signs and doorways; avenues appeared beyond corner streetlamps. And each day a little more sunlight came through the glass the men had cleaned. From the floor of the concourse, the still-dark panes on the top catwalks seemed to form an enormous but rising black shade.

4
EMPTY AS A KETTLE

1946

The double jobs of leverman and tar scraper left Joe useless for most activities at the end of the day. It was rare now for him to shoot the breeze with the guys at the Y; rarer still for him to pick up a pool cue or sit down at a poker table. At night, after he'd had a beer or two, he would settle, exhausted, onto his bed and listen to the radio. Sometimes he just looked at the sports pages. Often he studied the atlas Nora had given him. Occasionally he might also sort through the magazine pages she had saved. He wanted to figure out what she'd been thinking: What was the thread that had led her from stories about Russian troop movements and the devastation of North Africa, say, to the girl pilots of Avenger Field and close-up photos of enormous beetles fighting? Why the hell had she pulled out articles about a giant potato in Walla Walla, Washington, and a female dogcatcher in Westport, Connecticut?

One evening, irritated by his lack of understanding, and by Nora for leaving him with these riddles, he had one bourbon too many and threw a bunch of her clippings across the room. They flapped and scattered onto the floor, and finally Joe saw what he'd been looking for without knowing it: the other sides of the pages. What Nora had clipped weren't the articles but the ads: ads for Brillo scouring pads, Palmolive soap, a Sunbeam coffeepot. Everything she had torn out had to do with things that would furnish their apartment, a destination that now seemed every bit as exotic to Joe as the places he might someday travel.

On days when Joe was too tired to moonlight on the blackened windows, he would often find a seat in the little newsreel theater off Track 17. The world on the screen inside the theater was black and white, but what it lacked in color it made up for in fascination. Through that summer of '46, Joe watched newsreels about a new president in Argentina, a foreign ministers' meeting in Paris, a fencing instructor in Scotland, and the Major League All-Star Game at Boston's Fenway Park.

But on the simmering morning of July 7,

when the theater was jammed because it had air-conditioning, Joe was gut-punched by the images of another world entirely. Above the usual heroic newsreel music, there was footage of sailors shaving farm animals, applying supposedly protective ointments, and leading them grimly into crates and cages destined for ships. First came the pigs, being walked like wheelbarrows, then the goats and lambs. Along with the rest of the stunned audience, Joe next watched the first images civilians had gotten to see of an atomic blast. Nearly a year after it had obliterated more than 150,000 humans in Japan, the atom bomb was being tested on farm animals in the Pacific. The newsreel screen went white at the moment of impact, and the ocean was covered by a bright hat-shaped cloud that spread outward as another huge cloud grew from its center, high into the sky.

Sickened, Joe wondered why anyone would expect to find a patch of skin, let alone an animal, let alone a ship, after the blast was over. Joe thought back to V-J Day, to the night the Japs had surrendered. Like everyone he knew, he had rejoiced, not thinking too much about what it had been like on the ground when the bombs that ended it fell. Now, seeing the animals being led onto the ships was like watching a horrifying, twisted version of Noah's ark.

Joe was not the only one in the theater who went to Ralston Young's prayer meeting the next morning. Along with three or four others, Joe tried to describe the sense of helplessness, waste, sadness — everyone had a different name for the feeling.

Trying to fend off his despair, he had a drink that evening with a girl from the Rexall drugstore. Her name was Felicia. Her hair was perfectly coiffed. She was wearing orange lipstick, a bright-yellow blouse, and a checked jacket, but despite all that color, her eyes had no sparkle. She was funny, though: She bitched about her boss and gossiped about a new co-worker. Joe and she had a few too many, but there was nothing between them. He walked her out to Vanderbilt Avenue, waved a hand at a cabbie, held the door for her, and gave her money for the fare. He had never felt so desolate. Listening to her had only magnified what Joe had been fighting since the newsreel: a kind of anguish even deeper than loneliness.

As he watched Felicia's cab pull away from the curb, a phrase kept coming into his head: *empty as a kettle.* It was what his father had sometimes said when he came home from work. Damian would say, "My stomach is empty as a kettle," and then Katherine would say, "Well, don't blow your lid." Joe barely smiled at the memory. His emptiness wasn't hunger for food but for something bigger: for the feeling of being alive that he had known most completely with Nora. What would he do if she didn't return? Would he wait another year? Would he have it in him to leave?

A little bit tipsy, he wandered back into the terminal and up the elevator to the art school, one of the few places in Grand Central he didn't really know. He had been there only once, to arrange for Nora's classes; he'd never been in any of the studios. The first one, on his right, was labeled PAINTING in the same black letters used for the terminal's passageways. Opening the door, Joe certainly didn't expect to find people at this hour, but he was startled to see that the room was either being reorganized or dismantled. More than a dozen easels were stacked on top of one another. All the furniture — desks, chairs, benches, even a rolling chalkboard — had been moved to one side. There was still art on the walls, though: all four walls, in fact. Landscapes, portraits, and pictures of fruit were all mixed together, arranged by the sizes of the unframed canvases, which hung in tidy rows. Studying them, Joe quickly found a canvas he would have recognized as Nora's even without the "NL" in the lower right-hand corner. It was a painting of a Manhattanhenge sunset, small but surprisingly vivid. Staring at the bright white path of the sun she had painted, Joe felt drawn into the image, much as Nora had been drawn toward the sun. Taking a step forward, he let his fingertips run gently down the right side of the canvas, which he then straightened just slightly.

He took the stairs down past the commuter level, the maintenance level, the carpentry shops, and finally to M42. Even before he had sat down on a wood crate by the carved-out rock, dozens of the cats appeared, mewing by his side. Dillinger was nowhere to be seen; he had disappeared months before. Somewhere in the depths of this hollowed-out place, Dillinger had died, and rotted, and turned to bone.

A small black cat with one green eye and one gray eye sat, curled its tail around its forelegs, and seemed to stare at Joe expectantly. Joe didn't pick it up.

Trains and people had come and gone, and all Joe had ever done was smooth the way for other people's adventures. He felt the grave emptiness — like a missed breath or a missed heartbeat. It was the same thing he'd felt watching Finn's train disappear into darkness, or when he'd found Nora's letter and boxes on the day she left. He had lost so much, so many. He kept thinking that there was something he was supposed to do — say a prayer, eat a meal, have a dozen drinks — that would make these feelings stop. But as long as he stayed in Grand Central, he knew the only thing that could do that would be having Nora back with him.

5

SOME WELCOME HOME

1946

After three years, one month, and twenty-six days, Manhattanhenge sunrise filled the east window with light and brought Nora back to Joe. She flickered onto the floor. She opened her eyes, and it took her only a moment to rise, brush the ashes from her dress, and turn around. "A child of the Earth and the Everlasting." That was how Ralston Young defined a miracle. And there she was: the miracle that time or God or fate had granted.

She started crying the minute she saw him.

It was hardly the first time she'd broken through the in-between to come back to life on the marble floor. It wasn't the first time Joe had seen it. But now it seemed more amazing than ever. And now, after all they had been through, each of them knew what was at stake.

"Nora," he said, as he took off his coat and put it around her shoulders.

Her tears fell insistently. She shook her head.

"You were waiting for me," she said.

"Of course."

"But Joe —"

"What the hell else was I going to do?" He sounded frustrated, fierce.

They held each other tightly, just standing in the concourse, the fit of their bodies at once so fresh and so familiar. All other feelings — confusion, anger, doubt, relief — were momentarily welded into this one embrace.

"Come with me," Joe told her, taking her hand, which was as warm and electric as ever.

He walked her to an unmarked brass door a few steps up from the south balcony. Furtively, he unlocked it and led her into a vast private office.

He looked so much older, she thought. His hair was still black and full, his mouth still lovably cartoon-crooked. But his skin appeared thin and gray now, his cheekbones so pronounced that they seemed shockingly like the scaffold for an old man's face.

"How long have I been gone?" she asked him.

"More than three years," he told her.

It didn't make sense, given how old he looked. "That's all?" she asked.

"That's *all*?" he said. "It's been more than three years."

Nora tried to gauge his feelings, even as her mind raced.

"Is the war over?" she asked.

"Yes."

"Did we win?"

"Yes."

"And Faye? And the kids?"

"They're fine," Joe said.

"And you're still mad at me?"

Their eyes locked.

"Yes," he said.

Breaking away from his stare, Nora looked around for the first time, noticing the room they were in, which like so many of Grand Central's wonders managed to hide in plain sight. Around them were stained-glass windows, velvet chairs, divans, palm plants, a huge black safe, and a loft with heavy railings and a fancy painted ceiling.

"Where *are* we?" she asked, stalling, not sure she could face the anger in Joe's eyes or discover what time had done to him.

He stared back, impatient. She had never seen this look on his face. He had waited for her all this time. But why, if he felt this way?

"We're in John Campbell's office," Joe said softly.

Nora didn't bother to ask who John Campbell was. "Joe, I didn't want to leave," she said. "You know I didn't. I wrote you that. I thought it was the right thing to do."

"I lost you and Finn at the same time."

"Would it have been better if I'd stayed?"

"It would have been better if Finn hadn't died."

Nora sighed. "Wasn't it simpler when I left?" she asked.

"That's not the point."

"What's the point, then?"

"The point is you didn't ask me."

"You would have said no."

"Maybe not."

"But Faye —"

"Yes, Faye. I know," Joe said bitterly. "She told me she came to see you and that she told you to leave. I thought I'd go crazy when I found that out."

Nora thought of the look on Faye's face: the need, the pleading, the brittle pride.

"Did you forgive Faye?" Nora asked.

He nodded, his face softening just a bit.

"Then you're going to have to forgive me too."

He was leaning back against a huge oak desk, his workman's clothes nearly as out of place as Nora's flapper dress.

She took a breath and asked him the question she had just asked herself: "If you're so mad at me, Joe, then tell me: What did you wait around for?"

He looked up from the desk. "For this," he said, and pulled Nora close.

First there was that embrace, their faces pressed against each other's necks. Then she kissed him, and time skittered away into the corners of the room. They were immersed in the homecoming of each other's arms.

She held the back of his head with one hand and circled the nape of his neck with the other. They broke off for a moment, then kissed again. For Nora, virtually no time had passed since the day she had last seen Joe. But for Joe, it was as if he'd spent three years in complete silence and now, at last, he could use his real voice.

Then she asked: "How long would you have waited if I hadn't come this year?"

He said: "How long would you have wanted me to?"

"I wouldn't have wanted you to wait at all," she said. "Not if you'd found someone else."

Joe looked uncomfortable, but before he could say anything, Nora said, "No, wait. Did you? Do you have someone else? Are you *with* someone else? Is it Faye? Is it —"

"No," Joe said quickly. "I'm not with anyone. I'm with you."

Nora beamed. "Then I guess I'll stay awhile."

"No fooling," Joe said sternly. "If you ever leave like that again —"

"I won't, Joe. I promise," Nora said. "I'll never leave again without telling you."

"No matter what," he said, overwhelmed.

"No matter what," she repeated.

They held each other for a long time.

"So *that's* settled," Nora said. "But now what?"

"We'll get a Floating Key. But maybe —" He glanced up at the little loft.

"What's up there?" Nora asked.

"Oh," he said, his face finally relaxed. "There's a pipe organ and some couches. Mr. Campbell gets the musicians to play there when he gives one of his parties."

"And what else?" Nora asked, smiling, stroking the side of Joe's face.

"Well," Joe said, "all sorts of things can happen up there."

He picked her up in one motion and threw

her — fireman's carry–style — over his shoulder to head up the steps.

He had done this before: The night Nora flickered out at the Cascades, he had carried her over his shoulder, down all those flights of stairs. Levermen had to be strong, and Joe was. But now, even as he took the first few steps up to Mr. Campbell's loft, he could feel a muscle in his back stretch, tighten, and grip. He let out a cry and managed, just barely, to climb the last few steps before he dropped Nora onto one of the couches and fell like a statue onto the beautifully carpeted floor.

It wasn't funny. They both knew it wasn't funny, because in less than a minute it was clear that Joe was in real pain. But the contrast was so ridiculous that the first thing they had to do was laugh. Eventually, though, Nora led a somewhat hobbled Joe out of the Campbell office and down to the men's lounge off the waiting room. He was in no condition to find a Floating Key, so he gave Nora his coat and waited while she arranged a Biltmore room the old-fashioned way: with a reservation in her own name at the hotel's front desk.

Twenty minutes later Joe was settling once again into a hotel room with Nora, yet for the moment his only comfortable position seemed to be with his back on the floor and his calves on the seat of an armchair.

"Some welcome home," he said. "I'm so sorry."

"It could have happened to anyone," she said, at the same time trying to banish the thought that it might not have happened quite as easily to someone younger. "But you're going to need some things," she added.

"And you're going to need some money."

She knelt beside him. "Right pocket or left?" she asked.

"Right."

"Roll a little, please," she told him.

He did, with some difficulty, and Nora grabbed his wallet.

In the bathroom, greeting her unchanged young self, she washed her hands and used a bit of the lather to sweep her hair up into something that might pass as a forties-style wave. She was twenty-three. He was forty-two. "I can't think about that now," Scarlett O'Hara would have said. And what mattered most, Nora thought, was that she had left because of him, and now he was here because of her.

She had buttoned Joe's coat over her flapper dress, though its hem still showed. But apart from the concern that her appearance would attract attention, Nora was eager to be heading back to the terminal. As always, her time away had been like a play's intermission, when the next act might take place in any time frame that the playwright chose. In this case the curtain had come up with the action set "more than three years later." Nora needed to catch up, to reclaim her place in time.

Walking around, she looked for changes. Bill Keogh was no longer wielding the yellow chalk at the arrival and departures board. She saw only a few men in uniform. No one was playing the organ in the north balcony. The lounge was gone, as were Paige and the other volunteers. But the ceiling was still its spectacular shade of blue-green. The floor was still that pale pink-orange marble. The sense of space, grand and warm, was every bit as marvelous as it had always been. Alva was still at the coffee shop cash register. And at Bond's, where Nora went to buy the pastries and coffee, Big Sal was still holding court, dispensing comments and questions along with the baked goods. She was larger than ever, the folds of her stomach now nearly keeping her from reaching the counter. She did a double take when she recognized Nora.

"And where have *you* been?" Sal asked accusingly.

"Wisconsin."

"Why Wisconsin?"

"Family."

Nora handed Sal a dollar.

"Does Joe Reynolds know you're back?" Sal barked.

"Of course. He's why I came back. This Danish is for him."

Sal's droopy eyes narrowed to slits. She paused, Nora's change in her hand.

"You two finally getting hitched?" Sal asked.

"We'll let you know," Nora said.

"And what the hell are you wearing?" Sal called after her.

Nora hurried on to pick up the rest of the things Joe needed, happy to feel — even if it was by way of the terminal's chief curmudgeon — that some things were exactly as she had left them.

By the time she got back to the room, she was carrying the pastries, the coffee, ice, aspirin, sandwiches, and two morning papers. Joe was in exactly the same spot where she'd left him: lying on the rug with his calves on the seat of the chair.

Nora stood above him, smiling down. "You know," she said, "I've heard that armchairs are for sitting, Joe."

He spent the rest of the morning on his back, with breaks only to eat and drink whatever he could while leaning on one elbow. Nora suggested he go to the terminal's doctor, but that was the last thing he wanted to do. "Maybe the pharmacist could at least give you some painkillers," she said. She shook the bottle of aspirin she'd brought him. "Something stronger than this."

"A good laugh and a long sleep are the two best cures," Joe said.

"I'm guessing that's something Damian used to say?"

"My ma, actually. Would you mind going out again and bringing me back a good laugh?"

"And by 'a good laugh' I'm guessing you mean some Old Crow?"

"You still know me so well."

" 'Still'? Don't forget, Joe," Nora said. "Your three years have been something like three hours for me, tops. I haven't had time to forget."

He smiled. "Any bourbon will do," he said.

With Sal's reaction to her clothes fresh in her mind, Nora didn't want to face whatever Mr. B. might make of her current outfit —

even assuming he was still at the Lost and Found. She headed instead for a shop she had passed on her way to the drugstore. Babette's seemed a casual dress shop, just right for the moment's needs. But it had a BE RIGHT BACK AT sign on the door, with a cardboard clock that had only one hand.

Still wrapped in Joe's overcoat, Nora went to wait in the Biltmore lobby. It was noon now, but already the red leather banquettes were starting to fill with college-age kids, apparently on vacation and waiting for their lunch dates. Even back in the twenties, when Nora was still at Barnard, kids used to say "Meet me under the clock," and everyone knew where and what that meant — it was one level down and several leaps of romance away from the more practical "Meet me at the gold clock." The girls were now wearing flesh-colored stockings and high heels, chattering, giggling, and checking the clock every few minutes. Perfume and snippets of conversation floated above them.

"Do you think he's bringing Peter?"

"Where'd you buy that purse?"

"Is that clock always right?"

"How's my lipstick?"

They were so silly, Nora thought, but, eyes widening, she realized that though she had been coming and going from the terminal now for more than two decades, she was only a few years older than most of them. And Joe, at forty-two, was only five years younger than her father had been when he died.

Several of the girls gave Nora a once-over worthy of Elsie's most savage assessments. In return, Nora stood, trying to make herself look every bit as regal as Elsie, as if wearing a man's overcoat and slicked-up hair was all the rage, and they just hadn't figured it out yet.

Maintaining that posture, she hurried back to the dress shop, now open, where the saleswoman at the counter fortunately seemed much more concerned with her own appearance than with Nora's — or anything else. Even as Nora quickly scanned the racks for a simple, all-purpose outfit, the saleswoman peered into a countertop mirror, practicing different facial expressions, holding up different pairs of earrings, draping a scarf in different ways.

In the dressing room, Nora quickly tried on several tops and skirts. Nothing fancy. Nothing expensive. Just something that would make her look presentable. Joe was waiting for her, and she wanted to get out of her telltale blue dress as soon as she could, so she decided not to linger. She purchased an inexpensive blouse and skirt and a pair of sheer stockings. In the drugstore, she bought a poppy-red lipstick and a thin comb. In the ladies' lounge, which was completely unchanged from her last visit, she stepped into a stall, tore off the price tags, and put on the clothes. Making sure that no one was watching, she balled up her blue dress and threw it into the trash once again. She dabbed on the lipstick and used the comb to tease her hair into a wave. Then she picked up the booze at the liquor store and headed back to the Biltmore.

While Nora was doing these errands, Joe had fallen asleep on the carpeted floor and awakened to find that the ice Nora had wrapped in a washcloth had melted beneath his back. He managed, cursing and on his knees, to get to the bathroom, where he pulled himself up to the sink. He stayed in the shower for a full fifteen minutes, the hottest water he could stand beating down on his lower back. Between the ice, the aspirin, and the heat, he could feel his muscles starting to loosen.

When Nora walked in, she found Joe sitting in the armchair, wearing only his undershorts.

"Progress!" she said. "Getting dressed or undressed?"

"Dressed," he said. "But it's slow going."

"Well, you made it off the floor," she said. "That's a start."

"Not only that," Joe said. "I took a shower."

"Well, you'll be wanting a drink to celebrate, won't you?" she asked.

"You read my mind."

He saw her slim figure in the simple skirt and blouse she had bought. It had taken her just a few hours, but she had transformed herself with lipstick, clothes, and hair into exactly the person she'd been when she'd left. The years of their separation were apparently not troubling her: She was chipper and fiery — *his* Nora.

She brought the glass from the bathroom sink, poured the bourbon for him, clinked the bottle against it, and took a jaunty swig from the bottle.

"What is it?" she asked when she saw the look on his face.

"I just can't believe you're back."

In all their time with the Floating Keys, Nora and Joe had never ordered room service because they had never wanted to call attention to themselves. But tonight they were legitimate paying guests in a hotel. A heavyset waiter who looked too large for his vest wheeled in a cart covered in a damask cloth and loaded with stacked plates under metal hats, a red rose in a crystal bud vase, and a tub of butter with the Biltmore *B* stamped into its smooth top.

After he'd left, Nora removed the two metal plate covers and banged them together like cymbals. "Dinner is served," she said.

It was steak and eggs for Joe, spaghetti with meat sauce for Nora, and an unusual quiet between them as they sat down to eat. The silences in Joe and Nora's conversations had always been as soft as breath. This silence seemed almost harsh.

"Well?" Nora finally said.

"Well what?"

"Did you have anyone in your life while I was gone?"

Joe salted his eggs, took a bite, and salted them again. "No one who mattered," he said. "In the end."

"Did you finally get to travel at least?" Nora asked him.

"There was a war," he said.

They shared a long look. The ties between them seemed tangled by devotion and fuzzy with doubt.

"What about Faye?" Nora finally asked.

"What about her?"

"You still haven't told me how things really were," she said.

"Sure I did."

"All you said was that she was fine."

Joe cut into his steak. "What do you want to know?" he asked.

"I want to know how you felt, how the kids took it, how much time you spent with Faye —"

"Look," Joe said. "It was a hard time. We made the best of it."

Nora had so many other questions. Why did he look so old? Had he made love with Faye? Had he moved back to the Y? Had he moved back to Queens? Had he been with other women? She twirled her pasta around her fork and said, "I thought the two of you —"

Joe drank half his glass of beer. "It didn't work out," he said.

"I know she loves you. She loved you even when Finn was alive. I could tell. I remember that day you and she sent the kids to camp. And when she told me to leave —"

"Maybe then," Joe said. "Maybe for a while. But not now. Nora. I've never in my life been in love with anyone but you."

They never called room service to pick up

the table. At about midnight, Joe quietly folded the flaps down and wheeled it out into the hall.

6
THE DREAM APARTMENT

Joe went back to work the week before Christmas. He started with half shifts, but soon realized that standing was less painful than sitting or walking. Several passionate nights with Nora had done nothing to help his back, but they were well worth the price, and in any case lever pulling didn't require bending. It was a relief to work again, to sink into the rhythm of the track calls and the blinking board, to sweat under the lights and feel his strength returning.

Max Colton was no longer at the Biltmore, but Brian, the head bellman, found Joe a Floating Key and a room, and while he worked, Nora began to go through the boxes he'd been bringing over, one by one, from the Y. She started with a carton of clothes and was immediately struck by their slightly musty smell, the proof — not that any more was needed — that time had indeed passed. Aside from the smell, though, nothing had changed. There was still a button missing from her gray wool skirt and fresh cellophane around a sweater she'd bought but never worn. There wasn't that much in the box: a few skirts, a few dresses, a coat, some blouses and shoes. But it was exciting to think that, in her time since the accident, she had accumulated at least some history. Except for her clutch and bracelet, every item of clothing — every knickknack, purse, and pair of shoes — held a story that had started sometime after 1925. A person without a past is no more alive than a person without a future. Looking through her boxes, settling back into Grand Central, Nora felt that she once again had both.

She was delighted to see that Leon Forrester was still manning the desk at the art gallery. Unlike Joe, Leon seemed to have gotten younger in her absence. His formerly triangular shape had slimmed down into something more like a rectangle. His mournful face looked a little brighter, and it brightened further when he saw Nora. She gave him a quick hug and raced past the sculptures, the tapestries, and the many new works on the gallery walls. The stairway that

517

led up to the art school was dim, but she climbed it with enthusiasm.

What she came upon when she opened the door was the shock of a wasteland, bleak and deserted. Though the skylight had been partially scraped free of tar, the studios were dark and almost completely empty. In Nora's old classroom, the smells of paints and turpentine — not to mention Mr. Fournier's own spicy mystery sandwiches — had been replaced by an airless odor of sawdust and cement. All the tables, easels, and cabinets had been removed. There were no paintings on the walls. This was the first time Nora had seen how large the room really was, and the first time she'd noticed the floor, which was so flecked with paint droppings that it looked as if it had been strewn with confetti.

"Mademoiselle Lansing."

Startled, she turned to see Mr. Fournier, bent at an alarmingly greater angle than he had been three years before, but more dapper without his artist's smock.

"I thought perhaps you had vanished," he said.

The word startled Nora for a moment. "No, not vanished," she said. "Not for good, anyway. I just went back home for a while."

"This must be something of an unpleasant surprise, then," he said.

"What happened?"

"I was just at a meeting of the committee, and that sad fellow at the front desk told me you had come up here."

"No, I mean what happened to the school?" Nora asked.

"Well, the gallery is still thriving. The committee and I have seen to that. But the school closed last year. The war made it too much of a luxury to maintain."

"But the war's over."

"*Oui.* Thank heavens."

"And when does the school open again?"

Mr. Fournier frowned. "I am afraid it does not."

"But why?"

"The classrooms are being turned into some kind of training center."

"Training for what?"

"Who is to say? Come," he said. "But I will show you."

Nora followed him down the corridor to the last studio, where the contents of the other rooms had been stacked and labeled with various destinations: schools, churches, hospitals. Art supplies had been apportioned to each. Yet the job hadn't been completed. Dust had settled on most of the furniture, easels, and boxes, and there were a number of items that were yet to be packed up.

"It's such a waste," Nora said.

"Too true."

She was standing with Mr. Fournier beside a few tables where wide Irish oatmeal tins held brushes of all heights and widths. Wistfully, Nora reached for one and used her thumb to riffle the bristles, releasing little puffs of ancient colored powder that smelled like clay. She looked longingly at the half-used tubes of paint, the piles of rags, the stacks of dusty blank canvases leaning dejectedly against a wall and a door.

She didn't know how to convey the depth of the yearning she felt. She looked at the confetti floor, her eyes tearing.

"What is it, Miss Lansing? Have I said something to upset you?"

"Oh, no," Nora said.

"What is it, then?"

"It's just that I don't know where I'm going to paint."

"Oh, that. Well, surely you will find a studio of your own somewhere. You certainly do not need lessons, although there are other schools —"

Nora shook her head. "I could never afford my own studio."

"Your apartment, then," he said.

"No. It's tiny. And my — husband — he

gets sick from paint fumes."

"Ah. So you have married. Possibly this is why artists should never marry."

Nora smiled wanly but leaned toward Mr. Fournier conspiratorially. "Couldn't I just work in one of the classrooms?" she asked him softly. "I wouldn't bother anyone."

"Well, for a while you could, I suppose," he said. He looked over his shoulder, his eyes full of life.

"What is it?" Nora asked.

"I may have a much better idea," he said. "How good are you at keeping secrets?"

Nora laughed. "Probably better than I am at painting," she said.

"And how good are you at climbing?"

With a smile but no further words, Mr. Fournier began shifting the blank and gessoed canvases that were obscuring the door. As more of the door became exposed, Nora could see the words NO ADMITTANCE, hand-painted in bold capital letters that matched the style of the signs on the Grand Central passageways. Soon that prohibition could be seen in multiple spots on the door, in a kind of conversation of lettering styles and colors. NO ADMITTANCE. NO ADMITTANCE. Nearly at the bottom, in an elegant, italicized addendum, were the words *Except by Invitation.*

"Allow me, madame, to invite you," Mr. Fournier said.

He opened the door to a set of steps that led to an enormous empty attic with a thirty-foot-high ceiling and dusty, warped wood floors. The long walls were covered, nearly all the way to the ceiling, with faded painted figures: studies of men in chariots and women in blue robes, prancing horses with braided manes, sleek dogs and classical temples, ships and sails, clouds and waves.

"What *is* this place?" Nora asked, amazed.

"I believe this could be your studio," Mr. Fournier said.

Nora hurried back to the hotel room, where on impulse she unwrapped the two paintings of hers that Joe had kept in his closet at the Y.

When he came back from his shift, the winter sun had already set, and the room was mostly in shadow, but Nora looked younger and brighter than ever. Her two paintings were leaning, unwrapped, against the desk. Hurriedly, she told him all about seeing Mr. Fournier, and she asked Joe if he'd ever heard about the secret studio.

"Maybe," Joe said. "I heard some artist used to give parties up there during the twenties and thirties. I didn't know if that was true or not. Sort of like M42."

"I think Mr. Fournier is going to look the other way and let me work there," Nora said.

Joe smiled and shook his head. "Is there anyone you *can't* get to eat out of the palm of your hand?"

Nora laughed. "Meanwhile, it made me want to see these again. What would you think about my hanging them in place of *those* for a while?" she asked.

She was gesturing to two unusually ugly flower paintings over the couch.

"Nope," Joe said. "We're not going to hang anything anywhere till we hang them in our own apartment."

The apartment. Nora hadn't let herself think about it. For her it had been only weeks since Joe had told her that their dream apartment would have to wait.

"Have you been by the place?" she asked him.

"No."

"Do you know something I don't know?" she asked.

"I know a thousand things you don't know," he said. "I know about couplings and ties and relay systems and rotary converters and —"

"I mean about whether there's actually an

apartment available," she said.

"How about if tomorrow we take a look?" Joe said.

The next evening, Joe came back to find Nora ready to go. She was dressed in one of her favorite skirts, her copper hair upswept with the good brush and comb she had fished out of one of her boxes. He kissed her, held her coat for her, and together they strolled through the lobby and out onto the street.

The last time they had taken this walk it had been spring, not too long before the horrible night of Manhattanhenge sunset, when Nora had almost died for good. This evening, the snow was gray and yellow in the shadows and under the streetlamps. Nora had always loved the way the snow in New York could make everything seem clean and fresh: one large, gessoed canvas. Tonight her footprints and Joe's seemed like the first strokes of a painting.

At the apartment house, they waited for the super. It was cold, as cold as it had been the night Joe had first tried to walk Nora to Turtle Bay. Again — as when Nora had made this pilgrimage alone — it took a while for the super to appear. When he did, he was wearing the same, apparently ineffectual, hearing aid, but he didn't seem to recognize Nora.

"Haven't you heard?" the super said. "The boys came back. There's a housing shortage on. They're putting up Quonset huts in Brooklyn."

Nora turned to go, but Joe wasn't moving. He reached into his pocket, and Nora saw him slip the super a bill.

The move had the intended effect: Suddenly the impossible seemed worthy of discussion. It turned out that the super had some tenants on the second floor whose lease was going to be up in a few months.

"What makes you think they won't renew?" Joe said.

The super cupped his ear again, even though he was now the one speaking. "Oh, they've already told me. The husband comes home from the service, you know, and one, two, three, she's pregnant again. Kid number four. They're moving out of the city."

"Well, that's probably too many bedrooms for us anyway," Nora said.

"It's just the one," the super said.

"Three kids and two parents in a one-bedroom apartment?"

"Well, as I say, they're moving."

Another subtle greasing of the super's palm by Joe, a quick climb to the second floor, and now Nora and Joe were offering apologies to a pregnant woman whose children — there seemed to be more than three — were clamoring around her as she dished out spaghetti from an enamel bowl. Barely noticing the adults, the woman gestured kindly but vaguely to the living room. Not wanting to intrude any further, Nora and Joe stayed no longer than five minutes, but that was enough time for Nora to decide that the place was perfect. It had a kitchen that was just big enough for a table, a living room with a view of Lexington Avenue, a bedroom with two doors she assumed were closets. Through the partly open bathroom door, Nora could see there was a footed bathtub nearly as elegant as the ones in the Biltmore. Yet all this was covered — for now — by an almost comic-strip chaos of children's toys, baskets of laundry, newspapers, magazines, and groceries. There was nothing on the walls except room for Nora's paintings.

Drifting to sleep that night, Nora started mentally clearing the apartment of its current clutter and beginning to fill it, piece by imaginary piece, with the things she and Joe might have one day. Unlikely though it might be, she could see it all, and she had to smile at how appalled Elsie would have been at the décor: not the formal silk and velvet, the carved feet and burnished table-tops, of Nora's youth, but a place more like that wonderful attic room she had shared with Margaret in Paris. A bit of this and that: some cheerful fabric on the curtains and bed; chairs in which you could curl up, not slide off. She would have to figure out how to coach Joe for the shopping, but nothing would have to be an antique, or "the best," or "a great find," or any of the things that had made Elsie so proud of their home. Nothing would have to match. Joe and Nora had lived out of boxes in a series of rooms that changed just slightly from one to another; it would be enough just to know that whatever they had would be able to stay in one place.

The next day Nora started to search the boxes for the stack of pages she'd torn from magazines. Realizing they'd been rearranged every which way, she asked Joe, "Did you go through these?"

He nodded. "Sorry if they're out of order," he said. "One night when I was missing you so bad, I started to look through them." He laughed. "I didn't understand at first. I thought you were saving them for the stories. It took me a while to realize you were saving them for the ads."

Nora held up a page advertising small radios. "I guess these are all old models now?" she asked.

"You'll just have to find new ones," he said.

When Nora woke the next morning, she found, fanned out on the pillow beside her, the current issues of *Better Homes & Gardens, Good Housekeeping,* and *House Beautiful.* On top of the last was a note in Joe's careful block letters:

FOR THE DREAM APARTMENT
OF THE FUTURE MRS. JOSEPH
DAMIAN REYNOLDS

Nora delighted in seeing the little changes as she leafed through the magazines: a new eggbeater with a handle that tilted, an armchair that folded out into a bed, a coffeemaker with a glass pot. It seemed that the postwar world was exploring every way to make life sleeker, faster, and easier.

Alongside the photos and stories about home improvements and housekeeping were references to world events that Nora had missed. In the anonymity of her cozy seat in the newsreel theater, she spent the days before Christmas trying to catch up — to understand the world of 1946. She saw images of the Nuremberg Trials, with the placid faces of the German leaders as they were sentenced to be hanged. The seventy-five girls who competed for the Tangerine Queen beauty crown. Nora saw the running of the Kentucky Derby and a three-year-old boy who swam the crawl. And, in one segment that would eventually be of overwhelming significance to her, she saw the announcement that the United Nations — an alliance Joe would later explain — had settled on New York City as the home of its permanent headquarters. The announcer spoke with what seemed like even more than the usual gusto: "The international organization's wanderings are over. From Forty-second Street and the East River in New York, running north to Forty-eighth Street, the future skyscraper headquarters will occupy six blocks near historic Turtle Bay. Work of clearing the land for a magnificent world capital will start in a few months."

Nora had grown up at 229 East Forty-eighth Street, right beside the neighborhood that would doubtless bloom with these new buildings. Back in their room, listening to the radio, she let herself remember her childhood home. Her room, with the lovely

529

wallpaper and the flowery chandelier. The books on her shelves. The dresses in her closet. She saw herself taking her father's arm as he escorted her down the steps for her coming-out ball — how he had put his large, slender hand on top of hers, an extra gesture of reassurance and courtliness. What she wouldn't give for even five more minutes with him. Five minutes to tell him everything that had happened.

The music of Isham Jones and his orchestra came wobbling into the room, playing "Who's Sorry Now?" Brushing back the tears she never liked Joe to see, Nora wondered what her father would have said or done about her situation. Probably he would have shaken his head at Nora and told her that she came from a long line of people who made the best of whatever they were handed. Frederick would have smiled wryly and quoted Hamlet: "There are more things in heaven and earth, Horatio, than are dreamt of in your philosophy."

And what if she actually had *spent* five more minutes with Frederick? Five more minutes in that hospital room? Perhaps she and Ollie would have gotten on a different subway, or even found a taxi. Ollie would have lived. She would have lived. Would she have gone back to Paris? Would she have gotten to show a painting in Ollie's gallery, or some other? And would fate have somehow arranged for her to meet Joe anyhow?

Those were things she could never know. But one thing was undeniable. If she'd lived, she would now be free to see the United Nations firsthand as a forty-four-year-old woman. She wouldn't be hearing about it in a newsreel theater as a twenty-three-year-old spirit who was dreaming of a life with a man twice her age in a one-bedroom apartment that seemed equally out of reach.

7
SO LUCKY TO BE LOVING YOU

1946

Not counting the times he'd had to work shifts at the Piano, there had not been a Christmas in Joe's life that he hadn't spent in Queens. Some of his earliest memories, the ones that were telescoped deep in his brain, were about the original four of them — Damian, Katherine, Finn, and Joe — on Christmas Eve or morning. There had been church clothes and mass the night before, Katherine's ham for dinner, the tree to decorate, the carolers in the neighborhood. Little and large things had changed over the years of his childhood. The mismatched socks Katherine had once hung from the mantel had been replaced by store-bought red stockings. The wooden icebox, after the family got its first refrigerator, had become the place to store important papers, pictures, and all manner of broken things needing repair. The scarves and Erector sets and other gifts of Joe's childhood had been wrapped, before the Depression, in pretty paper, and the discovery of them Christmas morning had never disappointed a year's imaginings. It took an entire day to suck a candy cane. Joe knew that because every year he and Finn had raced to see who could finish first, and by the time either of them did, their lips would be numb and the color of roses, and the peppermint would have lost its taste.

Over time, inevitably, the cast of characters had changed. Katherine had died. Finn had married Faye. Mike and Alice had come along. Damian and now Finn had died. For the past three years, the family Christmas in Queens had been just Joe, Faye, the kids, and whatever church friends or neighbors came by.

Ever since Atlantic City back in the spring, Faye and Joe had talked on the phone but seen each other less and less frequently. It had been three or four months since he had been out to the house, but tonight, Joe assumed, the family would be expecting him.

"Christmas with Faye?" Nora asked as she saw Joe wrapping the requisite Erector sets.

"With the family," Joe said.

Nora nodded.

He put on a tie she didn't recognize from

their previous years — perhaps a gift from Faye, she thought.

Tentatively Nora asked, "Does Faye know I'm back?"

Joe shook his head. "Not yet." He took a breath and put his hands on her shoulders. "Do you want me not to go?" he asked.

"No, it's fine," Nora said. "Maybe I'll order from room service and see what waiter brings the tray."

Joe had one sleeve of his coat on now and didn't seem to know whether she was kidding or not.

"No, obviously you should go," Nora said. "We'll have Christmas Day together. Just like we did last year."

"You mean just like three years ago," Joe said.

Nora reached under a pile of her magazines to find Joe's red scarf.

"Be here when I get back," Joe said.

"Where else would I be?" Nora asked as she tied the scarf around him.

Joe laughed. "I don't like to think about that," he said.

Alice was fourteen now, her hair dirty blond, her face with that custardy skin of Faye's.

"Uncle Joe!" she called from the top of

the stairs, and ran down to greet him. She was wearing a red-and-gray dress whose skirt flared out like a Christmas bell.

"Did you bring my present?" she asked him.

"What makes you think you get a present?"

"It's Christmas!"

"Well, were you naughty or nice this year?"

"She was both," an unfamiliar voice said, and there, coming down the stairs, was a slightly chubby teenage boy, a shopping bag of gifts in his hand and a look of nervous pride on his face.

"Who's   ?"

"Uncle Joe!" Alice said exuberantly. "I want you to meet Rusty!"

Rusty put down the shopping bag, slung one possessive arm around Alice's shoulder, and stuck out his hand in the way that only a kid with his first girlfriend could. Reluctantly, Joe shook it. What business did any boy have thinking he was good enough for Alice?

She was taking coats off the stand in the hallway, handing the first to Rusty and putting the second one on herself.

"Where are you going?" Joe asked.

"Oh, I'll be back," Alice said. "We're just going to Rusty's to open some presents with his family. They're ridiculous. They open them Christmas Eve."

Rusty shrugged. "That's just how we do it," he said, and he picked up the shopping bag and grabbed Alice's hand. They were laughing about nothing as they walked out the door.

Joe wondered where everyone else was. The church crowd didn't seem to be on hand this year. There was no sign of Mike. He could hear sounds from the kitchen, though, so he figured Faye was there. When he walked in, he came face-to-face with a thin, smiling man who Joe guessed was in his thirties and a vet. The left side of his face was mahogany from what must have been a burn, and his jaw was slightly askew. But the injuries didn't affect his smile, which looked perfectly genuine. Faye at that moment turned from the sink, where she was elbows-deep in sudsy water. The place was pure chaos. Paint cans, rags, and brushes cluttered the kitchen counters.

All the colorful bowls and pitchers that Faye had long ago placed atop the cabinets had been removed and stacked on the table, as had the old framed maps and prints of Ireland that they'd been put there to hide. The wall above the cabinets had been painted a fresh white, but the rest of the kitchen was only half done, and the sting of fresh paint and turpentine was sharp and overwhelming.

"So this is why I'm not smelling Christmas ham?" Joe asked.

"I'm sorry, Joey. We thought we'd be finished!"

She had put on just enough weight in the past few months to make her look less like a waif. Or perhaps she had done something to her hair. There was something different, at any rate, and it took Joe a moment to realize what it was: Faye looked happy.

"Joe," she said, "this is Manny."

Another handshake with a proud suitor. Joe looked at Faye questioningly. Who was this guy? Why hadn't she told him anything about him? Faye smiled the smile of a survivor. Joe felt an unexpected stab of loss. It had nothing to do with romance. It was more that he felt he was losing Finn all over again, along with his family in Queens. Alice was already out the door on a date with this Rusty, and so far, Mike hadn't even shown up.

Dinner turned out to be an extremely dry casserole that Faye had kept warming in the oven much too long. Joe, Faye, and Manny waited an hour, then started without the kids. They ate in the dining room, where the crystal candlesticks sat on the table but the candles hadn't been lit. Neither Alice, who returned without Rusty or an apparent appetite, nor Mike, who arrived wearing his police uniform — obviously tipsy from whatever the precinct celebration had been — seemed to mind that virtually every Reynolds family Christmas tradition had been discarded. Joe had to wonder why he'd come at all.

He rode the subway back to the terminal with one of his mother's old maps of Ireland on his lap, and when he stood up, he saw that it had left a tidy line of gray dust on his coat.

Christmas morning, while Nora was still sleeping, Joe quietly removed her prized charm bracelet from the small first-aid tin in which she now kept her jewelry. He dressed in the bathroom and slipped out of the room, her bracelet in one pocket and, in the other, the brass Red Cap uniform button that Ralston had kindly given him without asking him why he wanted it.

The main machine shop in Grand Central was located one level below the lower concourse. Joe had expected it to be fairly empty on Christmas morning, but he was surprised to find it completely deserted. On a rangy Christmas tree just inside the entrance to the shop, someone had left a string of lights that pointlessly flashed red and green, like signal lamps on an empty track. As Joe walked past aisle after aisle of empty wooden workbenches, he found the quiet of the place unsettling. Usually it rattled, clanked, and screeched with the sounds of drills, tile cutters, saws, lathes, and hammers. There was none of that today, just the distant buzz of the subways and the ringing of the rails above.

Eventually Joe found the row of benches that had the small tools and the bright swan-necked lamps the men used for delicate work. There was barely a screw in Grand Central that hadn't been designed especially for Grand Central, and special things required special maintenance. Nora herself, Joe thought smiling, fit into that category.

Sighing, he climbed onto one of the tall metal stools and turned on the radio, dialing past a few programs to hear Bing Crosby singing, of course, "White Christmas." He took Nora's charm bracelet from one pocket and the shiny button with the initials G.C.T. from the other. He pulled down half a dozen sets of pliers before he settled on the two smallest ones.

With the greatest care, Joe used a plier in each hand to separate one of the links on the bracelet, opening it up just enough to slip on the brass button, like another charm. As Joe worked, the radio kept him company, with Bing Crosby, Frank Sinatra, and Sarah Vaughan.

He closed the link up tightly and, for good measure, used a steam valve to clean the whole bracelet. As he walked back toward the Biltmore, he was still hearing Sarah Vaughan's voice in his head:

Time after time
I tell myself that I'm
So lucky to be loving you.

He stopped at Big Sal's and bought two coffees and two pastries, then walked on.

I only know what I know
The passing years will show
You've kept my love so young, so new
And time after time
You'll hear me say that I'm
So lucky to be loving you.

Joe and Nora had Christmas lunch at the Oyster Bar, festive with its usual red-and-white-checked tablecloths, and seasonal with its large wreaths of juniper and red ribbons hanging between old portraits on the rich mahogany walls. They had clam chowder, French fries, and beer. They finished with coffee and apple pie.

Walking back through the terminal afterward, they stopped to listen to the Christmas choir. Joe stood behind Nora, encircled her with his arms, then reached around to kiss her cheek.

"Remember when you snuck into that choir?" he asked her softly.

"How could I forget it?"

"That was the first time I figured out I'd have to keep an eye on you."

"But not the last," she said, turning to face him.

"Am I going to be able to trust you when we have our dream apartment?"

"Trust me for what?"

"Not to go too far."

"So let me get this straight," she said, teasing. "You just want me to play it safe."

"And you just like playing with fire."

"And you just like keeping the matches hidden."

Joe laughed. The choir was singing "Angels We Have Heard on High."

"I am in love with a woman who flickers out like a lightbulb when she gets too far away from the power source in the building where I work," he whispered. "I am in love with a woman who was supposed to have died in 1925 and really didn't, but who could now be killed for good by a sunset on a May Manhattanhenge. I am in love with a woman who I'm sneaking around with in the Biltmore Hotel. And you don't think I'm playing with fire?"

Back in their room, Nora sat Joe down and told him to close his eyes. When he opened them, he was speechless at first. She had given him a small painting — done in oil paints and collage — of the terminal's middle window, her window. It was bright white with sunlight, light that looked like a stream or a river, so solid in its shape, so powerful in its movement through the air that it seemed strong enough to bring in Nora, a miracle, hope.

"Where did you do this?" Joe asked in wonder.

"Up in the studio that Mr. Fournier showed me."

"And no one bothered you about being there?"

"No one," she said. "Leon even helped me move an easel and a table and chair up there."

Joe held the painting up appraisingly.

"Isn't this as good as most of the art they sell in the Graybar Passage?" he asked.

"I hope so," she said.

"Maybe you really could sell this stuff."

"Do you think?"

"But not this one. This one we're going to put in the dream apartment."

"What about that one?" Nora asked, gesturing to the map of Ireland that he had left on the dresser.

"What?"

"That map in the frame. Can that come with us too?"

Joe said nothing. He looked almost embarrassed.

"I'm sorry," Nora said. "Did you not want me to see it?"

"I took it last night," Joe said. "My mother used to keep all these maps of Ireland above our kitchen cabinets. Faye's painting the kitchen, so she brought them all down."

"And she let you take it?"

"It wasn't hers to keep," Joe said.

"It's beautiful," Nora said, picking it up.

Joe shrugged. "It's Ireland."

"Do you ever want to go there?"

Joe shrugged again. "My parents always made it sound like we got the better deal, being here."

"And how were things with Faye last

night?" Nora asked, putting the map back down. She reached for some tissue from the bedside table and gently wiped the frame.

"She's got a fella."

"A 'fella'?"

"His name is Manny."

"Manny what?"

Joe laughed. "What, you think you know him?"

"Is it serious?"

"I don't know. She certainly acted like it is. And Alice has a boyfriend too," Joe said. "Rusty," he added, as if it was the name that bothered him.

"And —"

"And no more questions," Joe said. "It's time for your present."

When Nora saw her charm bracelet, she was confused. "You polished it up!" she said. "That's so nice."

"Look closer," Joe told her.

She rolled it over her hand to her wrist, as she usually did, and touched each one of the charms in turn — the gold ballerina, the skates, the artist's palette with the dots of paint — rubbing them as if one might produce a genie and grant a wish. Then she saw what Joe had added.

"Oh," she said, smiling at the shining button. " 'G.C.T.,' " she read. "Since when does Grand Central Terminal make suit buttons?"

"For the Red Caps," Joe said. "Ralston gave it to me."

" 'G.C.T.,' " Nora read again. "Girls Can — what?"

"Talk," Joe said.

"Tell."

"Touch."

She kissed him. "Tease," she said.

He turned on the radio. Snow fell, the sky dimmed, and they danced.

8
IF HE'D MOVED AWAY

1947

By the middle of January, Nora had already found a way to honor the New Year's Eve resolution she'd made: to look for a job with a salary so she could start saving for the apartment. It turned out that Hattie Pope — former general of the servicemen's lounge, still in uniform but now operating with a hugely diminished mission and force — was back at her original job, overseeing the Travelers Aid station.

She recognized Nora and gave her a blue-suited, cushiony hug. Mrs. Pope explained that she herself had one of the only paid positions for the Travelers Aid team. But Nora got the sense that the older woman was itching to wield a bit of her diminished power, and within a few weeks she had flagged Nora down near the barbershop to say that the New York Central was looking to hire some new tour guides.

"It won't pay much," Mrs. Pope said, "but it'll pay something, and I've already told them what a treasure you are."

It was a perfect job for Nora. She and the other new guides were all given scripts, but Nora hardly needed one. By now she knew the catwalks and the subbasements, the errors in the painted sky and the county in Tennessee where the floor's marble had been quarried. She knew about the Kissing Room, the idea of Terminal City, and the corkscrew staircase and exit beneath the information booth. For Nora, the challenge of giving tours was in remembering what *not* to tell. Visitors didn't need to know about the Campbell office or the morgue, and they weren't supposed to know about M42 or the small white lights on the rim of the information booth that subtly switched to red in order to summon police in emergencies.

Nora was leading a tour of fifteen out-of-towners on a Wednesday in February when she looked out from the north balcony and saw Joe crossing the concourse floor. There was nothing particularly unusual about that: She had seen him — even sketched him — dozens of times when he hadn't known she was looking. But today he was walking with four or five of his fellow levermen. They were all talking and laughing about something, and Nora realized, more as a painter than as a person, that she was looking at the colors and postures of middle-aged men. These were Joe's contemporaries, Nora thought. They were workingmen who, unlike Joe, no doubt had wives and children, cars and houses. These were regular guys who had shopped for furniture, picked apples in autumn, carried their kids on their shoulders, taken their wives to see *It's a Wonderful Life.* Happily or not, touched by the war or not, they had lived normal lives and had normal choices.

That evening, as Joe scanned the real estate ads in the *Herald,* Nora noticed what she thought were even newer lines on his face, including one spot to the left of his chin where three or four lines converged to form what looked like an asterisk. It was mesmerizing, in a way. When he looked up to read her a rental ad, she wasn't really listening. Mostly she was staring at this star-shaped wrinkle and remembering a French phrase that Ollie had taught her: *prendre un coup de vieux.* It meant that the signs of age could appear as suddenly as a surprise attack. How much longer would it be before Joe began to resent all the choices she'd stolen from him?

Joe Reynolds was only forty-two, but he looked, even moved, like an older man. Nora could no longer avoid the question: Wouldn't he have been better off if he'd moved away before she'd come back?

That question began to dominate Nora's life, the contradictory answers flaring through her mind: yes and no, no and yes, as if someone were standing by a light switch, relentlessly flipping it on and off. The question was insistent, punishing.

Nora was unpacking the last of the boxes from the Y when she felt the switch being thrown with more than the usual force. In this box were some of her sketchbooks, a stack of Joe's New York Central newsletters, his childhood Bible, her childhood diary, and the atlas she had given him for Christmas in 1943.

Eventually she would wonder if things would have been different if she'd never seen this book or if it had been better made. But during World War II, when the nylon in women's stockings had been used for parachutes, and the steel in the Trylon and Perisphere had been used for tanks, even paper had been in short supply: The good stuff was needed for packing guns and ammunition, and most books were printed on paper so thin it was nearly transparent. In the case of Joe's old atlas, there were numerous pages dangling off the spine like broken wings.

Nora meant only to straighten them, but pencil markings caught her eye. As she gently handled the pages, she had the sickening realization that virtually every one of them had at some point been annotated by Joe. Nora sank to her knees as she tried to take it all in. The hours he must have spent poring over this book. The care he must have taken to devise these special markings. Each page looked like a treasure map, cryptic and complex. Joe had framed some place-names with rectangles, others with circles or ovals. Some had stars. Still others were the hubs of wheels with spokes connecting to places marked by colored pencils that she guessed he'd found in one of her boxes. On the maps of Italy and Africa, Nora recognized the lines Joe had drawn to trace the places where Finn had been posted. Around the town of Medenine in Tunisia, Joe had drawn a square in black and, beside it, the letters *RIP, FDR*. That was mystifying at first: She remembered from the newsreels that President Roosevelt had died at Warm Springs, in Georgia. Then she realized that Medenine must have been the place where Finn had died. *RIP, FDR.* Rest in peace, Finnegan Damian Reynolds.

But most of Joe's markings were on maps of the United States. Nora noted the cities he'd singled out: Chicago, San Francisco, Boston, Philadelphia. She saw the sites he'd starred: Yellowstone, Carlsbad Caverns, the Grand Canyon, the Pacific Ocean, the Florida Keys — a map of what seemed like his deepest dreams laid out on other maps.

Holding the atlas to her chest, Nora didn't think she'd ever seen anything so beautiful or heartbreaking.

As far as she knew, Joe had never lied to her. She assumed he had left a few things out. There had to have been women other than Faye in the years of Nora's absence. But Nora didn't believe that Joe had ever purposely hidden anything that was truly important to him. So finding the markings on the pages of his atlas was nearly as shocking as it would have been to find a hidden bundle of love letters.

In a sense, each page of Joe's atlas was just that: a love letter to a site, a city, a country — or at least an expression of his longing to meet them, a longing that Nora knew she could never satisfy, only squelch. She had always known that Joe wanted to travel, but she was stricken as she tried to accept just how deeply he'd felt that desire. She closed her eyes and imagined Joe in his black coat and maybe a new scarf and hat. He had a suitcase in one hand and a starry look in his eye as he got off a train to see the sights: the Golden Gate Bridge, say, or Yosemite. But that was where Nora's vision stopped, because she had never seen those places herself and never would get to see them. And she knew that as long as she lived, Joe would never want to risk leaving her long enough to see them himself.

Coming right after her glimpse of him with the older men in the terminal, the atlas answered the question in Nora's mind and replaced it with another. Yes, she was certain, Joe would have been better off if he'd gone away before she'd come back. But that was beside the point now. Now she had to ask herself how she could get him to leave.

9

SOMEWHERE ELSE

1947

The secret studio that Leon and Mr. Fournier continued to protect for Nora quickly became a refuge, not only from the squalls of her tour guide job, but also from the torrent of her feelings about Joe. The studio had an allure all its own. Nora learned from Mr. Fournier that the sketchy figures on the walls had been made by an artist named Ezra Winter, who'd first worked in this space during the Great War to create camouflage patterns for the U.S. Shipping Board. After the war, Winter became well known for his murals, including — ironically enough for Nora — one in the lobby of Radio City called *The Fountain of Youth*. When Winter's work became too large for his Connecticut home, he reclaimed this space as a studio, promptly becoming as infamous for the debauched costume parties he gave there as he was famous for the works he produced.

Feeling more at home in the vast room, Nora imagined how she might someday paint these walls herself. For now, she left Winter's sketches untouched and worked on her own paintings. The canvases she used, collected from the former classrooms, had almost all been painted before and gessoed over. Often Nora saw, beneath the chalky coating, faint images of what the first artist had painted: someone's abandoned attempt at a still life, portrait, or abstract. These images, as it happened, were known as ghosts.

Nora increasingly saw her love affair with Joe as exactly this sort of ghost. The first image of them together — when she was twenty-three and he was just ten years older — had remained as a ghost beneath all the other layers of time and laughter, sex and strife, their gradual understanding of a singular event, and their shared, stubborn, impossible attempt to make the supernatural natural.

One afternoon in March, Nora snuck one of her new landscapes from the secret studio into their current room at the Biltmore and — without waiting for Joe's approval — hung it in place of a dowdy still life.

"What's this?" Joe asked when he came in from his shift that evening. "I thought we weren't going to hang anything until we got the apartment."

"Don't you like it?" Nora asked.

"It's beautiful," he said.

"It's England," Nora said. "You could go there, Joe."

"What would I do in England?"

"See England," she said.

A week later she added a second landscape to the room.

"England?" Joe asked when he saw it.

"Actually, it's the French countryside," Nora said. "You could go there too, Joe."

He tossed his jacket onto the bed. "Why are you trying to get rid of me?" he asked.

"Just tell me," Nora said. "If I hadn't come back, and once you'd known Faye and the kids were okay, where would you have gone first?"

Joe was silent, studying the richness of the scene Nora had painted, the layers of blue and purple — even green — from which she'd made a sky so deep and alive.

"You're not going to tell me?" Nora asked.

She saw, even with his back to her, that his whole body had stiffened.

"I found your atlas, Joe," Nora said. "I

saw all your markings and your plans and
—"

He wheeled around from the painting,
enraged.

"You had *no* business looking through
that!" he shouted.

Flustered, Nora countered, "You looked
through my things too!"

Joe shook his head emphatically. "You
know that's not the same. I didn't know if
you were ever coming back."

They glared at each other until at last Joe
looked away. Gently, Nora said, "Joe. Just
tell me where you'd have gone."

He opened a beer, drinking through the
silence.

"Please, Joe," she said. "You can tell me.
Please."

He took another sip of his beer and
sighed. "All right," he finally said. "You
want to know? I'll tell you. I'd get on the
Twentieth Century and I'd go straight to
Chicago. I'd take in a game at Wrigley Field,
and then I'd catch either the Zephyr or the
Golden State. Probably the Golden State.
The southern route. And I'd see Carlsbad
Caverns, with all the bats, and then El Paso
and Tucson and Phoenix and Palm Springs,
and I'd end up in Los Angeles, and then I'd
go to Santa Monica, and I'd put my toes in

556

the Pacific Ocean."

Joe was breathless, Nora wide-eyed. He might just as well have described the eyes, legs, and breasts of his ideal woman.

"The Pacific Ocean" was all Nora could say.

"Why don't you paint me a picture of the Pacific Ocean?" he asked, his jaw set hard.

"I don't know what the Pacific Ocean looks like, Joe. I've never *been* to the Pacific Ocean. I'm never going to get to go. *You* can go to the Pacific Ocean."

He put his beer down on the dresser, hard, as if the bottle could leave a stamp.

"And I can also go somewhere else to get a beer," he said, heading for the door.

"Joe!" Nora said. "I don't think you even know how much you want to go."

He turned back slowly and, helplessly, raised his hands. "And what the hell do you want me to say?" he asked. "What the hell do you want me to do? I'm in love with you."

"That's not my point."

"That's the *only* point."

"Joe."

"So tell me this," he said. "What would you do if you were in my shoes?"

Nora looked up at him, her eyes filled with tears. "I'm not sure I could have stayed this long," she whispered.

It wounded him. She'd known it would. He looked around the room as if the right words were hidden somewhere. Not finding them, he lunged for the door and slammed it, hard, behind him.

Alone, Nora curled up on the couch, hugged her knees, and started to sob.

She had meant what she'd said about leaving. Maybe it was her own confinement that made freedom seem so important. But Nora at this moment couldn't think of anything better or more important for Joe to have.

How could she give him that freedom? Should she try to make him jealous or angry? Should she become dependent, needy, nagging, someone he'd want to escape? Could she drive him away with bad behavior? Reluctantly, she started to think that the only way Joe would ever leave was if he knew she was gone for good.

Things changed between them. Nora now understood the depth of his yearning, and Joe now felt exposed. Still, a few days later, when the lights went down in the newsreel theater, he took Nora's hand, and in the darkness he kissed it. They saw a few cartoons, which were silly but fun, and they saw footage of police confiscating and burning pinball and slot machines. Next came an actress boarding a Chesapeake and Ohio train that would host "the first motion picture premiere on wheels." In the semi-darkness Joe could feel Nora studying his face, searching for a reaction. What was she hoping to see? Was he supposed to stand up, point to the train, and shout, "I want to go too!"?

He was about to ask her to cut it out when he felt her attention shift. Now it was his turn to study her face. What had caught her eye in this last story on the newsreel? It was just about the United Nations: a model of how the new buildings might look.

As the images rolled by, Nora dropped Joe's hand and sat up straighter.

"What is it?" he whispered.

"*Shh,*" she said, though there were only a few other people in the theater, and they hadn't seemed disturbed by his talking. "I'll tell you later," she said.

Nora didn't want to explain anything until she was sure of what she'd seen. Despite the coziness of sitting beside Joe in the theater, despite the fact that she couldn't quite imagine not being beside him, she was fairly certain that, in the images of the U.N. that had just passed before them, she had found the way to get Joe to leave. It would have to involve these buildings, a clear Manhattanhenge sunset, and a lie — the only one she would ever tell him.

In the evenings now, while Joe listened to the radio and scanned the papers, Nora would settle across from him and read or sketch. He couldn't quite make out her mood — or her focus. For several weeks now, when she was drawing, she didn't seem at peace, the way she usually did with a pencil in her hand. He didn't ask her about it. He figured she would say what was on her mind if and when she wanted to. For the time being, it was a relief that she'd stopped talking to him about travel.

Still, whatever she was feeling seemed to be pulling her further away from him. She spent more time in her studio, painting. She gave tours of the terminal nearly every day. She wasn't clipping magazine ads. They hadn't checked on the apartment in weeks. And they made love only now and then.

Joe had always thought that as soon as they had their own place, he'd ask Nora to marry him. Now he wondered if he should have done that sooner, or if he should do it now. He imagined getting Sal or Alva to help him put up white streamers and paper bells in the empty train car on Track 13. He could picture Ralston holding the Bible in his graceful hands, asking for the promises that went along with marriage. Would he and Nora be able to have and to hold? For better, for worse? For richer, for poorer? All that, they had done already, and Joe knew they always would. But in sickness and health? He thought about Damian, old and angry, bristling or brooding in his wheelchair. Time, as Nora all too frequently reminded Joe, was going to catch up with him too, though never with her. She was already starting to look more like a daughter than a wife. At some point she would look like a granddaughter. In the end, would she look like his nurse? Joe choked a little at the thought.

Then he remembered the last part of the marriage vows: until death parts us. Hesitantly, Joe asked himself: Had that already happened, years and years before they had even met?

In May, one late afternoon, he came off his shift and opened their hotel room door to find Nora kneeling beside the coffee table, an issue of *Life* open on the floor.

"So, um, what are we doing, honey?" he asked.

Nora pointed to the headline in the magazine:

U.N. Headquarters Will Rise
Out of Old Turtle Bay

"The main building is called the Secretariat," she said without a greeting. "It's going to be five hundred feet tall, Joe. Thirty-nine floors." Her face, usually so soft and relaxed, seemed to be drawn tight. She almost — just for a moment — even looked a little bit older.

From under the coffee table she produced a box of Whitman's chocolates and stood it on its end on one side of the coffee table. "This is the Secretariat," she said.

Next came the room's small radio with its arched speaker, which she placed on the table's other end. "This is Grand Central," she said.

Next she dealt a line of playing cards from one object to the other. "This is Forty-third Street," she said.

Finally, she closed the heavy drapes and turned off all the lights except one table lamp, from which she removed the glass shade. She knelt beside the table, holding the lamp at its neck.

"The sunrise?" Joe asked.

"The sunrise."

She lifted the lamp, moving it ever so slowly up to the horizon of the coffee table. Joe watched the radio and he watched the chocolates box, and even when the light-bulb sun had risen above the coffee table horizon, the box was blocking the light, which couldn't reach the radio. Grand Central was in darkness.

"Your window's going to be blocked on Manhattanhenge morning," he said.

"Whenever that building is finished," she said. "Maybe even when it's half done."

As if the gesture could hold back time, Joe lunged for the curtains, pulling them apart and bathing Nora and the whole display in light.

"Don't you see, Joe?" she said to him. "Once it's built, everything will change. *All* the Manhattanhenge mornings will be dark. It'll be like a cloudy day, but forever. It'll be the way it was when the mural was up, but forever. Or the servicemen's lounge, but forever."

A long silence followed as Joe took this in. Finally, and softly, he said: "If you stepped out of bounds by accident, you could never come back."

"I'd be caught in the in-between," she said.

"Forever," he said. His heart raced; he imagined Nora in the awful state she'd so often explained: forever bumping up against the barrier of a massive building, and not just any building, but one conceived as a lasting monument. Nora would be stuck not in the terminal's light and not in the ether's darkness, but in the gray in-between: the frightful, tortured place from which her only escape had been the entrance through the terminal's middle window. With the building blocking the sun, Nora — if she stepped out of bounds — would be like a train that had run into a mountainside, its engine forever running.

They looked at each other for a moment, silent in the dim room.

"Don't you see, Joe? It's time," Nora said at last.

"Time," he repeated needlessly.

"You know I'm right," Nora said.

"No."

"Time for me to go for good. So I don't risk the in-between. And you can live your life."

Joe shook his head. "I want to live *our* life," he said.

Standing there, looking so young but so resolute, Nora squared her shoulders and stared at him. "We know how Manhattanhenge sunrise has let me live," she said. "And we know how the sunset can kill me."

He said: "And what? You're going to *make* that happen? You're going to *choose* that?"

"Yes."

"You're going to walk into Manhattanhenge sunset?"

"Yes."

"All that pain again? And that heat?"

Nora merely stared back at him.

"That's suicide," Joe whispered.

Nora flung her arms around him.

He stood completely still, in shock.

"I promised I'd never leave again without telling you," she said.

He stepped back. "No," he said. "I won't let you."

"Joe, the longer we wait, the less life you'll have when I'm gone."

"I'm not ready to lose you," he said. "We've got to give this more time."

"Joe," Nora said. "I was supposed to have died twenty-two years ago. I was never supposed to have gotten *this* time."

10
YOUR HEART'S
BEATING SO FAST

1947

On the May morning of Manhattanhenge sunset, Joe woke to find Nora moving quietly around the room. In the dim light it was hard to see the expression on her face. She looked a bit like a shadow, and maybe she'd been that all along: something forever fleeting that couldn't have existed without the sun.

But could he really let her go? And more than that: Could he keep her?

From the moment he woke up, Joe felt the tightness in his chest that he'd been feeling for the past ten days. It had been that long since Nora had shown him her model of the U.N. Ten days since she had told him she'd rather die — truly die — than risk spending eternity in the in-between. Joe had argued his point again and again: Just wait. You don't have to go now. Look, the building isn't built yet.

She had been calm and unwavering: The sooner she went, the more life he'd have, and the less risk she'd have of being trapped.

Plenty of desperate thoughts had crossed Joe's mind as Manhattanhenge loomed. What if he locked Nora in the room? Feigned an illness? Pulled her back from the sun, as he'd done to save her four years before? But if he'd become the kind of man who could do any of those things, then he'd no longer be the man she'd loved.

In any case, she had made up her mind to die a true death, a final death. He knew he had no right to stop her, no matter how much he wanted to.

Now he said her name softly.

" 'Morning," she said, as if it were any old day. "You slept pretty late. Time to get up."

"Come over here first," Joe said to her. "Please."

He could see Nora toss her head back in that way that was so brave and moving. She climbed into bed beside him. She put her head on his chest.

"You fit just right," he told her.

"So do you," she said. "You always have."

They kissed for a long time and were quiet even longer. Neither of them had the heart to speak. They could hear a distant siren, then the rattle of some guest's breakfast tray

567

being wheeled down the carpeted hallway.

In his arms, without her makeup on, Nora looked even younger than twenty-three. Joe marveled, as he held her, that her face was still completely unlined, her skin still that pink-peach hue. Even the morning he'd first met her, when her lips were stoplight red, she had looked older than she did at this moment, despite all the time that had passed.

Was this really the last time they'd lie like this?

"Your heart's beating so fast," she said.

Joe knew that his only hope was the weather. If it rained; if the sky was cloudy; if just one tiny cloud blocked the Manhattanhenge sunset, then Nora wouldn't be able to die, and he'd have her at least for another year.

He stood up, heart beating faster, and opened the bedroom curtains. The sky was the color of pavement, with wide streaks of dark gray and blue. Joe was glad he was facing the window so Nora couldn't see the relief on his face. He turned back, the tightness in his chest easing. "Looks like rain," he said to her evenly.

Nora offered the thinnest smile. "It's early yet," she said.

"Of course."

"And you've got to get to work."

They had agreed that he should work today.

Joe understood that he couldn't persuade her to stay, and that it was time for him to stop trying. Down in the tower room, he could be Steady Joe Reynolds. He'd know what to do and how to do it, and best of all, he'd be underground, blessedly unable to watch the sky.

At the hotel room door, though, he hesitated. "What are you going to do all day?" he asked.

"Tie up some loose ends," she said.

He looked at her warily. She just smiled. "You'll be late," Nora said, and she was right.

She had her hand on the doorknob. Joe was trying to make himself leave, but now the tightness in his chest had become a tightness in his throat. What if the weather *did* clear?

"Do you want me to be there tonight?" he asked her.

"Not if you're going to try to stop me."

"Where do we meet?"

She smiled. "I'll be at the clock at ten past eight," she said. "If you're not there, I'll understand."

He started down the hallway but rushed back before the door had closed. He grabbed her by the waist and kissed her, deciding at the same moment that there was no way this kiss could be their last.

Belowground, in the tower room, Joe was counting on the Piano to give him his usual sense of control. But today that seemed impossible. The call-and-response was meaningless:

"Ladder X out of H."

"Ladder X out of H."

"Ladder X into 40."

"Ladder X into 40."

He worked with his usual speed and deftness, but the commands were barely words; they were sounds. He was only part of a machine — a machine that was unstoppable, a machine over which, Joe thought miserably, he had no real control. It was the tower director who chose the routes for the trains' comings and goings. The leverman's skill lay not in deciding those routes but in making them possible. No argument could take place between a leverman and a tower director. And this, as far as Joe was concerned, was the situation with Nora. She had chosen the time and place of her departure, and if Joe was doing his duty, his only job was to help smooth the way.

He checked the clock repeatedly. His shift would end at 7:30, and the sun would set at 8:19. He would have plenty of time to shower and meet Nora at the clock. And he wouldn't have to decide until the last moment if he could watch her go.

Meanwhile, Joe worked and waited, and he recognized what he was feeling. It was like the Manhattanhenge mornings when he had prayed for the skies to be clear so that the sunrise could bring Nora back to him. On those days, too, he had kept his head down and pretended it was just a regular day. But the worry had always been there too: the knowledge that, at a certain moment, his life would go one way or the other. Ladder X into 40. Ladder X into 38. Push, pull, the click of the levers, the smell of the sweat, brass, and oil. And in the end, despite any knowledge or love or hope or prayer, he would be at the mercy of the sun.

What Joe wanted to see, coming up from the tunnel into the concourse, was a swarm of people in rain boots and hats who were shaking out umbrellas while Gus and other workers scrambled to mop up all the puddles. What he found, however, was a view of a cruel blue sky, with only the smallest, most feathery clouds.

Nora was standing at the gold clock, as promised, and for the first time since she'd told him her plan, she looked nervous about it.

"I'm just going to ask you one more time," Joe said.

"You know the answer, Joe," she said. "Let me ask if you —"

"Yes, Nora," Joe said. "I understand."

He reached out to take her hand, her miraculous hand, once more an electric thrill. Together they started up the marble steps, surrounded by people hurrying outside as they buzzed and chattered about Manhattanhenge.

"I just don't know what I'd have done if the weather hadn't cleared up," one woman said. "I've come all the way from Jersey for this."

That gave Joe and Nora one last chance to laugh. Then, with a suddenness that nearly overwhelmed him, Nora crossed her wrists behind Joe's neck and kissed him so deeply that it could only have been for the first time or the last.

When she broke off the kiss, Nora tore away, bounding up the stairs and out the door, as if the energy of the sun was already driving her. By the time Joe reached the top of the stairs, Nora had passed the cabs on Vanderbilt Avenue and was running toward Forty-third Street. They had always looked back at each other when they parted in the concourse. This time, Nora didn't.

The sky had become a jazzy blue. The unexpected heat of a late spring day had made the air heavy, and the street smelled of tar. The sun made its slow entrance from the left side of the canyon. Only a minute or so remained. Joe started to run after Nora, but running was merely a reflex, and he made himself stop. She was free to make this choice. It was among the only freedoms she had.

The sun hovered between the buildings, a balled-up fist. Joe watched through tears while Nora lifted her arms from her sides as if she was taking in a last moment of joy. Then she fell to the ground.

"Nora!" Joe shouted, despite himself.

The sun opened its fist, stretched out its fingers, and all but pulled her forward.

Joe's last glimpse of Nora came just as the sun reached the center of the horizon and seemed to explode before his eyes, so bright he had to close them.

When he opened his eyes again, Nora was gone.

■ ■ ■

Joe was on his knees, sobbing. It didn't matter a damn to him if anyone was watching. He stayed on the street for a long time as the crowd slowly dispersed. He watched the sky darken, the trucks and cars turn to silhouettes. Then he walked back through the terminal to the Biltmore lobby, the place where he'd first brought Nora to stay; the place where so many other couples would have so many embraces. Crossing the plush, carpeted lobby, he felt he was walking on Nora's grave.

Back in their room, he saw that this time she had gotten rid of everything. There were no boxes, no clothing or combs or makeup. She'd left behind only her old blue purse. Joe sat in an armchair and opened it. He took the things out, one by one: her change purse, with some bills and coins; the silver case with the lipstick that had painted on her last kiss; and the passport, which he opened, seeing the swept-up hair and the cream-and-tea photo of a bright, free flapper girl.

It was not until Joe had removed all these things that he found the envelope in the bag.

Inside it was a ticket for the 20th Century
Limited.

11
THE 20TH CENTURY

1947

It took Joe a few days to get things in order. There was the job, the bank, the goodbyes, and the promises to Faye and the kids that as soon as he was settled, they could come and visit him. He wanted to go as soon as he could, to get away from the feeling that he would or could ever see Nora again. It didn't escape him that if he stayed, he would, oddly enough, feel haunted by her. He knew he could never come back to this place without his heart breaking.

The 20th Century Limited left at six o'clock every evening. Joe got a second suitcase from Mr. Brennan and filled it, along with the one he'd taken to Atlantic City with Faye. He left a bunch of things with Faye to send later, so he neither needed nor wanted a Red Cap to carry his bags or usher him down the red carpet and into the lavish wilderness of "the most

576

famous train in the world." He found his seat and watched the other passengers come aboard, the porters fussing around them and the Century Girls getting them settled. It was every bit as swank as he'd always imagined it would be.

When the train started moving, Joe gripped the armrest. He had neither regrets nor fears, but he also had no certainty. From the rumbling darkness under Park Avenue, the train emerged into a gleaming summer sky. Silver arrows shot off the windows of the receding skyscrapers. Then the river came into view, the Hudson River, which he'd never seen like this, all stretched out and calm. It looked like a piece of fabric that had been wrinkled and then smoothed flat.

Joe glanced around at the other passengers, marveling that they all seemed so unimpressed by the change from darkness to light. Some didn't even look up as the sky brightened the whole car. They just reached for their newspapers, unfolding them like maps, and for many, Joe realized, whatever they were reading was probably more interesting than the journey. For Joe, holding his armrest, forehead pressed against the trembling window, tears filling his eyes, the journey would be everything.

Only gradually did he recognize that what he felt was freedom.

For hours he watched out the window until the last light of the sunset turned the sky yellow and purple. Then the world seemed to widen, the fields blanketed by distant house lights that twinkled beneath a heaven of real stars.

12
ALL ABOARD

Nora was slim enough to be able to hide her whole body behind a column on the platform, and that is where she was standing as she waited for Joe's train to leave. She was confident he wouldn't be looking for her: not now, not ever. She'd seen to that. As far as Joe knew, she had disappeared into a fatal Manhattanhenge sunset.

That was the lie.

Nora had counted on Joe to want to watch her go, and she had counted on the sun to blind him just long enough for her to duck onto a side street, out of the path of Manhattanhenge. Still, she was taking no chance that he might catch a glimpse of her. She had spent the days since then hiding in her studio, pretending to Leon that she needed total concentration and solitude for the art she was doing. She had stashed some food and wine in various corners. Leon faithfully

579

brought her more food and even helped her scavenge the small couch that had been used by models for decades of life studies. For now, Nora would use it as a bed.

Peeking out from behind a column on Track 28, she watched the Red Caps loading bags into the passenger cars. The train was sleek, with fresh black paint and shiny rivets perfectly spaced. The conductor called "All aboard," and Nora gripped the column. As she did, her charm bracelet wobbled down her wrist, a wrist that was exactly as pale and smooth as it had been on the morning of December 5, 1925. Head bent, tears dropping straight to the platform, she told herself that with each month that passed, she would grow only more certain that she'd been right to make sure Joe had left — and right not to call him back now, no matter how much she wanted to. Someday she might have another love in her life, a life she would end only when she had tasted every drop of joy she could find in it. But no one would ever compare to Joe. There couldn't be another man with his rare, marvelous combination of kindness and strength.

The conductor's whistle blew. Two decades had passed since the accident, but Nora had experienced only a fraction of them. She was greedy for more life, the life she'd been denied. Though she knew it would require some tricks of hair and makeup to stay inconspicuous to the people she met, she also knew she would make friends. She knew she would eat, and laugh, and paint.

Nora Lansing, who would have had enough energy for two lives of normal length, was not even remotely done with this one. She would stay as long as she wanted, and when she left, it would not be on some random day, or by accident, to be locked forever into the in-between. When she left, it would be in a fatal Manhattan-henge sunset of her choosing, when she'd walk over the threshold of pain into what she had come to assume would be either utter darkness or some other kind of light.

The Red Caps were stepping away from the doors, which closed in quick succession. The train made almost no sound as it started to move. Joe was going. He was gone. Nora was hugging the column now, her arms wrapped around it as she watched the train pull away and saw the electric blue taillight disappear into the dark.

13
SOMEONE SPECIAL?

Many Years Later

The young man is tall and thin. He's probably in his late teens, though he might also be in college. His floppy hair is black as a bristle brush. He's wearing a black coat and a green-and-black-striped scarf, and he's pulling off his gloves impatiently as he makes his way through Grand Central Terminal. He's been here many times before. The fact that some relative of his once worked here as a trainman gives him a vaguely proprietary air, as if every time he comes, he's somehow visiting his familial home.

But today he is on a mission no different from that of the hundreds of other people who crowd the annual holiday fair. Gamely, he weaves his way through the other shoppers, scanning booth after booth. He stops at one selling Christmas ornaments. No good. Not good enough, anyway. He looks at silk scarves, handmade cards, bamboo bowls, and porcelain vases. Anyone watching him would quickly guess that a romance is involved.

He has almost made up his mind to buy a wooden music box when he sees something in the distance, on the opposite side of the aisle. He passes five or six other booths to get a closer look. What's drawn him in is a painting of the terminal, unusual in its focus. The most famous image of Grand Central — the black-and-white photograph he's seen so many times on postcards and in books — shows fluted columns of light pouring onto the floor from the half-circle windows. But in this painting, the light comes from the middle of the three larger windows, and it's beautiful and different. He stops when he sees the painting, as if imagining what his friend will think.

"How much?" he asks the young woman behind the counter. She's making change for another customer and takes a moment to answer.

"Sixty dollars," she says, and turns to face him with playful eyes and a lively smile. Her mouth is raspberry red and almost seems to glitter. She's more than merely beautiful.

"Sixty?" the young man says. "Maybe fifty?"

"Fifty?" she says. "Maybe sixty."

Sheepishly, he takes out his wallet and three twenty-dollar bills. She reaches across the counter for them, a crowded gold charm bracelet jangling against her thin wrist.

"Do you need it wrapped?" she asks him.

"No, that's okay. I'm in kind of a rush."

"Trying to catch a train?"

"No."

"Someone special?"

He smiles.

"Good luck," she says, and hands him the painting.

They thank each other and say Merry Christmas. A new customer is browsing through the woman's artwork now, but she keeps her eye on the young man, recognizing something familiar about him. She almost runs after him, but he's already hidden by the crowd, so she reaches for her sketchpad and a heavy charcoal pencil, and with just a few lines she captures the strong, solid look of him and the crooked half smile that another artist might never have seen.

ACKNOWLEDGMENTS

Writing this novel had certain things in common with the love affair of its main characters: an unlikely beginning, a stubborn attraction, and a bunch of unforeseen obstacles causing its many stops and starts.

Unlike Joe and Nora, though, I had an abundance of help along the way, and I have to start by acknowledging James Sanders — architect, historian, friend — who was the first person to tell me about Manhattanhenge and the first to give me a hint of Grand Central's secrets.

I am lucky enough to have friends who are not just generous and encouraging but really, really smart. Susie Bolotin, Sharon DeLevie, Lee Eisenberg, Darrel Frost, Peter Lurye, Dan Okrent, James Sanders, and Sally Seymour all read parts or all of different drafts and offered help and priceless insights. My niece Caroline Grunwald explained how to approach a horse. Her father, Peter Grunwald, patiently reminded me about the difference between story and plot. My sister, Mandy, checked in constantly.

In addition to becoming an outstanding source of encouragement and support, my friend and physical therapist, Marcus Forman, risked being put on a watch list when he used a surveyor's tape to measure the yardage in and around Grand Central. He and my doctors — Phillip Blumberg, Richard Cohen, Alexandra Heerdt, Jon LaPook, and Saud Sadiq — have helped me navigate the medical obstacles I've faced in the past decade. I am deeply grateful to them all.

I want to thank Chris Jerome, the copy editor anyone who dreams of copy editors dreams of (and what she would do with *that* sentence!). Beth Pearson brought rigor and sanity — a rare combination — to the production.

My agent, Julie Barer, is effervescent and brilliant; she was encouraging, insightful, and exacting from the start and patient even when I wasn't. My editor, Kara Cesare, got to know Joe and Nora so well that she eventually joined me deep in the weeds around them but fortunately helped me find the way out. Finally, Susan Kamil, Random House Publishing's boss of all bosses, said yes in the first place and eventually wielded a pencil that was part wand and part scalpel. I'll be forever grateful to all of these remarkable women. I would have loved to thank Barb Burg.

Betsy Carter has read, edited, de- and reconstructed this novel so many times that she could probably recite parts of it by heart — a heart that is as loyal as it is wise. This book didn't just get better because of her. It got written.

From the first beach walks we took on Martha's Vineyard to the last brownie crumbs we ate at Zucker's, my daughter, Elizabeth Adler, shared her wisdom, compassion, and benevolent logic, even as she challenged and eventually embraced the idea that not all love stories end the same way.

My son, Jonathan Adler, was still in middle school when I began this book, but as he grew up with it, he grew into one of the most clearheaded, precise, patient, and inspiring editors I've known (and I've known a lot of editors). I will treasure in particular several messages he sent me *from* the characters in this book, urging me to finish their story.

And finally, and always, there is Stephen, whose mind, strength, kindness, loyalty, and

love are as rare and miraculous to me as
Manhattanhenge light.

SOURCE NOTES

Among the many joys of writing historical fiction is the research involved in trying to get the facts right. Many special challenges accompany this joy, one of which is keeping track of where the facts end and the fiction begins. With that in mind, a few notes:

The names and occupations of the following characters are real: John Campbell, Bill Keogh, Louis Landsman, Mary Lee Read, Ezra Winter, and Ralston Crosbie Young. But what they say and do in the novel is invented.

Conversely, the art teacher Alphonse Fournier is a fictional character, but some of his dialogue comes from a 1934 pamphlet, privately published, that consisted of notes taken during a Grand Central School of Art class taught by an artist named Harvey Dunn.

Though there was a subway accident in 1925 and I've cribbed a paragraph from the

New York Times story about it, I have changed the date of the event and a number of the details.

Naturally, most of the books I consulted were about Grand Central itself — including Sam Roberts's wonderful centennial volume, *Grand Central: How a Train Station Transformed America,* and John Bell and Maxine Leighton's *Grand Central: Gateway to a Million Lives.* But no book was more important to me than the one I happened upon in the stacks of Columbia's Butler Library. This one was written by David Marshall and published in 1946; it is called simply *Grand Central,* and it is an incomparable guide to the place and its past.

About Manhattanhenge: Sometime after finding David Marshall's book about Grand Central, I had lunch with my friend James Sanders. James has never read a page he's forgotten, so I shouldn't have been surprised that he knew Marshall's book and remembered its beautiful description of dawn in the Main Concourse on several special days of the year. I had read about how the rising sun seemed to bring the ceiling to life, but I wasn't sure I understood why it happened so infrequently. That's when James introduced me to Manhattanhenge.

Once called the Manhattan Solstice or the

Solar Grid Day, Manhattanhenge is a celestial phenomenon that occurs when the annual progress of the Earth around the sun coincides with the geographical alignment of Manhattan and its street grid. On these days alone — which happen a few weeks before and after the summer and winter solstices — the rising or setting sun is perfectly centered between the buildings along the east–west streets of the city.

"But you can't see Manhattanhenge sunrise in Grand Central the way Marshall describes it anymore," James said, and by way of explanation, took out a pen and drew the sketch opposite.

That arrow going from the sun down Forty-third Street through the terminal represents the light of sunrise as it comes up over the East River and crosses the avenues, heading west. The high arched windows of Grand Central's Main Concourse, centered on Forty-third Street, allowed that light to shine through into the terminal. That is, James explained to me, until the United Nations Secretariat was built along the East River. At thirty-nine stories, the building was tall enough to block the light of dawn from reaching the terminal's Main Concourse.

It is Neil deGrasse Tyson who popular-

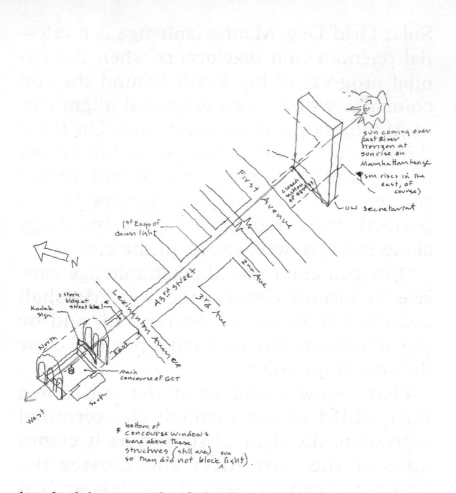

sun coming over
East River
horizon at
sunrise on
Manhattanhenge

sun rises in the
east, of
course)

UN secretariat

First Avenue

clouds
within
of 43rd

1st Rays of
dawn light

N

2nd Ave

43rd Street

3rd Ave

1 story
bldg at
street level

Kodak
sign

Lexington Avenue

North

East

Main
Concourse of GCT

West

South

bottom of
concourse windows
were above these
structures (still are) sun
so they did not block light).
                                 ^

ized this wonderful phenomenon, and for
the purposes of this novel, I have simplified
some aspects of it. For anyone who wants
to understand it more fully — or find the
dates on which you might see it in person
— I refer you to the American Museum of
Natural History website: www.amnh.org/
our-research/hayden-planetarium/resources/
manhattanhenge.

ABOUT THE AUTHOR

Lisa Grunwald is the author of the novels *The Irresistible Henry House, Whatever Makes You Happy, New Year's Eve, The Theory of Everything,* and *Summer.* Along with her husband, Reuters editor in chief Stephen J. Adler, she edited the anthologies *The Marriage Book, Women's Letters,* and *Letters of the Century.* Grunwald is a former contributing editor to *Life* and former features editor of *Esquire.* She lives in New York City.

lisagrunwald.com
Instagram: lisagrunwald
Facebook.com/LisaGrunwaldAuthor
Twitter: @lisa_grunwald